CW01175892

Kill Or Capture

Robert Dalcross

Published by Military Press (London)

ISBN: 9798323649365

www.robertdalcross.com

1) HMS Defender, A British Type 45 Guided Missile Destroyer, The Persian Gulf, Off Saudi Arabia

A blistering sun shone down from a cloudless blue sky. The sea seemed baked to idleness with never a breath of air to stir the surface. The only visible object from horizon to horizon was a sleek, grey warship moving at speed and cutting an arrow straight wound through the glassy calm water. On the flight deck, aft, a squad of Royal Marines were stripped to the waist and engaged in a form of ritual torture called calisthenics both to keep them fit and get them acclimatised to the broiling heat. Train hard, fight easy.

HMS Defender was a Type 45 guided missile destroyer belonging to the British Royal Navy and one of the most advanced air defence warships in the world. She was 498 feet long and displaced 8,500 tonnes yet had the radar signature of a rowing boat. She was also capable of speeds in excess of 30 knots while tracking several hundred supersonic airborne targets simultaneously out to a range of 250 nautical miles. A naval expert would immediately recognise the tall pyramid rearing high behind the bridge as air defence radar. For reasons which will become apparent, you need to know what armament the Defender carries.

Principally, she was designed and built to protect aircraft carriers from aircraft and missile attack while also being well able to operate alone on a wide variety of missions. Some years earlier, she had been tasked with protecting the US aircraft carrier USS George H W Bush as she carried out sorties against the terror group ISIS in these same waters.

Equipped with the Sea Ceptor CAMM ER anti-aircraft missile system and the Naval Strike anti-ship missile system she was capable of destroying any aircraft, missile, artillery shell, warship or combination thereof which chose to come within a range of 70 nautical miles. Her Maritime Warfare Wildcat Helicopters, though designed for maritime attack, could make life fairly miserable for a submarine too by dipping sonar or dropping sonar buoys to detect undersea threats and then deploying light-weight homing torpedoes to kill them.

To defend against line-of-sight threats, such as fast attack craft, Defender was armed with a pair of 30 mm cannon and the Phalanx radar-controlled roller cannon. Like a Gatling gun on steroids that can knock an incoming shell or missile out of the sky. If called upon to deal with trouble ashore then, of course, she had a compliment of Royal Marines, helicopter portable and equipped to fight and defeat anything they might encounter. Of course, if she was sent on a mission where the Marines might need to be transported as a unit the Wildcat helicopters would be replaced by the larger Merlins.

Should she be required to support her Royals ashore then on the fore-deck there was a 4.5 inch Mark 8 quick-fire gun capable of firing 45 pound high explosive shells out to a range of over 12 nautical miles at a rate of 25 rounds per minute. In 2011, HMS Iron Duke, a type 23 frigate equipped with this same gun, used it to destroy a missile battery outside the town of Misrata in Gaddafi-controlled Libya. It sounds like old-fashioned British gunboat diplomacy but they had been sufficiently foolish as to fire missiles at her.

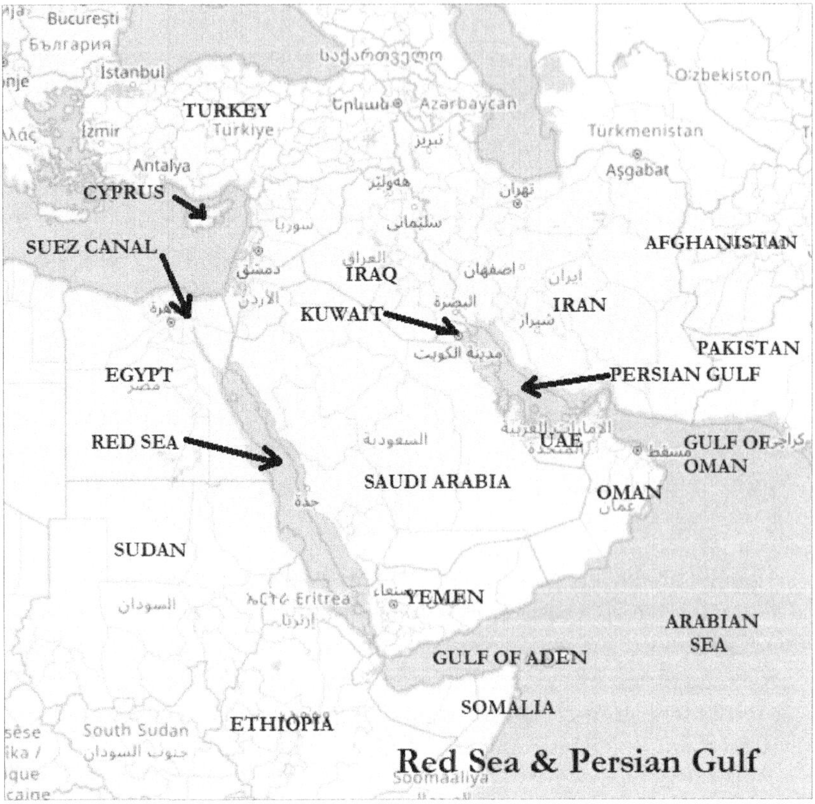

Two weeks previously, in the Eastern Mediterranean, one of her two Wildcat helicopters had left the ship and a specially modified Dauphin 2 helicopter had joined her from Cyprus. This aircraft, more or less radar invisible yet showing civilian paint and numbers which claimed Saudi nationality, was quickly hidden away in the onboard hangar where it remained out of bounds to all ship's crew.

Being fast, hardy and relatively spacious, the civilian-painted Dauphin 2s of 658 Squadron, Army Air Corps, are on permanent stand-by 24/7/365 at Credenhill, near Hereford, to ferry British SAS Troopers wherever they need to go at maximum speed and with minimum visibility.

This particular Dauphin came to HMS Defender packed to the gills with men and kit. She was flown by her Army Air Corps flight crew of two and, as was usual on extended away-missions, she brought her own pair of technicians for maintenance.

Heading up the passenger list was Colonel Mike Reaper of MI6, commander of this team. Mike was well over six feet tall and had the build of a top level tennis player. His background was special forces but his unusual talents had been noticed and he was transferred to the Special Intelligence Service (SIS), parent organisation to MI5 and MI6. Mike was made full colonel to be able to deal with senior foreign players and his claim to fame was his tactical genius, though he was highly skilled with all usual weapons and spoke several languages.

Sergeant Donald "Don Mac" MacLeish was a professional Glaswegian Scot. Don Mac amongst friends to distinguish him from the countless other "Jocks" and "Macs" in the SAS. He was of medium height with a weather-beaten face and a broken nose, badly set. Originally from the Royal Marines, he had served with 22 SAS for some years and transferred to E Squadron when he was promoted to sergeant. Mac was a desert warfare specialist and close combat instructor but his regular job in recent years had been as permanent bodyguard to Mike.

As a rule, members or teams from E Squadron were attached to MI6 agents when required, such as when they were in tricky spots overseas, but in this case Mac was on permanent attachment with Mike because he was almost permanently on important or difficult missions and he needed someone reliable to watch his back. Someone who knew how he worked and could keep up with him. Despite, or perhaps because of their obvious differences, the two men got on well. Mike claimed the reason he was given Mac was that he was the only Englishman who could understand his accent.

Agent Bradley Harrison was on secondment from GCHQ, the UK's intelligence, security and cyber agency where he worked on something to do with computers. He was a quiet type of person, the sort of young man you would not notice at a BBQ, and ill at ease amongst rough soldiers; but his presence, with his special skills, on this mission was vital. His friends in the "Dark Side", back at GCHQ, called him Brad but the SAS men all called him "The Geek." Strangely, their giving him this nickname was a mark of acceptance amongst them. He knew things they did not and they respected that.

Mac was technically in command of the four other men from E Squadron who accompanied them; Corporal Geoff "Geordie" Barnes, Corporal Mathew "Scouse" Halverson and two others. But in the SAS they played by "Big boys' rules;" if a man needed keeping in line he would have already been RTU'd, returned to his parent unit.

Not only are the members of E Squadron fearsome soldiers, they are trained in various unusual skills, street-smart and used to blending into the background in civilian clothes. Very often, they travel in plain sight as a sports team of some kind. Perhaps not a chess team.

In advance of their arrival the Captain of HMS Defender, Commander Graham Harmsworth, had instructed all ranks not to speak to the visitors unless addressed and specifically included the ship's Royal Marine detachment in that order because he knew there was a possibility that some of the Royals might know someone in the team. For obvious reasons a fair proportion of SAS recruits are from the Royals. And careless talk...

Following the arrival of the team, Defender sailed South through the Suez Canal, down the length of the Red Sea then turned North East to leave the Gulf of Aden and run up the coast past Yemen and Oman; cruising all the while at 18 knots. Three days later she changed course again to run North West into the Persian Gulf. So far the trip had been quiet and the guests no trouble.

The Dauphin flight crew had mostly stayed in their cabins or socialised with the other air-crew aboard. The SAS team were in the gym much of each day or running the deck with the ship's physical training instructors. Brad had apparently remained in his cabin glued to his laptop when he was not in the mess enjoying the high quality food aboard. It was not in his nature to speak to people without good cause.

The Captain had been informed by his executive officer, Lieutenant McGowan, that an electronics warfare specialist in the Defender's crew had reported a visitor had somehow piggy-backed the ship's secure satellite comms system to send and receive coded messages from God knows where. Mike told the Captain it was probably Brad chatting to his mates in "The Dark Side" at GCHQ over some encrypted line. Electronic warfare was instructed not to interfere.

It was 04:00 on a clear, calm and very warm night. The ship was steaming West of North. The port city of Dammam, Saudi Arabia, was 100 km off the Port beam and Iran was a little further off the Starboard while Kuwait and Iraq were 400 km ahead at the top of the Gulf. Habitually, Mac ran an eye over his team as they checked their kit. Quiet, methodical and professional. What else would they be? The Dauphin was out on deck and the engines were warming up.

Mike came on deck and nodded to Mac. Brad followed Mike like a clingy puppy, looking nervous. The team boarded the Dauphin and it lifted from the deck, but instead of climbing rapidly to avoid being seen or heard by seaborne traffic it put its nose down and headed North West almost skimming the surface of the calm sea depending on its stealth paint to avoid radar detection.

The team sat in canvas seats amongst the equipment as comfortable as they could make themselves. The pilot's steady voice came over the headsets built into their helmets. "We will cross the beach at Bubiyan Island, Kuwait, in 7 minutes and be over the border into Iraqi territory 9 minutes later Sir."

"Thank you Captain." Mike replied through his headset-mike without expression. His eyes were on Brad the Geek, "Sitrep Brad."

2) A Bunker Near Korosten, Zhytomyr Oblast, Northern Ukraine

On the outskirts of a heavily shelled Ukrainian city, close to the Northern border with Russia and protected beneath layers of reinforced concrete, was a "bomb-proof" bunker. There, six teenage fighters, amongst Ukraine's youngest defenders, fought their war from an assortment of laptops and tower PCs all cabled together on old, battered wooden tables.

Theirs was not the age-old field of battle, where men faced each other with rifle and bayonet, but a new form of conflict where size and strength mattered little, childhood ended abruptly and the lines between a game and an equally grim reality blurred. These six Ukrainian youngsters, thrust into this sobering maturity, fought with remote weapons, drones of various types donated from friendly nations, but the stakes were as high and as real as the tremors that shook their surroundings. They must hold this line against the advancing Russians or their city would fall and their families would pay with their lives.

In the bunker's dimly lit confines, old rules of command and advanced technology merged. Youth and experience blended, and a new style of warfare was being developed. It was a strange contrasting mixture of people, hardware and software. A place where innovation met tradition and the echoes of heavy artillery formed only a backing track to their assault on their enemy.

Every so often a shell detonated particularly close and the shockwave sent dust and whitewash flakes drifting from the bunker's ceiling, settling on maps and screens like harsh, snowy confetti. But this barely registered on the youngsters' determined faces. They were engrossed in their duties, consumed by the virtual battlefields displayed on their screens. The fighters remained intensely focused, their fingers gliding over keyboards and manipulating joysticks, guiding swift mechanical killers to find and slaughter their prey.

Their leader, a slightly less young man called Artem who once sold Western jeans over the 'net, navigated the narrow aisle between tables with a pronounced limp. A trophy from his time as an infantry officer. His stern gaze moved between the screens, ensuring that no detail escaped his eye. Despite the limp, his movements seemed confident, assured, each step resonated with a responsibility far beyond his twenty three years.

Commands and status updates echoed within the bunker's confines, bouncing strangely off the cold concrete walls. The youthful voices carried an unexpected calm authority, a sense of control amidst the chaos as they worked together to accomplish their tasks. "Target locked," Yulia announced, her voice steady. A ripple of anticipation ran through the room, followed by the precise, "Firing now," from a boy named Maxim with a deep scar across his ear.

Dmitro, his face bathed in the pale glow of a screen, navigated his reconnaissance drone along the enemy lines, spotting Russian tanks advancing. "Multiple targets sighted, heavy armour," he declared, his voice edged with grim satisfaction. "Engaging," intoned Daryna, guiding her drone low and fast, an almost silent predator armed with a shaped-charge weapon specifically designed for destroying armoured vehicles. "Tracking target," she murmured, then moments later, "Target neutralized." The words were delivered with an air of grim accomplishment. A brief shot of flames and twisted metal filled her screen from the aft cam.

Despite each successful hit the remaining tanks rumbled closer and the pressure settled heavier upon the defenders. "Drone lost," called out Dmitro, a sobering reminder of the approaching threat to the city's survival. There were some replacements remaining but not many. He quickly took control of a new machine. Their position must not be overrun or the city would fall. They were the unlikely guardians of their homeland, the collective embodiment of Ukraine's strongly independent spirit. The rumbling artillery might shake the ground around it, but within this bunker they stood firm, united by duty and driven by a cause greater than themselves.

In the far corner of the bunker two much older, senior officers observed the young warriors with a mixture of pride and concern. Their eyes, hardened by months of constant conflict, scanned the room, taking in the efficiency and determination of their young charges.

Colonel Petrov, a seasoned veteran of countless conventional tank battles, turned to his companion, Major Ivanova, his voice low and measured. "They're adapting well. Quicker than I expected."

Ivanova nodded, her expression unreadable. "Yes, but we mustn't forget, they are still children in many ways."

Petrov's eyes flicked back to the young fighters, his voice betraying no hint of emotion. "Children thrust into a war. It's not right, but it's necessary. Better they fight here than they are slaughtered by the Russians in the streets."

A tense silence settled between the two officers, filled only by the relentless chatter of keyboards and the distant thunder of artillery. The reality of their situation was all too clear; the war was evolving, and they had to adapt or perish.

A very young looking soldier looked up from his screen, his eyes meeting Ivanova's. A question was in those eyes, a call for reassurance. Ivanova could offer just a firm nod, a small smile. It was all she could give, a tiny spark of humanity amidst the cold machinery of war. But it was enough. He went back to his work.

The room's dynamics shifted as an alarm sounded, signalling a direct threat to the bunker. The youths' attention remained on their screens, their expressions perhaps hardening if that were possible. For Petrov and Ivanova the moment of reflection was over; it was time to fight again. Petrov turned to Ivanova, his voice firm. "Call out the close-quarters defence team. We may need to move quickly."

She nodded, moving towards the door, her steps brisk and purposeful. Petrov's gaze lingered on the young soldiers, watching them engaged in their digital warfare, their faces etched with determination and focus. As he followed Ivanova he realised he was proud of them.

The scene encapsulated the new reality of war, where youth and technology merged and the battlefield was both virtual and tangible. The stakes were as high as ever, the risks real and immediate. The fusion of old and new, of tradition and innovation, created a landscape where the rules were constantly changing, but the objective always remained the same: the survival of their nation.

3) An Alley Behind A Street Of Terraced Houses In Bradford, West Yorkshire, UK

In the darkening streets of an old Bradford housing estate, a gaunt, spotted teenage boy stalked through the shadowy alleyways like a sickly hyena, seeking out only the defenceless prey that it could manage to overcome. He had been named Wayne by parents who, in a moment of sobriety, thought he might make a footballer. They were wrong and he followed their example. His drug abuse had left him hard-of-thinking and frail, his body was begging for the next hit. Yet, right now, his primary focus wasn't the next shot, it was stealing the money to buy it with.

The immediate neighbourhood made a grim picture of poverty, a collection of terraced houses run-down on the outsides. But the only place first generation immigrants could afford to live. So they did. As nightfall blanketed the streets, a silence took hold, a silence broken only by the scuffing sound of Wayne's worn-out trainers on the cobblestones and the distant traffic of a main road.

Driven to burglary again and again by his craving, the boy had become adept at detecting potential targets for his petty thievery. Houses cloaked in darkness, void of any signs of life, these were the places he sought. Places where he could steal small, valuable things, quickly and undetected. Things he could easily sell for drug money.

His heart was pounding as he scanned each home, the tension playing its heady buzz in his ears. He was desperate, yet cautious, his motivation split between his desperation for another hit and his fear of getting caught, and perhaps badly beaten. Around here, they wouldn't call the police for a burglar.

Spotting a potential target at the alley's end, his pulse quickened. Its darkened windows and stillness suggested it was empty. With an addict's false sense of courage, he approached, his senses heightened, on edge. He stopped before a window on a garage, his quick breaths fogging the cold glass. It looked empty so far as he could tell. He peered over the wall, towards the house, eyes straining to detect any signs of activity.

Wayne never stole to pay for food or shelter, state benefits would always cover that. Robbing this home could provide him the means to satiate his crippling addiction; a laptop, treasured jewellery, or even some cash left carelessly by an absent owner. The mere thought accelerated his pulse, a toxic mix of fear, anticipation, and the ever strengthening hunger coursing through his veins.

4) A Ukrainian Battlefield North Of Rivne, 200 Miles West Of Kyiv, Ukraine

Winter in Ukraine was a relentless beast that seemed to freeze the very marrow in a man's bones. Raw Russian conscripts, boys scarcely shaved, shivered in their shallow slit trenches cut by hand into the rock- frozen ground. They found no comfort in their makeshift refuge. They knew that their temporary home was a mere joke of military strategy.

These boys had been thrown into a war they didn't want to fight with equipment that mocked the very idea of 'standard issue'. Their gear was dead men's clothes issued with a grim bureaucratic efficiency by a motherland now as distant and impersonal as the cold stars far above them. The clothing was indeed Russian, but there was not enough of it to provide a proper layered defence against the biting cold. Their boots, soles almost as thin as paper and as worn as their morale, offered almost no protection from the unforgiving chill that seemed to seep out of the ground.

At a sound, Viktor looked up into the sky above, a canvas of black and stars that now hummed with a noise that triggered a twinge of fear in his belly. He knew what it was, he had heard this sound before the massacre of his previous unit last week. It was the echo of rotor-winged predators: Drones, quite small but poisoned with lethal intent, scanning the scarred battlefield.

They hovered and wheeled like mechanical vultures, each armed with a light machine gun that would pour out a storm of bullets with a cold, methodical precision whenever it found a careless target. These were the hunters in this war, built by clever foreigners for this inhospitable wilderness. Viktor knew that he and his fellow conscripts were nothing more than their game, the quarry they hunted by night and by day.

Artem nodded to a couple of his comrades and, driven by a mix of courage and desperation, they opened fire on the spectres of death as they became visible, silhouetted against the stars high above. bursts of bullets from their AK47 rifles streamed wildly into the unforgiving sky, chattering on full auto, trying to swat the agile flyers from the air. One or two were shot down to cheers, but mostly the drones were too fast, too nimble, almost mocking in their evasion. They dodged the gunfire with a swiftness that seemed almost alien, before riddling all the boys with NATO .223 ammunition and moving on. Viktor lay face down on the snow, feeling the cold no more: Blood trickling from his mouth, his eyes staring, surrounded by his dead friends.

Alexei was driven by the numbing chill of stark terror, one of those few souls who tried to offer surrender. Their voices rang out, the words, "my sdayemsya", "we surrender," brittle in the cold air. It was a plea, a desperate gamble for mercy, a hope to see another sunrise. To make it home to their mothers and friends. But the drones didn't hear them. They had no ears for pleas nor eyes for the white flags. Their young controllers were as merciless with Russian soldiers as they were when they destroyed a pixelated alien in a computer game. Their hard eyes saw only targets, not flesh and blood beneath layers of inadequate camo. And their response was as chilling as the air itself; the abrupt, pitiless staccato of machine-gun fire, cutting short the pleas of surrender and silencing the heartbeats beneath.

Vladimir, his courage consumed by the fear gnawing at his insides, pressed himself deeper into the bottom of his second-row trench. He sought protection from the unforgiving earth, crouching down in a hopeless attempt at concealment. He held his breath, praying to the Russian soldiers' friend Saint Evgeny Rodionov for the whining drone above him to pass over, to spare him from its merciless onslaught. But he had no thermal poncho to hide his heat signature so his body shone out in the thermal imaging systems of the drones. They were running along the lengths of the almost empty trenches now. Killing anything that remained. Anything that looked alive, glowed in the thermal cameras. A brisk burst of automatic gunfire put Vladimir out of his misery.

This was the grim reality across Northern Ukraine. A reality carved in ice and fear, punctuated by the drone's merciless hum and the crunch of boots running on hard-frozen earth. Here there were few Ukrainian men facing the Russians, they were all in the East fighting the Russians face to face. Locally it was nothing like the comic book tale of an even duel between honourable men. It was Ukrainian boys and girls fighting Russian conscripts barely older than themselves. And just like every war, time and again, one side had the local advantage and slaughtered the other. It was a tale of survival, or the lack thereof, all over the cold, merciless battlefield.

5) General Nikolai Kuznetsov's Dacha Outside Moscow

In the frost-rimed expanse of his lavish dacha's grounds, in the open country just beyond the Eastern edges of Moscow, General Nikolai Kuznetsov, veteran of the Russian military and a formidable presence in the political landscape, was losing a game of tug-of-war. His adversary was a fourteen-year-old Borzoi named Laika, an old dame with greying hair that reflected the snow around them and possessor of an unwavering loyal spirit that made the old General's stern features soften with warmth.

With the Dacha's ornate spires and steep roofs towering behind him, Nikolai surveyed the frozen garden, his fur-lined coat resisting the biting wind that swept in from the plains. The snow-covered lawns and borders spread out before him were a symphony in white, a stark contrast to the comfortable, antique-rich interior of his magnificent abode. This was his home and his refuge, far from the gnawing games of power and the dangerous politics that occupied his days in the city.

Laika gave another determined tug and shook her head, her thin but powerful frame braced on her forelegs against the pull of the man she had for so long adored; her long thin tail whipping against the snowy ground, leaving swirls of white in its wake. A low growl vibrated in her chest, a playful challenge echoed with a rumbling chuckle from the General.

"Nyet, Laika," Nikolai gently reprimanded, his grip slackening on the dog's favoured toy – a worn leather tug. Even his icy blue eyes, hardened by years of command, softened at the sight of his old companion, her snout frosted with age but her spirit ever youthful.

The light had begun to wane, casting long shadows on the snow, painting the landscape with strokes of gray and deep blue. His breath hung in the air, a frozen testament to the searing chill, but he remained still, relishing these moments of solitude.

His mobile 'phone rang in his pocket, a sudden unwanted intrusion against the peaceful tableau. Without taking his gaze off Laika, he opened the connection. He listened, his features hardening, his grip tightening on the tug.

"Da," he replied curtly, a single word that carried the weight of command. It was a tone that had sent battalions into action, a tone that could shift the very landscapes of power. It was a tone Laika knew all too well. Sensing the shift in her master's mood, she released the tug and sat, her ears perked up, her eyes scanning the horizon, her silence an echo of the General's own.

Nikolai ended the call, a sigh escaping his lips as he pocketed the device. He looked at Laika, her eyes reflecting the dying light. "Duty calls, old friend," he murmured, scratching behind her ears. Their peaceful game had been a reprieve from the only battles he fought now - battles in the shadows, in the silent corridors of power.

As he trudged back towards the imposing silhouette of his dacha, Laika trotting loyally by his side, the weight of duty was another familiar companion. Yet, in the cold expanse of his Russian estate, against the backdrop of the gathering night, it was the soft panting of his faithful companion and the comforting crunch of clean snow under their feet that made the General feel invincible. This was the Russia he still fought for. A land of beauty, strength, and relentless spirit. Just like his old Borzoi, Laika.

6) **The Starlight Bar, Bradford, UK**

In the dim-lit confines of a rough Bradford bar called, for some long-forgotten reason "Starlight", the air was heavy with the mingled odours of stale beer, cheap cologne and simmering intrigue. Amidst the drinking, swearing patrons, mostly petty drug dealers, thieves and thugs, one figure distinguished himself by his age and dress. He was a middle-aged Russian named Alexei Volkov and he made a stark contrast to this motley collection of low-life.

Everyone here, pretty much, favoured hoodies and trainers but Alexei wore a suit, pristine despite the seedy surroundings, some might think it was a fortress of respectability around him. In reality, he would not stoop to hide amongst these dregs of humanity. His features were hardened, weathered by time and betraying a life steeped in shadow and secrets. He was a predatory creature from a world alien to this bar's patrons. Maybe it was how he moved or something in his eyes, but no one even thought about rolling him.

Across from Alexei sat his companion, a man of Pakistani extraction by the name of Riaz Khan. His broad shoulders and toned body hinting at a well worn gym membership. His skin was olive-tanned of course, but weather-beaten too, and his strong, dark eyes held an unyielding glare, a testament to his life as a first-line drug dealer, a kingpin in the world of illicit substances. Here was a man feared and respected locally and well beyond, but most importantly to Alexei, he was a man who got things done.

Between them, the talk was purely business, a delicate, secret negotiation defended by the hushed tones of conspiracy. Alexei, a Russian agent up from London and cold as the vodka he nursed, proposed a deal. He had a cargo of cocaine in the Docks at London, a shipment ready to flood the veins of Bradford. And his offer was simple yet perilous: There was an additive in this consignment, a chemical created in a laboratory which modified the effects of the cocaine. Test it on your customers, the expendable junkies of the city, said Alexei. And provide feedback to me. The risks were high, but so was the reward. The shipment worth £1,500,000 would be free and if he, Riaz, provided full feedback on the drug's effects he would be paid as much again. Very good pay indeed.

Riaz considered Alexei's proposal carefully, trying to control the greed pushing him to accept. His eyes flickering at the prospect of such hefty profits. Despite looking like a thug and appearing to enjoy causing pain to defaulting sub dealers, Riaz was a clever and streetwise operator; Alexei was not going to tell him why he was offering this shipment. There was no point asking as he would lie.

But Riaz was no stranger to risk. And what was the downside? Danger, after all, was the currency of his trade. He knew the implications well; the potential increase in turnover and demand, the heightened addictive qualities, the unpredictable side effects. The loss of any customers killed by the additive. Yet the lure of the deal was as potent as the substances he peddled. And this first shipment alone was worth eighteen months' profits on top of his already lucrative trade. How could he refuse? What was the down-side? A few dead druggies were neither here nor there. This sounded like a ticket to join the premier league.

Around them, life in the bar continued its monotonous cycle, ignorant of the outrageous pact that was taking shape. A heavy barmaid weaved through the crowd collecting empty glasses; beers were raised and the din of carefree chatter drifted across to the conspirators. A jukebox played a familiar tune, its thumping bass a contrast to the tension that simmered at the corner table.

As the deal neared its conclusion, Alexei slid a small vial across the table. It was a token, a sample of the additive-laced cocaine he could provide. The substance inside was as white and clean as fresh snow. As the terms of their deal; a dangerous cocktail of potential power and ruin. The dealer regarded it, a glint in his eye betraying his anticipation, a raptor scenting a new opportunity to feed on the weak. He could go away now and try the additive on a few punters. Or he could stay and cut the big deal. If he delayed Alexei might offer it to someone in Birmingham.

As their hands clasped in agreement, the Russian agent's eyes mirrored the frigid landscape of his homeland, as icy and unforgiving as the deal he had cut with Riaz. In this shoddy Bradford bar, two worlds had collided, two predators had found common ground. And, as the deal was sealed, so was the fate of many; their lives to be changed beyond recovery by this callous experiment.

In this dimly lit corner of Bradford, in the underbelly of the city's nightlife, the Russian agent and the drug dealer were about to change the future of Britain; and perhaps the world.

7) Khor Al Zubair, Iraq

Brad stared at his ruggedized laptop. "All good Sir. Target area quiet and the Turkey is at home."

"Is the local 'net up?"

"Yes sir, the government have not shut down their internet nationally for nearly a month and even if they did I should think the Turkey would still have access privileges"

"How does that work?" Brad opened his mouth and Mike raised a hand as if to fend him off, "No, I don't need to know."

The other soldiers sat quietly. Two of them appeared to be still asleep.

"Do you have the link to GCHQ Brad?"

Brad tried to keep the exasperation out of his voice, "Yes Sir, it runs through a satellite and is pretty much un-jammable – even if anyone knew the link existed."

The Pilot spoke again, "We are crossing into Iraq now and will reach our drop point outside Khor Al Zubair in 8 minutes Sir."

Mike replied, "Thank you Captain. Is the landing zone clear Brad?"

Brad stared at his laptop. "Sir, there is no life bigger than a rat within 3 miles of the landing zone."

Brad raised his voice instinctively for the pilot but still spoke through his headset-mike, "Captain, we have a go for landing."

"Roger that Sir."

The Dauphin looked like it was bringing a wealthy business owner home as it swung wide to the West of the fertilizer company and then between Khor Al Zubair and the steel works before coming in to land in open desert 3 miles North of town. Mac and his men worked silently but at speed to pass out four rotor drones each the size of a coffee table. Brad scanned his laptop for their vital signs and addressed Mike. "Drones are good, Sir." Mike looked at him for just a little too long and he swallowed.

As the drone rotors spun up the men passed out seven electric dirt-bikes. The drones lifted off the ground as if sentient and flew away in a flock towards Khor Al Zubair.

Meanwhile, deep within GCHQ, a group of four people, in their early twenties and wearing business suits, gripped their joysticks. They peered through artificial reality goggles and guided their respective drones towards the target. Their supervisor, a thin, balding man of perhaps 30, chewed his fingernails and watched a bank of screens showing blank desert.

In close to silence the team set off on the electric bikes across the flat sand towards Khor Al Zubair. Mac picked out the track from his mil-spec satnav and the men followed him, every man wearing night vision goggles. Mike and the SAS Troopers each had a small pack on their backs and a Heckler & Koch silenced sub machine gun, the sub-sonic 9mm MP5SD rated at less than 70 decibels, slung in front of their chest with a length of para cord. Brad carried just a small pistol, a light-weight 9mm Glock 19, in a holster on his waist belt and his rugged, milspec laptop in a bag slung around his neck.

A few minutes careful riding brought them to the edge of town. The target building was clearly visible through the night vision goggles despite the lack of moon. A modern, rather grand, two story villa with a portico on the front supporting a terrace above and set in its own lush garden of around half an acre. The team laid down their bikes beside a drone which had landed facing the target. They knelt in the pitch black, more out of habit than the hope of avoiding detection should anyone with night vision assistance look in their direction across the endless flat sand.

Mike turned to Brad. "What have we got?" Brad peered into his laptop where he toggled between views from each drone.

"The other three drones have landed surrounding the building so all access is covered Sir. There are two men that look like guards sitting by the front door."

"Okay. Mac, away you go."

8) Moscow City Centre, Russia

The Russian winter wind bit with unrelenting ferocity, its icy fangs gnawing on Moscow's architectural wonders, painting the capital in shades of frozen melancholy. Amid this frigid tableau, a fire kindled, fuelled not by wood but by indignant rage and despair, a flame burning in the hearts of the women of Moscow – the mothers, sisters and wives of conscripted soldiers.

Two women, Natalia and Zoya, stood side by side in the sea of protesters. Both mothers, both faces etched with a shared concern. They were there for a common purpose: Their sons, young men conscripted into the

Russian army to fight in Ukraine; to fight battles the people of Russia did not want to fight. Unequal battles against a foe which these young men were neither trained nor equipped to face.

Natalia, a woman of strong build and stronger resolve, clutched a photograph of her son, Artem, close to her heart. Her eyes, usually filled with a mother's love, now flickered with a fear she had never shown. She turned to Zoya, her voice barely above a whisper, yet laden with dread.

"Have you heard from Alexei?" she asked, her voice cracking with the weight of unspoken fears.
Zoya, a slender woman with a graceful presence, shook her head, her face pale against the biting cold. Her son, Alexei, was the same age as Artem, and the boys had grown up together. Now, they were in the same battalion, facing the same perilous fate.

"I received a letter two weeks ago, but nothing since," Natalia replied, her voice tinged with the desperation only a mother could know. "He said they were moving to the front lines. He tried to sound brave, but I could feel the fear behind his words."
Natalia's hand reached out to grip Natalia's, a silent gesture of solidarity. "Artem wrote to me as well," she confessed, her voice trembling. "He said they were ill-equipped, facing an enemy with clever machines and weapons they had never seen before. He's just a boy, Natalia. They both are."

Tears welled in Natalia's eyes as she nodded, the truth of Natalia's words cutting deep. "I know, my friend. I know. That's why we must make our voices heard. We must fight for them, as they are fighting for us."

The two women stood close, in the bitter cold their fears mingling with the winter air. Around them, the protest continued, voices chanting, raised in anger and desperation, but for Natalia and Zoya, the world had narrowed to their personal shared anguish.

Clad in black foreboding gear, the police were a phalanx of steel and frigid discipline. They descended like a midnight storm, wielding batons with an icy indifference that mirrored the harsh winter. Yet the women were unflinching, their courage undaunted, bodies bruised and bloody, some fell but their spirits were intact. They knew they were being watched.

The red on white snow told the story of their resistance and pain. Amid the bleakness, their spirit shone even brighter. Each baton strike strengthened their determination. The government cameras recorded their faces, but so did those of the protestors' hidden allies. And that message was carried far and wide across the electronic web.

Through the chill and the blows, the women's message spread covertly across Russian social media, into the hands of the Russian Resistance and into the hands of MI: They wanted their boys home, they wanted an end to the war, and they would not rest until they were heard. The people of Russian watched and they listened. And they passed the message on.

9) A Grand But Private Reception Room, Buckingham Palace, London, UK

The grand room in which Sir Rupert met with the King was steeped in tradition, a magnificent chamber within the heart of Buckingham Palace. The age-old wood-panelled walls echoed with the hushed whispers of conversations past, while the gold-framed, timeless ancestral portraits that adorned them bore silent witness to the ongoing dance of Royal power and strategy.

In his smart, pinstriped morning-suit Sir Rupert Grenville appeared to be a character pulled straight from a novel. A colourful character in a story recalling a long-past era of Britain's history where a gunboat or a regiment of foot was the answer to most diplomatic questions. In reality his appearance was deceptive. He was a figure polished to a shine by modern sensibilities, and set to task in a world where diplomatic power was usually exercised more subtly than in times past. A scalpel rather than an axe.

Sir Rupert was The Palace Security Manager, a nondescript title, and he headed up an organisation called the Palace Security Group, (PSG) which also had an intentionally modest and misleading name. The Palace Security Group was not a squad of old veterans who kept a watch for intruders into Palace grounds as its name might suggest. And Sir Rupert was not merely another faceless servant of the Crown but its sentinel, even its shadowy protector. In all but name, Sir Rupert was the King's Spymaster.

Standing behind the relatively public facade of the government's Secret Intelligence Service, yet entirely separate and operationally above that organisation, The Palace Security Group had its own mandate and its own set of rules. And it had agents, countless sources of information from loyal subjects in every government department, the Civil Service, the military, every major company and institution in the land and many more overseas.

Far beneath the Palace PSG had a network of bombproof offices connected to web and satellite for communications and to the "Underground" railway network for staff access. Daily access for the hundreds of carefully chosen staff loyal to their King and country who collated and acted upon that information according to the king's instructions. When all was considered and a plan laid, then a quiet word in the ear of a civil servant, a military officer or an SIS agent was all that was required to set in motion any intervention which might be thought required to bring the ship of state back on course.

Reporting directly to the King, and to no one else, PSG acted as a strong, silent rudder, steering the United Kingdom and its people clear of any icebergs and reefs which might threaten the stability of the King's realm. And those icebergs and reefs, in the modern world, might be anything from organised crime or foreign political interference in the UK's affairs to managing an insurrection overseas so as to protect a useful ally.

Rupert, with his resonant, mellifluous voice, voiced his suspicions, "Sir, I believe the Russians intend to deal a blow to the UK's reputation in retaliation for our support of the Ukraine against their invasion. I believe they intend to put pressure on us to withdraw our assistance. If you will take a look at this summary…," and handed over a single sheet of paper. On it he laid out his case, each piece of intelligence scrutinised and analysed with an astute eye and a mind as sharp as a blade.

The king scanned the summary. An eyebrow raised, "Mmmm, But I can see how it must look from their side. They don't want US missiles in Ukraine any more than the US wanted Russian missiles in Cuba. But we have no other option. Supporting Ukraine is the right thing to do and we will continue."

"Of course, sir." Sir Rupert's intuition, honed over the years, had given him warning signals that were hard to ignore. He knew the methods of the enemy and the lengths they were willing to go to meet their ends. He also knew his king and the inflexible moral code which guided his decisions.

The King listened attentively, as Sir Rupert filled in details from memory, his trust in his man total after so many years of loyal service. The spymaster's dedication was a reassuring constant in the erratic progress of global politics. His words, though carrying an edge of concern, also came with a plan, as ever there was a suggestion as to how the potential threat might be counteracted.

"…and so I believe the goal of their plan, whatever it turns out to be, will be to pressure us to withdraw our vote supporting sanctions against Russia at the UN."

"When the shoe drops, let me know immediately, wherever I am, Rupert."

"Of course, sir."

Though alliances across the world changed daily, shifting like sand, what Buckingham Palace represented stood firm. It was here that the wheels of intelligence spun to counter unseen threats and ensure the nation's course stayed steady, its people safe and prosperous. And ever by the King's side was Sir Rupert, the old spymaster, the watchful protector, always ready to go to any lengths to shield his country and its ruler from harm.

10) A Terraced House In Bradford, UK

The light from the street lamps barely made it down the narrow alley to where Wayne, now lurked. He lifted the gate-latch and entered the tidy little garden. There was washing left out, put on the line before someone went to work. A flickering lamp from a security light on a house across the road painted the home in an intermittent, ghastly light. But there was no sign of security lights or cameras here. Inside the walled enclosure, it was dark, deserted, all the windows to the house the same. Just what he was hoping for.

Approaching the window by the back door, he pulled from his pocket a thin, flat piece of metal bar - a crude window-opener. His fingers, though trembling slightly, manipulated it against the upper, smaller window frame with the dexterity of an experienced burglar. The catch yielded with a quiet click, a soft whisper of defeat that seemed thunderous in the silence of the night. Reaching through the open window with a thin arm, he opened the main window wide and froze, looking around for any sign of detection.

He slipped into the house, an unwelcome ghost in an unfamiliar home. Inside, the darkness was more profound, the quietness more deafening. But he was blind and deaf to everything except his objective. Dirty, skeletal fingers groped in the darkness, pawing over a family-worth of treasures. Anything he thought worthless he dropped to the floor.

Cheap porcelain broke, a lamp cracked on the hearth surround. The low-price furnishings in the living room clattered quietly as he tripped and stumbled over them. He froze after each accidental sound. But in the apparent chaos of his search a faint glow caught his attention.

Against the wall, on a cheap flat-pack table, sat a laptop and a phone, their screens turned off but betrayed by the faint red glow of charging indicators. The sight of them brought an unholy grin to his face, pulling taut his chapped lips, making his pallid skin even more ghoul-like.

He snatched the devices with a glee that was grotesque in its intensity, a triumphant golem-hiss escaping his cracked lips. His jittery fingers yanked the charging cables out, stuffing the devices down the front of his hoody with a sense of hungry urgency that belied his earlier carefulness.

The grim satisfaction that swept over him was palpable. These devices, insignificant as they might seem to some – though precious to their owners - were his lifeline, his ticket to the next hit that would temporarily dull his incessant cravings. The devices under his thin coat felt like a treasure, a lifeline in his pursuit of oblivion.

He exited the house as quietly as he entered, leaving behind a trail of needless destruction, an ordinary home defiled, transformed into a junkyard of broken objects and scattered belongings. The silence of the darkened home resumed its hold, the occasional gusts of wind through the still-open window a testament to the storm that had swept through its heart.

Back in the alley, Wayne disappeared into the shadows, a predator satisfied with his hunt, his sickness temporarily forgotten. The darkened home stood in his wake, a scarred victim of his desperation, its violated silence testifying to the relentless cycle of addiction, theft and destruction.

11) The President's Office, The Kremlin, Moscow, Russia

In the heart of Moscow, within the imposing Kremlin, a harsh overhead light illuminated an office, sparsely furnished in the regulation cold-war brutalist style. Seated at a massive desk was President Alexei Novikov, a bear of a man with a stern face and cold, piercing blue eyes. His heavy-set frame and towering height gave him an air of dominance, but his strength was more than just physical. Novikov was a talented and ruthless strategist, a grand-master in the game of global politics.

Opposite him sat the enigmatic General Leonid Petrenko, the formidable head of the GRU, Russian Military Intelligence. A gaunt, hawk-eyed man, his lean form deceptive. Behind the bemedalled uniform, the grey at his temples, lay a mind that thrived in the shadows of espionage and intrigue.

The room felt claustrophobic despite its size, the tension between the two men a tangible presence. Novikov, a bear cornered in his own den, had watched the shifting geopolitical landscape with growing resentment recently. The escalating conflict with Ukraine, his recent failed military campaign there, were cracks in his iron-clad façade. Cracks caused by strategic errors which were painting a target on his back for his political enemies, both foreign and domestic, to exploit.

His voice was a deep growl. "They think I'm weak, Petrenko," he seethed, slamming a fist onto the table, his fury barely controlled. "They think they can make a mockery of me, of Russia!"

Petrenko met the President's gaze with his own icy stare. "The United Kingdom supporting Ukraine, training their troops, supplying them with advanced weaponry... It's a blatant provocation," he said calmly.

Novikov nodded, a cruel smirk twisting his lips. "Advanced weaponry, artillery, armour, those cursed armed drones..." He spat out the last word with a bitterness that soured even the air. "Our soldiers are dying, being slaughtered like animals, while they celebrate in their grand halls."

"It was never about Ukraine," Petrenko interjected, his voice steady despite the dangerous topic. "It was about the United States keeping their weapons factories busy, about stopping our sales of gas to Europe and replacing it with their own, about keeping NATO in line. If you had allowed Ukraine to join them, we would have had their missiles on our doorstep."

Novikov's cold gaze hardened. "Exactly like Cuban Missile Crisis...but in reverse." His voice was barely above a whisper, yet it filled the room, icy and brutal. "And the US reacted to the placing of our missiles in their backyard with a threat of global war. We had to intervene, for the safety of Mother Russia. Now they paint us the villains. The Western world, led by their puppet media, always eager to point finger at us."

Petrenko nodded, considering how to channel the anger coursing through the President's veins. "We've always been their scapegoat, Mr. President, their excuse for military spending, but we're not powerless. We won't be trampled on. We have clever people of our own."

A long silence stretched between the two men, filled only by the ticking of a grandfather clock against the far wall. Then, Novikov's voice sliced through the silence, carrying with it an icy promise. "They've made their move, and we have suffered from their actions. But they forget, every action has a reaction. The UK have been pleased to act for the US to gain their favour and maintain unity, so they will face our wrath. Unlike the US, the UK is too timid to respond with more than words. So we will punish the UK, divide those two allies and revenge will be ours."

As the words hung in the room, the tension felt sharper, the shadows darker. Novikov, the old bear cornered in his den, was showing his claws. His growl echoed over the Kremlin walls, a menacing promise of a storm brewing on the horizon.

12) A Large Villa On The Outskirts Of Khor Al Zubair, Iraq

Two SAS troopers crept to within 50 feet of the guards and dropped them with a single shot to each head from their silenced MP5s. Closing with their targets, knives under the ribcage and into the heart then a twist ensured they were dead. The blood stops squirting when the heart stops. Mike caught Mac's eye and nodded. The team set off for the house, Brad's face a little paler.

The other two troopers quietly opened the unlocked door and stepped inside, weapons at the ready. The rest of the team arrived at the door. Three faint thuds marked the repeated discharge of the weapons inside and the team entered the house, dragging the two dead guards in with them. Already there were another three bodies on the floor in the hall. Two women in Western dress wearing carpet slippers and a boy-child of around 10 years old.

"Clear this floor" Mike instructed Mac. Brad stared at the dead child for a moment, a look of shock on his face. One of the troopers saw his reaction and commented without thinking, "This is not your X-Box kiddo."

Troopers opened each door in turn without further command. At one a trooper stepped inside and there was a round fired, then two more in quick succession. He came out again, face expressionless, "Clear."

"Upstairs now." Mike might have been trying to order a pizza without waking the baby. The troopers lead off upstairs and checked the rooms. There were three more shots fired and a brief expression of male surprise followed by the sound of a scuffle. Mike and Brad followed the troopers upstairs and into the room from where the noise had come. One of the troopers was pinning a swarthy, middle aged man to the floor. "Is this him, sir?"

Mike nodded to the trooper and turned to Mac, "Set up to hold a perimeter around the house please," then to Brad, "Tell Sunray we have caught the Turkey."

Mac led two troopers downstairs, leaving the one holding the man and one keeping watch at a window.

Brad opened his laptop on a table and tapped away for a few moments.

Mike knelt down and turned the man's face to see it more clearly. There was a small mole in front of the left ear. "This is definitely the Turkey." Mike stepped back and opened a camo bag. Pulling out a syringe, he filled it from a vial and held it up to the light, flicking the air bubbles out and squirting excess fluid into the air as he measured the dose. The man on the ground struggled but could not move against the trooper's joint locks. Mike injected the fluid into the man's buttock through his trousers and stood back, glancing at his watch.

The trooper holding the man down asked, "Do you want me to plasticuff him, sir?"

"No need, the sodium pentothal will have him chemically hypnotised in about 40 seconds so you can let go when you feel him relax."

The other trooper looked out of the window, changing sides to open his view. Mike watched the Turkey, as did Brad from behind his laptop, Brad's mouth a little open and dry. A minute passed and the trooper relaxed his grip then stepped back. Mike knelt down by the Turkey and spoke to the man in Farsi, his native language, their captive being Iranian.

"You are safe now Farhad. We are your friends and here to help you stop the American plot. But to help you we need the access code to your account. Tell me the code Farhad."

Brad sat at a table poised over his laptop. Already he had accessed the room's wifi and brought up the login screen for the Turkey's VAJA account through the local router, his access to the Iranian Intelligence main server.

"Tell me the code so we can help you Farhad."

Farhad began to cough, a common side effect of the drug. Then he recovered and mumbled something.

"Tell me again Farhad."

Farhad spoke quietly to Mike in Farsi. Mike turned to Brad, "EX1 9!F ?RS".

Brad typed the code into his laptop. "No, wrong code, sir."

"Farhad, tell me again, what is the access code we need to be able to help you run your network?"

Farhad spoke again, in Farsi, and accented one letter.

Mike intoned, "EX1 9!F ?OS"

Brad almost shouted, "We're in, Sir!"

Mike remained deadpan, "Are you absolutely sure we are in Brad?"

"Yes sir, we are in to their central database! We own the Iranian Intel network now!"

"Calm down Brad. Make sure GCHQ have the code this instant in case anything goes wrong."

"Done that, Sir – its automatic."

"Okay, fine." Mike lifted his MP5 and fired twice. One bullet hit Farhad's forehead between the eyes, the second the right eyeball. There was a splash of fluid from the bursting eyeball which splashed onto Mikes face. He wiped it off his cheek with a finger. Brad looked at Mike, an expression of shock on his face.

Mike smiled with no humour whatsoever. "Omelettes and Eggs, Brad. Listen, when this is found we want it to look like an assassination so leave nothing behind bar brass."

Brad had gotten a grip of himself, "Copy that, sir."

"I've been thinking Brad. You know when the Iranians find this chap dead, won't they close his account access and so on?"

Brad smiled grimly, "It will be way too late by then, sir. We will have access to all their servers and have copied everything on them within minutes. There will be a team working on this in London as we speak."

Mike shook his head, impressed. Automatic fire began a little distance away. Light weapons, multiple bursts. A window burst in as it was hit by fire. The trooper standing by it stepped sideways away from the flying glass and the men downstairs began to return fire.

13) A Residential Backstreet In Bradford, UK

The asphalt pathways were damp underfoot from the steady drizzle and the curtains of the humble terraced houses were closed against prying eyes and the evening city air. From the shadows emerged a gaunt figure, his skeletal frame a spectre amidst the glow of Bradford streetlights. This spectre was Wayne, a sorry apparition caught in the throes of addiction. His legs shook with anticipation as he crabbed towards his target, a shiny new black BMW purring quietly by the kerb. Its expected presence in the dilapidated backstreet felt to him like a mechanical beacon of hope.

In the car sat two case-hardened young men, each a stark contrast to Wayne. One, as white as the powder their trade revolved around, a craggy face toughened by the fists of life. The other, a dark-skinned man whose eyes shone with the cynical wisdom of street smarts. Their bodies bore the hidden scars of their harsh lives. Their alert posture told tales of countless battles fought against rival drug dealers, thieves, and the ever-vigilant police.

Around them, a cloud of paranoia swirled. The white man's gaze darted left and right through the windscreen searching the darkness outside the car, his senses pricked at every shadow and echo. He was an animal, a predator in the urban jungle, his instincts on high alert for threats that lurked unseen - and prey. His counterpart, the coloured man, followed a similar routine, his eyes flicking from the second rear-view mirror to the protective arsenal that waited ready within their reach. Knives, spiked clubs, cruel tools carried to support the survival instincts of these drug dealers. Lethal deterrents to any foolhardy thieves, or debtors who dared to cross them.

Wayne, repulsive and pitiful in his desperation, approached the BMW haltingly. His entrance on the stage was met with unmasked scorn from the dealers.

“What’cha doing Bro?” The coloured man scoffed, laughing at his trembling hands and the sweat that trickled down his dirty face. But the gleam in the dealer’s eyes betrayed their satisfaction at his dependence. His misery was their living, after all

Once he was in the relative safety of the back seat, their language morphed into a Jafaican slang as if to confirm the boy as an outsider. Their words slid between one another, a play of coded conversation, a medley of power and bravado that cut through the chilly night air. Their voices dripped with a lethal combination of indifference and menace, reinforcing their dominance over the trembling boy.

With a furtive exchange of his cash for two packages of the coveted white powder, the deal was done. Their scornful laughter followed him as he limped away, clutching his temporary salvation. The backstreet reclaimed its silence, left once again to the quiet hum of the BMW and the short wait for the next desperate soul sharing the twisted dance of survival and supremacy.

14) A Russian Military Laboratory, Shikhany, Saratov Oblast (Province), Russia

In the belly of a huge but nondescript industrial building, in the heartland of Russia, far away from prying eyes, there was a laboratory. A laboratory on a scale like few others; a research and production facility like a small town dedicated to chemistry.

The air was thick with a bitter, acrid stench, a telltale, perhaps, of malign purpose. Tubes, beakers, and vials, pregnant with crystalline powder and liquids of varying hues, were strewn haphazardly across the stainless steel counters. A testament, perhaps to the amorality of science.

Against this seemingly disorderly backdrop, and dressed in a stained lab coat, a strange figure stalked his lair of scientific endeavour. Old, but still tall, thin and round-shouldered, hair long and straggling over his shoulders, Dr. Lev Antonovich looked over rows of bent, working heads, checked measurements and readings, glared at sheets of records. His countenance, lined with age and obsession, flickered in the spectral light reflected from the complex glassware.

Antonovich inspected a Petri dish containing the latest iteration, a sinister additive designed to modify the effects of cocaine. The previous experiments conducted in the UK had yielded disappointing results. Too weak, too quick, too lethal - none had provoked the desired state of mind he sought to induce. But he was getting closer.

His icy gaze skimmed over a group of underlings huddled at a workbench, their fear almost palpable. They mixed compounds, measured powders, and condensed liquids always under his watchful eyes. Any mistake could spell disaster for the operation. And those at their level in the food chain would be punished. Severely.

A door clicked open, disturbing the working hum. General Kuznetsov entered, his large frame almost filling the doorway. His aura entirely filling the room. He strode over to Antonovich, his old fashioned steel-shod boots clacking ominously on the tiled floor. "What do you have for me Comrade Doctor? A success I can take to the President?" The General looked straight into his eyes, long enough to make a stronger man look down.

A shadow of fear passed over the Doctor's face and he shook his head, lips pursed, "Still not quite the result we are looking for Comrade General. I need at least one more test to be sure. Not more than two."

The General held his silence a little too long. He knew how to manipulate fear like a master artist handling a brush.
Antonovich's attitude changed, he was suddenly emboldened for no obvious reason, "Pressure, time, its all I hear! You want results now yet if the additive fails to achieve our goal we are lost and I carry the blame. What would you have me do?"

"I would have you get it right Comrade Doctor." The words cut the air like shrapnel. If a lizard could talk it would show more compassion.

Antonovich considered the scale of their upcoming operation. Millions of doses to manufacture and ship overseas. Then to be smuggled into the UK and distributed through a national network of drug traffickers. And then to be unleashed upon the unsuspecting addicts in the UK. All under the chilling shadow of the President's rage if they failed to deliver the required result. But first they had to get the formula just right. It must be right but it also must be soon. Yet each test needed to be on at least a hundred subjects and all of them normal drug addicts to produce reliable statistics on the effects.

Antonovich spoke calmly now he was sure of his ground, "I need time for one more test, maybe two. Neither of us will be popular in the Kremlin if the additive does not work properly." His thin lips curled into a macabre smile. He knew the General would share his reward and his blame according to their results. The additive was not just another intricate chemical compound. It was a weapon of mass destruction.

The General stared again for a little too long, but he knew the Doctor was right and felt the balance of power between them shift slightly. Still, his face remained impassive, he gave nothing away. "You must make your choices and your tests, Doctor. And we will expect to see the additive formula settled within the next two weeks."

The room echoed with the low rumble of machines, the clinking of glassware, the whisper of instructions, the occasional hiss of released gas The workers nearby were striving to hear the conversation.

As Kuznetsov left and the door slammed shut behind him, the horror of the monstrous plan seemed to hang heavy in the tainted air. A new war was about to be unleashed. Not on a battlefield but in the veins of the UK's vulnerable citizens.

15) A Large Villa On The Outskirts Of Khor Al Zubair, Iraq

They had just turned for the door when Brad looked up from his tablet and called out, "There are soldiers coming, sir!"

"Calm down Brad. No plan survives contact with the enemy. Have our drones hold them off and take out their leaders if they can."

Brad tapped rapidly on his laptop. "The soldiers have shot down two of the drones already, sir."

Mike's voice remained conversational as he looked over Brad's shoulder at the laptop screen. "I'm not surprised. These drones mounting MP5s are great for recce and the odd kill shot but too clumsy for tactical. Anyway, I would say these guys are Iranian Special Forces from the their night vision gear. Looks like they know what they are doing. Get me Eagle on voice."

Brad tapped rapidly into the keyboard and a cheerful, very relaxed and plummy British voice sounded in their helmet headsets. "Three Niner, Eagle Niner. What can I do for you chaps?"

Mike thought for a moment. "Eagle Niner, I need to escalate this contact. We have visitors arriving in some strength. Too many for us to deal with. I need them neutralising, Over."

"Jolly good. Wilco Out."

Squadron Leader William Naseby was sitting in a converted shipping container at Royal Air Force Station Waddington, Lincolnshire, in the East of England. He leaned forward a little as he adjusted his headset and looked closely into the screen through which he controlled the MQ-9A Reaper drone which, operating out of Ali Al Salem air base in Kuwait was already on station above the team and waiting to give fire support.

On his aircraft's bomb struts were six Laser JDAMs, laser guided bombs of 500 pounds apiece. Each of these bombs was capable, being of the newer type with pre-fragmented casing, of killing everything within an area of about 4 or 5 acres when detonating above open ground.

A burst of machine gun fire came through the window, ripping plaster from the wall opposite. Brad dived to the floor. Mike was already sitting on the floor with his back against the wall. He spoke to the Reaper pilot, "Eagle, we are taking fire from the South East at the Target Loc. Support now over."

"Three Niner, support is on its way as we speak gentlemen. Eagle Out."

A few moments later the building seemed to rock and the blast whipped the remaining window glass across the room over their heads like hail in a storm. Mike spoke to Mac over their unit net, "That felt like a JDAM to me. What do you think Mac?"

"Ah'm fair certain that wis a JDAM, sir." Brad looked at Mike as if they were crazy, which in a certain respect they were.

Mike signalled to Brad to follow him out the door and led downstairs. He shouted to the troopers spread around the outside of the house, "Okay guys, lets go home. Keep your eyes open" Another bomb struck some way off and a moment later shrapnel hissed over their heads.

Within the walled garden the tops had been neatly cut from three palm trees at increasing heights leaving them "sized off" like guardsmen. Outside the garden, the neighbourhood had been turned into a battle zone. Some houses were totally flattened and power lines were shorting out where they had dropped onto an ornamental wall. The team jogged back to their bikes.

16) A Filthy Derelict House In Bradford, UK

Full dark had settled over this suburb of Bradford, slightly improving the appearance of a low-rent housing estate now bathed in the sickly yellow glow of dim streetlights. Rats squealed as they scurried over half-eaten food in the rubbish-strewn alley. Wayne, his veins throbbing with anticipation, stumbled through the broken back door of an abandoned terraced house and into the shattered remains of what was once a family kitchen.

Years of abuse had stripped him to the bone and each rib stood out as a painful testament to his addiction. His eyes, sunken and ringed with shadows, scanned the room with a frantic desperation that belied his skeletal frame. His lips were chapped and bloody, curving into a grotesque grimace, revealing teeth yellowed by neglect. He looked more like a wraith, an apparition of the living, a spectre of the healthy boy he was, only a few years ago.

The kitchen, a grim tableau of decay, echoed the teen's own misery. Wallpaper, once bright and cheery, hung in tattered shreds from the water-stained walls, and a single, tattered net curtain hung from a rusty rail, shuddering in the draught.

With shaking hands, Wayne unwrapped a small package, the crumpled foil catching the sparse light that filtered in through the broken window. His grimy fingers trembled, betraying his desperation. He mixed the white powder with water in the bowl of a filthy spoon and laid it on a flat space amongst the detritus, his movements practised, mechanical, automatic. The anticipation was a fire in his veins, consuming his thoughts, making his heart pound in his chest. Picking a used syringe from the floor he sucked the mixture into the tube.

Wrapping a ragged piece of cloth around his arm, he knotted it. The skin there was mottled with bruises and lines of puncture wounds tracking veins, a physical diary of his downward spiral. He put a stick under the cloth and twisted to pull it tight and lift the veins. With one swift motion, he pushed the needle into a distended vein and injected the chemicals into his body. A brief grimace of pain flashed across his face, a wait of a few moments and it was replaced with a look of sheer bliss as the warm glow spread through his body.

Then he collapsed on the floor, unconscious.

17) HMS Defender, A British Type 45 Guided Missile Destroyer, The Persian Gulf, Off Saudi Arabia

HMS Defender cut through the flat sea at a cruising 18 knots. Within her, the crew toiled, cleaning, chipping paint, painting, servicing the machinery, standing watch and running the never-ending fire drills; all ever present features of life aboard a British warship.

The helicopter hangar doubled as a gym where Mike and Mac worked out alone on this early morning. The team were sleeping off a drinking session. Someone had a new son at home. Both men were pumping away on exercise bikes, avoiding the weights beloved of Royal Marines which built bulk and strength but sabotaged the ability to run or march long distances.

Mike was tall and athletic but looked lean with his shirt off, like a rather handsome pro tennis player; perhaps one with a shady background from the scars which criss-crossed his body.

Mac looked wiry but fit in his shorts with over-developed thighs and calves from years of intense work to improve his already superhuman performance when marching and carrying weight on his back.

The effort was steady, breathing was easy and regular for these super-fit men, easy enough to talk if there was something worth saying, "Every job comes with its own surprises," Mike remarked.

“Aye, always,” Mac responded, concentrating on keeping to his breathing pattern.

Mike continued, "No plan survives contact with the enemy." His words, a quote attributed to the great military strategist Helmuth von Moltke, hung in the air, a stark reminder of the realities of warfare.

No sooner had he spoken but action stations sounded, "Action stations, action stations. This is not a drill," came over the tannoy; then the hooter kicked off as the crew ran to their combat positions.

Mac looked calmly across at Mike, still peddling, "Weel, there's a hing fur ye."

"We're passengers Mac. I'll find an officer."

Mac grinned knowingly, "Aye, ye will."

Before they had time to move, the ship's chopper crew ran into the hangar and began to gather their kit at speed. Other sailors were moving around purposefully, presumably getting ready to launch the Wildcat, but the visiting Dauphin blocked access to the rear deck. Then the Dauphin crew arrived with their kit on.

Mike stepped out onto the rear deck where it was a little less busy. A bright sun shone from low in a clear sky; over the port bow as the Defender steamed South. Suddenly the Sea Ceptor system launched a CAMM ER missile from the bank of vertical-launch missile tubes on the fore deck. It accelerated vertically to Mach 4 in a couple of seconds and its course shifted to curve towards the North. It moments it was out of sight, the trail of smoke fading like a dream.

The ship heeled over as she turned sharply to Port and Mike grabbed a wire railing to keep his feet. The 4.5 inch gun turret moved sharply left and right, the barrel up and down, like a waking sleeper easing a stiff neck.

High in the sky, off the Port bow now and to the North there was the flash of an explosion, perhaps 20 miles away. Mac came up beside Mike, "Whit's that?"

"I think we just shot down an incoming missile Mac. Looks like we upset someone."

"Ah wonder ta?" Mac asked who that might be, rhetorically.

Another roar and smoke billowed out to Port from the front deck as another missile was launched. This time a Naval Strike Missile from the sloping, side-facing tubes immediately in front of the bridge. The missile soared a few hundred feet into the air then came back down and levelled off, tracking away to the North almost skimming the waves at just under the speed of sound.

"The sailors need twa jags, then?" Mac shook his head in mock scorn.

Mike chuckled, "The first missile was to shoot down something in the air coming this way. A missile probably. The second was a kind of smart cruise missile and is off to kill a ship, probably. Maybe a land base but I think it would be a ship."

"Fechtin's nae fun if ye cannae see the enemy, aye?"

"That's a point of view, certainly Mac. But I think we are killing an Iranian warship flying a false flag or perhaps a largish civilian vessel of some kind. Reason being, if they fired on this ship from Iran we would be at war now."

Moments later a flash like lightening lit the sky to the North from an explosion over the horizon.

18) A Street Of Terraced Houses, Close To The Filthy Derelict House, Bradford, UK

The Pakistani British family had spent their Saturday morning shopping; meandering happily through the aisles of the bustling local market, looking for a present for their little girl. The wife's bright green outfit, a pleasant blend of modern style and cultural tradition, billowed around her as they walked, while her husband's clothing was casual and entirely Western in style, a testament to their intertwined identities.

Their daughter Ayesha, nine years old next week, skipped along with them, her youthful energy shining through bright eyes and uncontainable laughter. As the trio made their way along the residential street and approached their modest home, the light of the morning sun painted the houses with a warm glow. It was the perfect picture of a peaceful family morning.

Not far away, Wayne awoke to the harsh light of day. The transformation of his features and temperament was immediate and dramatic; his eyes glazed over for a moment, then the hungry desperation in them was replaced by uncontrollable rage. He froze and his eyes went blank, staring at something only he could see. Then, with a primal scream, he leapt to his feet and ripped open a drawer.

His pupils were dilated, and the bloodshot whites almost hidden, but he focused with deadly intent and his fingers wrapped around the handle of a carving knife. A wild look on his face, he burst out of the house through kitchen door, the rage propelling him into the back alley. His anguished cries echoed and brought eyes to windows, but no more.

His gaze darted left and right as if searching. The alley was empty so he took a cut through a garage lot which opened out onto another, cleaner, street. A look of unfocused rage twisted his face into a grimace and he gripped the carving knife in a white knuckled hand. He saw the unsuspecting family, and broke into a run, heading straight for them.

The husband noticed him first, his eyes widening with alarm. He instinctively stepped in front of his wife and daughter, placing himself between them and the approaching threat. With a cry, he lunged towards the attacker. But the teen was faster, his drug-fuelled frenzy lending him an unnatural speed. He hacked downwards at the husband, catching him in the shoulder beside his neck. The knife slid in to its handle and the husband crumpled to the pavement. He fell backwards onto the shopping bags dropped behind him, their contents spilling out onto the pavement. His pumping blood ran across the flagstones and amongst his groceries.

His wife brought her hands to her cheeks and screamed, a sound of raw fear that echoed through the quiet street. Then, acting on instinct, she pulled their daughter to her, bending over and sheltering her with her body. Wayne was pitiless and turned his attention to the cowering woman, his knife rose and fell repeatedly, finding its mark time and again in her back with horrific precision.

Just when it seemed Ayesha would be killed too, the front door of a nearby house flew open. A group of Sikh men poured out onto the street, their turbans a swirl of colours in the morning light. One of them held a ceremonial sword, its long blade glinting in the setting sun. The others brandished smaller knives, the Kirpans which every male Sikh must carry in order to fulfil his oath to protect the innocent and the weak. With the fearlessness customary amongst Sikh men, they ran towards the assailant.

The sight of the armed men gave Wayne a moment's pause, and probably saved Ayesha's life, but his drug-addled mind was too far gone to recognise danger. He lunged at the newcomers, but they were ready for him. They surrounded him and took the advantage of numbers. There was a flurry of movement, the clash of metal against metal, and the assailant was disarmed, subdued and then pinned under the weight of several strong men.

Through their heroic intervention, the Sikhs had managed to overpower the crazed attacker without taking his life. As the police sirens began to wail in the distance, the men held the attacker down, their breathing still ragged, their hearts heavy with the knowledge of the horror they had just witnessed. A lady appeared from the same house as the men and held Ayesha to her, shielding her eyes from the horror of her dead parents lying in their own blood and groceries.

19) General Nikolai Kuznetsov's Dacha Outside Moscow

General Nikolai Kuznetsov sat across the mahogany dining table from his wife, Natalia. Their marriage was rooted in formality, a sturdy oak borne of deep-seated respect, companionship, and shared ideals. Nikolai was a strong figure, his life moulded by the military's iron fist. Yet deep beneath this firm exterior, there was a tenderness. He was a husband, a father, and at heart, a man who cared deeply about both his family and his country.

The war in Ukraine was not going as expected. Each day brought more casualty reports of young soldiers, the sons of Russia, lost in a conflict that was gaining negative attention worldwide. It gnawed at Nikolai. The numbers were not just figures; they were families torn apart, futures stolen. It was the sight of the Union Jack flying alongside the Ukrainian flags that stoked the fire of frustration within him. He knew that the UK's support, its advanced weaponry, its training – they were the hidden thorns tearing at his country's soldiers. His fists clenched at the thought. The UK would not escape unscathed; he would make sure of it.

Alexander, their only son, a dashing figure in his pilot's uniform, was a mirror of his father's younger days. But rather than a soldier, he was a fast jet pilot, a prestigious position that only fuelled Natalia's worries. She had seen the casualty reports, the list of names growing longer each day. Her heart clenched with the fear that Alexander's name might be added to that list. She knew he would take risks, do anything to impress his father.

As the dinner proceeded in their stylish, old-world dining room, Natalia mentioned her concerns. Her soft voice, usually filled only with warmth, trembled slightly as she spoke of the increased stress she had noticed in Nikolai. He had been working long hours, often returning home well past midnight. His health was a topic they both tip-toed around. A heart problem that had been kept under control was now literally a ticking time bomb as a result of the added stress.

She pleaded with him to consider retirement, to step away from battlegrounds and politics. "Nikolai," she said, her eyes filled with worry, "You've done enough for Russia, Nikolai no man could have done more. You should retire. Our son is risking his life every day because of this war but your risk is self-imposed. I have enough to worry about with him on the front line."

Nikolai's gaze softened as he looked at his wife. He reached out, cradling her small hand within his paws. "I can't," he told her, his voice filled with a regret he rarely showed. "Not yet. Not when there's still so much at stake."

Natalia watched as her husband rose, moving to the window that overlooked the distant Moscow skyline. He stood there, a silhouette against the glimmering city lights, the weight of the world on his shoulders.

"I need to ensure our country's security, its place in the world," he said quietly, more to himself than to her. "We must stand firm against this American-inspired threat, Natalia. It's not just about Ukraine; it's about the safety of our people, our son. The future of our country."

The room fell into silence, their concerns hanging in the air like an unfinished conversation. Both knew the sacrifices they had to make. Both knew the risks. Yet, they stood together, two pillars in the storm, anchored by their love for their son, their country, and each other.

20) A Street Of Terraced Houses, Close To The Filthy, Derelict House, Bradford, UK

The video of what had happened was replaying over and over in little Ayesha's mind. Her parents had been her world, her shield against all evils, and now they were no more. The man who took them was a demon, his crazed eyes and lethal knife an embodiment of a terror she would never forget, never get over.

The kind-hearted Sikh lady, Eknoor, gently began to lead Ayesha away from the scene towards her own home. Her heart ached for the child. She put her arms around her, whispering words of comfort and courage, knowing all too well they were lost in the tempest of the child's emotions. Around them, the street buzzed with alarm and confusion. The heroic men were still there, holding a limp Wayne, their bearded faces grim and their hands smeared with blood. Thankfully, none of it their own.

The wail of sirens echoed, growing louder as the emergency services drew closer. So Eknoor began to lead Ayesha back to where she might receive help. And as the flashing police lights painted eerie, dancing shadows on the brick façade of the terraced houses, a sleek Audi Saloon slowed past the scene.

Her detached mind fixing on random things as the shock set in, Ayesha saw a familiar face inside the luxury car, that of Mr. Iqbal, a man not of her parents' community, but someone she had seen near the local mosque during Eid. He was accompanied by three other men, a trio of half seen shadows in the late-night gloom. She froze and stared at them in horror.

They were laughing. Laughing, looking towards her parents bodies still on the pavement. Ayesha couldn't comprehend it. Their mirth felt like the cruellest joke, a brutal mockery of her tragedy. Her pain, her loss, was but a fleeting amusement for them. Their laughter a jarring note in the symphony of sirens and crying that filled the night.

As the car disappeared around the corner, the ambulance finally arrived. Medics leaped out, their faces a mask of professionalism hiding the heartbreak of attending one-too-many victims of senseless violence. As a lady tended to Ayesha, she felt detached from her surroundings, numb to the clinical touches and soothing words. The only thing that echoed in her mind was the laughter of the men in the Audi, a haunting soundtrack to the darkest day of her short life.

21) Billy's Restaurant, Mayfair, London, UK

The restaurant was of the kind where people without a title or connections can wait for months for a table. It was refined, it was expensive and it was discreet. So people who valued discretion ate there. People who were known by the public, and people who did not want to be known. The price of a meal would rent a family home for a month.

An aura of sophisticated elegance surrounded Yelena Ivanova, an invisible, ethereal glow that rendered the tall Russian lady mesmerizingly beautiful. Her distinct accent, which she could switch on and off at will, held a hint of the steppes, a touch of Moscow's high society and the subtle nuances of impeccable British education. Every syllable she spoke dripped with charm, so much so that men, even those of experience and high standing, were often left spellbound, speechless like teenage boys in her presence.

Currently accredited to the Russian Embassy in London, she was, in truth, an intelligence agent; trained from adolescence to be a lethal combination of beauty, brains and skill, the perfect weapon in the endless game of international intrigue. In her tailored skirt suit, Yelena embodied the sophistication of her diplomatic cover. Yet beneath the civilised exterior hid a predator's cunning, a merciless disposition as cold as the Siberian winter.

Sir Henry Atwood, the head of SIS, was a gentleman to the core. An aristocrat who carried an air of nobility as effortlessly as he carried the responsibility for the UK's national security on his shoulders. His family was ancient, his education the best, his club exclusive. His polished exterior, however, hid the scars of battles fought, not on the frontlines since his youth as a guards officer, but on committees, behind closed doors and in shadowy corridors.

A subtle tell-tale sign of their past encounters was hinted at in their intimate conversation. Yelena had slept with him once already and was working now to exploit the few chinks in his otherwise formidable armour. She was tasked with an ambitious mission: Her superiors wanted her to ensnare the actual head of the British SIS, a man with access to most of the UK's secrets both military and diplomatic. To compromise him with a temptation few could resist, her continued friendship and an exceedingly lucrative payment for a seemingly very, very insignificant favour.

A favour which, once granted could be parlayed into bigger favours, more useful betrayals by the careful use of implied blackmail. The threat of exposure if he refused to share the next, very slightly bigger secret. It was a classic trap, one where greed could quickly turn into a snare that would lock a man in, keep forever under their control, trapped by the threat of exposure and the consequent loss of freedom, family, wealth and reputation.

To accomplish her mission, Yelena played her role to perfection. Her voice, soft yet assertive, filled the air with sincerity as she delicately spun her web around Sir Atwood. She combined calculated flattery with delicate hints at their shared past, and their potential future, gradually leading the conversation to the point of her true objective.

"Darling, I need a card to get me into the MP's bar in the House. Can you get me one do you think?

Sir Henry raised an eyebrow at the outright request to break the rules.

"I would not ask but I have to write a report and you know my boss, the hag that hates me, she checks everything I do. I need to show her something for all the time I have spent with you. I know money is not important to you but there would be a substantial payment."

On the outside, it seemed like a harmless favour, a tiny deviation from protocol. The bait was laid out enticingly, the trap set. The lure of the reward, and the idea of it coming from someone he had become intimately involved with, might want to impress, could be enough to push him over the edge, to make him agree to her proposition. And if that were not enough, another night with her for sure.

As the stakes of the conversation became apparent, Yelena continued to hold his gaze, her emerald eyes reflecting a serenity that was at odds with the high-wire act playing out between them. But, in the merciless world of international espionage, the game was all about keeping one's nerve. And as she waited for Sir Henry's response, Yelena knew she had played her hand to perfection.

22) Thornbury Business Park, East Bradford, UK

The sleek Audi Saloon which had appeared at the family murder scene earlier was now a prowling beast as it navigated the rain-glossed streets leaving the city. It slid smoothly into a desolate, low-rent industrial estate wearing number plates belonging to a similar car owned by an accountant in Surrey. All the little businesses were closed at this time of night, except for one unit across the way from where they stopped. Inside the vehicle, five figures tensed for action. Among them, Faris Iqbal. He bore a stoic, controlled expression, a stark contrast to the loud, bragging, macho anticipation that bristled around him.

The car's doors swung open, and the men leapt out, running into the unit. Long blades and clubs were gripped tightly in their hands, brutal tools of their trade. Faris ran ahead of the gang like a man possessed, his actions driven by a real need to impress. His long, curved blade slashed one man, opened up the face of another, then he found a third target, and he plunged the blade in with brutal aggression. The other man's eyes widened in surprise, and then dimmed as his life bled out onto the cold concrete. The killer stepped back, a dark satisfaction creeping onto his face.

Methodically, the other gang members cornered the remaining occupants of the unit and stabbed or beat them to the floor. The scene was ruthless and bloody. Men fell like rag dolls, their bodies hitting the oily concrete, as the ferocious onslaught took them by surprise. Groans and cries of fear from the victims mixed with the heavy breathing and curses of the aggressors, the harsh grating of metal on flesh and bone.

Quiet had fallen in the unit. The rival gang was destroyed, the territory claimed. Faris's actions, as merciless as they were, had solidified his standing within his gang. Their nods and glances now held a new, respect for him. Their minds grasping a new, chilling realization. Faris Iqbal, their newly proven comrade, was not a man to be trifled with.

Leaving one of the defeated rival gang members writhing on the blood-slicked concrete and the others dangerously still, the triumphant gang swaggered back to their Audi. They had emerged victorious once again, only the night bearing witness to the savagery of their territorial claim. Faris, seated again in the car's plush interior, stared out of the window into the night, his reflection, and his mind, tainted by the brutal necessity of his actions.

Behind the hardened veneer of the ruthless thug, the MI5 agent was locked in a grim introspection. He had crossed a line tonight, spilled blood in the service of a higher purpose. He had no choice, his duty demanded it and he would be covered against legal repercussions, but his humanity recoiled at his first kill. The city's night seemed a little darker, its shadows a little deeper.

23) Riaz Khan's House, Bradford, UK

The house was new, it was big and it was gauche. It had pillars and balconies enough to give any footballer's wife a wet dream. Like a paste diamond in a yard sale, it sat in a small, high price enclave amongst the general austerity of Bradford housing. By any reasonable measure, this ostentatious display of wealth amongst relative poverty was in bad taste. But the owner clearly had money.

The house did not just reek of decadence. Today the air was heady with the pungent aroma of expensive cigars which entirely failed to cover the smell of various other drugs drifting with the noise through from the party room. Comfortably cocooned in expensive leather, in a room used as an office, laid back or acting so, two men wore masks of smug satisfaction from their raid on the rival gang's industrial unit. And this party was a little celebration. A reward for the crew and their contacts.

One of these men was the drug-gang leader, Riaz Khan, a man of massively powerful build, if just short of six feet tall. He had a distinctly hoarse voice and his cheeks bore the scars of smallpox from his youth in Pakistan. Besides the pox-scars, his face featured a prominent, jagged knife scar which had healed badly. Or had been rubbed with lemon juice to make the owner look tough. If it was lemon juice, it had worked.

Riaz lifted his attention from a home made video playing on his mobile phone and leaned forward towards his number two, Jacko, piercing the veil of tobacco smoke with a gaze that was as hard as the streets they ruled. "Our new boy, Fa (Faris), he's proven himself. Look at this."

Jacko looked over Riaz's shoulder at the video. He was a bull of a man with a strange, blank gaze, his obese hulking frame witness to many a battle fought and won. He watched the clip to the end and appeared to consider. He nodded, the unspoken agreement hanging heavily between them for a moment. Faris Iqbal had indeed proven his worth, proven his reliability by getting his hands stained with the same blood that bound them all. If he betrayed them in future he would spend time in goal because he had been discretely caught on a phone camera slashing and stabbing their enemies in the fight.

Beyond the closed doors of the private room, the sound of laughter and pulsing music filled the air. The house was filled with young people desperately trying to enjoy themselves, all members of the gang, hangers-on or their women. Or someone's women anyway. They lounged on plush couches surrounded by bottles and pizzas, their faces reflecting alternately joy and emptiness. The too-loud music pulsed from oversize speakers, drugs and alcohol flowed freely, and the scantily clad young white-women, caught like shiny flies in the web of this dangerous world, moved between the men with a drug-dazed complacency.

In their office, Riaz and Jacko continued deep in conversation. Their discussion centred on alliances with other gangs, drug distribution areas, control of streets and the always precarious balance of power with other big players. Faris Iqbal, now he could be trusted, would become an essential part of their operation.

The house, luxurious and sprawling, was more than a place to sleep or party; it was a stronghold and a headquarters. The opulent surroundings belied the ruthlessness with which this criminal organization operated. Every decision made within these walls reverberated through the streets for miles around, a game of chess played with human lives.

In the party-room Faris drank as little as he dared. He gave the impression of listening to the opinions of a drug-addled whore on the state of the nation. His cover was more solid than it had been before the fight but it remained vulnerable to compromise if he put just a toe wrong. His role demanded both participation in, and observation of, this underworld in order to stay alive and do his job. He now had become one of them, his actions driven by necessity but weighed down by the moral compromises required.

The night wore on, the house continuing to throb with unchecked excess. Drinking games and sex games passed the time between hits. Quite a few "guests" were passed out on the furniture. Some girls still danced around handbags. The sounds of revelry masked the underlying tension which went with the territory, a grim dance between pleasure and power, trust and betrayal.

Faris held a can in his hand and stared into a mirror nailed onto a wall for no obvious reason. His reflection stared back at him surrounded by the gilded frame. He knew that he had crossed into a world from which there was no easy return. The mission continued, the stakes were getting higher, and the final cost was, as yet, unknown.

24) A Tank Gunnery Range Near Scotch Corner, Northern England

In the chilly Northern British dawn, a vast, bleak, moorland training area stretched out; to all appearances a theatre of war dotted with shattered armoured vehicles waiting for the next round to commence. The scarred landscape rolled gently down to meet the sea some miles distant, its tranquil appearance broken by eight formidable, 75 tonne Challenger 2 tanks standing line-abreast on the firing point, their guns directed ominously towards the coast. The hulking silhouettes formed an intimidating steel curtain, their menacing presence dominating the landscape.

Major Charles Wentworth, a highly experienced British Tank Regiment officer, stood tall and lean, his considering gaze firmly fixed on the squad of Ukrainian soldiers gathered behind the tanks. A British lieutenant by his side and a Ukrainian Captain, his new charge, completed this trio of officers. Their postures were a little stiff, almost rigid, reflecting either the seriousness of their task or their cultural differences, yet a subtle camaraderie had begun to form as a result of the shared understanding which was growing between them as the tank-training progressed. After days of classroom-work learning the theory, today was the first day the Ukrainians would see a tank actually fire its main gun.

Strewn at the far end of the range lumps of twisted metal, the scrap of once-proud armoured vehicles, lay decimated by the force of the tank's firepower. Each distorted mass served as a silent testament to the devastating destructive power of the Challenger 2's Sabot rounds. A thirty inch, fin-stabilised, depleted uranium dart which travelled at nearly 6,000 feet per second and carried with it enough kinetic energy to explode one tank as if it were a bomb and then go on and destroy the next behind it. To the British present, the wreckage served as a visual reminder of the power under their fingertip control. But the Ukrainians had not seen the guns in action.

The fire control order came over the radio net to which all the men were listening, "3 1 Bravo, 3,000, armoured target to your front, 1 sabot round, await my order……fire."

The two British officers assumed a strange pose habitually, knees together and their hands cupped over their groins. A look of puzzlement passed across the Ukrainian officer's face. He moved half-heartedly to copy their motion, unknowing. The comfortable moment's silence was shattered by the deafening thud of a tank main gun, felt more than heard.

As the Sabot round, L27A1 APFSDS: known affectionately as the CHARM 3, tore through the air, travelling flat by its glowing trace towards the 2 mile distant target, the recoil rocked the heavy tank back on its tracks and the concussive force from the gun-barrel radiated outwards, an invisible wall of raw power. The veteran British instructors amongst the men had already covered their groins, a ritual born of experience.

The blast wave hit the unprepared Ukrainian soldiers standing behind the line of tanks. Unaccustomed to the shock-wave from the Challenger 2 main gun, a sensation not unlike being kicked in the face and groin simultaneously, they staggered and bent, their yelps of surprise slicing through the Rowanite 304 propellant smoke, aftermath of the blast. The expected reaction drew raucous laughter from their British instructors.

Then the Ukrainians joined in and the shared mirth amongst the young men served to lighten the gravity of their circumstances. Despite his stern demeanour, the corner of the Major's mouth twitched, an amused smirk playing for a moment on his lips; as close as he would approach to levity.

This light-hearted moment revealed a layer of humanity beneath the formal military façade and highlighted the beginnings of bond between the British and Ukrainian troops. The Ukrainian Captain exchanged a glance with the Major, his eyes reflecting his awareness of the interaction.

As the training continued, with more and more rounds fired by Ukrainians hurtling down the range, their ammunition handling drill became smoother, their accuracy increased and they began to understand the sheer might of these British weapons. With each passing hour, the bond between the men strengthened and their respect for each other deepened.

25) A Public Park In Bradford, UK

Not far from the centre of the bustling city of Bradford, a green oasis of tranquillity buzzed with life and presented an almost idyllic tableau of urban harmony. The sun, generous this day in its warmth, reflected from water and lent a shimmering glow to the park. Families, out to enjoy the sunny weather, were scattered across the pleasant expanse of lush green grass. Children ran free, their laughter a merry tune over the soft quacking of the resident ducks.

Around the boating pond, the joyous chaos of childhood unfolded. Small boys controlled the motions of their toy boats with intense concentration, their tiny vessels weaving across the calm water. A family, huddled together at the water's edge, threw breadcrumbs at a flotilla of eager ducks. Some of the web-footed creatures, more enterprising, eagerly climbed out of the water and waddled forward, snapping up the offerings with delight. Meanwhile, canines of all kinds, from bouncy terriers to lithe greyhounds, raced around, chased after tossed balls and begged for treats. Their exuberance was contagious, their antics drawing amused chuckles from owners and bystanders. The park resonated with the harmonic music of life, a happy microcosm teeming with laughter and activity.

At the edge of this peaceful scene, on benches set under trees, a group of apparently less-happy young men huddled together, their matching exercise-wear a stark contrast in this family environment. Their words, though delivered in the King's English, seemed to be crafted from a different patios to the familiar local dialect. They passed around a small pipe, its sharp scent slicing through the natural odours of grass and tree.

Suddenly, the tranquillity of the afternoon was brutally disrupted. The drug-addled young men started to argue, then began lashing out at each other. Fuelled by the additive within their cocaine fix, their hidden blades appeared and flashed in the sunlight. Transformed and driven by the narcotics coursing through their veins, the men lunged at each other with a feral intensity, their quick knives glinting red with blood. Driven by who-knows-what-urges the unwounded men spread out in a random star-burst and begin attacking innocent park-goers, their crazed eyes devoid of any humanity.

The atmosphere changed instantly under the impact of this horrifying spectacle. Families scattered, their happiness morphed to terror. A dog barked then whined as its owner was struck down, its playful bounding replaced with fear.

As the frenzied attacks continued, people ran and the park was rapidly deserted, the lingering screams and cries echoing ominously through the trees from the escaping figures. What was once a happy, family scene had become a tableau of horror with bodies on the ground, some still moving in agony, and blood trails on the paths left by those running to escape. The beauty of the day shattered by the brutality of the drug-induced frenzy.

26) The Disputed Sky Over Northern Ukraine

In the sky over the contested North of Ukraine Lieutenant Alexander Kuznetsov, son of General Kuznetsov, flew his SU-27 air-superiority fighter like a deadly falcon, demonstrating his superlative prowess as a pilot. The Mi-17 troop carrier helicopters, sluggish Russian remnants of the bygone Afghan war and supplied to Ukraine by the US from that benighted nation, were easy pickings for his ravenous bird of prey.

This brutal game of aerial chess was like shooting fish in a barrel and the modern Soviet-designed fighter jet totally dominated the aerial battle, if it could be called a battle, with ruthless efficiency. Select target, target locked, fire, target destroyed. Repeat. But Alexander's supply of deadly R27E air-to-air missiles had run dry. Still, targets continued to present themselves and the young pilot did not falter.

Switching to the fighter's GSh-301 30mm automatic cannon, he flew his metal bird closer to the remaining enemy. From point blank range he unleashed a stuttering burst of shells with a sound for all the world like ripping canvas played through a rock-amplifier. The explosive shells from the rapid-fire cannon tore into another Mi-17. Flames and black smoke, the falling carcass of a chopper, its crew and passengers now doomed, was another proof of his skills. From this range he could see the faces looking out of the windows as they fell. Some of them seemed to be looking directly at him, wide-eyed and open-mouthed. Were they screaming?

But his moment of triumph was short-lived. A sudden sharp explosion behind his cockpit sent a shiver down his spine. A flash of white in his peripheral vision, then the sickening shudder of the airframe. A deadly, hand-launched, Starstreak missile had found its mark. Its three tungsten alloy darts smashing into one engine then exploding and destroying the other. Another gift from Britain.

For just a moment a sensation of icy dread ran through Alexander's body as the stick went dead in his hands. The once arrogant roar of the jet turbines was now replaced by an eerie silence. For a moment his straining ears tuned in and he heard the wind whistle around his cockpit. His SU-27, once the eagle, the king of the skies, was now a falling bird with a broken wing.

Bracing for the shuddering impact of escape, Alexander automatically began the ejection sequence and in the slow-motion reality noticed his heart pounding against his ribs. The canopy above him jettisoned first, thrown clear by explosive plugs which burned the part of his throat exposed below his breathing mask. Then a deafening wind filled the cockpit and tore away the fumes. With a spine jarring kick from another charge the ejection seat propelled him into the open sky and away from his stricken, falling war bird.

A sudden moment of high-Gs as the chair's 'chute filled and then calm as the chair itself fell away. He checked the chute above his head was inflated, checked for crossed lines over the canopy without thinking. All good so far. His view of the battlefield shifted as he rotated, dangling beneath the parachute. The chessboard of the ground conflict sprawled out beneath him as he drifted towards it. Farmland, scarred and scorched, rose smoothly up to meet him, countryside twisted into a war zone. His descent, slow but inevitable, took him closer to that ground. And the reality of his situation crystallised in his mind.

The merciless irony was not lost on him. Moments ago, he had been the hunter, and now he was the prey, descending into the land of an enemy with little reason to love him. Little reason to keep him alive. Every reason to take the revenge on him for the invasion of their homeland, the deaths of their countrymen. A stab of fear gnawed at his belly for a moment but he pushed it down and prepared himself mentally for an impending confrontation with the enemy.

As his boots hit the earth he realised he was standing on enemy territory for the first time in his life and the weight of the situation sank in. He had seen many battlefields from above but never once from ground level. The hunter had become the hunted and the ace pilot would now have to flee for his life. The battlefield may have changed, but the struggle was not over for Alexander Kuznetsov.

27) Accident & Emergency Department, Bradford Teaching Hospital, Bradford, UK

Under the harsh glow of clinical lights, the Accident and Emergency department of Bradford Teaching Hospital resembled a scene from a war movie. It was an environment fuelled by adrenaline, a battleground of a different kind where life and death hung in the balance and the heroes didn't wear capes, or uniforms, they wore scrubs.

Nurses, the unsung heroines on this front line, darted between the curtained cubicles in an effort to keep up with the influx of patients. Their hands, steady and experienced, dressed an alarming number of superficial knife wounds themselves. More experienced nurses did the sutures. The deeper wounds were staunched and scheduled for surgery by a consultant to stem internal bleeding and clean out infection. The brutality of the injuries, the whispered stories of crazed violence and fear had become all too commonplace in their city.

The makeshift production line of healing operated with clockwork precision: Assess. Cleanse. Stitch or tape. Dress. Repeat. The nurses' faces, etched with exhaustion, were masks of stoic determination. Two of them, Sunita and Helen, stole a few moments from the organised chaos to catch their breaths.

The pattern they were observing was new and unsettling. Scores of victims of seemingly random attacks by drugged-up individuals. Drug-fuelled violence was no stranger to them, but this sudden surge, this epidemic, had them shaken. It was not uncommon for drug users to harm each other. It was quite usual for drug dealers to harm their competitors. But this was different, it was drug users attacking random, innocent people. Their patients' fear-laden eyes and trembling voices spoke of the terror that was gripping the city.

Sunita, her big brown eyes shadowed with concern, peeled off her bloodied gloves, her hands trembling slightly. "It's like they've gone mad, Helen," she said, her voice hushed. She was referring to the druggies, their motivation seemed to have changed from the usual desperate need for a fix to something more sinister.

Helen, with her cropped hair and piercing grey eyes, mirrored Sunita's concern. She was a seasoned veteran, her experience spanning many years of tending to the city's injured and ailing. But this, this unnerving onslaught of violence, was new even for her.

"It's like we're dealing with a different breed of addict, Sunita," Helen replied, her gaze unfocused for a moment as she grappled with the implication. "I've never seen anything like this before. It's not just the frequency of the attacks, but their random savagery."

“Yes, it is strange. Druggies steal from people’s houses while they are out, they don’t attack them.”

As they talked, their words were underscored by the steady background noises of the A&E department; the urgent beeping of monitors, the hushed whispers of reassurance from medics to patients, the stifled cries of pain. Someone was sobbing. It was a chilling backing track to their work that spoke clearly of a crisis unfolding.

They shared a look of mutual understanding. This was not just a series of isolated incidents but an escalating situation with the potential to bring civilised life in their city to a halt. The haunting images of the victims, their lives forever marred by the sudden violence, were front and centre in their minds.

A sudden call for assistance ended their conversation, and they plunged back into the fray, back to their roles as the last line of defence in this escalating war. The threads and needles moved in a rhythmic dance, stitching the city's wounds one patient at a time.

But as they worked, a nagging fear tugged at their hearts. This violence was a symptom of a disease rapidly spreading through the veins of Bradford, one that was far beyond their ability to heal with stitch or bandage. As the epidemic of madness fuelled by drugs continued to spread, the hospital's stark fluorescent lights cast long, ominous shadows over the future of their city.

28) Farmland Scarred By War, Northern Ukraine

Alexander climbed out of the ejector seat and looked around. He saw smoke from his crashed SU-27 rising over the false horizon of Ukrainian trees. His gloved hand instinctively reached for his issue sidearm, a Makarov pistol, no more than a desperate talisman against the odds lurking in the wilderness around him. Then he realized he was not alone.

A dozen menacing figures, Ukrainian irregulars by their half-uniform, had emerged from the trees. Their rifles were all levelled at him from fifty feet away. There was no love lost in this war and any excuse would be enough for them to open fire. Alexander understood the futility of any resistance so he dropped his pistol and raised his hands in the air, a universal signal. The Ukrainians would understand it. Would they accept it?

The irregulars approached with the caution of some predators. Suspicion and hostility rippled through the group in words Alexander understood only by their tone as they surrounded him. His hands were pulled behind his back and he felt the pressure of rough rope binding his wrists. Someone slapped him hard across the face, the taste of blood in his mouth came salty, and he was dragged to their truck.

Searched and stripped of his watch and money but not ID tags, he was thrown in the open back of the truck and three men got in the front. They set off along rough tracks amongst the trees for seemingly hours and it was growing dark when they stopped. Their destination was a grim, fortified concrete structure hiding furtively amongst the trees. His heart sank further. If this were Russia, the interrogation would come next and the grey walls of his new prison only echoed the coldness in his captor's eyes.

As they dragged him roughly from the truck, the crude laughter of his captors rang out and he heard the ring of mess tins as men were fed somewhere out of sight. Alexander's flying suit was now stained with dirt and blood and his body bore the weight of his capture like irons but his spirit, albeit battered, remained. He was a Russian soldier, a Kuznetsov. And in this forbidding Ukrainian detention, under the uncaring eyes of his captors, he would face his fate with the stoic resolve that his lineage demanded. Russian courage would not falter in enemy hands.

29) An Upmarket Room, The Clearmount Hotel, London, UK

In the soft, opulent warmth of an upscale London hotel room close to Whitehall, Yelena Ivanova, the strikingly beautiful Russian agent, and Sir Henry Attwood, the aristocratic SIS Chief, lay entangled amongst the silk sheets of a king-size bed. Beyond the soundproofed, triple-glazed windows, London hummed with a quiet energy, oblivious to the manipulative plot that was developing within those four walls.

Yelena, her stunning face gently illuminated by the ambient glow of a bedside lamp, gazed into Henry's eyes, her expression one of soft, sincere interest. With a voice that was as silkily enticing as it was strategically probing, she asked, "… and so I need your help Henry. I need a little something of no consequence to give to my boss. Just a titbit so she will keep me here in London… with you. Tell me, are the Brits going to buy the Israeli or the Turkish drones?" The seemingly innocent question floated through the air, its profound implications simmering beneath the surface.

Henry, ensnared in the heady blend of Yelena's charm and a liberal intake of alcohol, heard the words through a haze of smitten intoxication. He knew that this information was of no consequence. And he knew that it might keep this lovely girl in his bed for a while longer. His response was accompanied by chest-swelling pride, his voice heavy with the weight of self-importance. "I sit on some very influential military committees," he asserted, a little slurred yet unmistakably boastful. "I hold significant sway in the hierarchy," he added, laying bare his inflated perception of his standing. His need to show away to a lady.

A subtle, kindly smile danced on Yelena's lips. She adopted an expression of adoration, her almond eyes entirely failing to reflect the spark of victorious accomplishment she felt inside. She was acutely aware of Henry's family's ongoing financial troubles, a weak spot she had been briefed on and was now ready to exploit. Injecting a tone of gentle concern into her voice, she murmured, "I've heard about the difficulties your family has been facing, Henry." Her words hung heavy in the air, gently piercing through Henry's drunken stupor.

Her promise followed, laced with a tantalising assurance of salvation. "If you could just help me in this little thing, Henry," she paused for emphasis, "I might be able to help you regain your family's wealth."

She could see that this offer struck a chord in Henry's vulnerable psyche. The thought of restoring his family's dwindling fortune, and saving face among his high-born peers, was clearly too enticing to resist.

Blinded by the shimmering promise of financial redemption, and swayed by Yelena's bewitching allure, he made a dangerous pledge. "I will get you the order documents," he said, his voice unsteady but brimming with a resolute determination.

In the hushed sanctuary of the luxurious hotel room, a perilous conspiracy was taking shape. Under the cosy warmth of the bespoke bedcovers, a high-stakes gamble was being stealthily set up. Yelena could see clearly that Henry, with his wavering loyalties and insatiable hunger for money and power, combined with the weakness of all men, had unknowingly become a pawn in her strategic play.

As the hands of the ornate wall clock inched towards midnight, the contours of this secret alliance cast long shadows of an uncertain and potentially calamitous future. And everything was being recorded.

30) General Nikolai Kuznetsov's Dacha Outside Moscow, Russia

The Kuznetsov Dacha was about to become the stage for an emotional tragedy. This picturesque haven of quiet and calm, surrounded by miles of unspoiled forest, was about to bear witness to the raw, human anguish of two parents.

General Kuznetsov and his wife, Natalia, stood at the formal entrance gate as a uniformed courier arrived, saluted and delivered an official-looking envelope. The General returned the salute, took the letter, the two men saluted again and the courier left a little more quickly than seemed natural. Ever suspicious, the General considered that the envelope was too small and light to be a bomb. The courier would not have known if it had been anyway. The couple shared a concerned glance as there were only a few things this official delivery could signify, and none of them were good.

The General tore open the official seal, his hands uncharacteristically trembling. A deafening silence enveloped the two of them. Then the contents of the letter struck him like a sledgehammer, slicing through his life like a knife to the heart. He read aloud, "Pilot Officer, Alexander Kuznetsov has been shot down in Ukraine. He is presumed to be dead."

"No! No Nikolai, it cannot be true!"

A shockwave of grief stunned the couple. The General's weathered face blanched; normally a stoic figure even in the face of tragedy, his eyes glistened with an unshed tear. Natalia, usually a pillar of resilience, let out a heart-wrenching wail and clung to her husband, the reality of their loss tearing into their souls.

They staggered inside the house and he slammed the heavy door. Her sobbing echoed through the silent rooms of their home.

In his desolation a seething rage began to simmer. His eyes, now filled with a fierce anger, stared out the window and into the distance. "The UK supplied the Ukrainians with those damned anti-aircraft missiles," he growled, the veins in his neck bulging with his rising fury. The seeds of personal vengeance had now been sown in the fertile ground of his sorrow, each word feeding its growth.

His wife, now cradled in his arms, looked up at him, her tear-streaked face etched with pain. "What can we do, Nikolai? Is he really dead?" she asked, her voice barely a whisper.

The General, his heart filled with a heady mix of grief and anger, his walls of secrecy breached, chose to share an ominous state secret. "Those British, they will pay for our loss," he hissed. His words were razor-sharp, searing the air with their lethal intent. "We have a plan. An operation in progress that involves smuggling cocaine into their country. But not just any cocaine."

His face, hardened with resolve, bore a terrifying intensity as he continued. "We have created a chemical additive, a potent substance that will wreak havoc in the veins of their drug-using citizens. Drive them to murder all around them with a merciless ferocity. The trials are nearing completion and soon, our weapon will flood their streets."

Natalia, her sorrow momentarily eclipsed by the surprise, the words arriving out of context from nowhere, stared at her husband. Her heart pounded in her chest, a rhythm of dread, as she realized the scale of the murderous plan he was a part of. As the weight of their son's loss and the reality of the General's words sank in, the silence in the Dacha seemed to grow heavier, almost palpable. The echoes of their grief now joined by the ominous undercurrent of an impending war crime.

31) A Pensioner Couple's Bungalow In Halifax, West Yorkshire, UK

On the outskirts of Halifax, a pleasant Northern English town, stood a collection of comfortable bungalows designed specifically for the retired workers of the area. Tucked away from the hustle and bustle of the town, the house on the corner plot radiated a cosy, if slightly old-fashioned, charm. This comfortable abode was the "forever home" of Harold and Mildred Spencer, a sweet, aging couple who had spent their entire adult lives together, each line on their faces a testament to the passage of time and their shared experiences. Their well-loved home mirrored their quiet lifestyle, resplendent in the vintage aura that more than two decades of careful maintenance had bestowed upon it.

After their evening meal, the couple had sunk into the comfy sofa, their favourite spot in the little living room, and switched on the old tube television set. The room was set aglow by the flickering light from the screen which cast shadows that danced on the flowered wallpaper. The watching of the evening news with a cup of tea by their side was a ritual, an integral part of their nightly routine.

The headline news tonight, a shocking story of drug-crazed attacks spreading across West Yorkshire, struck them like a thunderbolt. They watched, mouths open, as the overly-sincere news-reader recounted terrifying stories of innocents, whole families falling prey to attacks by individuals high on drugs. The gruesome details, accompanied by disturbing footage of violent assaults, and shots of the knives and clubs used in the attacks, were a stark intruder set loose in their home.

Harold, his gnarled, millworker's hand instinctively reaching for Mildred's, wore an expression of disbelief. His silver brows furrowed, his watery eyes squinted at the screen as if trying to make sense of the madness unfolding just a matter of streets away. Mildred clutched his hand tightly, her knuckles turning white, her other hand covering her mouth in horror.

As the news continued, their living room, once a comforting bubble of familiarity and warmth, seemed to grow colder, darker. The photos of their grandchildren's antics, the aroma of Mildred's baking, the cosy clutter of their lives, all faded into the background. Their attention was captivated by the shocking scenes flickering on their television screen.

"Why on earth would anyone do such a thing?" Harold murmured, his voice echoing the question hanging in the air. Their bewilderment was palpable, This news highlighted the gulf between the tranquil life they had lived and this new, chaotic reality.

Mildred, a former librarian, shook her head in sadness. "Its the drugs, Harold, they're taking those horrible drugs." She shivered, her heart heavy with sorrow, unable to comprehend the behaviour of these lost souls. Their home, filled with the soft murmur of the television and the occasional clink of their teacups, now held a disquieting tension.

The remainder of the evening was spent in quiet contemplation. The couple, usually chatty and cheerful to the background of game shows, were each lost in their thoughts and occasionally exchanged worried glances. The harsh reality of the news report had thrown into sharp relief the shadow looming over their peaceful society. The disturbing images of violence, the chilling tales of drug-induced frenzy, had etched themselves into their minds, shattering the peace of their quiet evening, of their quiet lives.

32) The President's Office, The Kremlin, Moscow, Russia

Behind the huge desk in his sparsely furnished but impressively grand Kremlin office President Alexei Novikov was deep in discussion with General Leonid Petrenko sitting opposite him. Petrenko was head of the GRU; military intelligence, spy agency, overseas covert action agency, call it what you will. The room, this evening bathed in just the sombre glow of a desk lamp, was stained by the weight of countless ruthless decisions that had shaped their nation's fate.

With just a sharp rap as warning, the heavy oak doors swung open, and in walked General Kuznetsov, his uniform immaculate, his face an inscrutable granite mask. He raised his right arm, offering a crisp salute to the President, "You sent for me Comrade President."

With a nod, President Novikov acknowledged the salute. He looked straight at Kuznetsov for a little longer than was comfortable, even for the General. An extended moment of silence held its breath before the President delivered the unexpected news: "Before we begin, General Kuznetsov, I have good news for you. Your son is not dead, he is a prisoner of war, held by the Ukrainians."

Relief and happiness fought for control in Kuznetsov's face, and lost. His gaze hardened, betraying nothing, and his jaw clenched. The room swayed for a moment, as did the old warrior, as he took in the sudden change in his world, in his life.

With a nod to his old drinking partner, General Novikov almost smiled. Almost. "I am glad I am not offering condolences General Kuznetsov..."

The President cut in harshly, "Nevertheless, this happy news does not affect our reaction to the UK's interference in our Ukrainian special military operation by their support for Ukraine. The timings for our operation against the UK must be finalised."

Kuznetsov, his steely gaze mirroring his resolve, confirmed his position, as per the expected form, "The UK's transgressions will not go unanswered. Russia will make them pay." He then produced a letter from an inside pocket, opened it and delivered the required update from Dr. Antonovich, reading, "The field tests on the alternate versions of the cocaine additive are now complete. The most suitable for our purpose has been selected and even now it is in bulk manufacture at our facility outside Shikhany, Saratov Oblast (Province)."

The President smiled with his mouth, "Well done General, I knew I could rely on you to push this operation forward. When will the additive be ready for release?"

"Sir, if we release piecemeal the UK may find some way to mitigate the effects so, subject to your view, I thought to build up sufficient stocks of the additive and have them shipped by military aircraft and diplomatic package to the facility which mixes the additive into the cocaine. The facility can then mix in the additive as they receive cocaine through the usual channels and hold the completed product to send on in smaller packages at your order. In this way, our network of main dealers in the UK will all receive their shipments together, less an acceptable percentage stopped at the border, and all regions of the UK will be flooded with the cocaine-mix at the same time."

The President considered for a moment, "I was hoping you would have been ready in three weeks to coincide with our push on Kyiv but I will allow you to stick to your plans and expect an appropriate result General."

"Thank you Comrade President, I hope you will not be disappointed in the result."

"I too hope I will not be disappointed, General." A chill ran through the room.

Displaying the sudden, destabilising, change of mood for which he was well known, the President produced a bottle of premium vodka and poured a glass for each of them. The crystal-clear liquid shimmered under the lamp's light, reflecting the steely resolve in the men's eyes. They raised their glasses and tapped them together as this was not a funeral, the clink resonating through the room like a sombre toll. The President led the toast, holding up his glass, "To Mother Russian and her victory over the American Imperialists."

Then raising their glasses, the men repeated the key words in unison as tradition demanded, "Mother Russia and victory!"

33) Riaz Khan's House, Bradford, UK

Riaz Khan's gaudily opulent home, tucked away on its expensive new Bradford housing development, pulsed again with the frenetic beat of a loud, drug fuelled party

Cruising the rooms, their air clouded by a haze of excess and indulgence, Faris found himself greeted by and chatting with an assorted series of highly successful villains and characters of ill-repute. Word had got around about his performance at the fight and his stock had risen.

Amidst the roar of drunken laughter, the raucous music, and the clinking of expensive glassware, Faris's sharp mind remained keenly alert. He had to maintain his cover as he would die horribly if discovered; but he also had to find out what was happening. There was only one way to do that; get close to Riaz while he was talking.

The upscale living room was crammed with a garish display of wealth. A visitor might have thought the house was owned by a Premier Division footballer and the decorations chosen by his wife. Too-ornate chandeliers dangled precariously above clusters of fine leather sofas, gold-plated fixtures winked grossly under the dimmed, vary-hued lights. Paintings by named modern artists asserted their status on the mahogany-panelled walls. All paid for in cash with the huge profits which flowed from drug dealing in bulk. Money washed by its trip to Pakistan and back.

Shared between the press of colourful characters, young women stumbled from group to group in a drug-addled stupor and various states of undress, their hollowed eyes reflecting their wanton occupation.

In one corner, the bulky form of Riaz Khan, the man himself, slouched in a luxurious armchair, nursing a crystal tumbler of some amber liquid. A slight sneer repeatedly crossed his lips as he whispered instructions to a lanky lieutenant by his side. Faris, tucked unobtrusively into the shadow of an alcove only feet away, could see the Riaz's eyes; two cold shining orbs that darted between his guests and his lieutenant. And Faris could see his lips. Clearly Riaz was taking something tonight to keep his wits sharp.

Faris's ears pricked up as he caught fragments of the conversation drifting over the blaring music. Some parts he could hear, some meaning he captured through MI5-trained lip-reading. Riaz was discussing a sinister additive to their cocaine shipments, an ominous concept that made Faris's stomach tense. 'Additive'. The word stuck in his mind; this was something new and perhaps important. What would Riaz add to the notoriously pure cocaine he imported pretty much direct from South America?

One of the reasons for Riaz's success was the purity of his supply. A purity that gave his wholesale customers the confidence to pay him top dollar for a product they could "cut," lace with cheaper, Benzocaine dental anaesthetic, to improve their profit margins once a new customer was hooked.

Faris's mind raced, struggling to piece together more fragments of the conversation, his instincts causing his thoughts to focus on this unsettling revelation. But he must not show he was paying attention. He pulled a passing girl onto him and she giggled as he made an effort and fondled her.

Riaz's words revealed more, "…so remember, you make sure none of our crew use anything from future shipments. Tell them all to come to me for their personal supply. Tell them for the next month I will supply them all for free."

A tremor of dread ran through Faris when he heard the boss's reasoning. The unsuspecting end users of their product in the near future would react with unprecedented violence soon after using the contaminated product. This violence, he emphasized, would be far more brutal than anything they had witnessed before and cause the users to attack, and try to murder, anyone they came across. But his crew must not worry about the cost of lost customers because the reward they would earn for shifting this adulterated cocaine would buy them a Mercedes Sports each and, soon, apartments in Puerto Banus, Southern Spain.

Faris's mind whirled with the implications of what he'd overheard. The importance of the information hit him like a ram raider. This was not going to be a mere turf war or a rivalry dispute. This was a weaponized drug about to hit the streets of the UK. It must be part of a plot to trigger anarchy and instability on an unimaginable scale. And who was behind it? He felt a cold dread grip his heart. It was clear that he had to report this information, and fast.

The party continued around him, with its garish excess and raucous noise, but suddenly it seemed to fade into the background. The girl on his lap had passed out, the attention-seeking laughter of the drugged, dancing women rang hollow in his ears, and the opulent splendour of the surroundings felt stifling and suddenly distant. Faris knew that Riaz felt little for human life, he knew its value to the pound, but this move was ruthless, even for him.

Extracting himself quietly from the shadowy alcove, and avoiding the offer of another drunken girl, Faris made a swift, discreet exit from the room. As he stepped outside into the cold night behind the house, he pulled out his burner phone, looked at it and stopped; he dare not use it in case Riaz wanted to check the usage later. The party's muffled sounds echoed behind the closed door, an eerie soundtrack to the plot unfolding within.

The prospect of Riaz adding this "additive" to the UK's cocaine supply was as serious a matter as he could imagine. He absolutely had to report what he had discovered ASAP. But making contact from deep cover was fraught with danger. Faris took a deep breath of the cold air to clear his mind and headed for a gold-plated loo.

34) An Upmarket Room, The Clearmount Hotel, London, UK

The intoxicating scent of aged, single-malt whisky hung heavy in the air of yet another luxurious hotel suite, blanketing the room in an invisible mist. The bedroom, bathed in the soft glow of the bedside lamp, flickered with shadows that mirrored whispers and shared secrets. Sir Henry, sprawled out naked across satin sheets, traced the captivating silhouette of Yelena with his eyes.

She turned to him, her blond waves cascading over her bare shoulders, and touched him softly, her eyes reflecting a tension and vulnerability that had been absent until now. The air between them pulsed with anticipation as she voiced her plea. With a hint of desperation lingering in her voice, she painted a vivid picture of the dangerous game she was playing, "My boss suspects my intentions because of all the time I am spending with you, my love. She is questioning my allegiance and I need something more to reassure her."

Her words conveyed her fear consummately, but they made plain that, for her companionship to continue, she needed something more, another act of betrayal. But his ego, inflated by whisky and lust, seemed to shrug off the cost. He listened carefully as she confided about the potential punishment awaiting her if she were to be recalled to Moscow; a fate, she said, much worse than any he could imagine.

She looked directly at him, steadily, as she revealed what she needed next, "My love, I need you to get me the British plans for implementing the Australian CEAFAR active-phased-array radar on their warships, the state-of-the-art microwave-tile-based design. And the specifications of the anti-hypersonic missile laser that is to be fitted onto the Type 83 Destroyer." As she uttered these words, the room seemed to grow colder, the gravity of her request sinking in.

Henry pulled back, the request was so blatant, detailed and clearly planned ahead of time. A look of shock flickered across his face and disappeared. She wondered if she could have phrased the requirement better and continued, "This is just what my boss asked me for, directly. She has put me on the spot, beloved. Deliver or…" She left her potential fate hanging. "It is nothing to harm anyone darling. It will help maintain world peace. And I would not ask if it were not important to… us."

"You are asking a great deal Yelena." He shook his head.

"My boss knows this and has authorised a payment of £10 million pounds to your Swiss account on receipt of the documents. She hates me and doesn't believe that you will obtain them."

She felt his resolve wavering, and increased the pressure with the assurance that she would safeguard the documents from his previous transgression. The old "stick and carrot" game.

Sir Henry sat up and thought for a while, his eyes closed. The sum offered was enormous, enough to not only pay his family's debts but to leave a little over. Had she seen his bank statements? He turned to look at her, his gaze strengthened by the brash confidence that was his signature trait.

She continued, "If you can do this for me, darling, there will be more harmless little jobs which, now the rate has been set, will pay equally well."

Yelena watched his face as his internal dialogue ran. Doubtless, he was thinking that he was a man of considerable influence and obtaining such information was not beyond his reach. His mouth curved into an arrogant smirk as he reassured her. "I can get you what you need, but it will take me a week or so."

As he pledged his willingness to participate in this dangerous dance of secrets, the room felt smaller, the stakes higher. Yet, there was an unspoken understanding between them, a thread of mutual desperation weaving them together in their shared plight. In the dim light of the hotel room, two figures lay entangled, their fates now also irrevocably intertwined in a web of deceit, manipulation, and, apparently, desire.

35) Riaz Khan's House, Bradford, UK

In Riaz's house, that party world of frenetic energy and unchecked hedonism, it might seem easy to move or leave unseen, but it wasn't. Everyone with any part of the drug trade, and there were plenty of that type here, was always on the alert for betrayal. Traitors giving away secrets, prices or contacts. Or the despised police informer. So there was always someone watching, no matter how smashed they seemed.

Faris knew he was walking a fine line in contacting his base. Without comment, he detached himself from the wild chaos and staggered into the relative calm of a bathroom.

Once inside, Faris pressed his back against the door and a shadow passed across his face as his rigid composure faltered for a moment. He glanced up to the ceiling and over to the mirror, checking for cameras, didn't see one.

then his hand slid under his jacket, his fingers splayed across his ribs beneath his right arm, measuring. He began tapping out a rhythm, his fingers hammering repeatedly on his own skin in an intricate pattern. The almost silent action was muffled further by his shirt, a private rhythm unheard amidst the wild revelry of the party.

Then Faris leaned over the toilet. His fingers down his throat and face contorted with discomfort, he forced himself to be sick, spewing into the pristine toilet bowl, taking care to achieve a noticeable near-miss. There was no real nausea, no sickness, but he mimicked the actions perfectly. His body heaved loudly, the bitter taste of bile filled his mouth. The dramatic show would colour his face, redden his eyes, and justify his prolonged absence from the party. It would make an effective cover if challenged.

He cleaned up the mess roughly, carefully leaving a trace, and wiped his mouth. He splashed cold water on his face. Wiped it off. He paused for a moment, stared at his reflection, saw the determination etched in his eyes behind the bloodshot veins. His task was far from over, his mission deeply entwined with the chaos outside.

Exiting the bathroom, Faris found one of the gang members waiting to use the loo. The man scanned him up and down, noting the sheen of sweat on his brow, the pallor of his face and laughed. Faris offered a sheepish grin, "Too much whisky, bro."

The man seemed satisfied with the explanation, brushing past him without further inquiry. Faris returned to the party, his secret task well hidden, he thought.

36) A Dense Forest In Northern Ukraine, Close To The Russian Border

In the dark heart of a Ukrainian forest a Russian conscript unit, the 371st Guards Rifle Division, had set up a makeshift encampment huddled under trees in the hope of softening the cold wind. They were a ragtag bunch of about fifty teenagers and barely able to see adulthood on the horizon.

The unit was under the command of a keen but youthful officer, Junior Lieutenant Igor Mazakov, aged himself a mere twenty one years. The product of a military academy designed more to inculcate loyalty to the state than produce skilled leaders. Their NCOs were barely adults themselves either, selected by being the fortunate survivors of a previous Russian push.

Separated from their homes by thousands of miles, everyone bar the Lieutenant had been conscripted into the military by the Russian State and forced to fight for a cause they scarcely comprehended by an ideology they did not believe in. At that moment, their only solace came from the natural camaraderie of young men experiencing a testing hardship together.

The unit was spread over three narrow lines of trenches, their parallel zigzag design a testament more to fortune than to tactical skill. The trenches' bends would make it difficult for the men of a unit storming their position to clear the trenches by firing left and right as they crossed the lines. But they provided scant shelter from the harsh wind.

Barely visible, a tiny drone high above them buzzed its way across the sky. "Ha! They damned drones not see us here," Yuri commented, half way through a tin of cold goulash; opened with a bayonet and eaten with the spoon that every soldier soon learns to carry.

No one in the unit had the experience or training to know that a unit should consider the tactical situation before taking cover under trees. That even antique point-detonation mortar bombs would strike the branches above their trenches and detonate as deadly air-burst, sending deadly shrapnel downwards onto the men sheltering below in their trenches.

Scattered throughout the position they had built sturdier bunkers for sleeping and against artillery, their wooden roofs covered in earth offering a semblance of protection from the threatening, but so far distant, artillery barrages that had become a constant soundtrack to their lives. Thank God for the old Russian artillery shells the Ukrainians were using. Modern NATO 105 and 155 shells would be set to airburst over their heads or to produce bunker-busting, trench collapsing pressure by exploding underground.

A brew of strong, dark tea, sweetened almost to the point of syrup, was being passed around, its comforting warmth battling against the biting chill of the evening. They added lemon juice, the tang cutting through the sweetness and giving a welcome relief from the monotony of their biscuit, porridge and goulash diet. Several of the boys, their youthful enthusiasm having fuelled a poor decision, lay semi-conscious from consuming too much issue vodka, their faces ashen and ghost-like in the dim light. Their new friends would save them from hypothermia as the temperature fell further in the night.

Then came the dreaded sound. A low rumble at first, like a distant train pulling into a station, growing quickly in volume and intensity. The boys' faces morphed from confusion to dawning realization. It was the sound they had all come to dread, the harbinger of a heavy artillery bombardment.

Suddenly, their position erupted in a blaze of flash and smoke as the modern 155mm artillery shells found their mark. The explosive force of shells detonating ten feet underground collapsed the trenches and buried their occupants alive. Bunkers collapsed, their roofs flying into the air, splintered under the onslaught, their earth shields no match for the force of these terrible shells.

An airburst detonated 10 metres above the ground and a lethal hail of shrapnel ripped across the encampment, angling down and making mincemeat of the boys who had not found refuge in the doomed bunkers. Lieutenant Mazakov stared at the sky, mind numb and no idea what to do. Then he too was swept away in an iron-studded blast wave, his brief command brought to a sudden end.

Just half a dozen shells had fallen but in the blink of an eye they had transformed the makeshift camp into a landscape reminiscent of World War 1. A barren patchwork of turned earth, broken trees, shell holes and mounds, each one a tomb or a marker for the boys buried below or dismembered and scattered across the dark earth. Desolation now marked the spot where they had gathered in camaraderie moments before.

The drone returned a few minutes later to photograph the scene and switched from the infra-red which had highlighted the boys to light-intensifier for a good picture.

37) A Senior Officers' Bar, The Kremlin, Moscow, Russia

Tucked away amongst the grandeur of the Kremlin's ancient architecture, this was a high-end bar reserved for the Russian military elite; Colonels and upwards. It gently hummed with subdued, fairly civilized conversation and the occasional clink of glasses. Luxurious fixtures bathed the room in a soft light, and the rich aroma of expensive cigars drifted through the air.

Amongst the patrons were two particular men, passing middle age. Their grizzled features and heavily bemedalled military uniforms blending with the rest. They were both senior Russian Army Generals, both weathered by countless battles from the Chechen rebellion to the Afghanistan disaster, and both had spent half a lifetime safeguarding their motherland from harm. They sat close in a private corner, backs to the wall and watching the door like all old soldiers of any rank, nursing their drinks and engaging in hushed conversation.

Viktor Andropov, the one with the square-jaw and the eye-patch, broke the silence, "We can't let this continue. The President... if the war keeps going badly in Ukraine... or if he loses… he won't survive it."

His companion, Ivan Vladimirov, a heavy man with a cultivated stern countenance, nodded gravely, "I agree. He's being driven into a corner where he will be destroyed. It's a double-edged sword; either he steps back, accepts the US placing their missiles in Ukraine and loses respect at home for risking the safety of Russia, or he continues the invasion and is demonized by the West and hated by the mothers of our troops."

Viktor finished for him, "And if he loses in Ukraine it would be worse than if he did nothing. The public and the apparatchiki will unite against him."

"He needs to keep the US missiles out of Ukraine, their presence would drastically reduce our reaction time to an attack by the US. And the US will not even consider our position. They want everyone to forget about their reaction to our missiles in Cuba when they almost began World War III" Ivan took a long drink of neat spirit as if to wash the words from his mouth. It went down like water.

Shaking his head in sadness, Viktor went on, "It is a bad thing that we had to go into Ukraine. Their people were a valuable part of our nation until the US-funded revolts led them to break away and turn to the West."

"Ah, I recall," said Ivan, "The US promised them protection from us… Us! That elusive ghost of freedom and great wealth from trade if they would give up their nuclear deterrent. So they gave up their weapons and the US betrayed them as they always do. Established a corrupt system of paid-puppets to run their country, blew up the gas sales pipeline into Europe and cut off their grain exports."

"Now, for protecting his people, by keeping US missiles out of our back yard, our President is painted a monster in all the media run by the US. What else could he do Ivan?"

"Having painted him so, it has allowed them to impose global condemnation and sanctions. And sanctions mean hardship for the common people, not the political classes."

"There are rumours, Viktor, rumours the President is "overworking." That his mind is not what it was… He forgets details and decisions..."

Viktor took a long drink from his glass of spirit, the burn of the vodka doing nothing to ease the worry etched on his face, he nodded in acceptance, "The pressure he is under would break a Golem. To get Russia out of this corner someone might have to oust the President..."

Ivan stiffened at the treasonous proposal, his eyes hardened, "If that's what it takes to save our country, so be it. We cannot let Mother Russia be threatened!"

Their quiet words, spoken in that invisible corner of the bar, reverberated with the magnitude of their decision. They were not only choosing their own path but the fate of the nation as well.

As they continued their discussion as to ways and means, the murmurs in their bar, the clinking of glasses, and the hum of muted conversations further off served as a stark contrast to the gravity of their words. Unbeknownst to the rest of the patrons, the fate of their President and their nation was being decided within the confines of this bar. And perhaps in other bars across the capital as they spoke.

The Generals left their drinks untouched for a while and stared at their glasses, their minds preoccupied with the enormity of the decision they had made. The lives of their people and the future of their nation rested on their broad shoulders; and they were prepared to bear that weight, no matter the cost. As they departed together, the bar continued its normal rhythm. Though the two were not overheard, most of the other patrons were all too well aware of the storm brewing in their nation's corridors of power.

38) General Nikolai Kuznetsov's Dacha Outside Moscow, Russia

A gentle but cold wind was just bending the tops of the trees surrounding his dacha as General Kuznetsov alighted from his vehicle. The falling snow was caught by the breeze and shone in the security lighting by the house. He took a moment to drink in the beautiful, rural landscape – the sprawling snow-covered paddocks, the meandering stream now frozen hard, and the secluded dacha itself standing protected from the wind amongst the trees. This lovely place, far removed from the constant stress of his working life in Moscow city, gave him a feeling of peace, spread a balm over his war-weary soul.

His wife, that gentle, graceful woman, was waiting for him, her face fraught with worry. The moment he stepped through the gate, she rushed towards him. The tears that welled up in her eyes told tales of sleepless nights and anxious days, the painful burden of uncertainty gnawing at her heart.

They met halfway in a supportive embrace, two pillars of strength still seeking comfort in one another. The wind picking up again rustled the leaves overhead, a momentary distraction from the tension of the moment. Holding her now at arm's length, he looked into her eyes, portals into her fears and anxieties, and spoke the words she had been desperate to hear.

"He is alive, my dear," he whispered, his voice breathy with relief. Her eyes widened, a flicker of new found hope and joy igniting in their depths. He continued, "Alexander is not dead. He has been taken captive by the Ukrainians. He is uninjured, though he has taken a bit of a beating. Nothing he won't get over."

A sigh of relief escaped her, a tremulous smile dared to spread across her face. She clung to him, head on his chest, her body shaking as tears of relief streamed down her face. Their son, their only child, was alive.

"Can we reach him? Can we send him anything?" she asked, her voice wandering aimless and quivering with pent-up emotion. He nodded, assuring her that soon they would be able to exchange messages with their son.

Her mother's concern, however, did not end, "We must bring him home, Alexei," she pleaded, her hands gripping his arms tightly. Staring into his eyes, "Can't we do something?"

He held her gaze, his eyes showing that customary determination. "I will try to negotiate an exchange of political prisoners with the British. They have sway over the Ukrainians. We'll bring our boy home," he promised."And just remember, my love, that while being a prisoner of war is neither comfortable nor honourable, at least no one is shooting at you."

Arm in arm, they headed to the dinner table. A lantern of relief shone over the rustic dining room as they raised their glasses to toast Alexander's safety and his eventual return. Their conversation was lighter than it had been for weeks, their spirits finally lifting. Dinner that evening was a celebration of hope and of their commitment to bringing their son home. Despite the lingering uncertainty that must always accompany an ongoing war, that evening at the dacha was one of joy, relief, and promises of homecoming celebrations.

39) GCHQ, Cheltenham, Gloucestershire, UK

The three principle branches of the British Secret Intelligence Service all fall under the supervision of the Foreign and Commonwealth Development Office and are divided by responsibility as follows: MI5 deals with human intelligence, "HumInt" threats within the United Kingdom. They provide counterintelligence services, that is they counter foreign spies and terrorists operating within the UK. They also help the NCA with serious organised crime because there is often an overlap or interaction between snooping foreign intelligence services and the criminal underworld.

MI6 deals with HumInt overseas, countering threats which occur abroad against British interests, recruiting and handling spies to act for the UK interest and sometimes engaging in "disruptive" actions of various kinds to achieve political ends. Both of these units have their headquarters at Vauxhall Cross in London and are supported as required by members of E Squadron, 22 SAS Regiment.

In the modern day, however, the greater part of intelligence is Signal Intelligence or SigInt and comes from interception of communications between governments, foreign agents, businesses, universities, criminals and similar organisations. However they pass their messages, be that landline telephone, cell-phone, internet, radio or whatever, they are all vulnerable to interception. This interception and the collation of that information is carried out principally at the Government Communications Headquarters building, GCHQ.

It is said that GCHQ, or at least the AI that works there, reads every email sent and listens to every phone call made in the UK and can do the same when required anywhere in the world. If that is not true then the reality is not far short. Some very, very clever people work at GCHQ.

Beneath the remarkable ring-based architecture of the Government Communications Headquarters building, universally known as "The Doughnut', an air of steady concentration reigned. Inside and far below the innovative steel and glass structure, a network of interconnected operational hubs was abuzz with organised activity. Row upon row of state-of-the-art computer stations hummed, their screens casting a glow on the faces of the intelligence officers seated before them. Highly motivated people working tirelessly to collect and collate signals-intelligence from selected satellite, radio, 'phone, web, wifi and email traffic all around the world.

Among the many skilled signals analysts stationed at GCHQ was Amelia Darwin, a young lady approaching thirty years of age and a seasoned signals analyst and translator of several Asian languages known for her acumen and efficiency. As she sat at her workstation, her gaze fixed steadily on her computer screen, her fingers tapped an arrhythmic pattern on the keys. The vast digital world at those fingertips was her domain, and she navigated it with the finesse of an artist.

Suddenly, her screen blinked a warning. A high-priority signal-interrupt flashed its message across her screen and overrode her current task. This was not her usual recent fare of decoding military conversations in Mandarin, it warned of a covert message sent via a secure channel from a clandestine source. She pulled it up instantly. Recognising the significance of the warning header, a shiver of alertness ran through Amelia as she imagined the heroic, and doubtless very handsome, agent from whom it originated. Of course, she had never met him, never had any idea of his appearance or real name. Not even his cover name. All she knew was his operational designator.

It was a message from Blackbeard, an MI5 operative embedded within the underbelly of organised crime, he was in deep cover; long term penetration of some criminal or terrorist enterprise, his code name known only to a select few, his real identity to even fewer. For a split second she had an image in her mind of a dark-haired handsome young man in a dinner jacket with the collar of his white shirt open… then she pulled her mind back to her duty.

The message was brief, a succinct line of code. He required the immediate collection of a 'dead letter,' a method of communication dating back to before the Cold War which required a message left in a pre-determined location to be retrieved by another agent. Given the deep-cover of Blackbeard's operation, the use of a physical dead letter drop indicated the extreme urgency and importance of the information he needed to convey back to his handlers.

Decoded, the message read as follows: "Dead letter drop at site "B" to be checked daily p.m. from the 4th for one week or until message collected"

Immediately, Amelia notified her manager, James Barclay. A middle aged man of stern disposition and hawk-like features, he was no stranger to the perilous world of intelligence operations, being an agent handler himself in an earlier stage of his career. This unexpected communication from Blackbeard made him snap to attention, his sharp eyes scrutinising the coded message on Amelia's screen in an effort to read more than was there.

Understanding the implications, James gave a curt nod. "Pass it to the recipient ID at Vauxhall Cross immediately," he ordered, referring to the iconic Secret Intelligence Service headquarters on the bank of the Thames in London. "Check it is picked up as the agent's life may depend on this." There was no time for delay or error.

As Amelia relayed the recoded message through a secure cable with a high priority tag she felt as if the entire labyrinth of the Doughnut held its breath. Each bit of data travelled at the speed of light, carrying with it the weight of at least the interruption of a major crime syndicate, probably the life of a brave agent and perhaps even national security itself. Then she set up a phone call through her head-set to a certain live number to ensure the Blackbeard message was seen immediately. As the number rang she smiled with pleasure inside and savoured the experience of being right at the beating heart of all this. Blackbeard was really cute for sure. He probably liked cats too.

40) An Untidy Bedroom In A Large, Old House Set In Its Own Grounds, Surrey, UK

Tucked away in the pleasant green embrace of the Southern English countryside, an imposing mansion basked in the golden hues of early evening. Within its rather grand, stone walls, each room echoed with silent stories of the past, a reminder of the many generations that had called it home.

One such room, upstairs and to the rear of the house, belonged to young Daniel, a university student currently enjoying the tranquillity of home between the rigorous terms at Bradford University. Terms that he was struggling to cope with. His room, a blend of old world charm and youthful modernity, was his sanctuary. Heavy, dark mahogany furniture lined the walls, juxtaposing the bright posters of rock bands and colourful trinkets from university life. Slightly depressed, Daniel found the terms difficult as he was not a natural academic. His degree course in video animation, which he thought would be an easy way to placate his parents, was actually including a hell of a lot of study. His course work could wait for a while.

In the center of his room stood a large, four-poster bed, its duvet strewn with textbooks. His guitar lay propped against its footboard. The walls were lined with bookshelves brimming with everything from Marvel Comics to "Easy Lead Guitar Riffs," a mirror of Daniel's modest intellectual curiosity.

Amidst this tableau of late teenage life, Daniel was seated at a small desk under the window, the sun casting an apricot glow on his earnest features. In his hands, he held a delicate pipe, its bowl filled with a mixture of rich tobacco and a dusting of the fine, white powder he had brought home with him.

Displaying the finesse of a seasoned smoker, he filled his pipe, tamping down the tobacco and powder mix with practiced precision employing a little tool on a smoker's penknife. The illicit nature of the act didn't seem to weigh on his spirit, perhaps it was the thrill of the forbidden or maybe it was the promise of relief from his stress that made his eyes dance with a peculiar mix of trepidation and excitement.

Rising from his desk, he approached the window, drawing the heavy, velvet curtains right back. He unlatched the window, letting the fresh, country air blow into his room. The muffled chirps of evening birds outside mingled with the distant chatter of his family preparing dinner downstairs.

Leaning out into the breeze, he held the pipe to his lips, his fingers fumbling for a match in his pocket. As the match struck the smell of sulphur filled the air, its sudden, orange glow high-lighting his face. He held the flame to the bowl, a glow of hot ash appearing as he sucked the gasses into his mouth and held them.

As his pull ended, the smoke began to snake from the bowl into the air, carried away into the quiet serenity of the countryside. The white powder added an extra edge to the tobacco, a heady rush that coursed through his veins. With his head tilted back towards the sky, Daniel indulged in his secretive ritual, a young man on the edge of adulthood seeking solace in the harmless escape of his hidden vice.

As the sun started to lose its strength, painting the sky with shades of twilight, Daniel sat perched on his window sill. He continued to suck gently, making smoke rings dance in the soft breeze. Every pull from the pipe seemed to make him more alive, to take him further away from the reality of his privileged life and the demanding rigours of academia, into a world entirely of his own. A blessed relief.

Eventually, he would have to face his responsibilities, his work and his future. But for now, he found solace in the calm of his room and the sweetly intoxicating charm of his cocaine and tobacco-laden pipe. The sun would set, and night would fall, but Daniel, like the smoke from his pipe, was lost in the moment, floating on an intoxicating cloud of freedom, and youthful rebellion.

41) Ralf Burgin's Office, The Secret Intelligence Service HQ, Vauxhall Cross, London, UK

Mike walked the few hundred yards from the Tube along the Thames Embankment and up to the entrance of the huge modern building facing South across the Thames. Straight through security by card and retina scan, he strode through the polished hallways of Vauxhall Cross.

By way of an elevator, his path led him to a nondescript door that barred entrance to the office of his direct superior. Mike passed his hand over a scanner and the door eased open to reveal Ralf Burgin, Chief Intelligence Officer, stationed behind an antique oak desk which he had purchased himself. Ralf was a man fast approaching middle-aged with a grizzled beard and sharp eyes, quite young for his rank, but he gave off an air of seasoned competence.

Ralf looked up from his admin, a hint of a smile playing on his lips. He rose, gesturing to a decanter of whisky and two crystal glasses ready perched on a side table. The corners of his eyes crinkled, "Never too early for a good single malt, eh, Mike?"

"Its five o'clock somewhere." Mike joked.

He poured two generous measures and handed one to Mike. They stood for a moment, swirling the Scotch in their glasses. Then they each took a sip in unison, savouring the liquid gold. They were more than colleagues, they were as close to friends as the Great Game allowed, bound by years of shared secrets and a mutual respect born from navigating their treacherous world.

Ralf leaned back in his chair, his gaze a little serious then broke the companionable silence, "Mike, I have a job for you." His tone held a note of apology. "It's not your usual fare. Crossover op with MI5. Quite frankly, it's way beneath your pay grade, but I need it doing and I need it doing now. You were in town..."

Mike raised a hand, forestalling him. His expression a blend of amusement and nonchalance. "No need to apologise, Ralf. I'm not too proud to do some legwork."

Ralf exhaled, the slight awkwardness evaporating. Nodding his thanks he gestured at Mike to look at his screen. It showed the address of a public house, "Dog & Barrel, Westgate, Bradford BD1 2QR," and a photo of the frontage.

"I will have it sent to your secure email but the job is simple enough. Go to the gents at this pub ASAP and collect a written message left there. Probably in the toilet cistern, if that is practicable, but wherever he can hide a message in the gents. Check every afternoon for a week until you find a message." Ralf looked at Mike for his understanding.

Mike's eyebrows arched in mock intrigue. Ralf continued, his voice serious, "This isn't the usual domestic petty dealer crap. MI5 have had a good man embedded deep in a high-volume cocaine import and wholesale gang for some months now collecting info and trying to find out the sources, routes and big names. So this is likely related to a substantial cocaine shipment headed for the UK.

"But you don't actually know what the message is though? Mike was just wanting to be clear but it went across wrong.

Ralf looked slightly pained at admitting his own uncertainty, "Well... actually we don't, but a guy in deep cover would only contact us in an emergency so it is likely a big deal coming through or he has something else urgent to tell us."

"Might you want me to act on the message, stay on this job?"

"Depends what's in the message Mike. Could be. Let me have the message ASAP and if there is a job you can have it if you like the look."
Downing the last of his whisky, Mike stood, "Consider it done, Ralf," he offered a tight smile. "I'll take Don Mac with me and I'll be in touch." The two men exchanged a handshake.

42) A Comfortable Drawing Room In A Large, Old House Set In Its Own Grounds, Surrey, UK

The door from the kitchen was flung open and banged back against the wall, jarring the calm rhythm of the home. Daniel loomed in the doorway, face unrecognisable, eyes blazing with a wild, frantic intensity. In his bloody right hand, he brandished a large kitchen knife, point down. Its cold steel glinted ominously in the dim light.

The tranquillity of the drawing room was disrupted by Daniel's sudden, appearance. His father, a distinguished gentleman in his late forties, He been sitting comfortably in his favourite armchair, immersed in the evening newspaper. His head turned at the noise but before he could react, Daniel lunged at him, grasping him with his left hand and thrusting the knife into the top of his chest, downwards to the hilt with ferocious force.

His father's newspaper was flung down to the floor, a spread of newsprint pages. The only sound the victim made was a choking gurgle as the life ebbed out of him, bleeding out quickly in spurts from his severed artery. He died with his eyes wide in disbelief as he registered his son's twisted face. The quiet, pleasant drawing room now a horrifying scene of patricide.

Behind Daniel, the kitchen door creaked back against its hinges, the doorway framing a grisly scene: His mother lay sprawled on the gleaming floor of the kitchen, a grotesque circle of red pooled around her on the floor tiles. Her lifeless eyes stared vacantly at the ceiling, a look of pure shock frozen on her face. Another proof of her son's implacable fury.

As if awoken by the creak of the door, the living room was punctured by a deafening scream. Daniel's younger sister, Hanna, a petite, soft-spoken girl of sixteen, had stood mute and witnessed her father's death. She was rooted to the spot, her face pale, her eyes wide with terror, her lungs now empty. As Daniel advanced on her, she raised her arms instinctively, an instinctive but futile attempt to shield herself from the inevitable.

She screamed again, then, "Daniel! No! No!"

Ignoring her pleading cries, Daniel rained down savage blows with the knife. First to her protective arms then he got through to her body and she coughed blood. Each thrust, each slice, was a chilling testament to his inexplicable wrath. Her frail body crumpled under the relentless assault, her screams subsiding to choked whimpers. Then nothing.

The room was gripped by an eerie silence, broken only by the breathless panting of the murderer. Daniel stood, now frozen, amidst the nightmarish carnage, his chest heaving with exertion, the cold gleam in his eyes replaced by a vacant, unseeing stare. The knife hung limply in his hand, its blade greased by the scarlet stains of his horrific deeds. The knife dropped to the floor with a clatter.

The once vibrant living room was now a chilling crypt bearing the remnants of a family annihilated by one of their own. The sheer horror of the scene a foretaste of what the future held for the country.

43) 06:30, Entrance Gates to St. James's Park, London, England

Mike stood in front of the ornate, wrought iron gates guarding St. James Park. They were closed to the early morning air. He was wearing a long camel-hair coat over his suit against the chill and the brim of a fedora hat shadowed his face. His head was bent to his hands as if in study. A casual, or even not-so-casual, observer would think he was reading a small book or checking his phone messages.

Closing the book and inserting it into an inside pocket he stepped towards the kerb just as a black Jaguar saloon, with dark-tinted rear windows, pulled up in front of him from his right. The gleaming car's driver was hard-faced to be a chauffeur and perhaps forty years of age. Mike glanced left and right then opened the near-side rear door himself and climbed in so he was behind but across from the driver.

There was a bulkhead decorated with a coat of arms and glass windows separating the driver from the passenger space but the slider was open. "'Morning Johnny, how's the new plastic foot performing in this cold weather?"

The driver's reply was warm, even affectionate, "I can do anything bar tap-dance with it, sir. Just did a 25 miler for Pilgrim Bandits. You okay, sir?" A proud man, Johnny wanted the world to know he still had something to offer after losing a foot to an IED. He was involved in a fundraiser for the charity set up by ex British special forces to help badly wounded veterans.

"Mustn't grumble, Johnny" Pleasantries out of the way, Mike sat back as if in thought and Johnny knew better than to push the conversation. The car glided forward.

44) General Leonid Petrenko's Office, The Kremlin, Moscow, Russia

The office of General Leonid Petrenko, head of the GRU military intelligence organisation, was a cold image of stark functionality. Walls painted in institute cream and brown, surfaces bare of any personal touches, it generated an air of clinical, if sombre efficiency.

Behind a large, metal desk sat Petrenko, a man of intimidating stature, his grey eyes and severe features reflecting a lifetime of self discipline. The window was shuttered and the only source of illumination was the harsh, unforgiving glare of the fluorescent lights overhead. Under their scrutiny, he poured over a stack of reports, his brow furrowed in deep concentration.

General Nikolai Kuznetsov, a man also known for his iron will and calm style, stepped into the heavily secured office. An uncharacteristic tension tightened the sinews of his old but muscular frame, his broad shoulders hunched as if carrying the weight of an invisible burden. His habitual aura of command marred by a perceptible air of uncertainty.

Petrenko, a veteran intelligence officer with a steady, analytical gaze that betrayed years spent wading through the muddy waters of international espionage, glanced up from his desk and found Kuznetsov's face. His sharp features softened briefly at the sight of his old friend, yet he recovered quickly and remained steeled, ready to assert the difficult truth that his position demanded.

Without preamble, Petrenko gestured to the chair opposite him, an unspoken invitation for Kuznetsov to sit. The General did so, his movements displaying an unusual hesitancy. His stormy grey eyes sought reassurance in Petrenko's, a question lingered in their depths.

In the silence, Petrenko sighed, his hardened exterior revealing a hint of regret. He knew that his words would not help the turmoil churning within his friend. Yet, he was a man of duty, bound by the codes of his profession, and the necessity to remain objective in a world woven with subterfuge.

"Nikolai," he started, his voice carrying a rare note of apology. "I've received word from our people. There are no plans to negotiate for your son's release in the near future."

He paused, letting the words hang heavily in the air. Kuznetsov stiffened, his fingers drumming a restless tattoo on the armrest.

"There are others," Petrenko continued, striving and almost failing to keep his tone matter-of-fact, "political and intelligence prisoners of high value to the state, in line for exchange with the US and UK. Alexander's case just doesn't carry the same weight."

Kuznetsov's face was a hard mask, his eyes cold steel. For the merest instant, anger showed a fin. Then the tremor in his hand betrayed the impact of the revelation. The general was a stoic man, but the thought of his son languishing in an enemy prison gnawed at his self control.

"I understand," he said after an interval too long for Petrenko's comfort. His words carrying the weight of a father's helplessness. He stood abruptly, ready to leave. His rugged face was devoid of any emotion, but his eyes, those deep grey pools, were haunted by a grim realization. A desperate, unspoken prayer formed in the silence between the two old friends.

Petrenko watched the general leave, a genuine sadness etched onto his weathered features. As head of the GRU, he had made difficult calls before, many times, but the personal cost of this particular message was a bitter pill to swallow. "I'm sorry Nikolai. If I can do anything…"

As the office door closed behind the departing Kuznetsov, Petrenko sighed, his gaze drawn to a screen displaying some intricate web of geopolitical interests. He didn't see it. Today, friendship had collided with duty, leaving behind a trail of echoes. Echoes of regret, echoes of loyalty broken, and echoes of battles yet to be fought, perhaps. He regretted losing Nikolai as a friend but, more than that, he did not want to make an enemy of him. Not if there was going to be a leadership contest.

45) The Dog & Barrel Public House, Westgate, Bradford, UK

The Dog And Barrel was a black and white, timber-framed building of apparent Tudor vintage and stood on the corner of an alley in Westgate, close to the centre of Bradford. It had long held the title of roughest drinking hole in the city. Which was quite a feat given that Bradford, being the major drug dealing centre in the North of England, boasted the highest crime rate in the entire United Kingdom.

As they entered the bar, casually dressed in jeans, caps and warm jackets, Mike got a few hard looks. Some probably thought he was police, others that he was lost. Mac went to the bar and, after a word with the barman, slipped him a banknote.

Mike didn't blend in well with the usual clients, some of whom had their own teeth. Tall, athletic and good looking he stood out in a low dive like this, whereas Mac, being short, wiry and battered, with lines on his face well beyond his years, and a professional Glaswegian Scot to boot, fit in quite well.

Apparently a little drunk, they sat in a corner with a view of the door, backs to the wall and a bottle of Scotch whiskey on the table between them still in its brown paper wrapper. It was half empty. Appearances can be deceptive. Their bottle was half full of tea and had been wiped down with whisky for the smell. Mac had slipped the landlord a tenner on the way in to let them drink their own poison.

Though the place already contained a few drunks and smack heads, this being the afternoon it was barely a third full. A man in his thirties, heavily built and perhaps of Pakistani extraction though, this being a pub, not so obviously of the Moslem persuasion, left his friends at the bar and walked, slightly unsteadily, to the gents. Spider and Mac didn't watch him. A few minutes later he returned to the bar and continued a quite animated conversation about cricket. For those who have not spent time with them, men from the Indian sub-continent tend to favour cricket with the same almost religious passion that the ethnic British reserve for football.

Mac jerked his head back at Mike and got up very unsteadily to head for the gents. Moments later, Mike noticed a large, young white-man in jeans and T-shirt, with a ragged scar down his right cheek, detach from a group opposite and walk casually, dangerously, towards the gents. Almost imperceptibly Mike shook his head to himself and pursed his lips.

Inside the gents Mac lost his drunken shamble and moved quickly to the far cubicle which was empty. Inside he lifted the cistern lid and removed a small, sealed plastic bag with a little folded paper in it. Placing the bag in his front left jeans pocket he adjusted the strap over his shoulder for comfort and began to return to the door leading back into the bar.

This door opened firmly in front of him and the large young man from the bar entered. Mac stepped back from him. As the door closed on its sprung damper he pulled out a long flick-knife and opened it high, with a stylish flourish. "Give me your 'phone and your wallet old man."

46) One Canada Square, Canary Wharf, London, UK

One Canada Square, a towering monolith of steel and glass in the heart of Canary Wharf, was the London nerve center of the merchant bank AFM Capital Partners. High above the city, almost nestled among the clouds, Alexander Sinclair, occupied a spacious corner office. An office that was the epitome of corporate opulence with its polished hardwood furniture and large windows offering a two-wall panoramic view of the mighty Thames and the ever-moving landscape of London city.

Filtering in from beyond his heavy office door, the muffled sound of a bustling workspace formed a steady background to his thoughts. The rapid tapping of keyboards and muted phone conversations of the office workers painted an auditory picture of productivity and purpose. Yet, in the serene isolation of the executive's office, a different form of work was required.

Alexander Sinclair, Chief Financial Officer, was solitary by nature and weary from the long hours he spent pushing his financial schemes forward: company takeovers, initial private offerings, asset stripping, he oversaw them all. And he was responsible for their success or failure. He slumped in his executive chair, his posture betraying fatigue. His eyes, shadowed by prolonged strain and sleep deprivation, stared unseeing over the river, lost in the relentless pulsation of the city. Even though twilight had begun to paint the sky in hues of orange and purple, his working day was far from over.

A quick glance at his expensive wristwatch revealed the relentless ticking away of seconds. The New York markets were open until 22:00. He sighed, a breath heavy with the burden of high stakes gambits and expectations of success. No one would disturb him without invitation, a privilege he enjoyed as a senior executive. And no one would bear witness to this darker side of the corporate dream.

His hand reached out of its own accord for his desk's top drawer and withdrew a neatly folded paper. He carefully unwrapped it, revealing a small mound of white powder. Cocaine. His escape. His catalyst. His rocket fuel. The magic powder that made the impossible workload manageable, the stress bearable. It was his secret armour, worn as protection by so many on the unforgiving corporate battlefield.

His regular supplier had recently been arrested in Epping, a close call that reminded him of the precarious balance he was maintaining. But luck had smiled on him and a friend had brought him this gift from Leeds. Apparently, the dealers were running it straight from Bradford, uncut, and pure. It was a silver lining to the otherwise looming dark cloud of the Barings-Johnson takeover.
Using the fold in the wrapper, he carefully arranged the cocaine in a neat line on his highly polished, dark wooden desk. From his wallet, he withdrew a crisp, new £20 note and rolled it into a tight cylinder. With an ease born of practice, he bent over his desk, placing one end of the roll to his right nostril and the other to the white line. Closing his left nostril with a finger,

he inhaled sharply and the powder disappeared up the makeshift plastic tube.

The narcotic, uncut since it left Riaz, quickly passed through the nasal membranes and into his bloodstream. His heart pounded in his chest. Then the drug reached his brain and lit up his neural pathways as it always did. The fatigue was swept away, replaced by a surge of energy that made him feel invincible. He was alive again, ready to conquer another night of work, ready to play the big game and win.

Yet in the back of Alex's mind, a small voice whispered warnings of a precarious balance tipping, a price yet to be paid. But for now, the urgency of the immediate silenced the whispers, drowned in this chemical sea of vibrant energy and renewed vitality.

47) The Dog & Barrel Public House, Westgate, Bradford, UK

Mac looked at the knife and then at the face of the man holding it. "Ah, ye certain this is a solid plan, pal?" Mac sounded about as concerned as if he was considering a fish and chip supper.

Faced with Mac's obvious lack of fear, a puzzled look flickered across the young man's face for a moment before he recovered his frown and yelled, "Give me your 'phone you sad, old bastard!"

"Here you are laddie." Mac reached for his back pocket with his right hand and pulled out a rubber coated metallic cylinder some 6 inches long and something over an inch in diameter. With a flick of his hand it extended into a tubular steel baton of the type called an Asp by the police. It pointed at the floor to his right side initially.

Before the young man realised what was happening Mac broke the wrist of his knife hand and sent the knife bouncing off the tiled wall. On the horizontal backhand stroke he then shattered the bones of the man's face so blood squirted from his nose and his good hand moved towards his face. Then Mac's boot found his crotch and he tumbled forward to receive the baton across his neck. Mac stepped back to avoid the body which, now unconscious, dropped to the floor like a sack of potatoes.

Mac pushed a wall tile with the end of his weapon to collapse it and returned the Asp to his pocket. He dragged the man by one foot from where he blocked the door and eyed the knife on the floor speculatively, "Piece o' shite." He shook his head in disdain, left the knife and opened the door.

Mike was studiously ignoring the stares from the would-be-mugger's friends when Mac came out of the gents and walked unsteadily back to their table. "Stand to," Mac whispered under his breath. A military warning to be prepared.

The mugger's friends had clearly expected him to come out of the gents first, possibly without Mac. They all stood, some blocking the exit from the bar and one hurried to the gents.

"Oh dear," Mike said, quietly. "I can't take you anywhere you bloody drunken Jock."

"Fuck off Mike," Mac responded in good humour. "The laddie wanted ma 'phone."

"You didn't kill him did you? I'll be up all night on the paperwork."

"Naw, ah just skelped 'im a wee bit."

The hero amongst the thugs now stood in front of Mike, he was about the same height at around 6'4" but his stance was poor, off balance. His fists were clenching and releasing as what passed for his mind considered his options. His tongue ran over his lips momentarily, a sure sign of a blow coming. His right shoulder began to move back and he shifted his weight to his rear foot ready to swing a punch.

Mike's right foot lifted straight from the floor without telegraphing any preparation and made firm contact with the man's wedding tackle. He bent over forwards as Mike drew his closed Asp and struck him on the side of the head with the end of it. This blow to the temple switched him off without killing him. Then he flicked the weapon open and things became quite heated for a few moments but ended with three thugs bleeding on the floor and the remainder realising that the fallen were not close friends of theirs. Mike sat back down to sip his drink.

Mac had not moved from his seat to assist, "Behave yersel', Mike."

The door burst open and a call rang out, "Armed police! Do not move!" Presumably the landlord had made the call when the first thug went after Mac in the gents, so that was a useful thing to know in case they used the place again.

A dozen police officers were in the bar in a second; black, heavy external body armour, helmets, pistols drawn and held in front at chest height in the prescribed manner. Doubtless, highly trained as they were, they had never heard a round fired in anger. Any police officer in the UK who shoots a criminal is always taken off the armed work and investigated to placate the bleeding hearts. Then they are often prosecuted.

48) One Canada Square, Canary Wharf, London, UK

A few minutes after the cocaine had begun to improve Alex's mood, a second metamorphosis began to take hold of him. The genial mask he habitually presented to the world fell away to be replaced by an open-mouthed grimace of rage, his eyes lit up with a bestial fury, his breath came sharp and fast.

In a sudden, swift movement, Alex wrenched open his desk drawer and seized a pair of large, gleaming scissors. A gift from an old P.A. leaving to have a baby in the days when offices had paper. Their cold, metallic weight in his hand only seemed to further fuel his chemical-induced frenzy.

With something approaching a roar, Alex burst from his solitary office into the communal workspace opposite, that friendly hive of activity. His appearance sent shockwaves through the room and most of the staff froze in fright at the sudden noise and horrifying spectacle. Clerks and assistants, the backbone of the merchant bank and predominantly young women, then recoiled wide-eyed in terror as they realised their quiet, respected superior had become a madman in their midst. Several girls screamed at the top of their voices.

Alex lunged at the terrified girls, scissors slashing through the air like an enraged tailor. More piercing screams joined the first as he attacked his young staff indiscriminately, the deadly blades piercing the victims' bodies with relentless precision. Young women fell, stabbed from behind as the crowd blocked the doorway, their professional suits stained dark with their lifeblood. The dead and dying were hurled aside as Alex continued his rampage through the office, his movements fuelled by some unnatural, drug-induced strength.

A brave young man, a recent accounting graduate and now junior analyst, lunged at Alex in an attempt to end the bloodbath. But Alex's chemically-empowered might was beyond any ordinary resistance. With a savage thrust of the scissors, the young man crumbled to the floor, a fatal wound in his chest pumping dark blood.

Amid the fearful chaos, one young woman kept her head. Sally Gibson, another new recruit with curly auburn hair and a heart-shaped face, watched the horror unfold from behind her desk. Terror pounded in her ears, but she steeled herself, her hands shaking just a little as she picked up her phone. With trembling fingers, she dialled 999, her voice a whisper of urgency as she reported the horrifying scene,

"What service do you require, Madam?"

"There is a madman stabbing people in our office at One, Canada Square, floor 39. I need to go."

When she had hung up, she dialled the number for internal security, "Is that security?"

"Yes, security here, Ma'm."

"Floor 39. Mr Sinclair has turned into a madman and is stabbing people. For God's sake send some help."

With each passing second, her voice had gained a touch more of steel, a whisper of defiance against the senseless violence. As she put down the phone, she made her decision. The sound of sirens was faint but growing, a distant promise of rescue. But she couldn't wait, wouldn't be another victim.

Sally slipped off her heels and fled. The cold of the marble flooring chilled her feet as she raced towards the relative safety of the stairwell, leaving behind the scene of horror and death. Carnage caused by a once-respected executive lost in the merciless grip of the polluted drug.

49) The Dog & Barrel Public House, Westgate, Bradford, UK

It was Police Standard Operating Procedure: One armed officer remained by the door, covering the room, and one advanced towards Mike and Mac covered by the third moving out to his flank to maintain a clear shot at the potential target. The remaining officers spread across the room covering the clientele. Mike and Mac remained sitting calmly. Clearly the lead officer had either been told who to look for by their informant or he was smart enough to see where the eyes in the room were focussed. "Stand up and put your hands in the air!"

Mike and Mac, in almost parade-like unison, stood, turned to the wall and raised their arms above their heads, forcing the officer to come closer by their positioning. The flanking officer now crossed the room with an air of authority and moved as if towards Mike while the previous officer covered him. As he came close Mike whispered, "We are Special Branch and armed. Read the card in my left back pocket."

"What are you saying!" The search officer was high on adrenalin and not hearing clearly.

Mike, spoke again, quietly, "Get a grip officer. We are armed Special Branch so pretend to pat us down then get us outside and into your motor. Read the card in my back left pocket."

The officer finally came off the adrenalin, out of automatic mode and felt for the card. He read it silently then looked hard at the two men. He seemed to think for a moment then stood back and read something from the card privately into his radio, released the speech button and looked back to Mike. The other officers tried to watch everyone in the bar.

A long minute or two later his Operational Firearms Commander (OFC) must have done some quick checks as his radio responded into his earpiece. The officer on the radio listened, his eyebrows raised, an incredulous look passed briefly across his face. Then he searched Mike, ignoring the pistol and baton and not even checking his wallet. Then he did the same to Mac.

Apparently satisfied, he stepped back and nodded to the officer covering them. "Cuff these two and put them in the car."

50) One Canada Square, Canary Wharf, London, UK

In the centre of the communal office, Alex Sinclair stood almost like a statue. Almost, because his chest still heaved from his recent exertion; the sound of his laboured breathing harsh, grating against the relative silence enveloping the room. His arms, drenched in blood, hung by his sides; one hand still gripped the red stained scissors. His eyes stared into the distance.

The floor around him was littered with his victims and awash with their blood. A little blood spreads a long way and there was a lot of blood here. Young women mostly, helpless in the face of his frenzied attack. Some clung to life by a thread, their quiet whimpers coming faintly. Some lay still, eyes averted and held still by an instinctive survival response to an attack. Most lay still for another reason, their eyes wide open in a final, horrifying stare. The dying don't close their eyes.

A single young police officer in street uniform pushed past the frozen security men and into the room. He produced a yellow Taser and trained it on Alex while checking the room for other threats, his face was a calm mask but his eyes were wide at the horror. In a commanding voice he called out:

"Police with a Taser. Drop your weapon!"

Alex remained frozen, unhearing, the scissors still clutched in his grip, his eyes vacant and staring into some distance beyond the walls. Registering the lack of compliance, the officer took action. With a practised aim and a resolute expression, he triggered the Taser. The twin probes flew through the air to strike Alex's chest inches apart and connected him by fine wires to the capacitor in the weapon. There was a noticeable crackling sound and Alex's body convulsed violently as 50,000 volts coursed through his system. He went down like a sack of potatoes, the scissors clattering from his grasp to the bloody floor.

Repeated shocks were not required. Two more officers arrived, breathing heavily, as Alex fell and, practised, quick and efficient, they knelt on the floor to pin his arms behind his back and fit the cold steel of handcuffs to his wrists.

Then one arrested and cautioned him, "I am arresting you on suspicion of assault and attempted murder. You do not have to say anything but it may harm your defence if you do not mention when questioned something that you later rely on in Court. Anything you do say may be given in evidence."

The two officers then hoisted him to his feet, his body now limp and unresisting, a stark contrast to the monstrous strength he had displayed mere minutes earlier.

The urgent wail of approaching ambulances had followed Sally's call for help. At the first officers signal, the paramedics rushed into the room, their green uniforms a stark contrast to the grim, red-splashed scene around them. They moved quickly, systematically, working to stabilize the wounded. The room filled with a new energy, the feeling that the area was safe and the hope that some lives could be saved.

The arresting officers led Alex away, leaving behind the trappings of the terror he had unleashed. His glazed eyes remained open but now sullen. The rage was gone, replaced by the raw shock of a man coming back from insanity to face the consequences of his drug-fuelled actions.

More medical staff arrived, bodies were covered respectfully and carried away on folding stretchers. The surviving staff members waited according to the severity of their wounds as the medical professionals worked diligently, swift, confident actions a slight balm to the raw terror of the day.

51) General Nikolai Kuznetsov's Dacha Outside Moscow, Russia

As General Kuznetsov's secure motorcade glided along the tree-lined driveway towards his Dacha, his gaze scanned the familiar scene. A surge of warmth thawed his frigid mood as he thought of his wife Natalia, exchanging the hardened shell of the commander for that of a concerned husband.

His driver stopped the vehicle within the gates and close to the house's main entrance. Nikolai's large frame emerged from the vehicle, his steps purposeful despite the icy gale that threatened to steal his resolve. He paused for a moment, stalling, then cast a quick glance towards the snow covered expanse of his private wilderness before turning to meet his wife's worried gaze through the frosted window.

Natalia, a radiant figure against the bleak winter backdrop, greeted him with kind eyes but a restrained smile. The delicate lines on her face betrayed the years of worry, but her eyes, lovely as the first day he met her, held steadfast in their unwavering love for him. With a soft, sad sigh, she took his hand, pulling him into the warmth of their home. The moment the heavy outer doors closed behind them, the biting cold gave way to a familiar, comforting warmth.

As the couple moved from welcoming hallway of their home, lined with centuries-old tapestries and priceless art, and into his office the unspoken tension between them grew. The General's silence was a foreboding undercurrent in their otherwise mundane routine. Anna watched him, her concern deepening as he accepted the crystal glass of vodka she poured, his grip she noticed was tight around the glass.

Finally, Nikolai broke the silence. His voice, usually firm and steady, wavered slightly as he recounted his conversation with General Petrenko, head of GRU. The words hung heavy in the air, "Our son will not be exchanged in the near future beloved. There are other prisoners more valuable to the state who must come first." Then his tone change by an amount noticeable only to Natalia, "We should be glad that he is safe in the hands of the Ukrainians. At least he will not be harmed."

The news hit Anna like a piercing winter chill. Her pale face lost the little colour it held, her eyes welling up with unshed tears. Unused to sharing these feeling, Nikolai struggled to find the right words to comfort her, "He is safe where he is now. We will soon receive letters from him via the Russian Red Cross."

Natalia's response was sharp and cold, a tone she had never taken with Nikolai and a testament to the pain etched on her heart. "That is not what I have heard! The International Red Cross are being denied access to our soldiers held by Ukrainian in the countless camps spread across that God-forsaken country." Both of them knew that the Ukrainians were dragging their feet processing the Russian prisoners in retaliation for alleged Russian mistreatment of their own countrymen. And rumours were swirling about their mistreatment.

Nikolai's clumsy efforts to pacify his wife fell on deaf ears. The glimmer of hope in his voice was met with silent resistance, his wife's hardened expression refusing to waver. The General's eyes softened with regret, a stark contrast to the hardened officer that the world saw. He looked at his wife, his soul mate, her distress stirring a pain deep within him.

As he held her, his arms failing to provide the comfort he so desperately wished to give, he looked into her eyes. Those beautiful eyes, now filled with a despair stronger than his own, eyes that reflected a fear that was all too familiar in their world. It was in that moment, under the ornate arches of their luxurious abode, that the General, despite his immense power, felt a sense of helplessness creep into his heart for the first time.

52) An Anonymous Hotel Room, Edge of Bradford City, West Yorkshire, Northern England

The unmarked police car pulled up beside a public park, covered from view by some trees and about two hundred yards from the Bradford Mercure Hotel where the two men were staying. Mike turned to the senior police officer as they climbed out, "Thank you for the lift Chief Inspector. This will do us just fine. We don't want a tail following us back to the hotel."

Some criminals record and share the numbers of unmarked police cars. The last thing Mike wanted was to be seen walking from a police car to a hotel, so they did a lap around the place first to check for a single tail. Negative; and the local opposition would never be up to mounting a proper relay surveillance team. In any event, Mike had chosen this hotel because it was in a quiet area 4 miles out of the city centre and not easy to watch for anyone with that inclination.

Back in their twin room, Sweet, military-style tea in hand, Mike extracted Faris's note from its waterproof cling-film covering and spread it out flat on a small table. The handwriting was small and difficult to read despite being all in caps.

"Package doctored cocaine arriving Duquesa, Spain, on private yacht Esmeralda 17th August, evening. Believe additive already in imported cocaine is what is causing psychotic attacks around Bradford. Suspect Russian GRU Unit 29155 involved somehow and despatched this from Colombia to Nigeria, then overland to Morocco. Boat loaded at Ksar es Seghir. Much more bad cocaine to come soon. Blackbeard."

"Thit's nae far fae yer pal Russian Leo in Marbella, is it Mike?"

"No, its not Mac. But I would be surprised if he knew about it because this is treading on his patch. And I know he only supplies around the Costa Del Sol. The question here is what do we do about it?"

"Cannae huv the dealers grabbin' gear wi' the additive in ony amount or it'd be pure mayhem in the UK."

"Yes, it needs stopping, clearly. But we've been dropped into the middle of an MI5 op and we don't know the full story...."

"As a'ways"

"It looks like all these crazy attacks in the news recently are down to cocaine being doctored by the Russians. I am guessing its to embarrass our government on the law-and-order front as a punishment for our involvement in Ukraine. But whatever it is, our source needs to be protected as well. It might just be that our man was fed this info as a test and there is nothing on the boat. And if it gets searched our man gets his bollocks burned off with a steam iron before they get properly nasty with him."

"So whit dae we dae?"

Mike sat back and thought for a moment, "I think the best way to handle this is to tip Leo off and have him get his tame coppers to search the boat as if he thought he had competition. Then, if our shipment is real, the coke plus additive is stopped and even if it isn't then there is a fair chance word will get back Leo was behind the search and our man will be in the clear if he is lucky."

"Pish life bein' embedded, Mike. Cannae trust yer ain side no' tae grass ye up if the deal's worth mair than yer hide."

"You're not wrong mate. We've got the best job in the world.

"Aye." Mac managed to cram a sentence worth of cynicism into the one word.

"The first thing I have to do, Mac, like a good field operative, is report this back to Ralf. Copy him the message and my suggestion that we work through Russian Leo."

"Thit numpty will slap his name oan ony win an' take aw the credit."

"'Course he will Mac. But he will also take the stick if it goes wrong."

Mac shook his head in dismissal of Ralf's good parts, "We gaun o'er?"

"I should think so. When I get clearance from Ralf to cover it. Leo is a good mate of mine from Afghan times and I owe him one. He runs a string of girls in Marbella, and has a coke network around there now, but nothing too nasty so I've been able to get cover for him with Interpol and the Spanish as an informant. There is a good chance he doesn't know about this coke run because it would look like he had competition and he would have stood on someone's fingers already. I'll message Ralf now…"

53) General Nikolai Kuznetsov's Dacha Outside Moscow, Russia

The call was unexpected and shattered the fragile peace of the Dacha. Nikolai strode over to the secure landline and his features hardened at the sight of the callers ID: The President. This was not going to be pleasant.

The President had become known for his unpredictable attitude changes in recent times and they were getting worse. Nikolai threw a reassuring glance at Natalia before excusing himself; her silhouette disappeared into a drawing room as she fled the office. A deep breath before picking up could do little to prepare him for the rant he was about to endure.

On the other end of the line, the President, let rip, "General, what has happened to the production of the additive? Have you been on leave? Did you spend a little family time on the Black sea coast? Every day I have reports of our men dying in Ukraine. I have rioting in Moscow and now St. Petersburg. What of your promise to deliver? I trusted you!"

The General swallowed. Against the President's irrational anger, logical argument was futile and could be fatal. He waited for a moment of quiet, "Comrade Supreme Commander, I know this project has taken some time. You are right to be angry and call for results now. We have tested the last of the variants and have found the optimal formula to use in the UK..."

The President cut in, slightly mollified, "It is about time. The world does not wait for you Comrade General."

"Of course you are right, Comrade President. As we speak, our people in Shikhany are producing the final product in sufficient quantity to flood the UK."

The President was calming, "When will it be ready for distribution?"

As an experienced handler of the President, General Kuznetsov was ready with the exact figures, "Comrade President, The UK consumes over 150 tons of cocaine per year so we believe 40 tons will saturate the market short-term and achieve the optimum effect. As you know, the main cocaine trade to UK runs from Columbia, via Nigeria to Rotterdam."

"The President sounded impatient but on a more even keel, "I know that, of course."

"Our own purchases of Columbian cocaine are intercepted in Nigeria and taken to our facility there run by Colonel Petrenko, son of the General of that name..."

"Come to the point. When will it be ready?"

"Within twelve days sufficient additive will be produced and flown to Nigeria as diplomatic luggage, then mixed with our cocaine within the following week. Then it will be shipped to Rotterdam the week following and into the UK two days after that using our six main importers in the UK. Our product will be on the streets of the UK in less than three weeks."

"Is that your final timing, General? Three weeks from today? Can I rely on that?"

"Yes, Comrade President, I will have the additive distributed across the UK in three weeks."

The President's silence on the other end was deafening. "You realise the importance of this project, General? It will put great pressure on the UK government at the very least and most likely cause them to quietly reduce or end their support for Ukraine. They will not dare a repeat of this public outrage when we have demonstrated the effect we can create at will."

"I realise the importance Comrade President."

"Very well. If you let me down you will answer for it."

The line went dead before the General could reply. Nikolai looked at the handset then turned his head to the left and made as if to spit. Traditionally, in Russia, one should spit on the devil to ward him off and, of course, he is always on one's left side.

There was work to be done. Lives hung in the balance, not just the Russian troops in the field which the President had mentioned but those of his wife, his son and, of course his own. But even without that pressure, General Kuznetsov, the iron fist of his nation, would not falter now.

54) An Anonymous Hotel Room, Edge of Bradford City, West Yorkshire, Northern England

Their modest twin room was bathed in the dim glow of a single bedside lamp and the flicker of a TV as Mac busied himself with the British soldiers' tea ritual in the small kitchen area. The aroma of the sweet, milky brew drifted in the air, promising the familiar taste which had supported countless British soldiers on numberless operations for centuries.

Meanwhile, Mike, laid out on one of the beds, was watching a news story playing out on the television screen. "Hey, Mac take a look at this." His low, urgent call pulled Mac away from his task, the tone of his voice suggesting something more serious.

Mac turned just in time to catch the almost-hysterical news report on the screen. The young presenter was hamming up the terror like a pro: "There has been yet another brutal knife attack in Bradford by a group of crazed drug users in a city park. Young mother, Janine Walker, 23, and her baby girl, Cortnee, 11 months, were amongst the seven victims killed by a mass knife attack. The unexpected and horrifying violence erupted from nowhere..."

The young reporter was stressing the horror, and focussing on the female victims, to hold her viewers' attention. But the basics were all too true.

Staring at the ceiling, Mike whistled as he had a realisation.

“Mac, I heard last week from someone higher up the food chain that there would likely be some sort of plot by the Russians to embarrass the British government, and bring them down if they could, as punishment for supporting Ukraine against their invasion. Their aim would be to dissuade the UK from supplying weapons to Ukraine in future or voting for sanctions against Russia at the UN.”

"Aye, they're nae shy, the Ruskies. Mind the Novichok poisonin' they did tae publicly bump off a traitor in the UK a while back? Slow, messy way tae kick the bucket. An' on the telly tae."

Mike continued, “Right. Well, I’m guessing, that this crazy-making additive to the cocaine is the way the Russians have decided to get back at the UK. They are paying the major drug importers. A drug dealer only interested in profits would avoid causing trouble like this as the police would focus on his network. And he’d be killing his own customers.”

Mac was non-committal, "Aye. Me’be."

“Let me finish, Mac. Because this outbreak of crazies is mostly happening in West Yorkshire, and we know now there is a link with the cocaine, I think the Russians are supplying just one major dealer to test the additive. And when they are happy with how it performs they will roll it out through a number of dealers across the UK.”

“Aye, but if tha's true, whit wey hivnae the medics clocked oan tae the extra batty juice in the neds' bloodstream?”

Mike thought for a moment, "Well I’m not a pathologist but maybe the additive breaks down in the body after driving them crazy. Maybe no one told me yet. Anyway, before jumping to any conclusions, I accept that we need solid proof that the main dealer in this area is already selling cocaine with something in it, and that means getting ourselves a sample from a local dealer. Now big players control sizable territories. They don't allow other people’s imports to be sold on their patch. So, if we can buy some cocaine from anyone within the area of these recent attacks, chances are we'll be getting a sample from the main dealer in this area and it’s tainted with a test version of the additive that is causing the trouble around here."

Mac frowned slightly, clearly thinking about what Mike was saying. After a moment, he nodded, a look of grudging acceptance on his scarred face. "Aye, that's pro’bly true," he admitted.

"Well," Mike went on, the barest hint of a smile playing at the corners of his mouth, "Once we've tracked some buyers back to their supplier, we're going to have to go in and try to buy some."

"*We* ur?" Mac stressed the "We." He knew what was coming but played the game anyway.

"Well Mac, more *you* I should think. You look a lot more like a druggie than I do."

The room was silent for a moment, then Mac exploded. "Wha'?!" he exclaimed, his thick Glaswegian accent even more pronounced in his incredulity. "Ye hink Ah look like a pure junkie, aye?"

55) General Nikolai Kuznetsov's Dacha Outside Moscow, Russia

Alone in the opulent living room of their country Dacha, Natalia Kuznetsova nestled on the Italian sofa, her legs tucked up by her side and eyes fixed intently on the television screen. The rustic crackle of the wood burning in the imported iron stove filled the room, a pleasant contrast to the ice and snow outside. Yet it did nothing to warm her tormented heart.

The state news channel was broadcasting the usual propaganda; the Ukrainians were brutal captors. Pictures of haggard Russian prisoners of war, their faces bearing the imprints of beatings, cold, and starvation, were paraded across the screen. Each image was a cold stab, a painful reminder of her son Alexander's fate, a helpless pawn in a cruel game of power and politics.

Worry gnawed at the edges of her heart, morphing into a knot of fear, growing tighter with every passing second. However, more than anything, it was the overwhelming sense of helplessness that choked her, the horrific feeling of being a spectator at her own child's suffering.

An image of a hollow-eyed soldier shivering in a makeshift cell flashed across the screen, and Natalia could almost feel the icy chill that clung to his ragged uniform. For a moment she thought it was Alexander. She closed her eyes, the heartbreaking clips too much to bear, her mind filled with tormenting thoughts of Alexander enduring the same hardships. A lonely tear rolled down her cheek, trailing a damp path on her pale skin.

When she opened her eyes again, there was a different kind of fire in them. They were no longer glistening pools of fear and uncertainty; now, they held a steely resolve. Her jaw set firm, lips pressed into a thin line. She could not, would not, sit idly by while her son was trapped in a nightmarish existence, a pawn in a game he had no say in.

Her hands balled into fists in her lap, knuckles white against the soft fabric of her skirt. As a General's wife, she had long been a keen but silent observer of the world's treacherous dance of power. And she had learned a great deal. Now things were different, the stakes were personal. Her son was at risk, and she would not let bureaucracy and political machinations decide his fate.

Natalia lost interest in the propaganda. It had done its work on her emotions. She turned off the device, plunging the room into a silence broken only by the uneven crackle of the fire. She stood up, her back straight, her stance resolute. She had made a decision. The time for waiting and worrying was over. Now, it was time to act. Natalia was no longer afraid. The mother bear was angry and would move mountains if she had to; but she would find a way to bring her son back home. She would not allow her son to be just another face in the grim parade of war casualties.

56) A Run-Down Public Park, Edge Of Bradford, UK

Evening had fallen on the city of Bradford as Mike and Mac sauntered through a dilapidated suburban public park, their eyes keenly observing the park's less wholesome inhabitants. Two burly men of South Asian descent stood under a malfunctioning dim street lamp, engaged in a hushed conversation with a group of dishevelled teenagers. The exchange of secretive glances and the subtle passing of items indicated something illicit at play. Mike nudged Mac slightly, nodding towards the scene unfolding.

"Heads up Mac. Looks like we've got our dealers," Mike murmured. They tailed the pair discreetly, turning off the path and watching them walk to an ostentatious, modified Mercedes waiting with a driver, engine idling at the park's edge.

Quick on the uptake, Mac dialled in the car's registration number through a specially designed app on his encrypted phone. Within seconds, they received a reply from the Police National Computer; the vehicle owner's name, address and a warning note: "Subject flagged for drug trafficking and violence". Mac snorted in amusement, "Violence? This numpty's nae seen violence."

Their unsuspecting targets departed in the Mercedes. Mike and Mac returned to their invisibly modest Volvo estate parked some distance away. Programming the suspect's address into the GPS, they were on their way.

Pulling onto a narrow street, they noted the given address was a paint-peeling mid-terraced house in a rundown neighbourhood so they drove by and kept going. As they passed the door, a youth dashed out from the residence and ran down the street. Parking the Volvo discreetly a hundred yards away, they sat in the dark car.

"What I want you to do, Mac, is get in before the boys with the Merc come home for a resupply. We can see they also sell from home so I guess there will be at least one other person in the house. Probably more than one for security."

Mike hung back a short way from the house while Mac swaggered up to the front door and rapped his knuckles against the worn wood. A wiry, tough-looking man of perhaps an Eastern European persuasion swung the door open, a baseball bat gripped in his hand. He looked Mac up and down, clearly unimpressed at Mac's hunched, swaying form.

"What you want?" the man grumbled, a dangerous glint in his eyes.

"I'm after a deal o' coke," Mac said, keeping his tone neutral. The man snarled a profanity at Mac, but Mac was fast. Two fingers jabbed into the man's eyes before he could move, drawing a howl of pain. The man brought his hands up to his face and dropped the bat. Mac pushed him backwards into the house and followed him, clicking out the telescopic baton from his pocket and landing a quick, hard blow on the man's right arm. His broken arm came away from his face and left his neck unguarded so Mac struck him there with the ball on the tip of the weapon.

The drug dealer crumpled onto the floor, stunned from the blow to the nerve. Mac barely glanced at the gently twitching man, he scanned the room for other threats; nothing obvious. Mike arrived just in time to see Mac step over the fallen figure and take up position beside the interior door in case someone came through it.

"Go easy on them, Mac. I have to write this up." Mike closed the external door behind him and began to look around the room for cocaine.

"Fuck off Mike."

Just as he opened a drawer the front door opened quickly and three men piled in one behind the other. They stopped and stared for a moment at the surprise visitors they had found, thieves for sure. But they came to their senses quickly and drew their weapons. Sheath knives were not sufficient to scare their customers and potential thieves apparently as these men had various knives of a longer, more wicked looking design. There were blades with holes, serrated edges and a spike on the spine of one knife. But they were not knife fighters, not like the characters Mac and Mike had met in Russia and Eastern Europe.

The first man through the door had raised his huge blade high to cut downwards but before it began to fall Mac's Asp smashed his wrist and sent the knife flying. A backhand blow caught him across the face making him scream like a pig in a slaughter house. Mac kicked him backwards to corral and hamper his friends against the now closed door.

Mike drew his Asp and broke a man's knee in the standard crowd control technique taught to a certain kind of soldier. The ball at the tip then caught the man across his neck and he dropped to the floor. Mac took down the last with a cut to break his forearm followed by a backhand to the temple. Now there were four men on the floor and none of them were moving.

Just as the room fell silent, the back room door burst open and a hulking pit bull bounded in, teeth bared and growling menacingly. It latched onto the first drug dealer where he lay on the floor, its strong jaws clamping down. It began to shake its head side to side and "worry" the unconscious man.

"There's a good dog," Mike remarked dryly, eliciting a snort from Mac.

Mac approached the dog, running a hand down its back as if it were merely a playful pup, despite its jaws remaining firmly locked around the dealer's arm. The dog's eyes turned up to look at Mac and he spoke softly to it. While Mac distracted the dog, Mike rummaged through the room and located their prize: A bag of white powder which was almost certainly cocaine and another bag of light brown lumps something like brown sugar. This was almost certainly crack cocaine for smoking. He stowed the bags inside his jacket, patting it securely.

"Gonny huv tae tak this dug wi' us, Mike." Mac declared, a statement not a request. He gave the pit bull a friendly scratch behind its ears. It let go of the man on the floor and pushed its head against Mac. "Polis'll likely jist pit him doon otherwise."

Mike shot Mac a grin, "Since when did you become a dog person, you softy?"

Mac met his gaze for a moment before he replied, "Fuck off ye heathen!" Much to Mike's amusement.

Turning serious, Mike indicated with a toss of his head they needed to leave, "We need to get this sample to Porton Down for testing ASAP."

57) An Anonymous Hotel Room, Edge of Bradford City, West Yorkshire, Northern England

Mike had reported back to Ralf and awaited instructions. He picked up his second secure phone. It was an SIS issue covert device, its functionality far exceeding expectations from its nondescript exterior. But it did not come from the SIS. Logged in, he scrolled through the secure menu and located the specific coded contact he needed. His codename glowed at the top of the list, "Grim."

When asked once by a certain senior intelligence officer, he said he had never heard the play on his name before, but that it was amusing to a certain type of mind.

Seated on the bed opposite, Mac was busily wiping down the pit bull terrier with a towel swiped from the bathroom. He had just given him a bath in the human bath en suite the room. The dog had taken to Mac surprisingly well, it's once snarling front now softened with food bribes into contentment. Mac glanced across at Mike, "Snuffles hus hud his first bath, ah reckon," his tone betraying a hint of self-consciousness to Mike's trained ear.

"Snuffles?" Mike mocked. Don't make me laugh, I'm trying to work here," Mike tapped out his report; professional, concise, devoid of unnecessary details:

Suspect psychotic attacks a result of additive to cocaine.
Suspect this is local test for effect around Bradford before national roll-out.
Collected samples cocaine & crack within area of attacks.
Likely same dealer & drug as caused attacks.
Require sample testing. Will forward to PD.
Grim

The response came quickly:

Roger all.
Sunray requests meeting.
As soon as convenient.
Location 3.
Beefeater

Mike's eyes scanned the lines of text, his expression unreadable. He was being summoned for a personal meeting with his other boss, a first in his new position where anonymity and remote correspondence were usually preferred.

He raised a quizzical eyebrow at the message, his mind already turning over the potential reasons for such a direct encounter. Mac looked up from his canine grooming efforts, a question in his eyes. Mike gave him a non-committal shrug, "Have to see Sunray." Sunray is the military radio phonetic designator for the senior callsign, the unit commander on a radio net, and by extension used in general chat to refer to the boss.

For now, they focused on the immediate task at hand, getting the sample to Porton Down by a secure courier so it could be analysed. Mike wrapped the plastic bags of, presumably, cocaine and crack in a thick covering of brown paper obtained from a local newsagents. Mac scoured the room for their kit, as per standard operating procedure and placed the licked-clean plate in the sink. The pit bull, now clean, with a full tummy and looking somewhat less ferocious, padded over to Mike, nuzzling against his leg and wagging his tail. He gave him a final scratch behind a cropped ear before he too stood, ready to vacate the room.

58) Balmoral Castle, Aberdeenshire, Scotland, UK

There was a modest elegance to the room, decorated with that tasteful austerity common to all the King's private rooms. In the seclusion of the King's private office in Balmoral Castle, a meeting concerning a matter of national importance and requiring the most sensitive handling was about to take place between Sir Rupert and the King. A matter that threatened to shake the very stability of their nation.

It went without saying that Sir Rupert was of impeccable character and unfaltering loyalty to the crown, given his position as effectively the King's Spymaster; but he also had the brain of a maths professor, an eidetic memory and a knowledge of political matters which rivalled even that of the King.

The King sat at an antique wooden desk with a green leather top, its rich mahogany frame gleaming under the warm light from a leaded window. A chessboard was spread out in front of him, the scattered pieces telling a tale of a recently concluded game.

"Rupert," the King began, "I trust you had a pleasant trip up here?"

"Thank you Sir," Rupert replied. He was not a man for small talk and his eyebrows asked permission to begin the briefing.

The King noticed and half smiled to himself. "When you are ready Rupert. I will have your favourite tea sent in." The King touched a discrete button but looked to Rupert.

"Regarding the spate of attacks which have been occurring mostly in West Yorkshire recently, we have more intelligence. Sufficient now, I believe, to hazard a guess at the people behind the operation and formulate a response to it."

"Ah, good, it has been on my mind, I confess."

"The meat of the matter is that we believe the Russians to be testing an additive which, when mixed with cocaine, has a psychoactive effect. It turns the user into a crazed killer. They attack anyone they can find and kill them without mercy or thought for their own survival."

"That's rather nasty." The King waited for Rupert to continue.

"It seems likely that the Russians are close to completing a series of tests on variations of the active ingredient. Tests which have been run in West Yorkshire using the customers of a single importer of cocaine who is based in Bradford."

"Mmm..."

"Shortly, we expect the Russians to flood the UK market with their final admixture in an effort to create such murder and chaos on the streets that the government falls and we as a country are brought to a position where the public demand that we end our military support for Ukraine and our political support for measures against Russia at the United Nations."

"I will not allow that to happen willingly, Rupert."

"We have an MI5 agent in deep cover close to the man whom the Russians are working with to import these test samples. A drug wholesaler in the Bradford area. And we have arranged for Colonel Reaper to become involved apparently by chance when he had to retrieve a dead letter from that agent."

"Very good. The agent must be a brave man." The King pursed his lips, impressed. "I am glad you managed to get Reaper on the job too."

"Yes, Reaper actually worked all this out independently while he was on the edge of this operation so your nomination of him as a special agent with the PSG was clearly justified."

"Thank you for that Rupert." The King smiled.

"No, sir, I didn't mean…"
The King laughed, kindly, "No, I know you didn't but allow me a moment's levity."

"Yes sir, of course." Rupert was clearly discomfited by the break from formality. "Reaper has acquired a sample of the additive-bearing cocaine and it is being tested at Porton Down as we speak."

"Very good. And what are you proposing we do with this information, Rupert? You have never yet come to me with a problem and no solution in your hands." The King smiled with the intention of showing his trust in Rupert. A very sensitive man whom he valued highly and would go to great lengths not to embarrass.

"It seems to me that merely stopping drug shipments piecemeal as they enter the country would be fire-fighting and sure to fail eventually. Colonel Reapers efforts to follow up on the tip-off and stop one shipment in Spain will only buy us a little time even if it is genuine. So I believe we must put the Russians in a place where they feel they have to cancel the entire program. And the way to do that is to find proof of Russian fingerprints in this matter such that we can present it to the United Nations and embarrass them sufficiently that they deny their involvement and cancel the whole enterprise."

"That would be the optimal outcome Rupert. How are you going to do that?"

"There are two main routes taken by the cocaine which reaches our shores. One is direct from Columbia to Rotterdam by ship and then across the channel. If this is the case the additive must be mixed in with the cocaine pretty much at source. The other is by ship from Columbia to Nigeria and then either transhipped to a vessel bound for Rotterdam or taken overland to Morocco and then Spain. If the latter, then the mixing could be done anywhere along the route."

"I thought that was the case."

"So it seems to me that the rational move is to find where the additive is mixed in, raid the place and take samples, photos and other such proof as would convince the UN."

"That is probably easier to say than to do."
"It seems to me that the logical way to go is to investigate the source of the cocaine in Columbia first then, if the additive is not mixed in there, move on to Nigeria."

"I can see the sense in that. Can I guess who you are wanting to send to Columbia?" The King chuckled.

"Clearly, Colonel Reaper is the man for this job and he is already involved. He will doubtless want to take that Scottish person with him."

The King's smile widened, "You have something of a history with Sergeant MacLeish don't you Rupert?"

Rupert was clearly awkward, "He is an NCO in the British Army and as such ought to show more respect to his superiors...."

The King cut in quickly, good humoured, "Rupert, Rupert, Sergeant MacLeish is a rough diamond who has served me well. Served our nation well. I think we must overlook his little idiosyncrasies."

Rupert was clearly unconvinced, "Of course, sir."

"Ah, your tea is here Rupert."

59) The A74M, Main Road To Scotland, Northern England.

Under a blanket of stars, the Volvo Estate drove smoothly along the A74M at a steady 70 miles per hour.

The car's interior was cast in a green glow by the console lights which made the faces of its occupants look like ghouls. Mac was at the wheel, relaxed and settled in for a long drive. Mike sat in the passenger seat, eyes open but silent for a while and far away in his mind.

The back seats were down and sprawled on a generously sized dog bed, lay Snuffles the rescued Pit Bull. The massive canine was surrounded by an array of chew toys, squeaky playthings and a durable rope tug - spoils from a quick pet shop visit. He was fast asleep, his guttural snores providing a steady background to the drive.

Mike was back in the motor, "He snores just like you Mac.

"Away an' bile yer heid, Mike."

Mike chuckled, "There's the Carlisle sign. Be at the border just now."

Mac nodded in agreement then showed what was on his mind, "The courier must've goat the package tae Porton Doon by the noo."

Mike's gaze shifted briefly from the road to the passenger's rear-view mirror left of the driver's, a must-have for driving instructors and intelligence agents. The snoozing Pit Bull was in his view. A faint grin tugged at the corners of his mouth. "For sure. Your dog's snoring could wake the dead Mac."

Mac didn't turn to face Mike, his voice thick with humour. "If ye hink ye can drive better while Snuffles is up, pal, huv a go. Ye've no seen him when he's wantin' tae play fetch, ken?"

The dog snored on, oblivious. Mike rolled his eyes good-naturedly, adjusting his seat and trying to ignore Snuffles' log-saw rattling

60) General Nikolai Kuznetsov's Dacha Outside Moscow, Russia

Natalia sat in her study staring out of the window across the snow covered lawn and towards the trees beyond. It was a calm, feminine room laid out for meditation and writing letters to her friends. The daylight was fading and a distant house-light was already visible through the trees, their closest neighbour. She was almost alone in the large house, the only other occupant being a servant girl who was quietly preparing dinner.

Natalia was lost in thought. To her mind, a decision was required. In point of fact the decision was already made and she was summoning up the courage to act upon it.

Her shoulders straightened, the movement marking a conscious resolution. The awareness of her decision was reflected in her elegant features. With an apparently newfound determination Natalia flipped open her sleek, imported laptop, its screen casting a soft glow on her worried but resolute face. Her fingers began to dance over the keyboard, crafting a message:

"My name is Natalia Kuznetsova. I am the wife of General Nikolai Kuznetsov of whom I am sure you are aware. My son, Alexander, has recently been shot down over Ukraine and is currently a prisoner of war held by the Ukrainians. I have information of great value to you

regarding a drug-related action which Russia is about to undertake against the UK and will share this if you are prepared to arrange for my son's release and have it made to appear as an escape."

Completing the message on a text document, she paused, taking a moment to collect herself before switching on her virtual private network and navigating to the British SIS website. It was easy now she had begun. She found the portal, specifically designed for the receipt of anonymous intelligence information, re-read her message and then swiftly pasted it into the box provided. Natalia keyed in her email address for a reply, her fingers slightly trembling over the keyboard.

She took a deep breath and tapped the send button. There was a click that seemed to echo through the silent room. In her mind, the message flew across cyberspace, and as it did, Natalia exhaled slowly. Her plea for help, bundled with a promise of valuable information, was now in the hands of strangers, enemies, British Intelligence no less. She could only hope her message would find the right recipient. An enemy, no doubt, but an enemy perhaps willing to do business. She leaned back in her chair, the glow from the laptop screen now the only light piercing the growing darkness of her office.

61) Outside The Traveller's Rest Public House, Anderston, Glasgow, Scotland, UK

Mike and Mac stood before the shabby exterior of a public house in Anderston, less than a thousand yards from the River Clyde and by the North West (Drug) Recovery Communities building. The chilly Glasgow evening began to seep into their bones, warm and relaxed as they were from the long car ride. The pub, called the Dog and Pheasant since time immemorial, was old and worn with the paint on the window frames beginning to flake; but it was solid and defiant, like the hardy locals who filled it every evening.

The chatter from inside didn't pierce the thick walls and the edges of their world were swallowed by fog-laden gloom. Mike scanned and took in their immediate surroundings, the litter-strewn street and crude graffiti completely failed to brighten the deprivation, and his face momentarily betrayed his distaste. He masked his feelings as he looked at Mac and saw in his eyes the shine of a happy familiarity at what was probably the closest thing to a home he had ever known.

Mike, standing slim, unusually tall and relatively smart in his habitual attire of denim shirt, jeans and desert boots, entered first. His imposing presence filled the doorway and the chatter inside dropped quickly to an uneasy silence. Eyes lifted from pints and dominoes to fall on this stranger, unwelcome in their midst. The instantly tense atmosphere thickened, someone said, unfriendly above the silence, “Is it the polis?”

Then Mac, shorter, with his battered face and familiar horseshoe moustache, entered behind him. His scarred features and bent nose were home-grown, etched with Glasgow’s character and a regular sight in this pub when he had leave. As he stepped into the light, Snuffles beside him on a masculine platted leather lead, a chorus of recognition rippled through the room.

"Aye, it’s Don Mac," a voice exclaimed and the tension broke like a wave, leaving relief and camaraderie in its wake. Laughter and chatter resumed, the usual gruff tones now punctuated by cheerful banter. Mac navigated through the crowd, a warm nod here, a quick pat on the shoulder there, carrying with him an aura of affection that parted the sea of locals. Mike followed him to the bar, the crowd's curiosity still evident but friendly now, given Mac's company.

They reached the bar where a robust woman with lines of wisdom carved deeply into her face was pulling pints. Auntie Moira, the matriarch of this sanctuary, met Mac’s friendly expectant gaze with a stern expression of reproach.

"Ye never call, ye never write. But when ye want somethin'..." Her voice trailed off as she caught sight of Snuffles, pressed tight against Mac’s leg. His eyes were bright and hopeful, his tail began thumping against the worn wood of the bar as he basked in her attention.

"Well, aren’t ye a bonnie dog," she cooed, her mock harsh tone for Mac melting away as she reached out to stroke the pit bull’s head. The dog leaned into her touch, a whine of bliss escaping from him.

"We fund him in a pure bad way," Mac explained, his Glaswegian accent at home now, "Ah thocht ye might kin gie him a better hoose."

Moira nodded, her eyes twinkling and a well of care now apparent that belied her gruff exterior. "Aye, that we can, Mac."

Two tumblers of whisky appeared on the bar in front of the men, unasked.

Moira indicated Mike to Mac with her eyes, "Wha's yer bonnie pal?" Then she looked Mike in the eye.

Now it was Mike's turn to be embarrassed – by a totally confident older woman lacking any false front whatsoever. The evening wore on and Snuffles became the official pub dog, finding himself on the receiving end of kind words, pats and countless scraps of food. A sense of friendly contentment settled over the public house, the sense of community found in places where life has been hard and brought people together.

62) Balmoral Castle, Aberdeenshire, Scotland, UK

Mac had remained in Glasgow, catching up with aunt Moira and some old friends, while Mike set off alone, to obey the unexpected summons. The Volvo's engine hummed comfortably as he drove steadily North on the open A9. The road stretched out ahead of him like a shiny damp ribbon winding through the country landscape towards the Scottish Highlands. The formidable silhouette of Stirling Castle receded in his rear-view mirror as Mike drove on, bypassing the bustling city of Perth and the scenic towns of Coupar Angus and Pitlochry along the way.

The scenery underwent a dramatic transformation as Mike drove into the Highlands. Towering, heather-cloaked mountains and apparently endless pine forests by turns dominated the magnificent landscape, their sheer scale dwarfing the villages and lone farmhouses scattered here and there. He was entranced by the rugged beauty of Cairngorms National Park, its primordial vistas seemingly untouched by the fingers of time.

After a relaxing four-hour drive, Mike reached the royal estate of Balmoral. The wild, rolling hills and deep valleys had given way to idyllic hamlets and picturesque scenes straight from a postcard. The majestic mountains of the Highlands still loomed in the distance, framing the now more comfortable landscape. As he drove, Mike soaked in the pastoral tranquillity and fresh country air, such a welcome relief from the grimy urban sprawl he'd left behind.

Then, as if emerging organically from the landscape itself, Balmoral Castle swung into view. The regal granite fortress, a mass of close-set towers surrounded by 50,000 acres of verdant parkland and primeval forests, had served as a refuge for British royalty for nearly two centuries. Mike felt a swell of history and tradition wash over him as he took in the towering battlements and manicured grounds. This ancient castle actually looked like what is was, a royal sanctuary far removed from the modern world.

Pulling into the visitors' parking area, Mike was greeted promptly by a senior member of the castle staff. The man, dressed smartly in a traditional morning suit, failed to give his name in response to Mikes but ushered him courteously from his car. "The king will receive you when you have refreshed yourself, sir," he intoned, leading Mike towards the guest quarters.

Mike was guided through the wood-panelled corridors of the castle interior to a pleasant suite of rooms such as one might find in an English country manor. After the long drive, he gratefully seized the opportunity to shower and shave, ensuring he looked reasonably sharp and presentable for his royal audience. At least, he put on a pair of decent trousers and a shirt then topped it with a sports jacket. Picking up the ornate bedside phone, he dialled what amounted to the reception desk to signal his readiness. Shortly after, the same staff member arrived to escort him to the king's private chambers.

A flutter of nervous anticipation gripped Mike as they walked, an unexpected sensation for the usually unflappable veteran. But after all, it wasn't every day an ordinary guy met the king. He straightened his shoulders and self-consciously tried to keep his steps assured and steady.

At last, the staff member paused before a plain wooden door and gave a brisk knock. At the call of "Enter" from within, he opened the door, ushering Mike inside with a bow.

There, in front of a window and so framed against a panoramic view Scotland, stood the king. He was dressed in traditional Scottish attire; a smart kilt and tweed jacket combination that somehow looked right on him, seemed to blend seamlessly with his surroundings. The king looked happy and alert, as though he had just returned from a refreshing jaunt in the hills.

Stepping forward, the king extended his hand warmly towards Mike, a gracious smile on his face. "So very good to finally meet you in person, Colonel Reaper. I haven't had chance to arrange a meeting since you joined out little team."

Relief washed over Mike as he stepped forward to shake the king's hand firmly. Any lingering unease evaporated, replaced by a sense of interest in this singular, rather friendly man.

"The honour is mine, Your Majesty," Mike replied. "I appreciate you taking the time to see me, especially out here at Balmoral."

"Think nothing of it," the king responded amiably. "Balmoral holds a special place in my heart. I find these rugged hills very restorative." He gestured towards a plush sofa near the windows. "Please, have a seat. Can I offer you some tea?" This was a man who knew how to put his guests at ease.

"That would be most welcome, thank you." Mike sat, warmed by the king's graciousness and familiarity. As a uniformed attendant prepared the tea, the king settled into an adjacent armchair. "There is a sensitive matter I wish to discuss confidentially, one that requires input from someone with your unique experience..."

"Of course, I am at your service, sir." Mike listened intently as the king outlined the cocaine additive situation as he saw it, interjecting occasionally with clarifying questions. The warm tea sat untouched beside him, his focus absolute.

63) Sir Henry Attwood's Office, Whitehall, London

Whitehall is actually just a road in the centre of London, but amongst the many fine buildings which line it are a royal palace and many impressive government buildings filled with civil servants. For this reason the name of the road is commonly used to refer to UK government offices or British government administration as a whole. The grandeur of Whitehall, steeped in history and smelling of power, served as the backdrop for this meeting in Sir Henry Attwood's grand office.

His office was the epitome of stern British formality, a strong fortress against the unpredictable tides of global espionage. Sturdy oak panels lined the walls, insulating them from the cacophony of Whitehall beyond. Sunlight, diffused by the grand tall windows, painted a mellow glow across his desk, transforming the crisp documents into a landscape of light and shadow.

Sir Henry was head of the entire SIS organisation and answerable only to the Minister in charge of the entire Foreign Office. And then only nominally because ministers, while appointed by government to oversee departments, are unable to learn the workings of a huge body overnight, if ever. For this reason they must rely on civil servants to run the day-to-day and make many tactical decisions. And this gives the latter a great deal of power. As perhaps it ought, given the average ability of elected politicians.

There was a polite tap on Sir Henry's door and Chief Intelligence Officer Ralf Burgin, SIS, walked in, smiling grimly at his almost-friend as he crossed the floor to sit opposite Sir Henry.

"How are you, Ralf? I will have tea sent in." Ralf pressed a discrete button, a young lady's head popped around the door and took their order.

Ralf favoured his technical superior with a raised eyebrow before beginning the briefing upon which their discussion would focus. His voice betrayed a steely determination as he relayed the findings from their scientists at Porton Down, referring to his notes for the technical spec.

"The substance detected in the cocaine sample collected by Reaper in Bradford was unusual, unique even. It must be the product of a biologist at the cutting edge of psychopharmacy. It amounts to a sophisticated neuro-active compound, perhaps a tetrahydrocannabinol variant, C21H30O2, or an altered amphetamine molecule, C9H13N, blended with a psychoactive compound such as 3,4-Methylenedioxymethamphetamine (MDMA) or C11H15NO2, to create a potent, mind-altering cocktail…"

Sir Henry pulled a wry face, "Stay with the English please Ralf."

Ralf continued, "Sorry, Henry. It's a clever drug right at the edge of what is currently possible and created by someone at the leading edge of research. No similar substance had been detected in cocaine anywhere else in the country, confirming the deduction that it was restricted to this one Bradford dealer's supply chain. A dealer who continues under surveillance."

Sir Henry could come across as a good natured old buffer when he wanted to but anyone who took him at face value might lose their shirt, or worse. "A dealer would have to be crazy to add something like this to his product as it would draw attention from us or the NCA and lose him business. I think it was a state actor such as China or Russia. And that they are compensating the dealer for his trouble."

Ralf nodded, "A message from our agent Blackbeard suggested it was the Russians behind it, specifically GRU Unit 29155 of infamous repute. Before he knew for sure what was in the drug, Reaper said this was a test run in Bradford and a national roll-out would follow when they got the mix right."

Sir Henry chuckled, "Smart boy, Reaper, better keep an eye on him." They both smiled as if they had read how to form that expression in an instruction manual.

Ralf continued, "Given that this additive converts regular cocaine users into axe murderers it poses a significant threat to national security and social stability. The ripples would cause humiliation for the government and potentially threaten the country with anarchy should the drug go national…"

Sir Henry finished for him, "So my money is on the Russians. And the motivation, revenge for our helping the Ukrainians with weapons and training. I would guess they want to cow the government into ending their support."

"The Russians have the means and the motive, plus they have form for poisoning people operating in the UK. And they know our choice of response is very limited. I think we should assume it is the Russians until something proves otherwise. Reaper is already on his way or in Spain to interdict a shipment but that will only delay the operation a very short while, probably only days. It would make sense if the Russians are sending double what they need to distribute on the basis that half will be seized. "

Sir Henry paused as the tea tray was brought in and the young lady poured for them and withdrew. "It makes limited odds how far away the Russians are from a roll-out because we cannot do anything without knowing where it is coming from. Aside from the NCA, of course. I will have them briefed on this and they will doubtless stop some of the stuff coming into the country. But they are just looking for the proverbial needle until we have a tip off or something concrete to go on."

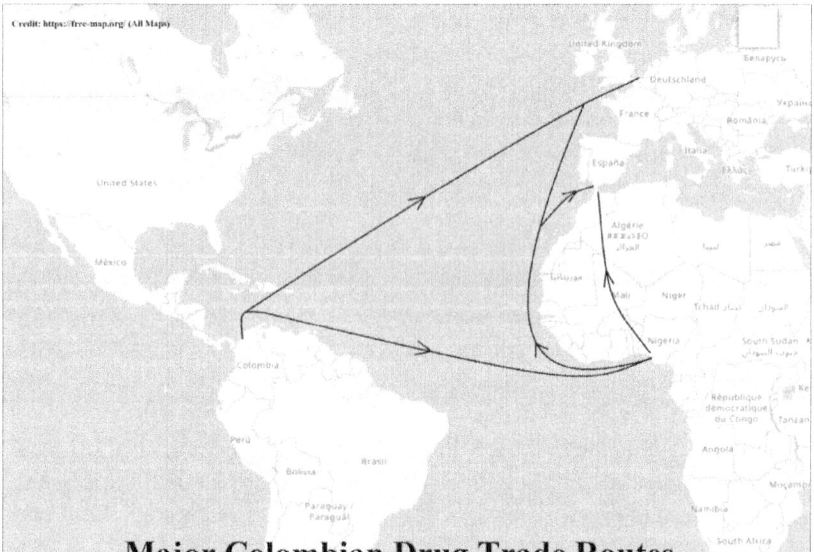

Major Colombian Drug Trade Routes

"I think our best bet is to start looking where the cocaine is coming from and try to find where it is having the additive mixed in. It presumably originates in Columbia, then comes to the UK directly by ship or to Rotterdam, or to Nigeria by ship then overland Morocco then Spain or its transhipped there and sent on to Rotterdam. But the volume of imports… is too big to do much with."

Sir Henry considered this as he bit the corner off a biscuit, "I think that our best bet is to send Reaper to Colombia and see if he can find any sign of the mixing plant there. I am sure we can get our friends at the DEA to give him a hand. And if that draws a blank then I think the next likely place for a mixing plant is Nigeria. That would be safer for the Russians."

The corners of Ralf's mouth turned down as if he were not convinced, " I would think Nigeria a better bet than Columbia as it would be so easy to set up there unnoticed."

"You may be right, Ralf, but we have good contacts with the DEA and a few dollars can buy a lot of quiet in Columbia. A check in Colombia would not take too long. We have to start somewhere so we will start there."

Ralf dunked a biscuit in his tea, "Without a crystal ball it could be either or neither Henry. I am okay with that. Wherever their mixing-plant is, we need enough evidence to embarrass the Russians in front of the UN so they will cancel their plot. That means some pretty hard evidence."

"When Reaper gets back from Spain send him straight on to Columbia. I will have a word with our friends at the Drug Enforcement Agency and call in a favour or two so they will put Reaper on the right track if they can."

Ralf considered this for a moment, "So you are going to tell the Yanks about the drug additive and what we suspect?

"Mmm. I will have to. It will gain us some brownie points anyway as the Russians might try something similar with them if it is not stopped here."

64) The Prime Minister's Office, Number 10, Downing Street, London, UK

At Number 10, Downing Street, official office of the Prime Minister, a pivotal meeting was underway. Prime Minister, Daniel Lawson, sat behind the famous desk, listening attentively as the head of the Secret Intelligence Service, Sir Henry Attwood, outlined details of the latest emerging threat.

Sir Henry had a talent for distilling complex intelligence matters into understandable narratives suitable to the attention span of a politician; narratives which, by happenstance, generally demonstrated how clever and indispensible the head of intelligence was.

"…and we have the results back from Porton Down and they confirm our worst fears. It is now proven that an enemy of this country is testing a chemical additive to cocaine in the North of England. This additive turns users of the drug into psychotic killers, driven to murder anyone in their sight."

The Prime Minister had a thousand things on his mind but Sir Henry's words focussed his attention. "My God!"

Sir Henry continued, "It seems likely that within weeks the tests of variations of this additive, which have been causing these random murders across the North of England, will be complete and the enemy will roll out this additive in cocaine sold right across the UK."

"Do you know who is behind this? Sir Henry?"

"Not for a fact, as yet, sir. But it seems obvious that it is the Russians and their motive would be to embarrass your government and force you to pull back from supporting Ukraine directly with military aid and also voting for sanctions against Russia at the UN."

The Prime Minister was not as slow witted as the media would portray him, "Mmm. Makes sense. And they have a history of direct intervention on our soil. What are you doing about it?"

"The solution seems to be to expose this operation and embarrass the Russians sufficiently to force them to call it off, given it is the Russians."

"Yes, we can never plug all the holes in the border defences against drug imports."

"Sadly, no sir. I am sure the head of the NCA is doing her best."

The Prime Minister's face sharpened instantly as he picked up the inter-departmental sniping. I hope there will be no points-scoring between agencies here Sir Henry?"

Sir Henry gestured his dismay that the PM might even consider such a thing. "Of course not, sir, we have already informed NCA of the threat so they are able to strengthen their defences but we do not expect them to plug all the holes."

The PM's voice was knowing, "No, of course not, Sir Henry." For all their failings, politicians can generally read people pretty well. Its what they do, after all.

Sir Henry ignored his tone and continued, "We believe that the best, indeed the only way to neutralise this threat is to find where the additive is being mixed with the cocaine. This seems likely to be in either Colombia or Nigeria. When we find the site we will know who is behind it and ought to be able to gather sufficient evidence to get it stopped."

The PM's attitude hardened and he spoke with something close to annoyance in his voice, "I don't want you sending in a bloody SAS hit squad again. After that last bloody operation I had to apologise to their head of state in person and pay him off with more foreign aid than I could easily cover for. There would have been less casualties if we had sent the RAF to carpet-bomb the whole place."

Sir Henry raised his hands and made calming motions, "Of course not sir. That operation met with unexpected resistance and our men had to defend themselves. But you will recall they did put an end to any ideas the government had of aiding the Islamists, didn't they?"

The PM was firm now, "They did neutralise the terrorists, but they also levelled an entire town Sir Henry. I don't believe they left a building standing or a goat alive and they scared the bejesus out of the government. I don't want anything anywhere near that level of violence to happen again. Do you understand?"

Sir Henry was smoothly placating, "Of course not, of course not sir. Anticipating your thoughts on this matter, after that terrible misunderstanding, I am just sending Colonel Reaper to recce the situation in Colombia and then Nigeria if that turns up nothing."

The PM had calmed down now, "Just the one team?"

"Well you know what our budget is, sir."

The PM produced a knowing look, "Of course, its always the low budget which prevents effective intelligence." Sir Henry opened his mouth to protest but the PM raised his palms and stopped him, "Okay, okay, I know. We will discuss your budget when we have seen the results from this operation. With limited funds I must allocate them where they are most useful." Henry was silenced by the obvious pressure.

The PM continued, "Reaper is a good choice from his past exploits. I assume that terrible Scottish person will be going with him?"

"Of course, sir. He always takes his bodyguard on jobs of this nature. Its standard SOP."

"Well keep them on a tight rein Sir Henry. I don't want any collateral damage or diplomatic incidents. But make sure you find the target and neutralise it. Now, I have another meeting starting ten minutes ago. You will excuse me?"

65) Duquesa Port, Costa Del Sol, Southern Spain

Duquesa was just another cheerful British ghetto on the South Coast of Spain. With the ongoing development of faux-Spanish holiday apartments on the landward side, Duquesa had grown from a few houses and a bar running along the coast road to become quite a sizable town. But the focus of activity remained the modest, rectangular Marina and the English bars and trinket shops which surrounded it.

There was a rule, perhaps enforced by some unelected British Ex-pat committee, that every British enclave in Spain was required have an Irish theme pub which was covered in shamrocks, displayed maniacally cheerful leprechauns and sold bad Guinness. Some foreigners thought this strange, considering the Irish had not been British for a century but both the British and Irish thought it natural. The only obvious Spanish influences in English ghettoes were the road signs and the bi-lingual waiters.

For 20 years the Russians had run the whores and drugs in Southern Spain and Leonid Sergei Domitov, ex-Spetsnaz Sergeant, had cheerfully plotted and murdered his way upwards until he controlled everything West of Malaga. Under his firm, paternal control holiday makers could drink their cold beer in peace and safety. Because there was absolutely no other significant criminal activity on Russian Leo's patch.

At a table outside the Duquesa Irish Bar Russian Leo, Mike and Mac were sitting at a tin-topped table around a bottle of decent, or at least expensive, vodka. The Marina was busy, one o'clock in the morning being early evening for Spain, but they had a good view of the seaward entrance to the Marina and the customs births. Leo was obliging Mac to listen to his collection of war stories from Afghanistan, several of which featured his spirited attempts to kill Mike. Clearly, Leo and Mike were old friends, united by a love of soldiering and a shared history, albeit mostly on opposite sides. But as Leo said, a war was nothing personal.

"Did Mike tell you about time he bring in Yankee missiles for Afghans shoot down our choppers Mac? Had string dozen camels loaded up Stingers was coming over mountains from Pakistan. We caught him good and fair. Mortared his people to Hell and back. Mike buried in camel guts!" Leo rocked with laughter, Mac laughed long and loud, Mike laughed somewhat less.

"Wait, we have visitor!" Leo nodded in the direction of a 60 foot flybridge motor cruiser which had just entered the marina and lined up for a quiet birth. "Watch this my friends. The police here are like taxi drivers, you pay them properly and they do their job very well."

A young man jumped ashore and began to moor the boat as the helmsman used the bow thrusters to straighten up against the berth. All quiet and smooth. No one taking any notice at all. Aside, obviously, from the 8 Guardia Civil police officers who suddenly appeared from nowhere, arrested the youngster at gunpoint and boarded the boat with him in front of them.

"They find cocaine. Make sure crew know they looking for cocaine not coming to me. Will make happy I think Mike?"

"Will make happy, Leo. As ever, I can rely on you. Thank you my friend. There will be E100,000 in your bank account tomorrow so you can have a drink on me."

"Thank you my friend. Now, let us drink wodka and spend time pretty girls. They waiting for us."

Then the Police began to file out of the boat and back onto the dock. Something was clearly wrong

66) The King's Private Office, Buckingham Palace, London, UK

The King was deep in conversation with Sir Clarence Alnwick, his Principal Private Secretary and most trusted advisor as Sir Rupert Greville, head of the Palace Security Group entered his private office. Both men turned to the visitor, "What news do you bring today, Sir Rupert?"

"Your Majesty, a plea for help from Russia. Specifically, from Natalia Kuznetsova, wife of General Kuznetsov. It came in through the open SIS website."

The King pursed his lips and shook his head in dismay at such a crude method of contact. Sir Rupert unfurled a transcript and read aloud,

"My name is Natalia Kuznetsova. I am the wife of General Nikolai Kuznetsov of whom I am sure you are aware. My son, Alexander, has recently been shot down over Ukraine and is currently a prisoner of war held by the Ukrainians. I have information of great value to you regarding a drug-related action which Russia is about to take against

the UK and will share this if you are prepared to arrange for my son's release and have it made to appear as an escape."

The King exchanged a grave look with Sir Clarence. "Sir," said the latter solemnly, "if Russian intelligence detected this plea, Natalia's life could be in immense peril. We must move quickly but tread with utmost care here." The King nodded. "If the Russians know about this, sadly, she is already dead; though she may still be breathing. What do you advise?"

Sir Clarence contemplated briefly. "I suggest signalling our potential willingness to arrange Alexander's release in return for intelligence on the drug plot. Kuznetsova likely knows at least critical details. However, overt pressure could both compromise this lady and endanger the pilot."

The king looked to Sir Rupert who nodded his agreement, then to Sir Clarence, "I completely agree," he affirmed. "but I am leaning towards having her boy released if that fits your plan." Then back to Sir Rupert, "Is the SIS aware of this yet, Rupert?"

"They will be by now, sir. But I came to you quickly, before they had chance to respond, given the matter's sensitivity."

"Very good. I am minded to approach the Ukrainians for the release of the boy immediately and make a response to Madam Kuznetsov that we agree to her offer. We will have that arranged if nothing has arisen to change our position by the time we are concluded here, gentlemen."

"Yes sir." Alexander tipped his head in a bow.

The King turned to Sir Clarence. "Now, to Russia's invasion of Ukraine. How do we increase support while avoiding open war?"

Sir Clarence's expression darkened. "A precarious balancing act indeed. I can advise nothing more than gradually increasing our military aid and supporting the sanctions proposed at the UN while actively pursuing covert diplomacy. We must cripple Russia's economy, reinforce Ukraine's defences, and empower Zelensky's negotiating stance, all while avoiding direct armed conflict with Russia."

The King nodded thoughtfully.

Sir Clarence bowed his head, waiting for the king to speak.

A knock on the door caused all three men to turn towards it. A footman opened the door from the outside and addressed the King, "Pardon the intrusion, Your Majesty, but the Prime Minister has arrived for your one o'clock briefing."

"Show him in, please." The King turned to the others. "We will resume shortly."

As the two men left the room, the Prime Minister entered and the King assumed an aura of calm. The PM bowed from the neck as custom dictated.

"Your Majesty, thank you for fitting in this audience despite your workload."

The King smiled graciously. "Overseeing the welfare of our nation is a shared duty Prime Minister, please, sit down and update me on key developments."

The Prime Minister carefully outlined recent events, policies and proposals, working from notes for accuracy. The King listened closely, asking pertinent questions. Their discussion was wide-ranging.

After an hour, the Prime Minister concluded. "Forgive my speaking at such length, sir."

"No need to apologize," said the King. "I appreciate your being thorough."

After the Prime Minister's departure, the King's countenance turned solemn as Sir Rupert and Sir Clarence rejoined him.

"Now, where were we?" mused the King. "Ah yes, the deteriorating situation in Ukraine. Have detailed options for increasing aid without provoking open war on my desk within three days."

"Yes sir," affirmed Sir Clarence.

The King continued gravely, looking at Sir Rupert, "Regarding the captured pilot Alexander Kuznetsov, closely monitor both our and Russia's intelligence services' actions in this area. If our people choose to do a deal with Mrs Kuznetsova let it go ahead and observe. If they stall or decline, have one of our people there step in and change their decision to move it forward." Then turning to Sir Clarence, "Clarence, make arrangements for the pilot to be released and transferred to UK as soon as possible. I think it is important to know all we can about this drug plot as it may become a significant problem."

Clarence nodded, "Sir."

"If I must act it will be with the utmost discretion, sir," Sir Rupert promised.

"I know it will Rupert. Keep me informed of any unexpected developments," instructed the King, rising to signal the meeting's conclusion. "We stand adjourned, gentlemen."

After a few amiable parting words, Sir Alexander and Sir Clarence withdrew, leaving the monarch alone to contemplate his responsibilities. He sighed heavily, as if feeling their full weight.

67) Duquesa Port, Costa Del Sol, Southern Spain

The scene unfolding before Mike and Leo was puzzling. Leo's deceptively keen eye picked up on the Spanish police's submissive body language as they exited the yacht; unusual considering their usual authoritative style. As Mike followed Leo's gaze, he saw the cause: three individuals behind the police officers brandishing what he identified as old AK47s from the wooden butts and fore-stocks on them. "Strange, having fireworks in the marina tonight. Those villains could shoot a copper and not be heard."

"You think Mike?" Leo speculated nonchalantly, eyes narrowing as he observed the unfolding scene. The roughened edges of his Russian accent added a layer of depth to the absurdity of the situation. The icy chill of the vodka provided a stark contrast to the heated spectacle playing out before them.

As he sipped his drink, apparently relaxed, Leo's gaze slid up to the apartments overlooking the port. His action was discreet, just a slight inclination of his head and a lifting of his hat as if paying his respects to an unseen observer.

No sooner had Leo's hat returned to his head than three gunshots echoed through the air. Hidden amongst the fireworks. The villains fell, their bodies crumpling lifelessly to the ground, dark pools of blood staining the dock beneath them. The surrounding civilians in the bars were blissfully unaware of the brief, deadly exchange, their attention claimed by the fireworks and their own merriment.

"Russian SVD fitted with a decent suppressor," Mike remarked, his voice unruffled. "Decent shots downhill." The tone suggested an appreciation for the marksman's skill. A soft smile creased Leo's features. He gave little away, but there was a hint of approval in his eyes.

As they watched the growing turmoil by the boat, a sardonic voice spoke up. It was Mac, his Glaswegian accent a sharp contrast in the Spanish setting. He made a simple declaration, "That will aboot do it."

68) Deputy Director's Office, CIA Headquarters, Langley, McLean, Virginia, United States

CIA Deputy Director Steve Walters reclined in his leather office chair, gazing out the seventh-floor window at the Potomac River flowing steadily below. A crisp rap at the door drew his attention.

"Come in," he called.

The door opened and a tall, muscular figure strode in. "Afternoon, Steve," it conceded in a gravelly voice.

"Randy, good to see you." Steve stood, shook the proffered hand firmly and favoured the visitor with a grin, "Please, have a seat."

Randy Coleman, deputy administrator of the DEA's Latin American operations, threw himself into one of the chairs facing the desk. Steve retook his own seat and folded his hands, piercing blue eyes fixed intently on the other man.

"I appreciate you making the trip over from VA, buddy. Something rather delicate has come up that requires the DEA's assistance."
Randy raised an eyebrow. "Something you did not want on the email record?"

Steve half smiled, "We've had a request from our British colleagues in MI6. They have an operative they want embedded within one of our teams targeting a certain Colombian cartel."

"For what purpose?" Randy asked warily.

"They've received intelligence suggesting Hernan Torres may be acting for the Russians by tainting certain cocaine shipments bound for Europe. Adding something extra to his product before it leaves the country. Something that turns the users violent. They need to interrogate him to confirm if it's true."

Randy's expression darkened at the mention of Torres. A powerful drug lord who had eluded lawful arrest for years. "I assume this operative would be embedded with one of our teams tracking Torres's network?"

Steve nodded. "That's the favour I'm asking. I know your men have been working for months to build a case against him. We'd like your team to take point with the Brit shadowing your operations."

Randy frowned, scratching his stubbled chin. "That could get complicated. We have actionable intel on Torres's location and we're preparing to move on him within the next few weeks."

"All the more reason for your team to spearhead this," Steve pressed smoothly. "The Brit can observe the takedown firsthand while your men execute the mission. Minimal disruption to your plans."

Randy considered this silently before responding. "Here's my concern. If we openly kill or capture Torres early, it could jeopardize the case we're building against his whole organization. Too visible."

He leaned forward, elbows on his knees. "But maybe there's an alternative. We share intel on Torres's location with the Brits. Let them try to apprehend him, then your man can get access for questioning if he is successful and not if he isn't. Either way, it keeps our hands clean."

Steve's eyes gleamed. "I like the sound of that. Smart way to maintain plausible deniability. And if the operation goes sideways..."

"It's on the Brits, not us," Randy finished with a wry chuckle. "I have to say, I like how you think."

The two men shared a look of perfect understanding. The unspoken arrangement was clear: If the Brit agent was successful, the CIA & DEA would get the intelligence they needed, while the DEA safeguarded their operation. If the Brit agent failed, and he was either killed or got taken prisoner, then it was all on the Brits and the CIA and DEA kept their hands clean.

Steve stood and extended his hand once more. "Excellent. We have an agreement. I'll let London know we're prepared to receive their man within 48 hours."

"My team will handle the rest," Randy assured as they shook firmly. "We'll brief our people on the ground and make sure their man gets a shot at Torres."

"Outstanding. Glad we could make this work." Steve walked Randy to the door and clapped him on the shoulder. "A pleasure as always. We need to play golf."

Alone again, Steve gazed out at the river as he dialled his phone. When the call connected, he skipped the pleasantries.

"Tell London the cowboys are saddling up down south. We'll ride this one together, but they better pick a man who can hang on."

Satisfied, Steve ended the call. Everything was falling neatly into place. The Brits would get their intelligence, if their man was any good, the cartel would be compromised, and the CIA and DEA would keep their hands clean. A win-win, forged through unofficial channels and unwritten rules.

His work now done, Steve loosened his tie and poured four fingers of whiskey from the crystal decanter on his desk. He smiled faintly. Just another day at the office.

69) Sir Henry Attwood's Office, Whitehall, London

Sir Henry Attwood sat at his sturdy oak desk in his Whitehall office, sunlight streaming through the tall windows behind him. A knock at the door heralded the arrival of Ralf Burgin.

"Come in, Ralf," Henry called, rising to shake the other man's hand firmly. Though Henry's role overseeing all of MI5 and MI6 gave him significant technical seniority he exercised it subtly when dealing with this man. Or at least he thought he did.

"Please, have a seat," Henry gestured to the chair across from him as he settled back down. "Thank you for coming on such short notice. A rather delicate matter has arisen upon which I would value your input."

Ralf nodded seriously, his hooded eyes bright with interest. "Of course, Henry. What can I help you with?"

Henry slid a printed email across the desk. "This message came in through our classified website, routed through multiple cut-outs and proxies. It's purportedly from Natalia Kuznetsova, wife of Russian General Nikolai Kuznetsov."

Ralf scanned the letter quickly, his expression difficult to read. "She's offering intelligence on the Russian plot to taint cocaine shipments entering the UK in exchange for assistance freeing her son from captivity in Ukraine. What a stroke of luck, if its genuine," he summarized.

"Exactly," confirmed Henry. "Her son Alexander was recently shot down while flying combat missions against Ukraine. He's now being held as a prisoner of war. I checked that out already and its true. Natalia wants him freed and sent home, either through a contrived escape or diplomatic transfer."

Ralf steepled his fingers contemplatively. "And what she's offering in return could be very valuable. Nikolai Kuznetsov likely does have intimate knowledge of Russian covert operations. But is it genuine? If it is true we gain an excellent confirmation that we are on the right track with the Russian plot at effectively the zero cost of freeing a Russian pilot. If it is not genuine, then what? Hard to see what they would gain by bringing our attention to a plot they thought we did not know about. Hard to see what we have to lose."

Henry nodded gravely. "My thoughts exactly, so we should run with it as if its true, I think. If I were her I would want him sent to UK, not home. But that is not our problem. No doubt the GRU is monitoring Natalia fairly closely as a matter of procedure. We'll have to act fast before they realize she's reached out to us and lift her."

"I can get someone at the Doughnut to reply to her message covertly and assure her we will get her son freed so long as she tells us something useful," Ralf replied, "We can tell her the boy will be free in a day or two if she sends us the information she has right now. She doesn't need to know that we want the info quickly before she is arrested. We should tell her she must either cooperate immediately and trust us to free him, or its no go."

Pacing to the window, Henry gazed out at the London skyline before continuing. "Of course. Getting the boy out of Ukraine is not a problem. Our diplomatic people can ask for his release as a returned favour and the Ukrainians will comply cheerfully. Neither they nor I could care less about another Russian pilot. But just in case Natalia is not arrested in the next day or two we do need to free her boy.

Turning back to Ralf, he said, "I will have the Ukrainians transfer the boy to our people and ship him to London. We can debrief him, in case he knows something and keeping it quiet is their goal, before quietly returning him to Russia if that still seems sensible in a day or two. It will show Natalia we're dealing in good faith until we've extracted everything of value from her."

Ralf frowned but couldn't argue with the logic. "Very well. I'll have our people reply appropriately to Natalia and get what we can out of her."

"Do it quickly, before the GRU gets to her," urged Henry. "This may be our one chance to uncover what General Kuznetsov is up to."

Ralf stood, recognizing the meeting's conclusion. "Understood completely, Henry. You know you can rely on my people to handle this delicately. The stakes are too high to hesitate."

Henry smiled tightly and gripped Ralf's hand. "Excellent. Keep me informed of your progress."

After Ralf departed, Henry stood at the window again, contemplating the sprawling city below. Sacrifices were always necessary in this business and sometimes the sacrifice was a man's sense of humanity. Natalia's fate was already sealed, whether she realized it or not. But Henry would be damned if he didn't extract every last drop of intelligence from her before she became another cold war casualty. Picking up his phone, he briskly set things in motion, "Get me the Foreign Office." Henry allowed himself a rare smile. The Great Game never slept, and neither did he.

70) A Concrete Bunker, Two Kilometres Behind The Front Line, Northern Ukraine

The concrete walls of the bunker shuddered as another Russian shell detonated nearby. Loose dust drifted down from the ceiling, filtering through the dim overhead lights. Brigadier Watson didn't even glance up from the maps spread across the makeshift table.

"Very well, gentlemen," he addressed the two British officers and a handful of Ukrainian counterparts gathered around him. "I want to finalize our plans to break through the Russian defences along this ridge."

His finger traced the line on the map where they hoped to cut the Russian line with a coordinated tank and artillery assault. The battle raged on just miles away, the distant thunder of explosions providing an ever-present soundtrack.

A young Ukrainian lieutenant straightened up from where he had been bent over a radio receiver. "Incoming reports show the enemy has reinforced their established position. At least two more companies of mechanized infantry supported by tanks."

Watson nodded, taking a sip of tea from a patterned china cup held carefully in his steady hands. A British orderly hovered nearby, ready to refresh anyone's cup.

"Thank you, Lieutenant." The Brigadier turned back to the group of staff officers and trainees, "Their defences are solid and quite well designed, but our combined artillery and armour will tear right through them." Watson's voice rang with calm confidence. "Major Phillips, what's the status of our artillery?"

"Ready for your command, sir," replied the British major briskly. "I have two batteries of 105s sighted in on the enemy position and a squadron of Ukrainian BM-21 rocket launchers standing by."

"Excellent." Watson's eyes crinkled with satisfaction. "Time to give Ivan a proper thrashing. You may commence firing at..." He checked his watch. "...1415 hours. Give them everything you've got for a full 15 minutes to soften them up. Subject to our counter-barrage artillery being on-line then."

"Yes sir! I will confirm counter-barrage now sir." Phillips nodded sharply, an eager glint in his eyes.

The bunker trembled again as another enemy shell exploded outside. Sergeant Jenkins steadied the illuminated map with a swift hand.

"Begging your pardon, sirs," he said in his pronounced Welsh accent. "But Ivan seems rather upset today."

Watson smiled thinly. "Nothing we can't handle, Sergeant." He surveyed the intent faces around the table. His own weathered features bore the marks of decades of service, but his back was ramrod straight.

"Right, while our artillery turns the enemies static position into a collection of smoking craters, Major Clark will direct our Ukrainian friends' tank squadrons in a flanking manoeuvre through this gully, here, shielded from view."

Watson traced the gully on the map with a long finger more suited to playing the piano, perhaps. "The Challengers will pop out right behind their lines and catch them in a classic pincer movement." He grinned wolfishly. "We'll crush their armoured infantry against our artillery bombardment like a nut in a vice."

Appreciative murmurs rippled around the table. A young Ukrainian lieutenant exchanged a meaningful look with his comrade, clearly impressed by the audacious British plan.

Watson checked his watch again. "It's time. Major Phillips, please give the order to commence firing."

Phillips sprang into action, grabbing the handset to issue firing orders. Moments later, salvos of artillery shells streaked through the sky toward the ridge. Blasts sent up harsh, grey clouds and flying debris amongst the enemy positions, muted thuds transmitting through the bunker's thick walls.

Sergeant Jenkins refilled the officers' teacups, the fine china absurdly civilized amid the organised chaos. Brigadier Watson maintained his air of stolid command. His erect posture and composure presented the iconic picture of British calm.

When the final barrage died down, he addressed Major Clark. "Now, Johnny, take your tanks, sorry, guide the Ukrainian tanks in while they're still reeling. We'll be monitoring your progress closely."

"On our way, sir!" Clark snapped a salute and exited swiftly, calling for his driver. A stirring, throaty roar filled the bunker as a pride of tank engines burst into life outside.

Watson turned to a technician monitoring a bank of screens. "Link us to the helmet camera of the officer commanding the lead tank. I want to observe the assault directly."

"Yes sir, linking now." The young corporal worked rapidly, pulling up a slightly jumpy live camera view. The war seen through a Ukrainian officer's eyes. The picture swung and rocked with the ship-like movement of the Challenger tank, edges of the angular turret and the length of the barrel filling the frame as the fearless officer took the dangerous but effective option of commanding his tank with head and shoulders out of the commander's hatch on the turret.

"Excellent work." Watson's voice was steady, belying the anticipation they all felt. "Today we strike the Russian army a grievous blow. For King and country, gentlemen." He nodded to share the weak British military humour with his Ukrainian compatriots.

Jenkins refreshed the Brigadier's teacup one last time as the British tanks roared into action. Come what may, the savouring of a proper cuppa would carry on. Explosions and flame, cart-wheeling turrets and burning bodies filled the screen as enemy vehicles were ripped apart by crushing blows from hypersonic sabot and high-explosive shells.

Meanwhile, in a sprawling bunker complex not far distant, another British Staff Officer was playing his part in supporting the heroic Ukrainians. He had a troop concentration underway in readiness for the recapture of a certain border city. Major General Jones-Wallis leaned over a rough-hewn desk, his brows knit in concentration. The screen in front of him was marked with symbols indicating helicopter groups, reserve troops, useful landing areas and fuel dumps.

The rapid tap-tap-tapping of keyboards provided a relentless background rhythm, accented by the distant rumbles of war. British NCOs conferred in hushed tones over laptop screens glowing in the dim light. At the other end of Jones-Wallis's desk, Ukrainian officers debated strategy, their voices swirling with native cadence. Individual soldiers crisscrossed the bunker, responding to commands, carrying messages with fluid precision.

At the center of this hive, the General traced his planned manoeuvres on the map with his gnarled, old fingers. Helicopters refuelling here, collecting men here and dropping them here. Trucks bringing in supplies here. A convoy lost to Russian artillery here. A replacement en route. Timings down to the minute. The nuts and bolts of good strategy. Not flashy, not glorious but absolutely vital to the success of any military operation. His two British subordinates stood nearby, sipping tea from matching pristine china cups. The sharp clinks of porcelain were jarringly loud amidst the bunker's throbbing hum.

Each time a nearby Russian artillery shell shook the bunker, the tea cups rattled, dust sifted down, yet the British officers were unperturbed, their focus unbroken. Their quintessential British stoicism in the face of adversity impressing even the tough Ukrainians.

After one close explosion rocked the bunker violently, a Ukrainian officer glanced at his unflinching counterparts, shaking his head with wry admiration. "Bozhevil′ni brytantsi," he murmured to his comrade, lips twitching in a faint smile.

The General briefly met the Ukrainian's gaze, acknowledging the quip with a flicker of a smile, "Dyakuyu" he said, with a trace of an Eton accent. The Ukrainian looked as if he had seen a ghost. Then Jones-Wallis's steady hands were back to implementing the agreed strategy, gathering men and materiel for an unstoppable orchestrated assault which would shake the opposing Russian forces to their core.

Hours passed, the atmosphere in the bunker thickened as Zero Hour approached. The echoes of distant artillery, soft voices, and tapping keys coalesced into a single rhythm, an overture counting down to a deadly dance. Soon the band would strike up.

71) GRU Listening Post, National Guard headquarters, Moscow, Russia

The glow of computer monitors provided the only illumination in the sparse basement room. Junior Lieutenant Ivan Kozlov leaned back in his chair, removing his headphones and rubbing his eyes. Hours of listening to intercepted communications always left him fatigued.

"It was routed through an encrypted channel into the UK SIS website, but it was from a random civilian source. A woman asking for her son to be freed from captivity in Ukraine. She claimed to be a General's wife."

That piqued Anton's interest. "Let me see."

Ivan pulled up the message transcript and turned his monitor so Anton could read it. His eyes widened as he scanned the plea for prisoner exchange and the tantalizing offer of classified intelligence in return.

"My name is Natalia Kuznetsova. I am the wife of General Nikolai Kuznetsov of whom I am sure you are aware. My son, Alexander, has recently been shot down over Ukraine and is currently a prisoner of war held by the Ukrainians. I have information of great value to you regarding a drug-related action which Russia is about to take against the UK and will share this if you are prepared to arrange for my son's release and have it made to appear as an escape."

"Anything interesting?" asked his colleague, Senior Lieutenant Anton Federov, without looking up from his own monitoring station.

"The usual chatter," Ivan sighed. "Although..." His forehead creased as he considered the last transmission he'd intercepted. "There was one message that seemed rather unusual."

Anton raised an eyebrow. "Unusual how?"

"Bozhe moy," Anton muttered. "This woman claims to be General Kuznetsov's wife. And what she's offering could compromise state secrets." He looked sharply at Ivan. "Have you reported this up the chain of command?"

Ivan shook his head, face reddening slightly. "I wanted to verify it first. Make sure it's credible."

"No time for that. It needs action either way, and fast," Anton insisted. He stood abruptly, grabbing his uniform jacket. "This is too sensitive, it needs to go straight to the top. Get your coat, we're going to HQ."

Moments later they hurried from the underground facility into the biting Moscow night. A black sedan waited by the curb, summoned by Anton's urgent call. They slid into the warm backseat, engulfed by the smell of leather and cigarette smoke.

"GRU Headquarters," Anton ordered the driver curtly. "And make it quick."

As they sped through the mostly deserted streets, Ivan fidgeted nervously with his hat. Reporting something this explosive to the feared GRU headquarters made his pulse race. But Anton was right, the message was too critical to leave unreported. And too sensitive to report by email or telephone.

The imposing building loomed out of the darkness, floodlit against the night sky. Ivan craned his neck, taking in the bleak architecture. He had never actually been inside before. They flashed their IDs at the gate and were promptly waved through.

Minutes later, they were being ushered into the cavernous office of Colonel Volkov, head of Signals Intelligence. His sharp eyes quickly noted their unease. Both young men stood rigidly at attention until told to sit.

"This had better be important," Volkov said coldly. "I don't appreciate late night interruptions."

Anton spoke up, explaining the intercepted message and its implications. Volkov's expression darkened as he examined the transcript. Ivan held his breath, not daring to move a muscle.

"If this is legitimate, it confirms the suspicions we've had of General Kuznetsov's loyalty," Volkov said at last. "His wife would have access to many state secrets." He contemplated them both with an icy stare. "You were right to bring this to me. We must control the situation quickly."

The young Lieutenants exhaled in unison.

Volkov picked up a secure phone and issued rapid orders to have Natalia Kuznetsova brought in for interrogation. Replacing the receiver, he turned back to Anton and Ivan. "Well done, both of you. I will ensure you are commended for this. Now, return to your posts while I handle things from here."

Dismissed, they departed HQ with tangible relief. The night air never felt so fresh. As their car sped back through the darkened city, Ivan finally allowed himself to exhale fully. Glancing at Anton, he managed a shaky smile. "All in a day's work, right?"

Anton clapped him on the shoulder. "We did our duty. Not an easy thing, but vital for the Motherland. Get some rest tonight. I have a feeling things are about to get very busy."

Ivan nodded, sobering at the thought of the coming fallout. As the centre of Moscow receded around them, he stared out into the night, mind churning. They were small cogs, but they had set big wheels in motion tonight. For better or worse, only time would tell.

72) Sir Henry Attwood's Office, Whitehall, London

An unassuming knock shattered Henry's reverie. A reverie in which Yelena's legs played a significant role. Ralf Burgin stepped in.

"Ralf," Henry greeted him, a nod giving the signal for the intelligence officer to sit. "We've got a response from Natalia."

Ralf's eyes flicked upwards, dark irises lit with expectation. "Ah, Natalia! What's she saying?"

"She's willing to trust us, Ralf. She wants us to get her son out of that damned Ukrainian prisoner of war camp." Henry grinned at the implications of the deal. "She's given us a container-load of info, all paid in advance."

Ralf nodded, his focus sharpened like a small hawk zeroing in on a field mouse. "Go on."

"She says that her husband, General Kuznetsov, has been running their operation to destabilise our government. That they've developed some kind of psychotropic drug, a compound that turns people into killers when mixed with cocaine and that it is almost ready for general release."

Ralf stiffened, "That confirms our reasoning about the attacks then," he muttered, fingers drumming on the armrest. "and that they've only been testing it so far."

Henry nodded. "That's not all. The mixing operation is being run out of Lagos, Nigeria. A GRU colonel is overseeing it." He handed Burgin a file, the name of the Russian GRU colonel emboldened on the cover: Dimitri Petrenko.

Ralf whistled, "That's Head of GRU, Leonid Petrenko's son, isn't it? Who said nepotism is dead in Russia?" He grinned at his own wit then, shaking his head, thumbed through the first dossier that Henry had passed across. "This ties up everything we've suspected so far, Henry. The origin of the additive, the Russian connection, the link to Nigeria..."

"But Natalia is in a precarious position," Henry added, with the extreme understatement of his type. "We don't know what the Russians have on her."

"I think we have to assume Natalia will be arrested in a matter of days unless some guardian angel stopped the GRU Signals bods from intercepting her messages."

"Of course Ralf, so we need to wring her dry of information. But in case she does survive, we need to ensure we do not seal her fate. She would be a massively valuable source in the future if she survived, and now she has told us this, we own her."

"Agreed. Keeping her as a source is worth even a day or two's delay in catching the Ruskies putting in the additive." Ralf closed the file, his expression one of steely determination. "So, we can't tell Reaper about Nigeria yet."

"We have to let him continue in Columbia and find his own way in case the Ruskies have people there. If he discovers the Nigeria angle himself, fine. If not, we tell him to try Nigeria only once he's done in Colombia or Natalia is arrested. We should to do anything we can within reason to avoid compromising Natalia's safety."

"Exactly." Henry sighed, rubbing his temples. "She will be an invaluable asset if she evades detection by the GRU."

The two men fell silent, their minds a whirl of strategy and planning, of contingencies and what-ifs. Outside, the sun continued to stream into the room, oblivious to the weighty decisions being made under its warm rays. The desk was like a chessboard, and every move would dictate the ultimate fate of pieces spread across three continents.

73) General Leonid Petrenko's Office, GRU HQ, Lubhynka Square, Moscow, Russia

A sharp knock disrupted the rhythm of Petrenko's thoughts. He looked up, an expression of surprise flickered across his face almost instantly replaced by a mask of professional detachment. The door opened, revealing the tall, slim figure of Natalia, her normally vibrant presence diminished by the ominous silhouette of two large, stern men standing behind her. As she moved into the room under their watchful gaze, a heavy tension hung in the air, as though the very office held its breath.

Leonid fixed her with an icy stare. "Leave us," he dismissed the guards with a wave of his hand. They abandoned Natalia and departed swiftly, the metal door booming shut behind them. "Natalia, have a seat." His tone was polite but his eyes were hard as stone. She sat gracefully across from him, back straight and chin upraised.

Leonid remained silent for several long moments, building tension. When he finally spoke, his voice was lethally quiet. "It seems you've been rather busy making new friends abroad." He slid a transcript of her encrypted plea across the desk. "Asking British intelligence to intervene and rescue your son? Offering them classified information in exchange?" He tsked, shaking his head. "What were you thinking, Natalia?"

She met his icy glare without flinching. "I was thinking of Alexander, as any mother would. Saving his life is worth any cost to me." Defiance flashed in her eyes. "I have no regrets, and you cannot intimidate me."

Anger kindled in Leonid's chest at her audacity then it was drowned in admiration for her courage. He let nothing show, of course. "Your actions have caused grave damage, you foolish woman. What you've told the British jeopardizes Russian security." His hand clenched unconsciously on the armrest. "And your betrayal has doomed Alexander. He will suffer greatly thanks to your scheming."

Natalia paled at the threat but lifted her chin proudly. "I did what any parent would do to protect their child. Punish me if you must, but leave Alexander be." Her voice shook slightly but did not waver. "He is innocent."

Leonid scoffed. "Innocent? He is a second rate pilot detained in Ukraine through his own errors, in a war you seem content to prolong with your treachery." He stood abruptly, pacing across the room, "What did you think the British would do with the intelligence you gave them, Natalia?" His tone grew sharper. "Use it to undermine Russia, of course. Just as you have undermined your husband's distinguished career. Ruined him."

Halting in front of her, Leonid bent and placed his hands on the arms of her chair, encaging her. "You are a fool if you believed they would actually assist you. Or that your betrayal would free Alexander." He bent further, closer, eyes boring into hers. "There will be consequences for your disloyalty. Grave consequences." Straightening, he walked to the door and opened it. The guards re-entered immediately.

"Take her to the North wing holding cells. No contact or comforts." Leonid kept his gaze fixed coldly on Natalia. "Spend some time contemplating your shameful choices."

The guards seized Natalia's arms, hauling her up brusquely. As they led her away, she called over her shoulder, "My only regret is not acting sooner! Alexander's life is all that matters to me."

The steel door slammed shut, cutting off any reply. Leonid stared at it for a long moment.

Reseating himself, Leonid began considering his options for a counter-operation, a small smile playing about his lips. He would feed British intelligence carefully crafted misinformation apparently through her.

But first he had to run through the effects of Natalia's treachery for the effects upon many matters. She was in reality an acceptable loss with benefits; on the plus-side her arrest sent a message to any influential citizens who might waver in their support for the state while, at the same time, providing useful leverage over the unfortunate General Kuznetsov.

On the negative-side, as a result of her betrayal, the British merely knew two weeks in advance what was coming. They could do nothing to stop the drug distribution. Their people had rights and the protection of the law, after all. Was that it? Was that all? It seemed so.

Idly, he wondered how long Natalia would cling to her defiant courage once subjected to interrogation in the cells below. No matter, she was merely a pawn on this grander chessboard. All pieces were expendable in the Great Game between nations. Losing a rook did not mean forfeiting the match.

Leonid allowed himself a cold smile as he prepared his next moves. The British thought themselves so noble, but they would find only ruin at the end of this chase. For the Motherland, any sacrifice was justified.

74) St. James's Park, City Of Westminster, London, UK

The morning sun glinted off the tranquil surface of St. James's Park Lake, a strangely peaceful oasis in the middle of London's old city and opposite Buckingham Palace. Sir Henry stood at the water's edge, tossing handfuls of seed to the ducks gathering expectantly around his feet. The familiar ritual soothed him, providing space to ponder recent troubling developments.

The crunching of gravel signalled an approaching visitor. Henry glanced up to see Ralf walking purposefully towards him. With a subtle nod of acknowledgement, Henry turned his focus back to the ducks while waiting for Ralf to draw near.

"Morning, Ralf," Ralf greeted casually, taking up position at the water's edge beside him and producing a bag of duck-food. "I see the ducks are benefitting from your generosity as always."

Henry's mouth quirked with wry humour as he flung another handful. "At least they're happy for the crumbs I provide. Our human counterparts abroad haven't been quite as receptive lately."

Ralf gave a low chuckle. "Yes, diplomacy, even human decency, seems in short supply these days. But that's precisely what I assume you wanted to discuss?" He shot Henry a meaningful look. "Do you have an update on a certain cooperative venture underway overseas."

Henry kept his eyes on the ducks but his head lifted almost imperceptibly. "Our American cousins have come around on the matter of cooperation."

“Oh, jolly good.”

"Indeed. I've received word that the DEA is prepared to support Reaper's operation down South. Once he has been captured they'll facilitate access to the prime target for interrogation, Torres." Henry raised a knowing eyebrow. "Quid pro quo, as always with them of course."

Ralf nodded thoughtfully as he brushed a little seed-chaff from his hand. "Right then. Well, we always aim to be good partners, even if our books balance a little unequally." He turned fully to Henry now, dropping any pretence of unconcern, "I trust you've negotiated an arrangement to our benefit but which leaves our hand invisible? Plausible deniability and all that."

"Naturally. In exchange for their assistance in capturing the cartel boss Torres, Reaper will provide the cowboys with any worthwhile intelligence produced by the interrogation." Henry's expression turned shrewd. "A fair bargain secured through quiet channels without official fingerprints."

They shared a look of perfect understanding before taking their customary leisurely walk around the lake. To any passerby, they appeared two well-dressed gentlemen enjoying the park. Only the most perceptive observer might detect the subtle tension humming beneath their relaxed exteriors. "Any further whispers from Natalia?" Henry inquired casually. "Her insights have proven so valuable."

Ralf's expression clouded briefly. "Sadly, our songbird has changed her tune. After confirming the intel on the cocaine business she volunteered further information on another matter which I do not think can be genuine. I believe she has been arrested." He shot Henry a grave look.

Henry nodded grimly. "Shame. Her knowledge could have helped unravel some tangled threads."

"Quite."

Henry turned them back towards the park entrance, "Well then, I must be getting on with my day. I will pass along your regards to our mutual friends across the pond. And please give Reaper my best. His mission is critical in many ways."

"I will relay your sentiments," Ralf assured. They parted near the gate with an amiable handshake, then Henry watched his almost-friend disappear into the bustling city. Alone again amidst the swirling currents of intrigue, he felt the full weight of his responsibilities settling upon him once more.

Shaking himself free of Natalia, Henry walked briskly towards SIS headquarters, his mind moving to the next pressing matter requiring his attention. Ready or not, events were accelerating abroad and at home.

75) General Leonid Petrenko's Office, GRU HQ, Lubhynka Square, Moscow, Russia

Within the stark confines of his GRU office General Leonid Petrenko sat ramrod straight behind his desk, his attention wholly captured by a series of intelligence reports. An abrupt rap at the door broke his concentration, a shadow of annoyance crossed his face and his eyes flickered to the door. "Enter," he summoned curtly. The door creaked open to admit a tall figure in uniform, Colonel Anatoly Sidorov, who promptly snapped to attention.

"Colonel Sidorov reporting as ordered, Comrade General," he said, his voice echoing from the room's bare walls.

"At ease, Colonel." Petrenko gestured with the back of his hand to the chair opposite his desk. "Your promptness is appreciated. A pressing matter necessitates our attention."

Sidorov folded smartly into the chair, back rigid as a plank, his eyes conveying keen interest. "General, I stand ready to serve."

With a measured movement, Petrenko slid a dossier across the desk. "This pertains to the recent interception of a cocaine shipment in Marbella. A shipment containing a modified sample of cocaine being sent to test a new shipment route into the UK. I suspect this was no mere chance, not a jealous local dealer protecting his patch but a calculated act by British Intelligence or their lackeys."

As Sidorov skimmed the report, a frown puckered his brow. "You believe we have a mole in the supply chain, Comrade General?"

"That's the possibility I'm leaning towards," Petrenko affirmed, his fingers clasped together forming a temple. "Besides our people in Africa, the shipment's course was privy only to a select few within the gang running our distribution network in the UK."

Petrenko locked eyes with Sidorov, his stare penetrating. "It seems probable that someone tipped off British Intel about this shipment. So the insignificant cost of a package of drugs has potentially uncovered a threat to the main distribution effort we are about to launch. A very worthwhile trade if true. So, if it exists, the security breach in Bradford must be discovered and sealed."

With a slow nod, Sidorov absorbed the weight of the revelation. "It has serious implications if confirmed. But it does seem likely the case. Your orders, General?"

"I propose deploying an agent from our London Embassy to visit our dealer in Bradford. There he can utilise whatever means seem appropriate to quickly reveal any British informants amongst the gang."

A thoughtful expression replaced Sidorov's initial surprise. "A sound course of action, General. Yet," he paused, choosing his words with care, "given the recent fiasco with Natalia Kuznetsova, wouldn't our focus be better directed towards containing that fallout? The Brits are likely more invested in the Nigerian thread than our Bradford operations."

A momentary flicker of irritation marred Petrenko's stern features. "You refer to Kuznetsova 's treachery, Colonel?" His voice descended into an icy growl. "Be assured, her betrayal is being addressed. The price of disloyalty to the Motherland is severe. The British may chase ghosts for all it matters."

His voice softened, the sharp edge to his words blunted. "But you are correct in essence," he said, "we mustn't grow lax on securing our other operations. Have a clever agent despatched to Bradford immediately. I do not wish to lose that foothold."

Chastised, Sidorov bowed his head in acknowledgement. "Of course, General. I'll have London dispatch a good man to probe matters in Bradford without delay. Any traitors within their ranks will be found and dealt with."

"That is what I expect of you, Colonel," Petrenko said, holding the Colonel's eye a little longer than was comfortable before rising from his seat, a clear signal for the conclusion of their meeting. "Ensure you keep me updated on the agent's progress. You're dismissed."

Sidorov swiftly exited the room, his mind whirring as he considered potential agents for this critical mission. London would decide on the agent and he would be responsible. As ever. Or perhaps not. A residual unease clung to him about being forced to redirect his resources to confirm what might just be a hunch, especially when the looming shadow of Kuznetsova 's treason seemed far more significant to this operation.

But questioning Petrenko's judgement was out of his purview. Even a Colonel in GRU was merely a chess piece being manoeuvred on a board of shadows and subterfuge, a cog in the vast machinery of espionage, propelled by the currents formed by even higher powers. But there was something he could do to ensure a positive result and protect his position.

Back in his office, he made a secure call to his deputy. "Prepare a cover and travel documents for Agent Volkov. He has another assignment waiting in England..."

The intricate gears of the spy network started churning once again, overseen by the iron hand of those orchestrating the great game of international intrigue. Sidorov was but a small fish navigating the tidal currents in an ocean far too vast and treacherous for a secure life.

76) Guaymaral Airport, North Of Bogota, Columbia

The C-17 Globemaster III transport plane touched down on the hot Colombian tarmac with a bone-jarring thump.

"Any landin' ye can waak awa frae," quipped Mac habitually.

The huge ramp to the rear of the fuselage was lowered like a castle drawbridge and the air, still thick with the raw scent of jungle vegetation at an elevation of 8,400 feet, swept in like an unwelcome guest. The loadmaster began directing the exit of the line of military vehicles from the fuselage. Mike and Mac grabbed their gear, took a steadying breath of the warm, damp air and stepped out of the shade into the shimmering heat, their combat boots ringing down the walkway and then crunching on the gravel.

As they emerged from the belly of the beast, a squad of men clad in combat gear approached them, the glint of the DEA insignia catching the sun on their caps. The leader extended a calloused hand, his firm grip betraying the strength of a man hardened by a military life.

"Chief Agent Douglas, DEA" he greeted, his sharp, eagle-like eyes scanning the pair with a professional interest. "Welcome to Colombia. We've been expecting you gentlemen. Let's get you out of this heat."

The stifling jungle air gave way to the refreshing chill of an air-conditioned unit within a nondescript prefabricated government building, the DEA's local stronghold. In this cool, sterile environment, far removed from the dense, oppressive heat outside, Douglas ushered them to a table laden with food and refreshments.

"Help yourselves," he suggested, settling into the leather chair behind a table. "I know it's a long flight down from Houston in a Globemaster."

After hydrating themselves on fruit, Mike and Mac listened as Douglas outlined their mission. "So, your superiors have informed you about Hernan Torres and his... lucrative cocaine business, I take it?"

"That's correct," Mike confirmed, his eyes as hard as granite as the two men weighed each other up. "Our brief is to apprehend Torres and gain intel on his operations, particularly those pertaining to his exports to the UK."

Douglas nodded, steepling his fingers on the desk. "Our intelligence has located Torres. We'll provide the necessary support to ensure you reach him and get out unscathed."

Mac, his face impassive, raised a curious eyebrow. "An' whit's wi' the braw offer? Whit's the snag?"

Douglas looked at Mac, not unfriendly but puzzled.

Mike cut in, "My cynical colleague is wondering why you are making this gracious offer?"

Douglas, leaning back, gave a thin smile. "Plausible deniability. It's crucial that any forensic evidence or witnesses point to your operation, not ours. After the capture, we'll be more than happy to assist in the interrogation. Think of it as a courtesy amongst allies."

Mike and Mac exchanged a knowing glance. "That's a kind offer, Chief Agent Douglas," Mike responded, his voice smooth. "We appreciate your generous assistance in apprehending this mutual target."

With the mission's parameters now set, Douglas clapped them on the shoulders. "Get some rest guys. You move out at 0500."

Once Douglas left them, Mike turned to Mac, his voice low, a cautionary undertone softening his words. "The Yanks are pleasant enough, but remember, Mac, we can't fully trust their spooks. They have already changed the game from their catching the target to us doing it ourselves. 'Plausible deniability' also means we take the fall if something goes wrong. We need to keep our eyes open."

Mac took a long drink of water, his eyes filled with understanding. "Nae doot aboot it, Mike. This feels pure sketchy, but orders ur orders. We'll dae thir mucky joabs an' watch oor ain backs."

They spent the rest of the day sequestered in the DEA compound, pouring over operational details, security layouts, reconnaissance footage and novel support equipment. Their target's compound, a fortified bunker nestled deep within the jungle, was a formidable challenge, but neither Mike nor Mac were strangers to such missions.

Night fell over the Colombian rainforest, the nocturnal chorus of the jungle a stark contrast to the quiet of their temporary quarters. Lying on their cots, Mike's gaze was fixed on the ceiling, his mind mulling over the operation, his senses attuned to every minor sound in the unknown surroundings. Tomorrow, they would step back into the heat, into the danger. For tonight, they had only the cold comfort of anticipation.

77) General Leonid Petrenko's Office, GRU HQ, Lubhynka Square, Moscow, Russia

General Petrenko sat rigidly behind his desk as two guards admitted General Kuznetsov to his office. Kuznetsov saluted his technical superior. "Comrade General, how may I be of service?"

Petrenko's craggy features remained impassive and stern. "At ease, Nikolai. Please sit."

Suppressing his unease, Kuznetsov settled back into a chair across the desk from his old “friend”. This unexpected invitation did not bode well.

"I will get directly to the point," Petrenko began, his tone icy. "It seems your wife Natalia has been engaging in certain...unauthorized communications with the British intelligence agencies."

Shock rippled across Kuznetsov's face. "British intelligence? What are you saying, Leonid?"

Petrenko slid a transcript across the desk. "We intercepted encrypted messages from Natalia to MI6 pleading for help. Offering classified information in exchange." His eyes bored into Kuznetsov's. "She claims it is to free your son Alexander from Ukrainian custody."

Kuznetsov blanched as he scanned the damning document. One huge hand came up to cover his face. "Alexander... Natalia must be desperate for word of our son." He met Petrenko's gaze pleadingly. "I swear I had no knowledge of her actions, Comrade General. You must believe me."

Petrenko's expression remained stony. "Your personal integrity is not in question, thus far. But your wife's betrayal has endangered state security." He looked at Kuznetsov for just a little too long before continuing. "Natalia is being detained for interrogation. The severity of her punishment will depend greatly on your own loyalty and service in handling your ongoing operations."

Kuznetsov paled further at the implied threat. "Leonid, I implore you. Our families have been friends for decades. Can you not show leniency?" His voice dropped urgently. "Help her, for the sake of our years together."

For a moment, Petrenko's harsh attitude seemed to soften. He halted and sighed. "Out of respect for our history, I will...see what I can do for her. But make no mistake-" His eyes flashed dangerously, "the Motherland must come first. Betrayal cannot go unanswered."

"Of course, Comrade General," Kuznetsov acquiesced, though his haggard features betrayed his dismay. "I understand sacrifices must be made for Russia."

"See that you do." Petrenko moved briskly to the door. "Serve the Motherland well, Nikolai. Only devoted service can mitigate the consequences of Natalia's treachery."

The door closed with an ominous finality behind him. Outside the office, watched by the uncomfortable guards, Kuznetsov lowered his head into shaking hands. His loyal, devoted wife imprisoned as a traitor. His only son held prisoner in some Ukraine hell-hole. It was too much to bear.

And yet, he knew Petrenko's words were true. There could be no room for sentimentality or weakness. Natalia's insane action demanded consequences, regardless of motives. Who could he speak to in a bid to get her lenient treatment?

Straightening slowly, Kuznetsov began to walk and mechanically considered the main operation. It was all he could do to help his wife. Somewhere, British agents were doubtless pursuing leads from Natalia's intercepted messages. He could not allow their meddling to disrupt Russia's plans to bring down the British government.

With an effort, Kuznetsov returned to his office and forced his roiling emotions down, encasing his breaking heart in a shell of duty and resolve. The general worked late into the night, fortifying himself against despair with the cold comfort of patriotism. His family would pay a terrible price, but Russia, Russia would endure.

78) Riaz Khan's House, Bradford, UK

The sleek black rental BMW slipped urgently through the streets of Bradford. Alexei Volkov and Vasily Karpov were far from home in this English city, but their hard eyes took in every detail. Their suits and long coats would have marked them as outsiders to the tracksuit-clad youths on the sidewalks had they left their car but they would rather have stepped into a swamp.

Rounding a corner, they spotted their destination, a large modern house, fashionably garish and worth many times the cost of the average house in the area. As the Russian agents exited the BMW, the pulsing bass of rap music reached them. Vasily glanced distaste at Alexei. They strode up to the front door, Alexei ringing the bell and Vasily watching behind them.

Moments later the door jerked open, revealing a large, bearded, scowling young man. "Yeah? Whatchu want?" He looked them over with disdain.

"We are here to see Mr. Khan," Alexei said coldly. "Please inform him."

The punk spat on the ground at their feet. Very close to spitting on their shoes, a killing insult to a Russian.

"Riaz don't meet with your type, grandad. Now piss off."

He moved to slam the door but Vasily jammed it open with his foot. Their eyes locked, tension crackling. Then a voice called out, "Let them in, Tariq."

The youth backed down sullenly as Riaz Khan himself approached. He welcomed the Russians with recognition in his eyes. "Alexei! Saw you on the camera. Wasn't expecting you in town." He glanced at Tariq, "They're friends, no need for trouble."

Tariq reluctantly let them enter, shadowing them down the hall. Several hard stares followed their passage, but no one stopped them. At an office door, Riaz waved Tariq and the Russians inside.

As Vasily smoothly closed the door, Alexei turned to their host. "Apologies for arriving unannounced, but a sensitive matter has come to our attention."

Riaz's eyes narrowed in query, but before he could respond, Vasily drew a silenced Glock G44 .22 and shot Tariq point-blank through the heart and then centre of face before he fell. The expanding bullets, a type used by assassins, burst the heart and scrambled the brain but did not exit the body. The sound of the pistol was as quiet as an air rifle being discharged so inaudible in the next room. The body dropped to the floor like a sack of potatoes.

Shock flashed across Riaz's face. "What the hell…"

Alexei cut him off. "Merely establishing proper respect." His tone was glacial. "Discourtesies cannot be tolerated."

Vasily kept his pistol aimed at Riaz, who raised his hands slowly. "Alright, you've made your point. Now explain how you are going to get out of here alive." His jaw was tight but he kept his composure.

Alexei withdrew a small scanner wand from his coat. "We believe your organization has been compromised by MI5." He began scanning Riaz for a transmitter. "We are here to identify their agent."

Riaz's gaze cleared, understanding dawning. "MI5 has turned one of my men?"

"So it seems. My scanner will detect any implants they use to communicate." Finding nothing, Alexei glanced at Tariq's body. "With your permission?"

At Riaz's nod, he scanned the corpse. "Clean. Now summon your lieutenants one by one. We will uncover this mole."

Riaz called out, and three of his hard-eyed soldiers entered. They only saw the pistol-wielding Vasily once they were in the room and under its power. On Riaz's assurances, they submitted to scanning without resistance.

Then a final man was called and entered, Faris Iqbal. Alexei scanned him routinely until the wand beeped under his right armpit. "Well, well. It seems we have found a traitor."

Riaz looked stunned. "Impossible! Faris has worked for me loyally for years. He killed an enemy in a fight only last week."

Faris's face was blank.

"Loyal to king and country, perhaps," Alexei remarked dryly, "But MI5 agents are not gentlemen. Hold him tight and strip off his shirt." At his instruction, Faris was seized, pinioned and stripped to the waist, revealing no visible implant. Nevertheless, the scanner beeped insistently at a spot below his arm pit. Alexei examined a readout from the wand on his 'phone. "A sub-dermal chip," informed Alexei. " Probably activated by tapping patterns on the skin. Very advanced."

Riaz shook his head in anger and disgust. "I never would have doubted him! What should we do with the backstabbing swine?"

Alexei glanced at Vasily and looked back to Riaz then said simply, "We will take care of it. He has a need for a ride in the countryside." Their newfound reputation left no doubt as to the prisoner's fate.

Riaz nodded. "Get him out of my sight." To his men he added, "And dump that piece of trash too." He prodded Tariq's body with his shoe, lip curled in anger at the thought of MI5 infiltration.

79) Deep Jungle, The Approach To Hernan Torres Compound, North Eastern Colombia

In the dark, almost suffocating thickness of the jungle, two figures moved with caution. Mac led Mike, his frame slightly hunched, scanning the shadowed path through the crossover thermal imaging and image intensifying night-vision goggles they both wore and which gave the world an eerie green tinge. Behind him, Mike followed carefully, trying to place his feet in the prints left by Mac.

The only sounds were the rustle of leaves, the rattle of insects and, once, the distant, plaintive cry of some unseen creature being murdered.

Their clothes faded them into the night: Thermal-suppressing camouflage kit and silenced sub-machine guns, HK MP5SDs, held at the ready. On their chest, head, and back, electronic markers invisibly signalled their innocence to the sensors of friendly forces, human and robotic.

Ahead and behind them, like mechanical guardians, stalked a pair of LS5 Panthers, each the size of a tiger but painted to match the jungle. Sleek and practically silent, these infantry support robots were the evolution of officially-cancelled military prototypes, now armed with artificial intelligence and formidable weaponry.

Controllable by voice, signal, or console, their night vision systems constantly scanned the terrain for threats. With the capability to see, hear, smell, assess, make simple decisions and carry heavy loads, they followed the orders of the two soldiers almost like soldiers themselves.

Suddenly there was a whisper in both men's headsets. The voice of the lead Panther, calm yet alert, "Romeo Alpha, approaching target." The lead Panther stopped, and Mac's hand instinctively went to his ear, a nod passing between him and Mike. The rear robot too had stopped, its mechanical muscles presumably tensed, chain-gun pointing to their rear, ready for whatever lay ahead, or followed behind.

Without a word, Mac reached into the lead robot's cargo pannier and withdrew first a tiny multi-rotor recce drone, then a larger, boxy package while Mike unstrapped a much heftier combat drone from the back of the rear Panther. This drone was bulky, the size of a small table, a light machine gun mounted beneath it.

With a stealthy grace, both men stepped aside from the track. The rear Panther passed them and both machines then moved forward in unison, creeping silently to positions that would allow them to focus suppressing fire on a compound lying hidden just a few yards ahead. The entire layout of the target was known to all four of them from the drone reconnaissance film they had studied, or uploaded, the night before.

Mac's whisper cut through the stillness, a command to the headset, "All call-signs, assault position alpha ready." His usually thick Glaswegian accent barely there.

Mike's blue eyes narrowed and he smiled to himself at Mac's loss of accent while talking to the machine. As he prepared the larger drone his movements were precise, every action a testament to his long hours of practice. "Ready to launch," he confirmed into the mike, his voice a soft growl. The jungle seemed to hold its breath, waiting. The compound, filled with unknown dangers, lay just beyond their sight.

With a final nod between the two soldiers, Mac launched the little reconnaissance drone, the whirr of its tiny multiple rotors totally inaudible above the call of insects.

The Panthers stalked off quietly to their assault positions like exceptionally dangerous cats.

80) Riaz Khan's House, Bradford, UK

With a steely glint in their eyes, the Russian agents, Alexei Volkov and Vasily Karpov, set to work binding Faris. His face was still quite pale, despite being slapped a few times by Riaz, but his eyes remained hard and unyielding, he was not giving away any emotion at all. They tied his wrists and ankles with a ruthless efficiency, gagging him with a piece of cloth stuffed into his mouth and tied there which effectively muffled his voice but allowed him to breath.

Dragging him by the feet, as if he were an inert sack, Vasily made his way to the back door of the house. Alexei made his way to the front door, pausing to exchange a final nod with Riaz Khan whose eyes were filled with a mixture of anger and contempt for Faris. The Russian agents' intrusion into his domain had embarrassed him, had exposed betrayal in his ranks, and the sting of it was palpable in the room.

Outside, Vasily found a high-walled drive and garden where the black BMW was waiting, its engine purring softly. Alexei had brought it around, its boot now yawning open like the mouth of a predatory beast.

Working together, the Russians loaded the MI5 agent into the boot of the car, his bound body fitting comfortably into the ample space. The car's suspension dipped very slightly under the weight then levelled automatically.

Riaz Khan watched the car leave from the front doorway, his face still twisted in a grimace. As the car's lights retreated down the street, he spat on the floor, the taste of betrayal still bitter in his mouth. His eyes narrowed and he turned back into the house, the door closing with a definitive thud.

The BMW wove through the quiet streets, leaving behind the urban sprawl, heading out of town. They drove in silence, the tension in the car almost tangible. Every few moments, Alexei glanced in the rear-view mirror, ensuring they were not followed.

Finally they reached their destination, a secluded spot surrounded by towering trees. The car's headlights carved out a small clearing, and they stopped. The only sounds were the distant hoot of an owl and the soft crunching of gravel underfoot as they dragged their prisoner from the car boot.

The MI5 agent's eyes were wide but defiant as Vasily drew a knife, its blade glinting ominously in the dim light. Alexei held him, his grip like iron, as Vasily, guided by the wand, carefully cut into the flesh six inches below his right armpit.

The agent's body tensed, his face twisted a little at the pain, but he bore it bravely and made no sound. The knife worked with precision, and soon the tracking unit was extracted, a small piece of technology that had been implanted to save his life yet which had marked him as a traitor.

The wound was a couple of inches long and quite deep so blood seeped from it initially, but the Russians were unconcerned. Vasily pressed a large adhesive dressing over it to stop the flow of blood.

Returning Faris to the car boot, they drove away, their minds already focused on the next task. Behind them, the dark forest swallowed the evidence of their work, a secret hidden among the trees. A few miles away Vasily wound down his window and tossed a small item out to be run over time and again on the busy road. The tracker element crushed and well away from its last potential signal in the wooded area.

81) Hernan Torres' Compound, North Eastern Colombia

The first Panther, call sign Romeo Alpha, had taken up position on high ground overlooking the walled enclosure which housed the Cartel leadership. It lay like a camel and scanned the surrounding area, thermal and image intensifier sensors lifted high on an extending pole and seeing everything despite the pitch blackness of the night. Images were loaded on the team net to be seen by Romeo Bravo, Mike, Mac, and thanks to a circling Predator drone high overhead, God-knew who else back at base. Sentry positions at each of the compound corners were empty. No heat signatures from human bodies anywhere.

The second Panther settled down overlooking the main access track to the compound, an unmade road sufficient for a 4x4. It lay with its legs tucked underneath its body, its sensors scanning right and left. Nothing but a group of roosting parrots and some small quadrupedal creature in the nearby jungle glowing faintly on the imaging sensors. Some sort of monkey.

Mike and Mac had crawled forward to within sight of the compound. It was pitch dark so sight meant thermal imaging or image intensifiers. Mac spoke over his headset to the two Panthers, "Hello Romeo Alpha and Romeo Bravo, This is Romeo Niner, Sitrep re life-signs over."

The Panthers replied instantly with female voices, uncomfortably attractive, "Romeo Niner this is Romeo Alpha, no life-signs within compound out."

"Romeo Niner this is Romeo Bravo, no human life-signs within area of operation out."

Mike was listening in on the radio net, "I thought at least Alpha would spot the sentries, Mac"

"Aye, he seems tae huv a braw view ae the toors an' inside the compound awricht."

"What can you see from the recce drone?"

Mac concentrated on the heads-up display in his left eye-piece. "Guid visual intae the compound but Ah cannae see a livin' thing, Mike. Sumthin's no richt here."

"Anything from the High Drone?"

Mac switched the input on his eye-piece to show a view from the Predator drone circling high above them and set to watch the area around the compound. "Ah kin jus' see us... Ah kin see a wee bit heat frae the Panthers... Thar's nuhin frae the compound at aw, nor onywhaur within a couple hunner yairds, 'cept maybe fur a few monkeys... sma' an' gaun too fast tae be human."

Mike's face indicated he was not happy with the situation. "There is nothing for it but to go in and see what we can see buddy."

The two men broke cover and jogged over open ground to the compound wall. Mac made a back and Mike used it to spring up, grab the top of the wall and swing himself up. He turned around and stretched down to allow Mac to catch a hand and pulled him up beside him like a pair of acrobats. They were on a parapet, a walkway running around the whole wall surrounding the compound. Inside there were several store houses, a tractor, a farm-type trailer and a large single story dwelling.

Mike scanned the courtyard and saw a camera mounted on the wall of a building. "That's something we didn't see Mac. If it is live then they know we are coming."

Mac pulled a face, "We'd ken by noo. Thar should be guards in aw the toors an' that bunk hoose o'er there should be fu' o' them. Torres should be snoozin' in that hoose wi' at least wan burd an' a couple ae staff. Drone says the bunk hoose is empty. Ah cannae see through the roof ae the hoose fur some reason."

Mike looked resigned, "This all feels wrong. But we can't just go home and leave it. Cover me and we'll clear the house. If they knew we were coming there will be booby-traps. Scan the path to the house for mines."

"Aye."

Mike jumped down from the walkway into the compound and over to the dwelling. The main door was under a canopy but visible. Mac waited for him to arrive safely left of the door then followed him. Arriving at the opposite side of the door, Mac unslung the box he was carrying and fiddled with it.

Scanning the wall and door while peering into the small screen on top he concentrated for a moment. "Nae a body inside, Mike, but thar's sumthin'... Haud oan a mo."

"Take your time Mac."

"Thar's a booby trap inside, Mike. Looks like a couple ae slabs ae PE wired up tae this door."

Mike chuckled, "Its just as well we didn't knock then. Someone did know we were coming. I wonder what else they have set up to welcome us?"

Just as Mike spoke a feminine voice spoke into their ear-pieces, almost seductive, "Romeo Niner, this is Romeo Bravo, there are 29 humans carrying automatic weapons advancing on the compound over."

"Ah wonder whit deviant decided tae mak the killin' machines wummin?"

Mike smiled in the darkness.

Mac looked to Mike, "They must've been hidin' unner heat-proof sheets, the bastarts. Should Ah huv yon beasties take 'em doon?"

Mike nodded. "In your own time."

Mac spoke into his Microphone in English, "Romeo Alpha, move to support Romeo Bravo left flanking. Romeo Bravo, fire for effect on humans outside this compound, continue with suppressing fire as required. All call-signs Romeo, fire at will. Over."

"Romeo Alpha, moving now, out."

"Romeo Bravo. Firing now, out."

Romeo Bravo stood and moved its position slightly to give a better field of fire over the humans approaching the compound, their assault rifles at the ready. It opened fire with long bursts from its Bushmaster 7.62 chain-gun. Bodies fell to the ground, others scattered and threw themselves down. The survivors were pinned in place, movement would mean instant death.

Meanwhile, Romeo Alpha sprang up from its position and galloped like a camel around the far side of the compound to a higher position which permitted it to fire down onto the humans from their flank. Arriving, it had a clear view of the remaining live humans, trapped and cowering from its partner's fire.

A young man in a dark T-shirt and straw hat took careful aim with his AK47 and let loose an accurate burst at Bravo Alpha. A few bullets bounced harmlessly from its armour. Methodically, it killed the hero, then all the remaining survivors with short bursts of chain-gun fire.

"Well that's you and me out of a job Mac." They had watched the end of the drama from the gates of the compound, positioned ready to assist in repelling the attackers, but the Panthers efficiency had rendered their support unnecessary.

Mac picked his teeth with a sliver of some plant. "Weel, that wis a fuck-up, wisn't it?"

82) Deputy Director's Office, CIA Headquarters, Langley, Virginia, United States

CIA Deputy Director Steve Walters settled back in his plush leather chair, casting his eyes out of the window and over the sprawling view of the Potomac River below. He thought about his predecessors paddling to work from Sycamore Island by canoe in the '70s to dodge the road traffic. A vague reflection danced on the water, casting a hypnotic glow that was swiftly overruled by the important matters at hand.

The sharp sound of a knock on the door roused him from his contemplation. He straightened in his chair, his piercing blue eyes taking on a new intensity. "Come in," he called. The door swung open to reveal Randy Coleman. His tall, muscular frame and rough-hewn features were not softened by his grim expression. He was clearly unhappy about something and greeted Walters in a voice as gravelly as the riverbank outside, "Afternoon, Steve."

"Randy, good to see you again." Steve rose, clasping the proffered hand with a firm grip that conveyed both greeting and gravity. "Please, have a seat."

Randy sank into the leather chair across from Steve's desk. The two men, familiar with one another's characters and their shared enemy, locked eyes as Steve broached the awkward issue.

"I appreciate you coming over from VA, Randy. Better we speak off the record again given the fiasco down South. I wanted to talk off the record about this op because I smell a rat. Just so I know we are on the same page, when the Limeys made the assault on Torres's compound and the capture exactly as we agreed they found the compound was empty and there was a booby trap and an ambush waiting for them. If they were not so switched on they would have been toast."

"I know that."

Steve's voice held a note of concern, but his eyes were focused and calculating. "Someone obviously tipped Torres off about that raid. I'm troubled, Randy, by what this implies. I believe we have a mole somewhere in our ranks."

Randy's dark brows furrowed, and his fingers drummed on the armrest. "I have to accept that word of the operation must have reached Torres somehow. That's pretty much certain. But I don't like to think one of my men has gone over to the other side. We both know that the trouble with fighting Cartels is the huge amount of money they have. They can buy anyone who is open to getting rich. What I don't get here is that whoever informed Torres must have known it would compromise them, or at least show there was a mole in our organisation."

"Perhaps what they stood to make from saving Torres' neck was so much it was worth the risk." Steve leaned forward, his voice carrying a blend of urgency and control. "Clearly, I don't yet know who the mole is, but I must do something about it. Our entire operation in Columbia is compromised by a mole who was high enough up to know about that op. They might have access to anything we do."

"For sure."

"I have come up with a plan to fix this though. I want to set up a new operation for another attempt on Torres. And have every single man on the operation watched by our spooks. It ought to serve three ends: Catch Torres, flush out the mole, and act as a sort of apology to the British."

Randy raised an eyebrow. "An apology?"

Steve nodded, his jaw set firmly. "The ambush does look like a failing in our intel from the outside. But worse, it could look to the Brits like we have a mole and that would lead to all the repercussions you can imagine for cooperation. This next op will be supported by my people as well as yours. I want to set up a prisoner exchange of one of your captured agents from Torres to what looks like one of his big clients. We have someone who can put the idea in his head and he will find that irresistible. Playing the big man with a US buyer. I hope the Limeys are up to it because what I have in mind will really put them to the test. And best of all, it has no down-side."

Randy considered this, his mind processing the strategic and political implications. The room was filled with the faint ticking of an old clock.

Randy finally responded, his voice resolute, "I'm good. We can support that,"

"Good man." Steve patronised his sort-of-friend out of habit, his eyes narrowing. "We'll probably catch the mole, we'll certainly learn something, and if the Brits are successful this time we all get what we want… And if they fail, it's on them, again."

The two men shared a knowing glance, the unspoken understanding settling between them like a pact. They shook hands once more, sealing the agreement.

"We'll be in touch about logistics," Steve assured Randy, his voice carrying the weight of the promise then warming, "A pleasure as always."

As Randy departed, Steve returned to his seat, his gaze once again drawn to the river outside. The water's relentless flow seemed to mirror the unyielding march of events, and he found himself contemplating the twists and turns that lay ahead.

He snapped out of his reverie and dialled a number on his phone, his voice crisp and businesslike as he spoke into the receiver. "Tell London we are having another shot at Torres." Compliance muttered through the earpiece and he put the phone down.

Then he scrolled through a directory on his laptop and dialled another number. "Jim, its Steve. I need a full electronic surveillance job on Randy Coleman, the DEA man. Check him out for comms to anything cartel related. And you'd better put a good HumInt team on to tail him too, he's a wily guy. Its eyes-only so have any results sent direct to me by secure."

With business concluded, Steve allowed himself a moment of satisfaction. The game remained the same but the play required to win points had changed and the stakes were higher than ever.

Pouring himself just two fingers of whiskey from a crystal decanter, he reflected on the day's work. The faint smile that touched his lips was from a mingling of triumph and caution. This was no ordinary day at the office. The Brits would get their man, the cartel would be undermined, the CIA and DEA would keep their hands clean and, most importantly, they would catch a mole who had probably been working from within their ranks for some time. A good outcome.

Steve took a slow sip of his whiskey, the warmth spreading through him. This was why he joined the CIA; the thrill of espionage and diplomacy, the delicate balance of power and trust. Well, power anyway.

83) **Defence Science and Technology Laboratory, Porton Down, UK** Porton Down is a "Science Park" covering some 7,000 acres in the South of England. It is officially home to two British Government facilities; the Ministry of Defence's Defence Science and Technology Laboratory(

DSTL), known for over 100 years as one of the UK's most secretive and controversial chemical and biological weapon research facilities, and a site of the UK Health Security Agency which works to protect the UK from both "natural" infectious diseases such as Ebola and the other kind such as Covid.

The site is also home to various other private and commercial science organisations and is expanding to attract other companies. Some commentators of a cynical mindset say this is because once research is handled by private companies the researchers are free from having to reply to questions posed under the Freedom of Information Act 2000.

In short, Porton Down has researched, developed and manufactured chemical and biological weapons for a very long time and they are good at it. Very good. This is where the nerve agents Novichok, Sarin and VX were analysed and studied after their deployment in the UK and elsewhere by Russia recently. Being one of the most secure areas on the planet, lots of other British government agencies take advantage of the facilities. Amongst them are the Secret Intelligence Services.

Some of the people who work at Porton Down are unusual, perhaps a little eccentric.

And they do some odd things at Porton Down.

"How are you feeling Katie?" Professor Nigel Tribble sounded genuinely concerned. But his eyes betrayed him. Katie was rather tall and very blonde. She looked almost like a female athlete with slightly more muscle than most. Very attractive if you like strong women.

Professor Tribble was not attracted to strong women. Or to people of any kind for that matter. He did like cats though. One he had caused one to grow elongated fangs like a small Sabre-toothed tiger and then written a Thesis on it for one of his advanced degrees relating to biology and genetic engineering. In the scientific community he was respected rather than liked. His genius caused a lot of important people to cut him some slack. And his usefulness caused them to cover up his indiscretions. To paint his picture more fully, Professor Tribble was a useful genius with some odd ways and made a lot of people uncomfortable close up.

"Not too bad, considering." Katie spoke English with what might have been an Eastern European accent and she seemed friendly, considering she was naked and confined to a room about fifteen feet on a side with a built-in open toilet; and the Professor was speaking to her through bars.

"How is your dinner Katie?" The professor nodded at the leg bone she was gnawing through their conversation.

"Nice and tender but not as satisfying as the food yesterday." Katie did not seem too upset about this. She stretched and her muscles rippled. Tribble thought of a leopard.

"No, its from a young gentleman to see if you could tell the difference."

Katie shrugged, "I prefer the girl-meat."

"Is your skin itching at all?"

"No, not itching, but why am I growing hair all over my body?"

"It seems I made a little mistake Katie. The synthetic hormone that gave you that wonderful body and sharpened your senses seems to have a fault. Still, your eyes are lovely."

"Oh, thank you Professor."

Professor Tribble looked to his young assistant, a very intent young man with a clipboard. "I am going to get a coffee and think for a while." He nodded towards Katie, "Have this one euthanized please, Jeremy."

Jeremy nodded and the Professor walked off towards the canteen. Katie lowered her meat and stared with wide eyes. "You are going to kill me?" Her voice rose as she called after him, "Why?" She stood with her mouth open.

In the canteen, the Professor made a coffee using his own private percolator then sat alone at a table and ran his eyes over the gene expression map on his tablet, searching for the error. "Damn!"

84) Campo, Norte De Santander, Colombia

Hidden in the shade of dense bush Mac sat motionless with binoculars held to his eyes. An M4A1 assault rifle with a laser fitted to the SOPMOD rail lay by his side, the muzzle raised on a tree root to keep it out of the dirt. He was watching the road which ran across his field of view some 200 yards downhill and beyond a coca field.

Dressed in old, ill-matching camouflage pants and shirt he looked, at a glance, like a drug cartel soldier. Except for the US Special Forces rifle. A broad brimmed camo hat covered his head from a sun, strong despite the cloud. By the road Mike, dressed in denim and with a Stetson pulled down over his face, sat on the ground with his back to the tyre of a pickup truck parked under a tree. Two other men were in the crew-cab and at least one had a rifle of some kind. The Mac lowered his binoculars and breathed out through pursed lips.

Sharing Mac's shade were three other men in camouflage. One to his left was dozing behind an M110 rifle, another behind the two of them, was watching out to their rear and the third was concentrating on a comms

tablet. To his right, resting on its bipod, was another M110, also chambered to take a 7.62 x 51mm cartridge. Mac had chosen these 800 metre-range, semi-automatic sharp-shooter rifles for their relatively high rate of accurate fire. More accurate than assault rifles, more rugged and a faster rate of fire than a true sniper rifle.

The Mac checked his wristwatch, grimaced and turned to the man beside him. "Check the drone is on station Charlie." He suppressed his accent to a level understandable by his colonial team.

"On it Sarge." Charlie pulled out a gadget which looked something like a TV remote and pressed buttons. A red light showed and figures on a tiny screen. "The Reaper is right over us 2 miles up and circling. The Hellfire missiles are armed and keyed to your laser."

"That'll do. Stand by Matt." Mac nodded to the man behind the other rifle, then to Charlie, "Check the extraction team are in position." He glanced at the laser projection unit attached to his rifle which would, at the touch of a button, lay a laser dot on any target within line-of-sight and bring a Sal Hellfire II Missile down on it like the wrath of God.

Charlie picked up the radio handset, "Hello Nine Zero, this is Nine One over."

The handset responded, clear as a bell, relayed through the MQ-9 Reaper drone high above them, "Nine Zero send over."

"Nine One. Confirm the extraction team are in position over."

"Nine Zero. Wait.... Wait.... That is affirmative over."

"Nine One. Copy that, out." Charlie lowered the handset and caught Mac's eye. "At least we can rely on the cavalry," he said in a Southern drawl.

Two more pickups came into view heading for Mike, a skull logo painted crudely on their doors, the Sinaloa cartel emblem. All the windows were down and long weapons poked out of some. There were heavy machine guns mounted in the back of each vehicle with a couple of men to each.

Heavy Russian DShK 14.5s by the look of them. Both vehicles slowed as they neared Mike. He lifted his hat to see them. He stood and they parked one behind the other some 30 feet away. The passenger door opened on the lead vehicle and a comic-book Mexican bandit stepped out to meet Mike, himself dressed like a comic-book Texan. He spread his arms as if in welcome.

Mac clicked his tongue. "Damn. Too close fur Hellfires. That's three hunner grand we've saved the Yanks. Yer gonny huv tae use the RPG, Tom. Take Matt fur a quick reload an' pit a rocket in each ae the cartel pickups oan ma first shot. Aim low tae keep shrapnel frae hittin' the Colonel's team. An' move oot 20 metres tae oor West flank so ye dinnae hit me wi' yer back-blast."

"Put a rocket in each truck on your first shot. Aim low. Fire from 20 yards over there. Wilco Sarge."

"Aye, that's whit Ah said."

Tom picked up the RPG rocket launcher and caught Matt's eye. Matt flicked himself onto his feet from the prone position and picked up four rockets with the propellant sticks already attached. The two men made off at a crouching jog.

Mike smiled and beckoned the bandit leader towards him. "Come out of the sun Fidel."

Fidel walked away from his vehicle towards the tree under which the Gringo now stood. "So, Mr. Parker, we meet in person after all these years."

Mike nodded, "Its good to finally see you Fidel. How's business?"

"Times are hard Mr. Parker. The patrols on the Texas border want more money every month. Young men are always trying to kill me but I struggle on, you know."

Mike laughed. "Same old story Fidel. I made 50 million dollars out of our trade last year so I know you made more."

"Perhaps I am not starving Mr Parker." Fidel grinned and showed a gold tooth. I asked you to meet me here because it is safer than Mexico. I couldn't risk getting your present taken from me now could I?"

"Happy to come and see some of your farms Fidel. I guess your cartel owns most of North East Columbia now?"

"Not so much but we Mexicans are keen investors here. The government is more forward thinking than at home."

"I've seen that at work on the way here Fidel. Handled me like a VIP everywhere I went."

"You are our honoured guest Mr Parker. Now let me show you your present." Fidel turned to the nearest pick up and threw his head back as a gesture to someone inside. "Miguel, bring me the pedazo de mierda."

Miguel climbed out of the front cab door, a sullen look on his face, and slung his AK47 across his back. He turned, opened the rear cab door and leaned into the vehicle then, with a heave, pulled out a body which fell onto the floor without a sound. The body was cuffed with hands behind and tied with rope at its feet. Miguel dragged it by the feet the few yards to Fidel and spat on it theatrically before walking back to the vehicle.

85) Empire Industrial Estate, Bradford, UK

In the heart of Bradford's industrial district, the bustle of industry was in the air. The maze of garages, shipping containers, and warehouses was alive with the constant movement of cars, vans, and small trucks.

Men, mostly of Indian or Pakistani descent, navigated the chaos, their clothing stained with motor oil, paint and the wear of labor. Some stood outside the units, taking a break to smoke and share a brief respite from the toil. Signs advertising car tires, auto-breaking and spares, window replacements, and plumbing adorned the walls, giving a face to the everyday struggle and craft of the area.

A stray cat roamed the estate, its eyes darting with natural curiosity, searching for prey or watching the goings-on in a world it could never quite grasp.

Into this world of grit and industry drove a sleek BMW, not looking out of place among the assortment of vehicles. Fancy cars were not a rarity here; this was a place where successful young men could afford fancy cars and took pride in their machines, lavishing them with modifications, care and attention.

The BMW navigated its way carefully through the labyrinth, finally pulling into an open garage door, which was promptly closed behind it by a bearded worker, his eyes moving left and right but his face unreadable.

Inside the garage, the atmosphere was tense. The Russian agents stepped out of the car, their eyes cold, their movements slightly stiff. They were met by Riaz Khan, he nodded a greeting without smiling, his face stern and his eyes sharp. Several of his gang members loitered, a palpable sense of expectation in the air.

With no ceremony, the Russians opened the car boot, revealing the bloody and bound body of Faris. His eyes, filled with terror and pain, avoided those of the men around him as he groaned through the dirty rag stuffed in his mouth.

Khan's voice cut through the silence, filled with a chilling calm. "I would like to video the slow death of Iqbal and post it on social media to show others the price of betrayal."

Volkov nodded in understanding, his voice as cold as ice. "I can understand that; it is the Russian way, but this man must talk to us before he dies."

Khan managed a tight smile. "Of course. I understand. We can't have spies disrupting the operation. Just make the bastard suffer before he goes."

"We'll dispose of this vermin," Volkov assured. "Then you can get back to business without British eyes watching." He clasped Khan's shoulder with one strong hand. Almost human. "The Motherland appreciates your cooperation against our common enemy."

At his command, two of Khan's men brought a wooden box, its shape and size eerily reminiscent of a coffin. As it was placed on the waiting trestles, Iqbal's eyes widened with a terror that reached into the very depths of his soul.

Without a word, his body was lifted and dumped into the box, the sound of his moans filling the room. The lid was screwed down quickly with a cordless drill, each screw adding a little more finality to his fate.

Outside, the world continued to turn, unaware of the cruel dance that had just played out behind closed doors. The men returned to their work, the noise and chaos of the industrial estate swallowing them whole, as if the events of the garage had never occurred.

But for those who had watched, the memory would linger, a lesson about the lengths to which some would go to protect their interests and assert their dominance. It was a world where betrayal was met with the harshest of punishments, where mercy was a foreign concept, and where the price of disloyalty was blood, pain and death.

86) Campo, Norte De Santander, Colombia

Mike looked down at the body which was now, by the breathing, pretending to be unconscious. "This cagar has cost me some good men," he said with a thick Texan accent. He kicked it savagely twice with his ornate, square-toed cowboy boots before continuing, "How the Hell did you catch it?"

"Ah Mr. Parker, the DEA are so clever now. He worked for the Jalisco Cartel in distribution before he came to me with their secrets. I killed more than 50 of their men through what he told me and gave him a good job. Never let it be said the Sinaloa do not repay debts! But look how he repaid me!"

Mike shook his head at the body and kicked it again. As it moved under the blow he saw the front teeth had been taken out and the fingers broken. The right eye socket was a mess.

"And all the time he was passing our secrets back to the Feds, the sneaky bastard." Turning to Fidel he continued, "There are some serious questions I want to ask el Zurullo here before I make an example of him. Then I will share the video with people who need to know that spying on us does not end well. I will send you a copy my friend."

Mike turned, beckoned to someone in his vehicle then nodded at the body. A heavy, swarthy man in a combination of camo and denim climbed out, slouched over and dragged the body by its feet back towards his vehicle like a sack of rubbish. Then Mike lifted his hat a little and wiped his head with his free hand.

At that signal Mac squeezed off a single shot which hit Miguel in the centre of his face as he peered out through the open truck window. The back of his head exploded. A second later an RPG rocket hit the same vehicle, roasting everyone inside and throwing the machine gun crew clear. A rear, crew-cab door on the second vehicle opened and a man rolled out before a rocket destroyed that too.

Fidel saw the assumed look of shock and horror cross Mike's face and turned to see the destruction of his vehicles. As he turned Mike caught him under the throat with his left hand and stamped hard with his left foot beside the knee bringing him straight to the ground. Stooping over him Mike locked his wrist, spun him face down and secured him with cable ties, hands behind his back.

Firing steadily at a rate of 1 round per second, Mac took down the escapee from the truck and put a bullet through each of the gun crew members, dead or alive. Rising to a kneel from his firing position, but still watching the fire zone, he picked up the radio handset. "Nine Zero, Nine One. The Chicken is in the coop. Team lit. Extraction now Over."

"Nine One Nine Zero, Copy that. Extraction minutes three over."

"Nine One Copy that. Out." Mac spoke loudly to be sure all his men heard him, "Light up laddies." Then he pulled a match box sized item on a strap from a pocket and fastened it on top of his head with the strap under his chin. It looked vaguely like a caver's head-light worn wrong.

Suddenly the hard-to-forget crack of heavy machine gun bullets passing just over his head caused him to drop flat. Then the stream of bullets moved off towards Matt and Tom. There was a short yelp followed by cursing from over that way. Mac scanned the hills opposite but could see no telltale smoke from an oiled gun barrel.

A last single round fired marked the end of a belt. There was a gap between the crack of that round and the thump of the gun firing so Mac knew it was about half a mile away, but where exactly? He picked up the handset again, "Nine Zero, Nine One we are taking fire from half a mile North of this loc. Probably a 14.5 chopper killer. We need a hot extraction from the road. Moving now over."

Nine One, Nine Zero. Copy that. Out.

"Sarge. Tom's taken a hit." Mac crawled to where Matt was bent over Tom in a hollow that gave some protection from direct fire. He was putting a tourniquet on Tom's upper arm because the lower part had been ripped off by a heavy machine gun bullet striking the elbow.

87) GCHQ, Cheltenham, Gloucestershire, UK

Amelia, the signals analyst, worked steadily transcribing an apparently harmless conversation between two men in London. They spoke in Gujari rather than the usual Urdu but she followed every word. Even the joke about the mother-in-law. Which wasn't funny. Suddenly, her screen blinked and a white warning screen flashed up, obscuring what she was working on. "Warning, signal loss. Agent Blackbeard."

Without conscious thought, Amelia instantly followed the drill. It might be life or death for the agent. For "her" handsome agent. Her fingers flickered over her keyboard as she notified her manager, James. In moments he was at her side. The unexpected breakdown in communications from Blackbeard's implant had changed his mood from relaxed and in control to just how he felt when he worked in the field; a predator on good days and a hunted animal on the others. His eyes read and re-read the simple message on Amelia's screen as if they could wring something more from it. The transmitter had pulsed once and died. The location was a road running through woods and out of town.

"Its probably not him going behind shielding so its either a rare technical malfunction or the agent was compromised." He spoke his thoughts aloud for clarity then nodded to Amelia, "Pass it to Vauxhall Cross immediately," he ordered. "MI5 needs to check on their boy."

88) Campo, Norte De Santander, Colombia

Mac assessed the injury with a practiced eye then his words came, calm and in control, "Gie him morphine an' a drip. Keep the stump up high. The choppers'll be here ony time noo. Let them tak control o' the groond then we'll leave aw oor kit but weapons an' cairry him doon the hill."

"Okay Sarge."

As he spoke the sound of heavy rotors began from nothing and rose quickly in volume as two unmarked, black painted, DEA Black Hawk helicopters came in low over a nearby ridge. One climbed to give cover and the other hugged the ground as it approached Mike's position at speed. The hidden machine gun opened up again and the tracer came closer to the lower chopper than the crew's friends would have wished.

From above, the pilot of call sign Charlie Two could follow back the tracer and see roughly where the machine gun was positioned. Over his headset he called his Crew Chief gunner. "Can you see the Lights on the Friendlies Chief?"

The Crew Chief / Starboard gunner had her infra red sensor overlaying her visor. Below it she wore a face mask brightly painted like a fanged skull. "Got the Friendlies Boss. They are on the bank to the West I can see two, no three Candles together."

"Okay Chief, I am going to swing around and give you a shot at that pesky gun."

"Thanks Boss. 'Preciate that."

Charlie Two banked left and the target swung into the Chief's view. Sitting in the open doorway her infra red sights lit up a hot machine gun and six glowing human shaped bodies clustered around it despite they were otherwise hidden by bush and shadow. A single long burst from the M134 7.62 x 51 6-barreled minigun laid fire onto the target at a rate of 6,000 rounds a minute. She watched the warm bodies break up and splash under the intense fire impassively. "Target dead Boss."

As Charlie Two circled overhead, keeping watch like a Rottweiler, Charlie One landed amongst the coca plants by the road and two of the crew leaped out to help Mike and his men get Fidel and the DEA agent aboard. Mac and Matt ran down the hill towards the chopper carrying Tom between them through the coca plants. Charlie ran behind carrying an M110 in each hand and more weapons slung across his back. Mac and Matt passed Tom into the arms of a soldier bending inside the chopper doorway then he, Matt and Charlie climbed aboard.

The Crew Chief and lifted his visor and looked to Mike. "That everyone Sir?"

Mike looked to Mac and raised his eyebrows in question. Mac Nodded. "That's all of us Chief."

The Crew Chief spoke into his headset to the pilot, "When you're ready Boss."

89) DP World London Gateway Docks, River Thames, East Of London, UK

Rain splattered down on the glistening concrete and tarmac of the DP World London Gateway, a sprawling monolith of technology and industry sitting a convenient 25 miles downstream from London's centre. The colossal quay cranes, standing as tall as the London Eye, loomed over the landscape like ancient sentinels guarding the heart of Britain's maritime industry.

A hum of machinery and the regular clang of metal on metal filled the air as the port's 60 automated stacking cranes performed their endless dance. Artificial Intelligence coordinating their movements with the 180 transaction bays for trucks and loading or stacking their shipping containers for maximum speed and efficiency.

An articulated lorry, robust and grimed from many miles of travel on wet motorways approached the gate, its wet 40-foot shipping container gleaming under the combination of electric and early morning light. The driver readied his driving licence, Port Licence and Vehicle Booking Pass for the gate operator.

"Bay C38 please," the gate operator called out after scanning the Vehicle Booking Pass, her voice crisp and professional, but her eyes softened by a smile of acknowledgment and the awareness he was right on time for his loading slot.

"Thank you, darling," the truck driver responded, his accent revealing him as a local, his voice tinged with familiarity and warmth. Glad of someone even slightly familiar to talk to. The gate lifted, and he navigated the intricate maze of London Gateway with practiced ease.

Driving towards Bay C38, the scenery was marked by the precision and elegance that gave the port its reputation. This was a place that lived and breathed efficiency, boasting the UK's longest rail terminal and an operation so slick that many found it disorienting. But not this driver. He'd been here hundreds of times, he was a seasoned pro in this industrial ballet.

As the truck pulled into the bay, a manned loading vehicle, something of a heavy duty forklift for containers, waited. Its operator shot a mock salute at the driver's helmet, a gesture of camaraderie that was returned with a wave.

Dropping out of his cab, the driver's safety boots hit the ground with a thud. He released the clips securing the container to his flatbed trailer with swift, practiced movements and stamped his feet to get the blood flowing. The road to Watford Gap Services awaited him and if he was away quickly there was still time to get there for a full-English before the rest demanded by his tachometer.

The loading vehicle's operator skilfully positioned his machine, lifting the 25-ton container with a smooth, controlled grace. Soon, it would be aboard the Maersk Reliable, docking right now from Cape Town. The ship was already carrying over 17,000 containers and capable of taking on hundreds more before gliding out again as the same tide turned, a titan of efficiency and speed.

An automated camera scanned a tag on the sealed door of the container, registering its presence in the port's computerized logistics system. All above board. Customs were pre-cleared, it was just another of the thousands of "boxes" processed smoothly each day.

As the container awaited the approach of the gantry crane to load it aboard ship, the truck driver took one last look at the bay, his eyes passing over the intricate machinery and the endless stretch of the port, a world he felt at home in. It was a fleeting moment, but one that connected him to the rhythm of this industrial marvel, to the heartbeat of a system that never stopped.

With a wave to a fork-lift driver and a last glance at Bay C38, he climbed back into his cab and headed towards the exit gate, leaving behind the most technically advanced container port in the UK. The rain continued to fall, a soft drumming on the roof of his cab, and the hidden cargo began its 25 hour journey towards Rotterdam.

Inside his pitch black coffin, inside the container, clueless as to his destination, Faris felt the very slight rocking movement and another wave of dread ran through his cold, aching body.

90) Defence Science and Technology Laboratory, Porton Down, UK

Inside the cold walls of Professor Tribble's underground laboratory at Porton Down, the hum of some high-tech piece of equipment made a somehow fitting background to the varied tasks being carried out. Shelves lined with chemical vials, microscopes, and complex machinery gave notice of experiments in progress and reflected the peculiar genius of the space's chief inhabitant. Jeremy, a diligent young PhD biochemist, should have been fixated on a microscope, but his attention occasionally wandered to the more interesting spectacle playing out a few feet from his station.

A very robust dentist's chair, fitted with restraining straps, held a captive that didn't belong in the conventional medical realm. Indeed, a captive who very much did not want to be there at all: Hernan Torres, the notorious Mexican Cartel Boss. Torres's eyes, filled with rage and terror, darted around the room, while his mouth spewed threats in rapid Mexican Spanish. "My lawyers will bankrupt you and you will be locked up for your life. I have friends here in high places."

His profane protestations filled the laboratory, clashing oddly with the sterile surroundings. The scientists and security officers in the room maintained their composure; they had all seen something similar before.

Professor Tribble, a man with a mind so intricate some thought it a little out of kilter, stepped across and looked down at Torres eyes with an expression of cold curiosity. The expression and the level of concern one might expect of a scientist about to do something to a lab rat. Standing beside him was Ralf Burgin. His face too was impassive, then a slight smile dared to play around the edges of his lips as he spoke in fluent Spanish, his voice dripping with controlled menace.

"Lawyers do not count for anything here Torres. In this establishment you are playing with the big boys. And there are no rules." The words seemed to cut through Torres's anger, leaving him in a sullen silence. He looked from Burgin to Tribble, his eyes widening as he grasped the gravity of his situation.

"I don't believe you. What are you going to do?" he asked, his voice hoarse, barely more than a whisper.

"You will be interrogated under sodium pentathol," Burgin replied smoothly. "It's quick and painless, and it will reveal your deepest secrets."

Strangely, Torres's body seemed to relax at this assurance, and he even ventured to add, "Such a confession, under drugs, will not stand in court. My friends will pay for my release. It will happen."

"I'm sure you have good friends, and nothing to worry about," Ralf smiled, his voice dripping with false reassurance. Torres's eyes closed briefly. The calm before the storm.

"Please go ahead, Professor," Ralf commanded.

Tribble moved forward, his hand rock steady as he injected Torres's upper arm with an almost clear liquid. His eyes flicked to the sweeping second hand of the clock on the wall. "About a minute will be sufficient."

Torres's head dropped to his left shoulder, his breath slowing. A minute passed in silence, filled only with the soft whirring of machinery and the muted clinking of lab tools. Monitoring his vital signs, Tribble nodded, "He will be amenable now, Sir."

Ralf turned to Torres, his voice now gentle but firm. He questioned the cartel boss in perfect Castilian Spanish, probing for information.

Torres replied in his accented Mexican Spanish, the words flowing easily, his defenses completely destroyed. He seemed pathetically eager to help a friend. Such is the effect of sodium pentathol.

"I want to help you get home soon Hernan, so you must answer my questions."

"My pleasure, senor."

"How do you ship your cocaine to the UK Hernan?"

"We ship from the port of Cartagena on the Caribbean to the port of Lagos, Nigeria as part of our rice exports. From there our wares go by freighter to the port of Tarifa in Spain. From there overland, normally by train to a container port in Rotterdam in the Netherlands and then by container to London."

"Have you been adding anything to your wares recently Hernan?"

"No, senor, never. My cocaine is first quality and pure so I can command the best price."

"Is there anything else you can tell me about your shipping?"

"Would you like to know the names of the ships, senor?"

"I don't think that will be necessary, Hernan. Thank you."

"You are very welcome, senor," Torres murmured as the interrogation ended, his eyes glazed and vacant in the drug induced trance.

Burgin turned to Tribble, his voice clipped. "That will be all. Thank you professor."

Tribble injected a dose of methylethylglutarimide, "This will bring Torres back to normal consciousness almost immediately, sir." The excitement in Tribble's eyes was impossible to ignore as he looked at Torres with something akin to hunger.

Torres opened his eyes and looked at Ralf with a definite alertness, "Well? Did you learn what you needed to know?"

"Can I have him now, please, sir?"

Torres looked at Tribble, then at Ralf and he appeared worried, "What does he mean?"

Ralf's smile was polite, but his eyes betrayed a momentary hint of discomfort. Tribble's brilliance was matched only by his strangeness, a characteristic that often made interactions with him unsettling. First he replied to Torres, "Remember, Torres, big boys' rules? We are done with you now."

Torres visibly relaxed.

Ralf continued, "He is my present to you, Professor. Enjoy."

Tribble's response was almost childlike in its enthusiasm, his hands rubbing together in glee. "Oh, thank you, thank you, sir!"

A momentary look of horror flashed across the face of a tough looking MOD police officer. Then it was gone and his face blank once more.

Torres realised what Ralf meant, "No, you can't do that! No…"

Ralf turned and left the laboratory, followed by the MOD police officer to leave Tribble with his new "subject," the door clicked shut, sealing the secrets within. In this laboratory, Professor Tribble's planned experiments continued and Hernan Torres awaited his turn.

91) St. James's Park, City Of Westminster, London, UK

St James's Park, in the heart of London, was gently alive with the muted sounds of nature on an early, pleasant morning. The sun was still low in the sky, casting a golden glow on the tranquil waters of the pond. Flocks of ducks swam lazily, creating soft ripples on the water's surface. Towering trees adorned with lush green leaves framed the scene, while the distant murmur of traffic hinted at the already bustling city beyond.

Sir Henry Attwood stood at the pond's edge, his eyes narrowed in concentration as he methodically tore slices of bread taken from the paper bag clutched in his hand. The ducks, apparently aware of the upcoming ritual, gathered around, their beaks agape, quacking expectantly.

As Henry tossed the bread into the water, the ducks lunged, their beaks snapping, a cacophony of quacks and splashes. A happy smile tugged at the corners of Henry's mouth as he observed their antics, momentarily lost in the simple joy of it all.

A figure approached, the crisp sound of leather soles on gravel announcing his presence. Ralf Burgin joined Henry, pulling a plastic bag of locally purchased bird seed from his coat pocket. He began to feed the ducks a couple of yards away, his movements more measured and controlled.

Without looking, Ralf spoke, "White bread is bad for ducks you know, Henry."

Henry looked across, his eyes twinkling with mock contempt. "Ducks so enjoy bread, Ralf. There is little enough joy in the world," he remarked, his voice dripping with meaning.

Ralf looked up from his ducks, a hint of amusement in his eyes. "I had a result from Torres," he said evenly, ignoring Henry's quip.

Henry's face broke into a genuine smile. "I hear so, Ralf. And then you left him with that creature Tribble. How do you sleep?" he asked, his tone light but probing.

Ralf's face remained impassive, his eyes betraying nothing. "Tribble is a valuable man, so I keep him happy, I pander to his little foibles."

Henry laughed quietly and shook his head, his eyes wide with mock disbelief. "Foibles! What did Torres say, exactly?"

Ralf's expression tightened. "He is not adding anything himself to the cocaine. His transit route goes through Nigeria, Port of Lagos, and I think that is where we will find the drug being doctored."

Henry's brows furrowed, his mind whirring. Nodded to himself, "Fits with what Natalia told us. So it might be true. I think we can safely ask Reaper to take a look now we have our sources covered with the Torres capture."

Ralf nodded in agreement, his face blank. "Natalia is likely dead now anyway. Are you going to brief the CIA with what we learned from Torres?"

"I don't think so, Ralf, as far as the real shipping route is concerned anyway, but they will be interested in what we know about the cocaine additive. It will keep them happy for a while. They don't need to know about the Russians being in Lagos in case they put some men on the ground there and get in our people's way."

Ralf's lips twitched into a brief smile, attempting humour. "All we need is a battalion of shaven-headed marines breaking up the place before we have a chance to do what is necessary."

"Indeed, Ralf, indeed." Henry's voice grew firm, his eyes sharp. "Send Reaper and his Scots terrier off to Nigeria to find out where the adulteration of the drug is taking place and have him draw up a plan to collect evidence of their activities. Embassy will support them, I'll pass word on that. And I will thank our American friends and pass them a titbit to keep them sweet."

With those final words, the two men exchanged knowing glances, their faces reflecting the weight of the decisions made. They turned back to the ducks, their thoughts perhaps shifting back to the peaceful scene before them.

92) The Nigerian Port Authority Offices, Alakoro Marina Street, Lagos, Nigeria

Phillip Babatunde slipped another memory stick into the computer purring away under his busy desk. His fingers danced briefly over the keyboard and he hit Enter. A graphic appeared on screen, the bar quickly filling with green as the information was transferred. With a few deft clicks, a detailed record of all the shipping that had passed through Lekki Deep Sea Port in the last month had been transferred to the stick and he slipped it into his pocket. This ritual had become something of a routine over the last year, a quiet secret that brought great comfort to his pockets.

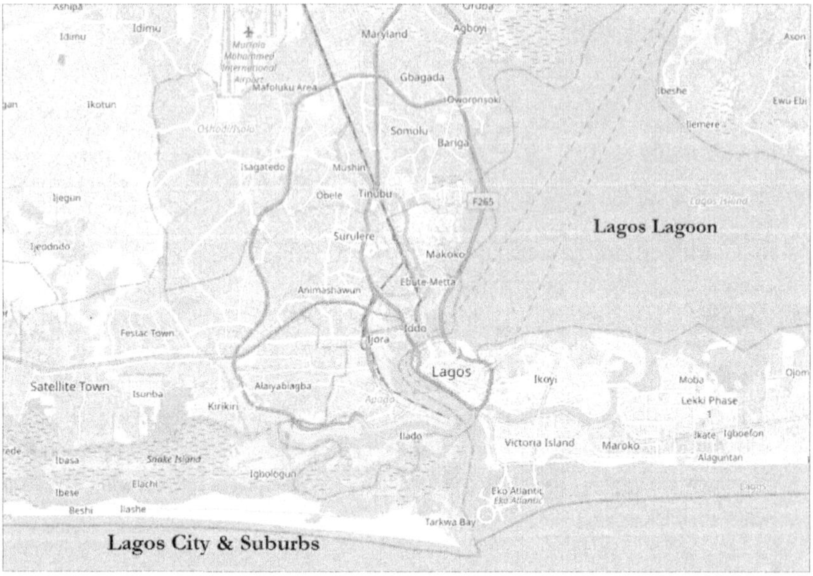

The Nigerian Port Authority was a grand establishment which faced West over the seaway entry to Lagos Lagoon, a towering behemoth of concrete and steel controlling the sea ports which connected Nigeria into the very arteries of world trade.

The port itself was a bustling hub of activity, with around 1,000 medium-sized freight vessels carrying 5,700,000 tonnes of cargo entering and leaving the Lagos port complex each year. Petroleum tankers glided in and out from the refinery area, bulk freighters and container carriers arrived at their berths and the giant cranes reached down like the arms of mechanical titans, unloading and loading containers with relentless activity.

The building Phillip worked in was a marvel of engineering, built by the Chinese, like so much of the infrastructure in Lagos, and funded by their mysterious deals, their investments buying them dominance and more than half of the port business. But what did Phillip care for politics? That was a game played by rich men in high towers. It was here that Phillip had found his calling, working dutifully for three years now since the new, extended port opened.

No, all Phillip wanted was to provide for his children, his wife and his girlfriend, and the port had been good to him in that regard. Though payment of the regular salary was four months behind still, Phillip had found a way to make ends more than meet. Through a peculiar twist of fate, he had come to assist both the British Embassy and the Russian Embassy in acquiring detailed records of shipping, crew, cargoes, and related matters.

"You're helping international business, Phillip," he repeated to himself, a contented smile spreading across his face. Both of his contacts had told him that same thing so it must be true. He knew he was doing something valuable anyway, something that paid twice. And best of all, these foreign businessmen paid on time and in cash every month.

With an hour to go before the end of his shift, Phillip settled back in his comfy chair, his gaze drawn to the large window opposite. A ship was being pushed into her berth by tugs as the derrick cranes loomed like watchful sentinels, ready to descend and pick up their next load. "One day," Phillip whispered, his eyes narrowing with longing, "I'll visit those distant, glamorous places like Rotterdam and London."

The port was a gateway to the world, a place of dreams and opportunities. As he watched a vessel being dragged out into the main fairway, ready to steam over the horizon, Phillip felt a thrill of excitement at the unknown and marvellous prospects that lay beyond his home shores. But for now, he was content with his small but significant role, a small but happy cog in the machine that fuelled the very pulse of global trade.

93) Ralf Burgin's Office, SIS headquarters, 85 Albert Embankment, Vauxhall Cross, London, UK

The view from his penthouse office at SIS headquarters on 85 Albert Embankment Vauxhall Cross was breathtaking, overlooking the busy River Thames with Vauxhall Bridge to the left and, opposite, the city's age-old structures and towering skyscrapers. Here, ensconced in a stylish office adorned with beautiful classical furniture and the finest art, sat Ralf Burgin. To be fair to him, he was almost as big a player as he thought he was.

Ralf looked up from his desk as the door swung open, and his sharp eyes met Mike's intense blue gaze. Mike's lean and athletic figure blocking the doorway for a moment as he habitually scanned the room for threats before entering.

"Mike, come in, please," Ralf said warmly, standing to greet his guest, an arm indicating a comfortable seat across the desk. Though his front was overtly friendly and relaxed, there was a hint of tension, there was something he was uncomfortable about lingering just beneath the surface. Mike mentally flagged that fact.

Mike strode across the room, his desert boots silent on the woollen carpeting, and took the seat across from Ralf. His lanky frame was relaxed, but his mind was alert. He knew Ralf well enough to sense that something important was coming.

"Well done picking Torres up for us Mike. Thanks came in from the CIA bods too. You impressed a few people over there."

Mike shrugged non-committally, "Some good men there," Was this just a standard "stroke" from Ralf or did he feel guilty about something?

Ralf leaned back in his chair, "The final interrogation of Hernan Torres confirmed some of our suspicions. Torres isn't actually responsible for the additives in the drug shipments, but he is shipping pure cocaine to Lagos, Nigeria, in cargoes of rice. That's the usual drug transit country for his wares and many others, so it's very likely where the additive is being added. Its certainly the next place to look."

Mike nodded non-committally, absorbing the information. He was no stranger to the world of espionage, and he understood the layers of deception and misdirection that often came with the territory. What Ralf said was likely true as far as it went.

"We suspect the Russians are behind this plot and therefore must have some kind of warehouse in Lagos to do the actual work, perhaps a rice wholesale business of some kind because the cocaine comes in rice shipments." Ralf continued, his voice measured." But we need incriminating evidence, cast iron proof of their activities to show at NATO and get broad support for pressure against the Russians. Something to definitely incriminate them."

The room fell silent for a moment as the gravity of the situation settled in. Mike's mind was racing, piecing together the puzzle. He could sense there was more to the story, but Ralf's face revealed nothing.

"I want you to go to Nigeria," Ralf finally said, leaning forward. "Find out where the drugs are being doctored and who is doing it. The first priority is to get some good photos of the operation and the people there. Shutting the operation down would be a bonus, but we can discuss that when we know what's happening for sure. Oh yes, and it needs doing in the next few days before they release the crazy-powder onto our streets."

Mike's eyes narrowed, and he studied Ralf for a moment. He had a nagging feeling that Ralf was being economical with the truth. But he accepted it; this was necessary or habitual in intelligence work.

"Understood, Ralf. I'm glad there is no pressure." Mike replied, his voice steady. "I'll get to the bottom of this and find the evidence we need."

Ralf smiled, though his eyes remained guarded. "I know you will, Mike."

With a firm handshake, they sealed the agreement, and Mike stood to leave. As he made his way to the door, he glanced back at Ralf, who was already absorbed in his paperwork.

The mission was clear, but the waters were murky. Mike knew he was being sent into a potentially unfriendly situation with limited support and probably not all the facts that Ralf knew. Still, it could be worse. He could be polishing Ralf's chair with his trousers.

As he stepped out of the office and onto the Thames Embankment to stretch his legs, he felt a surge of anticipation, excitement.

94) Interrogation Room Beneath GRU HQ, Lubhynka Square, Moscow, Russia

Faris Iqbal's breath hung in the frigid air of the cell and he shivered as he awaited his fate. The room was a dismal place, painted cream above the 1 meter line and dark brown below. Doubtless part of the softening process, the cold had seeped into his very bones. He had been in there for what felt like an eternity, left to ponder the situation he had found himself in. Standard police tactics. Intel too.

Finally, the heavy door creaked open and two armed guards stepped in. Their faces were stern, their eyes cold. "Prikhodit!" With a curt head-jerk, they gestured for him to come with them. Faris rose, his joints aching from the chill, the wound under his right arm sore. He was led between the guards and out of the cell.

They walked through endless corridors, a maze of lifeless walls and dim lighting, all in the same depressing decor. The sound of their footsteps echoed through the hollow spaces, a constant oppressive atmosphere. Up several floors, then they took a lift, a mechanical groan announcing their arrival at their destination.

The interrogation room awaited them, as stark and devoid of warmth as the cell. Two hard-faced GRU officers were seated at a table, their eyes like shards of ice as they appraised Faris.

"Sit down," one of the officers commanded, his voice devoid of emotion.

Faris took a seat, avoiding their eyes and doing his best to appear scared and humble. He knew he had to play his part convincingly.

"We know who you are," the other officer said, his voice dripping with contempt. "You're a spy for MI5."

Faris's eyes widened, and he put on an act of confusion. "Nah, mate, you got it all wrong," he said, slipping into street patois. "I ain't no spy. I was just a paid informer for the Feds. They was going to lock me up for drug dealing, but they gave me a way out, innit?"

The GRU officers exchanged a glance, their faces unreadable. "We don't believe you," one said coldly, in perfect English with a slight Russian accent. "You are an MI5 agent, and they fitted you with their tracking equipment. You will labour in a Gulag camp for the rest of your life if you do not confess."

Faris's heart pounded in his chest, but he stuck to his story. "I swear, that's all there is to it. Don't the Feds use that kit all the time? I ain't no secret agent. Just a bloke trying to get by."

The interrogation continued, the GRU officers pressing him, accusing him, but Faris never wavered. He knew that any sign of changing his story would be his downfall. He padded out his cover with some memories of his family. His little girl.

Finally, some hours later, the officers seemed to have had enough. With a curt nod, they dismissed him, and the same guards escorted him back to his cell.

Once Faris was out of the room, the GRU officers leaned back in their chairs, their faces relaxed into thoughtful expressions as a junior brought tea brewed in the Russian style.

"I think he was telling the truth," one of them said, his voice tinged with a hint of disappointment. "He was just a police stooge."

The other officer nodded, a frown creasing his brow. "It seems we might have been mistaken. The NCA do use informers and equipment like this. No matter, he was never going to be more than a pawn for whoever was running him."

"I do not think he is worth any more of our time, Yuri. We should send him for processing."

Back in his cold cell, Faris let out a breath he hadn't realized he'd been holding. The ordeal was over, at least for now. And no torture, which was good. He knew that he had played his part well, but the fear still gnawed at him. What would they do with him? Have him disappear into the endless Russian prison system? Please God no.

The eyes of the GRU would be watching him right now, cameras anyway, and he knew that he would have to tread carefully and keep playing his part if he wanted to survive. And get home to little Maryam. He was a pawn in a game much larger than himself, caught between powers that could crush him without noticing. All he could do was hold on to his story and hope that it would be enough to see him through.

As he settled back onto the hard bench, he noticed he was shivering again. But hope remained. He couldn't shake the feeling that something would happen to change his circumstances for the better. It was early days yet so still time for the diplomats to earn their corn. Surely he wouldn't be left in a cell for life?

95) The King's Private Office, Buckingham Palace, London, UK

A liveried footman opened the gilded door, its Georgian opulence glittering in the soft lighting of the corridor. Mike stepped through into the King's private office once more, the muted sound of his footsteps resonating in his head like an intruder in some sultan's inner sanctum. Memories of the time when he had been recruited by his namesake, Uncle Michael, an old family friend, a retired Major General, to work directly for the King, flashed through his mind. The mission statement had been clear: "You will support the King's efforts behind the scenes to watch over his people."

Mike didn't think it strange that he had never seen the King even once until the previous month. He had expected to be merely a cog in a vast machine, never laying eyes on the boss. Yet here he was, meeting the King himself for the second time in just two months. Was something bigger afoot? A promotion perhaps? Pride showed a dorsal fin to ego. The thought was not unwelcome.

The King was alone in his office, a spacious room adorned with tasteful art and filled with the gentle scent of aged wood and a trace of… perhaps aftershave. He stood to greet Mike, his hand outstretched, his eyes filled with genuine warmth. Mike was still slightly unsure of the proper protocol with a king, but he managed to come to attention and bow slightly from the neck before advancing to shake hands. Trying to watch himself from the outside, Mike thought the King seemed a decent man, Certainly a smart one.

"Thank you, Colonel," the King replied, smiling. "I've heard what a good job you and Sergeant MacLeish did in Colombia. Well done."

Mike mumbled something self-deprecatory, a faint blush colouring his cheeks.

"I've also heard about your next mission in Nigeria," the King continued, his voice growing more businesslike. "I'll be watching events carefully."
Mike carefully said nothing.

"Let me paint the picture as we see it here. You stop me if you think we have it wrong. The Russians are attempting to destabilize the British government by adding a substance to cocaine that turns users into murdering psychopaths. The population would be overcome by fear and horror, and the government would likely collapse in the face of such chaos and the media attacks and back-biting which would accompany it. The purpose of their operation is to put pressure on the government of UK to cease their resistance to Russian moves in Ukraine."

"That seems to sum it up Your Majesty."

"Sir is quite sufficient in private, Colonel." The king spoke kindly, "They've been testing modifications of this additive in Bradford. Very soon they're expected to go national. We must prevent this at all costs."

The King caught Mikes eyes and looked through him, "It is likely there is a hidden Russian base in Nigeria where the cocaine from Colombia is being laced with the deadly additive."

"That's what I have been told, sir."

"We have believed this to be the case for a while but could not have you go there direct due to the risk that would cause for another of our sources. To sum up," the King said, his eyes locked on Mike's, "it is supremely important that you find out where the Russian base is and get some hard proof of what they are up to. Probably you have a week to achieve this. Should you need additional support, you can rely upon my people. Military, diplomatic, or technical assistance, whatever is available. Call my people on our secure channel for support."

"So in essence, I should continue my mission for SIS as per their instruction but I have Palace intel, military and diplomatic support if I require it?"

"In a nutshell, yes, subject to the usual political restraints. Good luck Colonel."

Mike left the King's office, a flurry of mixed emotions churning within him. The trust and confidence placed in him by the King moved him deeply, but the weight of the mission also laid heavily on his shoulders. Lagos was big, almost twice the population of London, and the port itself had an immense commercial area. How could he possibly uncover the Russians' hidden base? Doubts nagged at him, but he pushed them aside. Once on the ground, he would learn more and the guys at the embassy always knew what was happening on their turf. That's how things usually worked.

As he strode through the beautiful rooms of the Palace, Mike's mind was a whirl of thoughts and plans as determination set in. He would not fail his King or his country. The game was afoot, and he would play his part.

96) Correctional Wing, Lefortovo Prison, East Side Of Moscow, Russia

Faris Iqbal's life had shifted dramatically since his transition from the cold, unforgiving depths of the GRU's interrogation complex to the outskirts of Moscow, where he was now imprisoned in a civilian detention center. Gone were the dark brown and cream-painted walls of his cell, replaced by a space equally as austere in white, but filled with quite a pleasant mix of characters. Certainly pleasant compared to the people he was dealing with in Bradford.

The gangsters and hardened criminals were there, certainly, their faces etched with a lifetime of ruthless choices. Russia was a hard country, after all. But the majority of the inmates were ordinary people, incarcerated not for violent crimes but for their political beliefs or resistance to the war in Ukraine. It was an unusual blend that gave the prison an atmosphere less dominated by brutality and more governed by a collective resistance to state oppression.

What struck Faris most was that omnipresent feature of Russian life; the corruption that seemed to seep into even the bleakest corners of the prison. It was as if the very fabric of society was woven with bribery and trade, creating a thriving internal economy. Here, almost anything could be bartered, from food to clothes, cigarettes to paper. If one knew how to navigate the system, privileges, even relative comfort were within reach.

Faris was shrewd enough to play this game and play it well, he came from a line of traders and it was in his blood, so life was rapidly getting physically more comfortable. He knew the value of silence and the power of listening. By ensuring that no one knew of his near-native understanding of the Russian language, he used a type of Pigeon-Russian to become an invisible observer, a dealer privy to whispers and secrets. His quiet facade and fair trading won the trust of many and allowed him to glean information that might someday prove vital.

But surviving was only a temporary part of the equation. Faris's future remained shrouded in uncertainty. Interrogation seemed to be behind him, but at any moment, he could be shipped off to a labour camp, his existence reduced to an endless cycle of toil and suffering.

He had learned much, but the path ahead was still unknown and potentially awful. Every day was a delicate dance, balancing between the need to keep his head down and the instinct to learn and plan for something more. In a world where silence was his armour and information his currency, Faris continued to navigate the intricate maze of prison life, all the while knowing that his true challenge lay in what awaited beyond those walls. What came next.

As days turned into weeks, the urge grew within him to act, to find a way out. He held it down. For now, he was merely a spectator of no importance in the system and he should keep it that way. An escape attempt would be stupid. But the time might come when he would be able to take control of his destiny and he would be ready. Until then, Faris Iqbal must remain the silent observer, his spirit unbowed and his eyes always watching, always learning.

97) Defence Science and Technology Laboratory, Porton Down, UK

Ralf 's Audi Q7 SUV glided smoothly over the asphalt, a machine of precision and comfort that matched his meticulous personality. The country roads that led to Porton Down were scenic and picturesque, a stark contrast to the facility's grim aura. As he approached the armed security point, Ralf's stern expression did not waver. He knew what lay ahead; he'd been here many times before.

Without a word, he handed his SIS ID to the gate guard, receiving a respectful salute in return while the car was scanned electronically and his face run through recognition software. The guard's eyes avoided Ralf's, acknowledging the power and authority he held. The gate creaked open, and Ralf drove through, his mind turning to the task at hand.

Porton Down, with its history of secrets and experiments, felt like a place touched by darkness. Even the beauty of the drive down from London, following the M3 from the M25, couldn't insulate him from the chill that settled in his bones each time he arrived. But today's visit was essential. He needed to keep Professor Tribble happy and motivated. A peculiar man, Tribble, but a genius whose work had bolstered Ralf's career and would continue to do so if he played him right.

Ralf navigated the familiar corridors and made his way into Tribble's lab unannounced. The security at Porton Down was a paradox; impenetrable on the outside but surprisingly lax once within its walls. At least in this sector. Even Ralf didn't know about the cameras "manned" by AI which measured his every step.

Tribble looked up from a bench where he appeared to have been working on a severed hand, the fingers extended straight by wires. His face momentarily clouded with confusion before recognition dawned. "What can I do for you, sir?" he asked, his voice tinged with curiosity.

Ralf knew exactly how to handle Tribble. With a smile that didn't quite reach his eyes, he began to lavish praise on the scientist. A young lady assistant nearby rolled her eyes, but Ralf was undeterred. He knew what made Tribble tick, knew how to manipulate his vanity.

"The work you're doing here," Ralf said, leaning in, "is vital to British security Professor. The Prime Minister himself sent me to check on your progress with the additive found in the cocaine seizures in the Bradford area."

Tribble's reaction was almost visceral. He purred like a contented kitten, his smile widening in a way that sent a shiver down Ralf's spine. He spoke excitedly, slipping from Latin to Greek and back to English as he did so. Detailing his findings of four chemical variants, each capable of turning a cocaine user into a crazed, fearless killer, reminiscent of the legendary Viking Berserkers.

"Some of the variants work quicker than others, some last longer once in effect, some work on everyone and some not," Tribble added, his eyes gleaming, "but they all lead to the user snatching up any available weapon and attacking anyone they can find. The drive is so strong and out of conscious control that they begin hacking at themselves if they are denied a victim."

Ralf's mind briefly stumbled over the implications of that last statement. How did Tribble know such specific details? Then it hit him. He knew very well that Tribble had been testing this drug on human subjects right here in the lab. It would be ironic if this had been tested on Torres.

“I have something to show you, sir,” Tribble waved an arm to follow, nodded to an assistant, and headed away. Ralf followed him, half dreading what was coming. Tribble lead Ralf along a corridor and into a small room with a large armoured viewing window opening into another room. Presumably the glass was a mirror from the other side.

A youngish woman and a middle aged man, both with a rather weathered appearance and tattoos, were secured into strong chairs, each by a metal clasp around their necks. The young assistant entered the room accompanied by two armed guards and injected the woman in the arm. The assistant stepped out and was followed closely by the obviously nervous guards, the door locked behind them.

Tribble pressed a button and released both the restraints. The two subjects remained in their chairs staring around them, clearly they had recently been placed there. The man turned to the woman and said, "What's the crack here? You good?" The woman said nothing and the man stood, then walked around the room, a trace of confident swagger in his step.

A few moments later the woman leapt from her chair and attacked the man like a wildcat. She raked his face with her nails then, showing far greater than usual strength, she smashed his head against the edge of a work surface time and again until blood splattered and his legs gave way. He had been totally unable to withstand her assault due to her overwhelming strength. When he hit the floor she found a light stand and began beating his limp body with boundless energy.

Tribble caught Ralf's blank eye, "Of course, they were vagrants that we use merely for experiments."

Suppressing a wave of revulsion, Ralf nodded, carefully thanking Tribble for his diligence. He couldn't afford to let his personal feelings interfere with the mission. Tribble was a necessary tool, one that Ralf had to wield with care.

As he left the lab, the unsettling nature of Tribble's work lingered in Ralf's mind. He thought of the sailing trip that awaited him with old Robin in Southampton, a temporary escape from the dark shadows of Porton Down. But he knew that he couldn't completely shake off the feeling of unease. It clung to him like a silent whisper, a reminder of the price paid for national security – and personal power.

Behind him, Porton Down stood as a fortress of secrets and transgressions, its walls hiding a world where morality was a negotiable commodity, and where men like Tribble thrived. Ralf knew that this was part of the game, a game he had chosen to play, no matter the cost. He didn't have to like all of it.

98) A Cell Beneath GRU HQ, Lubhynka Square, Moscow, Russia

Natalia Kuznetsova's small cell was dark brown and cream. The institutionally painted, concrete walls closed in on her like an endless winter. The one window high on one wall, less than a foot across and wire-reinforced, frosted glass with one iron bar. She sat on the hard bed, her body wrapped in an old army blanket over an expensive but thin dress. A shiver ran through her that had nothing to do with the temperature. Her eyes, vacant and distant, stared unseeing at the wall, her mind adrift.

Images of her stern but loving husband, Nikolai, filled her thoughts, followed by the smiling face of her beloved son, Alexander. Her heart ached with a mixture of love, fear for him, uncertainty. She never allowed herself to ponder her own future, focusing instead on her prayers to God for Alexander's safety. The knowledge that her actions would have caused problems for Nikolai weighed on her, but not too heavily as she knew her husband could handle whatever came his way. He was a survivor.

The sudden metallic clack at the door jerked Natalia from her reverie. The door swung open on stiff, protesting hinges, and a different guard stepped into thc ccll. His face was expressionless, his eyes devoid of warmth or sympathy. Natalia sensed something amiss.

“What is your name, Comrade?”

"Natalia Kuznetsova," she replied to his question, her voice steady but laced with an undercurrent of concern. "Have you heard anything of my son, Alexander?" she asked, unable to keep the desperation from her voice.

“No.” The response was cold, detached.

The guard's instructions were curt, his tone final. Natalia knew what was coming now. A chill ran down her spine, but she showed no fear, no emotion. Her face was a mask of calm bravery as she looked into the guard's dead, unseeing eyes. There was no humanity there, no compassion. He told her to turn around and face the wall. She did so, her body obedient, her mind strangely detached.

The sound of the leather holster cover unfastening was loud in the silence of the cell. Natalia held her breath, her body tense, her heart pounding. She knew what was coming, yet there was no thought of escape, no plea for mercy.

The shot from the Makarov was swift and merciless. It tore up through the back of her neck and through her brain stem, bringing instant death. Her body crumpled to the tiled floor, her left eye popping out and hanging from her cheek in a grotesque testament to the brutality of her execution.

The guard's movements were methodical, practised, as he replaced his pistol in the holster. He searched Natalia's clothes, his hands rough and impersonal, looking for cash or valuables. He removed her wedding ring and placed it in his pocket. The only thing worth taking. Her life had been reduced to a mere transaction, her death a cold and calculated act.

As he left the cell, the door clanged shut, sealing away the evidence of a life extinguished. Natalia Kuznetsov's body lay on the floor, a tragic end to a woman whose only crime was her love for her family and her faith in her beliefs. The sound of the guard calling for a cleaner echoed along the corridor.

Outside, the world moved on, oblivious to the horror within the cell. The guard went to make his report, his face impassive, his conscience untouched by the execution of a traitor. But in that small, cold room, the echoes of the shot lingered, a haunting reminder of a system that valued power and control above human dignity and compassion.

99) Unit 23a, Badia Industrial Park, Lagos Ports Complex, Lagos, Nigeria

Lagos city, on the sea coast of Nigeria, West Africa, is a place of contrasts. The city has developed around a huge natural deepwater harbour, Lagos Lagoon several miles in extent, which is now a hive of shipping activity. Modern skyscrapers cluster and scatter across the landscape like an archipelago of isolated, protected islands with, between them, huge waterways spanned by modern bridges, areas of thriving industry and a ground-cover of tin-roofed shanty towns.

The ubiquitous rusting corrugated iron and ancient handmade brick was the trademark of Lagos. A thriving place of, officially some fifteen million, but in reality twenty four million souls crowding in from the countryside and all striving for a taste of the good life that money can buy so cheaply in Nigeria. And some were doing very well indeed.

But poverty and endemic corruption made life difficult for the average citizen so they grew up strong and streetwise. If you built more than a street stall and had no contacts, someone would take it away from you so why bother? But despite their struggles, the average Nigerian was a happy and welcoming person. It is just that some of them were so poor and desperate they had to rob and steal to feed their families. Life could be very cruel in Lagos.

The Badia Industrial Park sat within the heavily gated security of the Lagos Ports Complex and fronted onto a seaway leading into Lagos Lagoon. This mile-wide stretch of water is chiefly a highway for huge ships and forms the main access into Lagos Lagoon proper; which is so huge it is more like an inland sea. But even this entry-way has multiple berths for oil tankers along its Northern perimeter.

West along the shore was the Apapa Bulk Terminal and opposite, across the water, was Lagos Island and Freedom Park. But all that could be seen through the polluted air over the water was a scattering of sky scrapers behind the newly constructed Ring Road. A colossal super-highway of eight lanes built on concrete stilts which ran the length of that shore. The traffic was already so heavy it looked like a car park.

A hundred yards from the water, and hidden away on a cul de sac amongst countless identical siblings, sat Unit 23a. Truck sized roller shutters and a steel pedestrian door gave access at the front to a flat-topped, concrete box with a walled compound behind. Above the triple-height warehouse space was a floor of offices with windows all around, accessed from the warehouse by an open stairway attached to the wall inside. Without the number, stencilled-in two foot high white paint letters on the road-facing wall, 23a would be indistinguishable from a thousand other units in the area. But inside it was a different story.

Out to the rear of the unit, inside the high-walled compound, there were several more sheds and shipping containers all on concrete hard-standing. The tall vehicle access gate to the rear had been custom made in sheet steel for additional privacy. A near-new pick up truck decorated with a few dents was parked by the gate.

Inside the warehouse, pallets were neatly laid out in parallel rows across one side of the concrete floor and most were stacked with sacks of rice. An idle butane-gas powered fork-lift truck stood ready to move or load them onto a visiting lorry. There was a forty foot shipping container, locked, which gave a little added security or privacy for goods in need of more discrete handling. And finally, the whole operation was visible from a porta-cabin office against the back wall, an oasis of calm, a refuge of air-conditioned cool air in a hot dusty workplace.

Within the office were three white men in what Russians considered to be appropriate tropical wear. Light slacks and safari shirts wet with sweat. Half a dozen Nigerians clad in various shades of rag moved sacks around under the guidance of another Russian. Casual labourers without papers, they were glad of another day's pay for easy work in the shade.

Unit 23a was a storage and trans-shipping facility, totally invisible amongst countless others of its kind. And therein lay its value. If there were any one thing to distinguish 23a from its fellows it might be the small satellite dish hidden at ground level in the compound, away from prying eyes.

To the knowledgeable observer it was of a slightly different type to the ubiquitous satellite TV dishes nailed to almost every building, and it was aimed at a different point in the sky to the rest. This because it was pointing towards a Russian communications satellite. But no passer-by ever looked over the high wall. In any event, few of the locals were space-scientists; and they were all too busy making a living.

One of the men in the makeshift office, Colonel Dimitri Petrenko sat at a folding table, half a mug of strong but cold coffee beside the lap top he was concentrating on. Columns of figures covered the screen as he checked the progress of their work in the warehouse. Then he tapped a key to show a map; the next incoming shipment of rice from Columbia. Mostly rice, anyway. The last satellite update showed the ship approaching the coast but Phillip had not yet notified the embassy of its arrival.

Dimitri was dragged from his concentration by a tap on his shoulder from a younger man. He turned, his eyes expressing first a query, then understanding as he was handed a note. There was no salutation and it was unsigned, as ever, but it was clearly from his father General Leonid Petrenko.

His dad was head of the dreaded GRU, but a good old guy all the same, and he missed him on this posting. But this was not the regular, "How's it going son," note, which came in every week, it was a warning. And a warning from his dad ought to be taken very seriously.

"The British captured Torres so they must have known their cocaine originates Colombia
And now they know that it passes through Lagos.
They do not know about our man in his operation.
They know, or will assume, your operation exists.
They are sending a picked agent, a Colonel Reaper, to find your location and recce or terminate you.
He will be working with minimum support and undercover.
Capture him and send him to me if you can.
Otherwise kill him.
I will have our embassy support you.
Be careful, he is a smart and dangerous man."

Dimitri spoke quietly to his father across the miles, "Spasibo papa." Thanks Dad.

100) La Veranda Restaurant, Bluefish Hotel, Oju Olobun Close, Lagos, Nigeria

In the dimly lit room, a partitioned chamber filled with the lingering scent of cigars and the weight of confidential conversations, Phillip Babatunde was a study in composure. He portrayed a caricature of a Nigerian Port official of sharp intelligence and even sharper dress sense. His attire was meticulous, a tailored suit that shouted professionalism. His eyes, filled as ever with the glint of shrewd calculation, were fixed on George Fitzwilliams, an even younger man, the refinement of public school education etched into his every word and gesture.

George, a junior field officer for MI6 and attached to the British Embassy in Lagos as an agent handler (Handler of sources or informers), met with Phillip monthly to make a routine exchange of currency for shipping intelligence. Sitting across a table in a pleasant bar, taking a drink and making a modest payment in exchange for a pen-drive was a way of keeping a low level agent (source) on a retainer while bringing in low level intel. Yet this meeting was far from routine. It was unexpected and urgent and might win Brownie-points for George with his superiors if he played it well. The almost masked urgency in George's eyes betrayed a need that went far beyond their usual transaction.

"Phillip," George began, his voice bearing a crisp home-counties British accent, now underscored by a seriousness that cut through the room's still air. "The matter I bring before you today concerns something of more significance than our usual business. It is of great importance to my government and requires your unique expertise."

Phillip's eyes narrowed, his mind already reacting to the flattery and imagining the potential for profit. The room seemed to contract, the walls closing in as the gravity of George's unusual intensity settled over them.

"The Russians," George continued, his voice a hushed whisper, but charged with energy, "are planning a criminal conspiracy. They aim to smuggle drugs into the UK from Lagos, and we need to stop them. We need to know where they might be operating from. And you, Phillip, with your connections, your local knowledge could be our key to unravelling this plot."

The charge around the table was palpable, the words hanging in the air like a tangible entity. Phillip regarded George as he appeared to consider the offer. From his eyes, Phillip's mind was a whirlwind of thoughts, his intellect assessing the implications of the request and fighting a losing battle with his ambition. He had already made his decision but was trying to play it cool.

"I understand this is an extraordinary request," George added cautiously, his eyes searching Phillip's face to extract more feedback from their depths. "But if you could assist us, there would be a significant bonus for you."

Phillip leaned back, the leather chair creaking in response, his eyes never leaving George's face. "This request might be considered to carry some risk, to be a venture into a world that transcends mere… business…" It was a challenge that beckoned to the core of Phillip's being, his ego. He might be joining the big players now! What was this worth? What might it lead to?

George thought to himself, "This chap should never play poker."

"I will do what I can," Phillip finally replied, his voice firm, resolute. "I don't know anything at present, but I will inquire. I will try to find where the Russians are doing this."

A smile broke through George's serious façade. He manufactured a fleeting expression of relief and gratitude and allowed it to run across his face. "Thank you, Phillip," he said, extending his hand, the handshake a seal of their agreement.

As the two men parted, each considering the implications of their undertaking, the room seemed to breathe again. Phillip Babatunde, the Port official, had stepped into a new role, a player in a high-stakes game of international intrigue, a game where the rules were unwritten, the risks uncharted, and the stakes immeasurably high. He was a secret agent and he was excited.

101) Bradford Interchange Railway Station, Bridge Street, Bradford, UK

Within the bustling complex of the railway station in Bradford, a franchised café stood as a haven for travellers and locals alike, a place where the aroma of freshly brewed coffee mingled with the muffled sounds of trains and human activity. At one of the tables, a man sat, greying at the temples, raincoat wrapped against the outside weather. A solitary figure lost in thought, his eyes fixed on the glow of his phone, a steaming cup of coffee in front of him.

The headlines on the news channel were grim, the words a stark testament to a reality that seemed to be spiralling out of control. "Government Loses Control Of Inner Cities," the headline screamed, the subtext detailing the random violence spreading across Lancashire. A call for an election, a plea for a new, more competent government that could stem the tide of unrest, was the undercurrent that ran through the article.

The man's eyes narrowed as he read, his mind grappling with the implications, the weight of the words settling over him like a shadow. The coffee, once a source of warmth and comfort, now seemed to grow cold, forgotten in the face of the disturbing news.

As he pondered the gravity of the situation, a sudden scuffle across the way jolted him from his thoughts. The sound of shouting, a scream, a discordant note in the symphony of everyday life, cut through the air, followed by a sight that sent a chill down his spine.

A dishevelled man, his eyes wild, his face contorted with rage, brandished a knife, slashing at passersby with a ferocity that seemed inhuman. Panic erupted, people scattering in all directions, their faces etched with terror, their screams a haunting echo of the violence that had been unleashed. The man bent over a fallen woman and stabbed her repeatedly.

Amidst the panic and chaos, heroes emerged. Railway staff, ordinary men and women thrust into an extraordinary situation, rushed toward the danger brandishing brooms and a shovel, their faces set with determination, their actions a testament to human courage. Like some ancient formation of pike men, they pushed the assailant from his victim.

Moments later the transport police arrived with a swiftness that spoke of their readiness, their faces grim, their movements precise. The crackle of a Taser filled the air, the sound a punctuation mark to the madness, as the assailant was subdued, his body convulsing, then falling limp.

The café, once a place of respite, had become a front-row seat to a play of horror, a microcosm of the societal unrest that was tearing at the fabric of the nation. It was caught on dozens of phone cameras and would be plastered across the 'net in moments. The man's coffee sat untouched, the headlines on his phone a prophetic warning of the violence he had just witnessed.

As the police secured the scene, specially trained railway staff tended to the wounded. Passers-by began to process what had just occurred and the railway station returned to a semblance of normalcy. An ambulance arrived to take the victim away but the scars remained, both physical, blood on the floor, and psychological, a haunting reminder of a world on the brink, a society in need of healing, a government in need of direction.

In the midst of it all, the man at the café table sat, his face pale, his hands now trembling, the headlines on his phone mirrored a living reality. The call for an election, the plea for a new government, had taken on a new urgency, a cry for change that resonated with a poignancy that went beyond mere words. The troubles were real, the violence a tangible entity, and the need for action had never been more acute.

102) The Kaly Cocktail Bar, Akin Adesola, Victoria Island, Lagos, Nigeria

In the heart of Lagos town, where every night the city's pulse beat with a vibrant, relentless rhythm, lay a certain select bar, The Kaly Cocktail Bar. It was part of the restaurant sharing that name yet separate, a sanctuary of elegance amidst the bustling chaos of Lagos nightlife. The soft glow of chandeliers bathed the room in a golden hue, the clink of glasses a delicate accompaniment to the mutter of hushed conversations.

At a secluded corner table, two men sat, their faces illuminated by the soft candlelight, their expressions a study in mutual understanding. Phillip Babatunde looked across the table at Sergei Stepanov, his usual contact from the Russian embassy. Sergei's eyes, usually filled with a gentle diplomat's charm, were fixed on Phillip, and Phillip could see a hint of urgency in their depths.

He was unaware of the hidden layers that lay beneath Sergei's exterior, the secrets that were woven into the very fabric of the man's being. He did not know that Sergei was a GRU agent, a master of subterfuge and manipulation. All he knew was that Sergei was a man of some influence at the Russian Embassy, a man who could open doors and offer opportunities. A man who paid him on time every month double what he received from the British and who could potentially make him a lot more money.

This meeting was almost totally unexpected by Phillip, a sudden message from Sergei had asked to see him on a matter of some urgency. "What could it be?" he thought, "Something to do with the Russian drug plot George had mentioned perhaps?"

"Phillip, my friend," Sergei opened, "I have a favour to ask of you."

"Ask me anything, Sergei. You know you can rely on me."

"I know I can Phillip. And that is why I am asking you to let me know if anyone British approaches you and asks for information about a Russian undertaking or base here in Lagos. The truth is, we are protecting some political prisoners who are fleeing from the British and they want to recapture and torture them."

"Sergei," Phillip began, his voice filled with a pride that resonated with his sense of self-worth, "I must tell you, the British have already approached me. They are looking for a Russian base in Lagos, seeking information about Russians engaged in unusual activities around the port."

Sergei's face remained impassive, his eyes never leaving Phillip's face, but there was a subtle shift in his expression, a tightening around the eyes that betrayed the weight of Phillip's words.

"Thank you, Phillip," Sergei replied, his voice smooth, his accent a melodic lilt that belied the gravity of the conversation. "Your information is valuable and I will arrange for a bonus to show our gratitude. We must meet again tomorrow. There may be a new job for you, a task that could perhaps save some brave souls from the cruelty of the British.

And, of course," he added, a smile playing on his lips, "it could earn you a year's salary for a night's work."

Phillip's heart skipped a beat, excitement surging through him, a heady blend of anticipation and greed. The prospect of becoming an important player, a key figure in a game that transcended mere business, was a lure he found magnetic. The money, a sum that could transform his life, was an added incentive that made the offer irresistible.

"I will help you all I can, Sergei," Phillip said, his voice filled with determination, his eyes shining with ambition. "You have my word. I will say nothing to the British."

Sergei's smile widened, a knowing expression that spoke quietly of a victory won, a pawn successfully hooked, "I knew I could count on you, Phillip," he said, extending his hand, the handshake a seal of their agreement, a transaction denoting trust. Usually.

103) The King's Private Office, Buckingham Palace, London, UK

Within the regal confines of Buckingham Palace, a place where history whispered through gilded corridors and time seemed to stand still, the King worked quietly at a laptop in his London office.

Sir Rupert Greville, entered the room, his patent leather footsteps a measured cadence on the polished floor. The King looked up from his desk; his face, usually a mask of calm assurance, bore an expression of concern, a hint of urgency that was not lost on Sir Rupert.

"Your Majesty," Sir Rupert began, his voice a respectful timbre, his words carefully chosen. " How may I assist you?"

The King's eyes fixed on Rupert's old face, a silent acknowledgment of the gravity of the situation. "Rupert, old friend, are you aware of the MI5 agent Faris Iqbal?"

Sir Rupert's face remained impassive, his eyes lifted and moved to the right in search of memory, but his mind was already sifting through the layers of information, the intricate web of intelligence that was his domain. "The last I heard, sir, he had survived the initial interrogation by the GRU and presumably convinced them he was not an agent. He had been sent to Lefortovo prison on the outskirts of Moscow. It is likely he will be left there, forgotten, unless moved to a labour camp or offered as an exchange for a Russian operative. Probably he will stay at Lefortovo."

The King smiled sadly and nodded, his face reflecting a satisfaction that was tinged with concern. "You are always up to date, Rupert." A pause filled the room, a silence that seemed to hang in the air, laden with unspoken thoughts. The King's eyes settled on Sir Rupert's face. "I want steps taken to recover Faris," the King said finally, his voice filled with a quiet determination. "He has been a good operative, outstandingly brave and a loyal man."

Sir Rupert's face betrayed a hint of surprise, a subtle shift that spoke of his better understanding of the complexity of the situation. "Your Majesty, there are others of greater value that we should recover first."

The King's face hardened one notch, his eyes filled with a resolve that was both regal and human. "That depends on how you value your people, Sir Rupert. I value courage and loyalty. Bring him home, please" The King's words were a flat command, a decree that resonated with a power that went beyond mere legal authority.

Sir Rupert's face reflected his understanding of his King, his acceptance of the task. "As you wish, sir. The exchange for Alexander Kuznetsov, son of General Nikolai Kuznetsov, has not yet been accomplished so there would be a certain irony..."

The King's expression silenced Rupert's attempt at levity.

As Rupert left the room, he thought how strange it was, a king troubling so much about a nobody. Then he realised that was what made him who he was. A man Rupert would die for.

104) The RFA Fort Victoria, East Atlantic, 450 Miles Off Liberia

Captain Graham McLeod stood on the bridge, his eyes scanning the wide expanse of instruments with a practised interrogation. His gaze, sharpened by years of experience, sought out any sign of trouble, any hint of uncertainty in the faces of the watch on the bridge. But all was settled, the night had been quiet, and his ship was running smoothly.

The Royal Fleet Auxiliary Fort Victoria was a colossal vessel that cut through the ocean's waves with a grace that belied her immense size; a marvel of engineering, a testament to human ingenuity. Measuring nearly seven hundred feet in length, a hundred feet in width, and displacing over 31,000 tonnes, she was a behemoth, a giant that dwarfed the 6,900 tonne Type 26 frigates that often accompanied her.

Her onboard weaponry was impressive; a formidable arsenal that included Phalanx radar-controlled chain guns, GAM-BO1 20mm guns, and Browning .50 calibre machine guns. Yet, these were merely for defence against the small fry of the sea. Fast boat attacks.

Her true strength lay in the three Merlin helicopters she housed in their comfortable hangars, each one loaded for submarine, and the two ship-killing Wildcats, armed with Sting Ray torpedoes, a 12.7mm calibre M3M cabin-mounted machine gun, and Martlet and Sea Venom missiles. Every one a very real symbol of power at sea.

But offensive capabilities, the Fort Victoria was not a combat ship. She was a Replenishment Oiler, a fleet support vessel that carried the lifeblood of the fleet. Her cargo included 12,000 tonnes of heavy fuel oil, 120,000 cubic feet of ammunition, and 104,000 cubic meters of dry stores, ranging from food to replacement uniform buttons. She was the beating heart of the fleet, the ship that kept all the others at sea, enabling them to perform their duties, whatever in the world those might be.

Today, however, Captain McLeod had a special mission to perform, a detour that added a touch of spice to his voyage as happened now and again. Currently off the coast of Liberia, West Africa, and heading South, he was expecting a Merlin to arrive tonight from an undisclosed asset, bringing two men to join him, a Colonel and an SAS Sergeant.

Unlikely as it seemed, this sounded very like the same chaps he had hosted before and supported on an operation. They were to be his guests for a couple of days, to enjoy his hospitality as the Fort Victoria changed course to steam East at a rate of five hundred miles a day and reach a suitable position to put them ashore quietly by boat on a Nigerian beach.

The thought brought a smile to Captain McLeod's face, a wistful expression that spoke of his excitement at the thought playing at secret squirrels again. The smile widened slightly as he recalled the excellent, "Boys-Own" operation he had been involved in where the Spook Colonel Reaper, his Sergeant and an SAS team rescued a girl from the terrorists in Yemen.

Well, the Admiralty had given the orders, and he would carry them out, his unlisted complement of Royal Marines ready, as ever, to assist with the task. And he hoped it would be Mike Reaper again. Nice guy.

"Call me when our guests arrive, number one,"

"Yes sir," that officer replied, his voice a respectful acknowledgment of the Captain's order.

"And tell my chef to arrange something nice tonight for one guest please. You will join us won't you?"

"Thank you sir, of course."

"And have a word with the President of the Senior Rates Mess to invite the NCO accompanying the Colonel to dine with them. Make him welcome."

With a final glance at the instruments, Captain McLeod left the bridge, his mind already focused on the mission ahead. It ought to be quite straightforward having his Royals put someone ashore on a friendly beach.

The Fort Victoria continued her voyage, a graceful giant gliding through the ocean's waves, her mission a line-entry in a story that was woven into the very fabric of international intrigue and power.

105) The Kaly Cocktail Bar, Akin Adesola, Victoria Island, Lagos, Nigeria

In the Kaly Cocktail Bar, the clink of glasses made a civilised background to private conversations and an early Phillip Babatunde awaited his meeting with Sergei Stepanov. The dim lighting, the soft hum of muted conversations, and the subtle scent of aged wood and rich leather provided a fitting 007-esque backdrop to the intrigue that was about to unfold.

Sergei Stepanov arrived with a purposeful stride, his eyes fixed on Phillip, his expression unreadable. As he took his seat, the weight of his full, somewhat disconcerting attention settled on Phillip, a pointer to the gravity of their meeting.

"Phillip," Sergei began sincerely, his voice projecting a smooth timbre that belied the urgency of his words, "I have recommended you to our embassy as a man with great ability and our ambassador has chosen you for a very special job. A task that will earn you a year's salary."

Phillip's eyes widened, excitement mingling with anticipation. The promise of financial reward, coupled with the allure of becoming a significant player in international intrigue, was a temptation he could not resist.

"You are to tell the British," Sergei continued, his words carefully chosen, his tone measured, "that you have heard of some strange Russians who have a warehouse somewhere on the Lagos Port Complex, overlooking the Lagoon. You are not sure exactly where it is, but you know that these Russians frequent the lounge bar at Rock View Hotel every Friday evening."

Sergei's eyes fixed on Phillip's face, his expression intense, his words a carefully woven tapestry of deception and manipulation.

"A friend of yours, a waiter at the hotel, has heard them speak of 'their guests,' of “Columbian Rice”, and of “illicit shipping to Europe” when they have been drunk. You must say that your friend thought they were criminals, being different from the other Russian businessmen in Lagos, who usually gather at the Freedom Hotel by the Landmark Centre event venue as you probably know."

Sergei's voice dropped to a whisper, the words a secret shared between conspirators, a plot that transcended mere business. "This story," Sergei said, his eyes never leaving Phillip's face, "is not too obvious a lead, but it will catch the attention of the British. It is vitally important that you convey exactly what I am telling you."

Phillip's mind raced, the implications of Sergei's words settling over him like a shadow, a realization of the complexity of the game he had become a part of. "I will do it," Phillip said quickly, his voice firm, his decision made. "I'll will accomplish the mission."

“Now, tell me what you have to tell the British, so we have it clear.”

“A friend of mind who works as a waiter at the Rock View Hotel, in the lounge bar, told me that there are some strange Russians who might be criminals. They gather there on a Friday night rather than at the Freedom Hotel where most Russians drink. When they were drunk they spoke of having strange guests, illicit shipping to Europe and Colombian rice.”

Sergei's face broke into a smile, a knowing expression that spoke of victory and success. “I imagine you must earn about 5,000,000 Naira a year in your management position…”

Phillip’s eyes betrayed his gratification at this overestimation.

“And I would not want it to be thought that we Russians are anything but generous with our friends, so I have persuaded our embassy that your services are worth somewhat more than this. So 10,000,000 Naira will be paid to you in cash within days of completing your mission, Phillip. I knew I could count on you."

Phillip’s eyes grew wide at this excessive payment, worth more than two years salary to him. Surely, the Russians must think him a valuable secret agent. As the two men parted, the Veranda bar maintained its facade of elegance and sophistication and the undercurrents of their conversation were washed away in the night air. But the web of secrets and deception had ensnared Phillip Babatunde.

He had actually become a bit-part player in the great-game of international espionage, a pawn in a complex dance of power and manipulation. But, as is so often the case, he had no idea of the goal to which his services contributed. The promise of money, the allure of intrigue, and the excitement of playing a role in an exciting world that transcended mere business had drawn him in, and now there was no turning back. Like so many men before him.

Sergei Stepanov, the mind behind this plot, had played his hand with precision, as ever.

106) A Sandy Beach Near Akinlade, 15 Kilometres East Of Lagos, Nigeria

Off the Nigerian shore near the little settlement of Akinlade, and fifteen miles South of the entrance to Lagos Lagoon, the dark water was momentarily disturbed as two heads emerged, almost indistinguishable against the blackness of the night. Faces concealed by breathing apparatus, heads encased in black neoprene wet-suits, these were no ordinary swimmers. These were Royal Marines from the RFA Fort Victoria, masters of stealth and reconnaissance.

One of them raised a night vision viewer to his eyes, and scanned the shoreline with meticulous care. His gaze swept over the palm trees, the rubbish piled near the beach, the thatched huts that stood in the middle distance. Nothing stirred, no hint of movement betrayed the presence of anyone who might see them. The coast was clear.

They closed the shore, stumbling moving through the low waves in that ungainly manner that even experts cannot avoid wearing swim-fins. Once ashore, they removed their head coverings to enhance their hearing, took off their fins to enable them to walk like humans, and padded up the beach, their eyes alert for any sign of trouble; silenced Glock 17 pistols ready in their hands.

Once amongst the palms they split up, taking positions fifty yards apart, their trained eyes quickly assessing their surroundings. A building site for a holiday complex, an area that looked like a local market, all deserted and silent. One swimmer produced a waterproof radio, holding it to his ear, his voice a soft whisper in the night. "Hello Catfish, this is Turtle, position clear, over."

The reply came back instantly, a distant acknowledgment of success. "Turtle, Catfish, on our way, out."

Minutes later, the faint sound of a well-silenced four-stroke outboard reached their sharp ears. Then it cut out as paddles took over. A Rigid Raider, twenty-one feet long and matt green, cruised quietly towards the shore paddled by four Royal Marines. Its low, black and green fibreglass body was the ideal vehicle for a stealthy landing, its design a testament to lessons learned through decades of covert operations.

Aboard the boat were six strapping young Royal Marines in total, faces blacked up, clad in combat gear and armed with Knight's Stoner 1 (KS-1) assault rifles. Incongruous amongst them, Mike and Mac, dressed casually in jeans and T-shirts. As the boat rode up onto the sand, the two men climbed out, dry-shod, followed by their packed civilian rucksacks passed over the bow.

With a wave to their escorts, Mike and Mac walked up the beach, their steps purposeful, their minds focused on the mission ahead. The swimmers reappeared from landwards, raising hands in casual salute while jogging quickly down to rejoin their boat. They pushed it back into the water, ready to turn and motor away.

Mac and Mike squatted by a palm tree, their eyes scanning the surroundings, their senses alert to any sign of danger. "Clear here, Mike," Mac said, his voice a soft murmur in the night.

"Then we had better double in and meet our embassy driver."
As they moved further into the shadows, the beach returned to its nocturnal silence, the waves lapping gently at the shore, the palm trees swaying in the gentle breeze.

107) The Red Bear Bar, Ulitsa Sel'skokhozyaystvennaya 19, Moscow, Russia

Nestled among the bustling streets in the heart of Moscow, with its finger on the pulse of city life, stood the "Red Bear" bar. It was a place full of locals, regulars, a place where people could speak without any great risk of being overheard. Or reported.

A group of young friends found solace in the corner booth, a refuge from the world outside, a place where they could share their thoughts and fears over a glass and without judgment.

The topic that weighed heavily on their minds was the news of the terrible losses in Ukraine, a subject that stirred emotions of anger, frustration, and sadness amongst them all. A group who would ordinarily argue over the colour of the sky, they were united in their opposition to the war, knowing that their friends were being conscripted to fight in battles they could not win, to be sacrificed against better-equipped, better-trained, better lead troops.

Yuri, the most vocal among them, leaned forward to be heard, "It's madness," he declared, his voice trembling with emotion. "We have no issue with the Ukrainians; we should be friends with them, not enemies."

Ivan nodded in agreement, his eyes dark with concern. "Our boys are being sent to a slaughterhouse," he said, "The press would have you think they are just numbers but they are our friends, our brothers."

Tatiana's eyes filled with tears as she thought of her younger brother, recently conscripted and sent to the front lines. "I wish our military were out of it," she whispered, her voice barely audible. "This war is a tragedy, a senseless waste of life."

Alexei, ever the philosopher, looked at his friends, his expression thoughtful. "We are caught in a web of political games," he said slowly, his words chosen with care. "Our leaders are playing with our lives as if we were mere pawns on a chessboard. We must find a way to make our voices heard."

The conversation continued, the friends sharing their thoughts, their fears, their hopes for a future where peace would prevail and friendship would replace enmity.

As the night wore on in the "Red Bear" it became apparent that many others shared the same views. An opinion becoming all too common for the comfort of the political class.

108) Unit 17, Apapa Industrial Estate, West Of The Lagoon, Lagos, Nigeria

The A1 dual carriageway, bustled with early morning traffic. It was flanked by the commercial sprawl of Lagos and branched off at Mobil Road where the solemn, unfriendly-seeming embassy driver who had answered their phone call dropped Mike and Mac without a word. Their destination was the Apapa Industrial Estate, a maze of warehouses and manufacturing units that thrived within a mile of the docks.

With packs slung over their shoulders, they embarked on a brisk walk, the rapid beat of their footsteps betraying their impatience to find and settle in to their new base. The industrial estate loomed ahead, an assembly of buildings that bore the unmistakeable marks of commerce and light industry.

Among its neighbours, a smallish warehouse unit stood, rented privately and at short notice by the British Embassy: Unit 17. It was a nondescript structure, its exterior betraying no hint of its use. But they had been assured by the military attaché's staff that inside there would be an old 7.5-tonne truck and with it a driver named Maxwell whose discretion and loyalty could be relied upon.

As the two men approached, the roller doors fronting the unit were up, revealing the truck's battered face. The sound of a spanner reached their ears, a rhythmic clinking from underneath that suggested something mechanical was receiving personal attention.

"Hello there. Is that Maxwell?" Mike called, his voice carrying through the open space.

From underneath the truck, a slim, overalled figure rolled out and sprung to his feet with an athletic grace. Maxwell's face lit up in a happy grin, and he extended an oily hand. "Hello, I am Maxwell."

Mike shook the hand, unperturbed by the grease, and introduced himself with a warmth that immediately bridged the gap between strangers. "I'm Mike and I have heard good things about you Maxwell."

Maxwell's response was immediate, his words tinged with pride, "I hope you have Mike, I have worked for the embassy many times. When they want something done off the books, I am the man they call."

"Maxwell, we have a few things to sort out here, do you want to carry on with what you were doing and we can chat later?"

"All good, Mike" Maxwell grinned and climbed back under the truck.

Maxwell's skills as a mechanic, his attention to the truck's maintenance tied in with his glowing recommendation from the embassy and his quiet singing as he worked spoke of a man who would be good company. This was not lost on Mac who nodded in Maxwell's direction. "He's gonnae be a handy wean, Mike. Ken's his stuff wi' motors an' the toon."

Mike nodded, his mind already elsewhere, "I'll set up comms if you want to take a look around and get your bearings."

Mac nodded, "Right ye are."

109) House Of Commons, Palace Of Westminster, London, UK

The British government was faced with a rapidly growing public discontent. Due principally to their perceived inability to control the spate of Berserker-like attacks that were occurring, mainly in the North of England. Attacks which had formed the basis for a great many hysterical news stories.

The media's ability to make this one issue the story of the month, and their decision to attach the Berserker label, had amplified the public's fears to such an extent that it had turned the public's opinion from this being a matter in need of attention to almost a national panic.

In Parliament's wood-panelled rooms, a series of focus meetings had taken place. Politicians on both sides of the House, advisors, law enforcement, and medical experts all gathered in committee, their expressions serious, voices measured. They were well aware of the situation's gravity, the high stakes involved, and the pressing need for resolution. Obviously, they were not privy to what the SIS people knew about the Russian connection.

Prime Minister Daniel Lawson, an experienced politician with a reputation for composure under pressure, found himself at the center of a very negative media scrutiny. A recent tabloid report of him taking time to play golf on a Sunday had added fuel to the fire. The opposition was critical, the media demanding, and trust in the government continued to plummet.

During a Parliamentary debate, the opposition leader had voiced the concerns of the people to score political points, "This Berserker drug has become a scourge," he declared. "The government's failure to control this crisis is a betrayal of the people. We demand answers, we demand action, and we demand them now!"

The galleries were populated with journalists, activists and citizens, all attentively following the proceedings. The atmosphere was tense, filled with anticipation.

The Berserker drug issue, initially a localized problem, had turned into a matter of national concern, partly due to the media fanning the flames into an inferno of fear and partly through enemies of the country using the public's fear to their own advantage.

110) <u>Tuesday 20:23</u> La Veranda Restaurant, Bluefish Hotel, Oju Olobun Close, Lagos, Nigeria

In the sophisticated ambiance of a La Veranda, Phillip Babatunde, port official turned double agent, found himself seated across from George Fitzwilliam of the British Embassy. The two men were about to engage in a conversation that would further entangle Phillip in a web of international intrigue.

Phillip, carefully maintaining his composed exterior and sincere expression began to recount the story given to him by Sergei Stepanov, the Russian agent he had met with at the Kaly Cocktail Bar. He chose his words with caution, ensuring that the details were presented exactly as he had been instructed.

"I have come across some information that might be of interest to you, George," he began, leaning slightly forward with slightly too much familiarity. "I've heard of some peculiar Russians who seem to have a warehouse on Lagos Port Complex, overlooking the Lagoon. The exact location is unknown to me, but these men drink in the lounge bar at Rock View Hotel every Friday evening."

His voice steady, Phillip continued, "A friend of mine, a waiter at that hotel, has overheard them talking about 'their guests,' mentioning something about Columbian Rice and illicit shipping to Europe. They've spoken of it when they've been rather inebriated. I couldn't help but think they were criminals, especially since they don't associate with the other Russian businessmen in Lagos, who usually gather at the Freedom Hotel by the Landmark Centre event venue."

George listened intently, absorbing the information, his expression betraying no reaction, no hint of the importance he attached to this information. He reached into his pocket and handed Phillip a wad of cash under the table, a gesture executed with practiced ease. The amount was significant, equivalent to a month's salary for Phillip. Yet Phillip's eyes remained unmoved, his thoughts already on the far greater compensation promised to him by the Russians for performing this task.

Inside, Phillip felt a thrill of excitement, a sense of importance from playing a role in this complex game of espionage. His conscience was untroubled; he saw his actions as merely shifting the balance of business interests, an action he deemed fair play in the world of international politics.

George, however, seemed to detect a hint of tension in Phillip's mood. He looked at Phillip, his eyes searching, a question forming in his mind.

"Is something troubling you, Phillip?" George asked, his voice tinged with concern.

Phillip's response was swift, a rehearsed explanation at the ready. "My wife is expecting a child, George. It's a time of joy, but also of concern."

George's face softened, and he offered a smile of understanding. "Congratulations, Phillip. I wish you and your family all the best."

George walked from the hotel calmly and around the corner. Then he punched the air and exclaimed, "Yes!" This was important. All the junior staff and Agent Handlers at the embassy had been tasked with finding the Russian base as a priority and he had just cracked it. This would look good on his report and be another significant step towards promotion.

111) The Federal Military Memorial Cemetery, Mytishchinsky District, Moscow, Russia

On the outskirts of NE Moscow, in a cemetery that spread its arms across a great expanse of solemnly decorated earth, a scene of collective mourning was taking place. The occasion was sombre, the air heavy with grief; it was a mass funeral for nearly a hundred young conscripts who had fallen in the Ukraine Special Military Operation.

The crowd, a sea of civilians mixed with soldiers, gathered around the fresh graves. Among them, a mother named Alexandra Petrovna stood out, a figure clearly in the grip of sorrow, lost in her thoughts. Her face, pale and lined with grief, mirrored the pain that had settled over the crowd. Her two remaining sons, Alexei and Dmitry, stood stoically by her side in their uniforms, eyes fixed on their mother, their hearts aching with empathy.

Elena, a friend of Alexandra, along with other family members, surrounded her, offering comfort through their presence. Elena's soft whispers provided solace to Alexandra's anguished heart, while the gentle touch of relatives provided warmth in the cold Moscow air.

The ceremony unfolded with a dignity that transcended mere formality. Prayers filled the air, hymns resonated in harmony, and tears flowed unchecked. As the caskets were lowered into the earth, a silence fell over the crowd, punctuated only by the soft sounds of weeping. Each face reflected a personal loss, each tear a testament to the void left by the departed.

The total absence of officers among the mourners was conspicuous and added a layer of complexity to the scene. Their scarcity seemed to speak to underlying tensions, perhaps an orchestrated move to avoid confrontation with the crowd. At any rate it added a note of discord to an otherwise united expression of grief.

As the crowd began to disperse, the reality of the loss settled in. The graves, once empty and waiting, were now filled and decorated. And the young men who had been taken from their families were now at rest.

The cemetery, a place of finality and reflection had become a symbol of the human cost of war. The pain etched on Alexandra Petrovna's face, the support of her sons, the comfort of her friend Elena, measures of the conflict's toll spread across the nation.

In the days that followed, the cemetery would return to its quiet solitude, but the echoes of that day would linger. The memory of the fallen would live on in the hearts of their families, and the grief would become a part of the nation's collective consciousness.

112) <u>Friday 21:44</u> An Alley Beside The Freedom Hotel, Downtown Lagos, Nigeria

Downtown Lagos was in full party swing as Friday night came to life. The streets were filled with vibrant colors, lively music, and the unique, rich aromas of Nigerian cuisine. People from all walks of life were enjoying the end of a hard working week and losing themselves in the city's pulsating energy.

In the midst of this cheerful, bustling urban landscape, the Freedom Hotel stood as a beacon of elegance and sophistication. Located near the Landmark Centre, it was a favoured haunt for a certain type of businessmen, but also for shady locals and tourists alike.

Inside the hotel's plush bar, a group of Russian men were engaged in boisterous conversation. They were celebrating something, their faces flushed with happiness, their voices loud and carefree. The clinking of glasses and hearty laughter filled the air as they toasted to friendship, to success, and the future.

But not all was as it seemed.

In room 28, on the second floor of the same hotel, two Russians were hunched over a table filled with high-tech equipment, making a stark contrast to the jovial atmosphere below. Their faces were tense, their hands steady and sure as they worked. The room was filled with the hum of computers and the weight of expectation. They were waiting, watching, ready for what was to come.

Outside, the night was alive with possibilities. Among the crowd, the two British operators, Mike and Mac, made their way barely noticed through the bustling streets. Dressed for a night on the town, they blended seamlessly with the revelers. But their minds were focused, their senses heightened.

As they approached the Freedom Hotel they casually observed the Russian men in the bar. Their eyes took in the details, their minds catalogued the visible clues. They continued down the alley, surveying the area, taking note of access and exit routes, preparing for the task ahead.

Unbeknownst to them, the Russians were waiting. Hidden in the shadows, two drones lay in ambush. Sleek and predatory, they were armed with Taser-type stun guns, capable of delivering a debilitating shock. The action came in a flash, without warning as it so often does. Mac spotted one of the drones above Mike and his instincts took over. With a rapid, fluid motion, he drew his Glock and fired a single, precise shot, holding position in case a second shot was required. The drone went down, its control center destroyed.

Mike, too, reacted with lightning speed a moment after, his automatic movements a product of endless training and experience. He sidestepped the falling drone and took aim at the second above Mac's head. His shot was true, and the drone crashed to the ground, but not before delivering its electric payload into Mac's neck. Mac fell to the ground, his body convulsing, under the effect of 50,000 volts.

An instant later there was a single crack and a sniper's bullet threw Mike against the alley wall and he fell to the floor. A perfectly placed shot to the centre of his chest from a Russian SV-98 rifle.

113) <u>Friday 21:53</u> An Alley Beside The Freedom Hotel, Downtown Lagos, Nigeria

The outcome of the sniper's shot was evident in Mike's twisted expression as he lay on the ground. The ribs around his sternum and the surrounding tissue were bruised and he was winded. But it was by no means a dangerous, let alone a fatal wound. Advanced, light body armour with ceramic plates concealed beneath his jacket had absorbed the worst of the impact and prevented penetration by the Russian 7.62 high velocity bullet, driven by a powerful 54 mm cartridge.

But the effect was still like being kicked by a horse. The small hole left in his sports jacket was a tangible reminder of how close he had come to meeting his end. But a more serious injury than anything relating to the shot was the blow he had received when his head had struck the wall of the alley.

A few minutes later, Mike began to move and his coughing broke the relative silence of the alley, a harsh, ragged sound as he struggled to regain his breath. The world seemed to sway around him, his vision was blurred and his senses dull. Every breath was a battle, each inhalation a burst of fire in his chest.

The Russians had already vanished into the night by the time Mike found the strength to lift his head and shoulders. He looked around groggily, his eyes scanning the shadows, his mind working to piece together what had just happened. Mac was nowhere to be seen. The memories were there, withdrawn and lurking just beneath the surface, but they were obscured by the haze of pain and disorientation.

As he lay there, unable to drag himself to his feet, the night life of Lagos continued unperturbed. Laughter and music drifted through the air, a discordant melody that seemed to consciously ignore the sound of a few shots. Very often city people would ignore a single shot but more than one and there was panic. This city was clearly different, was oblivious to a few shots, its inhabitants lost in their revelry, their lives untouched by the violence that had unfolded in that hidden corner of their urban landscape.

Three Nigerian men approached along the alley, presumably an off-the-cuff attempt to rob him. He knew he was fair game, being a white man who might be found drunk and disabled while in possession of a wallet. Mike picked up his pistol from where it had fallen beside him and pointed it at the men. They turned around and calmly walked away.

Slowly, with a determination born of necessity, Mike pulled himself upright by gripping a fall-pipe, his body protesting at every inch gained. The world was still spinning, but he knew that he had to get back to base, had to make sense of the ambush. The Russians had captured Mac and taken him to who-knew-where?

114) <u>Friday 22:33</u> Unit 23a, Badia Industrial Park, Lagos Ports Complex, Lagos, Nigeria

In the stark, concrete interior of Unit 23a the room on the top floor had became a place of interrogation. Mac, bound with cord to a steel-tube chair, his face and body bearing the red welts of a beating with canes and plastic piping, resisted his tormentors with a stoicism born of SAS counter interrogation training and sheer Glaswegian toughness.

The interrogation team, two Russians, were a study in contrasts. One, burly and clad in a vest, wielded a heavy, flexible plastic pipe with brutal, practiced efficiency. His face, contorted with scorn and anger, gave the impression of a personal hatred. The other, more smartly dressed, possessed a cold, calculating style, his questions delivered with a chilling precision.

"Tell me why are you in Lagos!" the smartly dressed Russian demanded, his eyes fixed on Mac, his voice devoid of emotion.

Mac followed the first rule of counter interrogation; don't make up a story, don't say a word. His face was marked by the violence of the interrogation, his nose, broken and bloody, and the gap where two teeth had been knocked from his upper jaw was dripping blood onto his lips. Yet, his total silence and rule two, his eyes, downcast and averted from his interrogator's gaze, showed he was following standard operating procedures. And his training served him well. One word leads to many and many words lead to breaking.

The beating continued, the burly Russian's blows falling with relentless force, the slap of rubber meeting flesh echoing through the room. Each strike was a test of Mac's endurance, a challenge to his willpower, a demand for his submission. His left cheek split under a blow.

But Mac's resolve held firm, his body absorbing the punishment, his mind focused elsewhere, passing the time until he lost consciousness. He thought about Snuffles eating a bag of crisps and chasing the bag around the floor. He knew that his silence was his strength, that his refusal to speak was his way to buy time, that his ability to endure was his shield, his one protection from execution.

As the time dragged on, the tension in the room grew, the atmosphere became charged with a palpable sense of frustration and anger. The smartly dressed Russian's questions grew more insistent, his tone more demanding, but Mac's silence remained unbroken.

Finally, the ordeal came to an end, the promise of further interrogation hanging in the air like a threat. "The Captain will return on Monday." The smartly dressed Russian said, his voice cold. "Then we will see what you have to say."

Turning to the man with the pipe, he continued, "Handcuff him with both hands around that pipe over there." He nodded in the direction of a steel pipe running down the wall near the row of windows.

Mac was dragged by strong arms and cuffed to the pipe but left sitting on the same chair. It occurred to him that this was a strange act of consideration. Then he was alone, his body aching, his head spinning but his spirit unbowed. Mac knew that he was not really alone. He knew that Mike would find him and Mike would come for him.

115) **<u>Friday 22:38</u> Unit 17, Apapa Industrial Estate, West Of The Lagoon, Lagos, Nigeria**

The streets of Lagos were still alive with people and the distant sound of nightlife entirely failed to distract Mike from the burden that rested on his shoulders as he staggered onto the main street.

The journey back to the base had been a blur, the local taxi driver's casual assumption that he was a drunk hurt in a bar fight, a fortunate convenience considering how quickly things had unravelled. Mike's mind replayed the ambush, the self-created mental video of Mac's capture haunting him, his own perceived failure to shoot down the second drone quickly enough to protect Mac gnawed at his conscience.

Maxwell had still been working on his truck when Mike arrived back at the unit and had seen his injuries. Mike's eyes, usually sharp and focused, were clouded with pain, his attitude solemn, his movements uncharacteristically sluggish. Maxwell showed his concern by brewing a mug of warm, sweet tea unasked.

Mike turned to his laptop and established a connection to the satellite that linked them to SIS through GCHQ. Wincing at the movement's effect on his ribs, his fingers flew over the keyboard as he reported the ambush and Mac's capture in a terse text message.

"Ambushed recce-ing Russians
Mac captured, self lightly wounded
We need to recover Mac before they can extract any information
Request a surveillance aircraft to overfly Lagos and locate Mac through his implanted tracker
This should also lead us to the people behind the drug additive
Grim"

116) **<u>Saturday 06:31</u> Unit 23a, Badia Industrial Park, Lagos Ports Complex, Lagos, Nigeria**

Mac sat on the steel frame chair and rested his head on his arms, supported as they were by the handcuffs. He lifted his head and spat some congealed blood onto the floor and shook his head to try to clear his thoughts. Then wished he hadn't. He lifted his hands, moved the fingers, "Still some blood pumpin'."

He listened for a moment. The guards had called again a few minutes previously and kicked him to be sure he was awake. It was quiet now and they were probably downstairs having a brew. Time to make a move. He slid his left foot from in front of the chair to around the side and pushed the chair back a little further from the wall and pipe to his front. Then he lifted his foot, as if he were crossing his leg over his thigh, and rested the outside of his left boot on his right knee. Making a gap between his arms he leaned his head forward and grasped the cuff of his trousers with his teeth and winced at the pain. But he pulled the cuff up to expose the top of the boot.

"Amateurs." He thought to himself. A trained guard would have taken his boots. He strained and bent further, gripping the doubled edging at the top of his boot with his teeth. It was stiff but he could get at it at least. He stopped and listened, all was quiet below. But as he listened he realised it was getting light, "Damn, it's ower late noo."

117) <u>Saturday 09:21</u> Unit 17, Apapa Industrial Estate, West Of The Lagoon, Lagos, Nigeria

In the dimly lit interior of the unit, Mike stared intently at the screen of his laptop, reading again the decoded text response from Ralf. As if the reading could change it. The message remained clear and unequivocal:

"The surveillance aircraft will take about two days to organize.
No other support from SIS or the military will be available,
the risk of offending the Nigerian government is too great,
the possibility of a serious diplomatic incident too real.
You must not do anything which might cause an incident yourself.
Grenadier"

The realization that he was not only on his own, but that his hands were tied, sank in like the cold, hard truth that it was. Was this Ralf's decision? Was he being leaned on from above? The almost-quiet room, filled only with the quiet hum of his laptop, seemed to close in on him. Maxwell watched from a distance, an oily rag clutched in his hands.

Mike's face betrayed the turmoil within. His mind ran over possibilities and impossibilities, his thoughts were repeatedly distracted by the urgency of the situation and his fury at his superior's lack of concern for Mac. With a sigh, he turned to Maxwell, his voice filled with a mix of disdain and resolve. "My boss won't support a rescue for Mac," he said, the words heavy with implication.

Maxwell's expression changed to one of resolution as he took in Mike's words. "I will do all I can to help rescue him," he declared, his voice firm, his eyes meeting Mike's, "I have friends I can speak with tonight. We will find the Russian base and Mac will be there."

"Thank you Maxwell, at least I can rely on you my friend."

The reality of the situation had become clear. It was descending into the usual military cock-up when politics gets involved. Probably there has been a directive from higher up the food-chain to avoid a diplomatic incident at all costs and that had been interpreted by Ralf or Ralf's boss as "do nothing."

Unless Max's friends came up with something almost immediately, Mike could not begin to plan a rescue for Mac until he had word of the results from the AWACs aircraft which would invisibly over fly Lagos in two days' time. Mac might be dead or talking by then. Even if he were still alive, with no support, the odds were massively against a successful rescue attempt undertaken by Mike alone. The stakes in this game, though, were very high; Not just Mac's life but the future of Britain.

As he continued to think through the situation, the reaction from Ralf was starting to appear strange. It was strange, wasn't it, that there would be no support from SIS for Mac's rescue when surely they had expected right from the beginning to have to assist in neutralising the target of this operation? Surely they were aware that rescuing Mac was an integral part of neutralising the Russians operation and therefore aligned with the goal of this operation?

For no obvious reason, an old intel saying drifted into Mike's head, "Twice is coincidence, three times is enemy action." Was there a traitor, a foreign agent in the chain of command?

118) Saturday 09:23 Kaly Restaurant, Akin Adesola, Victoria Island, Lagos, Nigeria

Phillip's anticipation was palpable as he settled into a secluded booth, his eyes scanning the room for any sign of Sergei. The meeting had been arranged with minimal notice, but the promise of a massive payment had outweighed the frustration of missing a date with his girlfriend. He would buy her a dress.

Within the sophisticated ambiance of the Kaly Restaurant, a place of relative calm in the already bustling heart of Lagos, Phillip prepared for a breakfast meeting that promised to be both lucrative and satisfying to his ego. Early as it was, the gentle hum of conversation filled the air, providing a backdrop to an encounter that had the potential to make Phillip the player he had always wanted to be.

Sergei, had chosen this locale originally for its discretion and elegance. As a seasoned agent handler, he knew the importance of appearances to new agents and the value of conducting business in a setting that offered the trio of confidentiality, comfort and ego-support to nervous informers.

When Sergei finally arrived on-time, his entrance was unobtrusive, his face composed. With a practiced ease, he slid into the seat opposite Phillip, his eyes briefly meeting Phillip's before shifting to survey the room.

"Mr. Babatunde," Sergei began, his voice respectful, smooth and measured, "I trust you are well?"

"I am indeed, Mr. Stepanov," Phillip replied, his tone almost controlled, betraying the excitement that bubbled within him only to an attentive observer such as the one in front of him. Sergei produced a bulging envelope, its contents were concealed but its significance was clear. Phillip's eyes were drawn to it hungrily, his heart quickened at the sight, the anticipation of reward mingling with a premature sense of triumph.

"You have done well, Mr. Babatunde," Sergei said, his voice conveying approval as if to a favourite dog that had performed a trick. "Your cooperation has been invaluable, and we wish to express our gratitude quickly and in the hope that you will assist us further in the future."

Without a flourish, Sergei slid the envelope across the table, its path smooth and deliberate. Phillip's hand trembled slightly as he reached for it, the weight of the moment settling upon him.

Crassly, he opened the envelope and glimpsed the contents. His joy was uncontainable and produced a huge grin which took over his face. The sum was substantial, far beyond what Phillip had dared to hope for. It was a windfall, a bounty that would change his life.

With a newfound confidence, Phillip looked into Sergei's eyes, his gratitude transformed into temporary allegiance. "Mr. Stepanov," he declared seriously, his voice filled with conviction, "I am honoured to be a part of this… enterprise. The Russians truly understand the proper way of doing business. You have my loyalty."

Sergei's smile was enigmatic, his response measured, his embarrassment invisible. "We value loyalty, Mr. Babatunde. We reward those who serve us well."

Breakfast concluded with a sense of satisfaction and a promise of continued collaboration. As Phillip left the bar, his future looked bright and his step was buoyant. He had crossed a threshold, had entered a world of intrigue and opportunity. The Russians had rewarded him handsomely, and he had pledged his allegiance.

119) <u>Saturday 09:55</u> The King's Private Office, Buckingham Palace, London, UK

In his private office the King was engrossed in his work, his mind focused on the myriad tasks and responsibilities that came with his position. A discreet knock at the door broke his concentration, and Sir Rupert Greville entered. His face wore an expression of concern.

"Your Majesty," he began, addressing the King with the salutation used by all staff on the first meeting of each day, "I bring news from Nigeria." The King looked up. The situation in Nigeria had become a matter of great concern and the fate of MacLeish and Reaper weighed heavily on the King's mind.

"MacLeish is captured by the Russians in an ambush," Sir Rupert continued, his voice steady, his words carefully chosen. " Reaper has been wounded by a rifle bullet striking his body armour in the chest area. He likely has broken ribs, possibly concussion. We do not yet know how the Russians were able to achieve this."

The news was troubling, the implications far-reaching. The King's face, usually a mask of composure, betrayed a hint of frustration.

"The SIS have told Reaper it will take two days to get an AWACS there," Sir Rupert added, "But also that there will be no military support for a rescue of MacLeish. I believe the opinion of the Prime Minister with regard to not offending the Nigerian Government has caused them to waver in their support for the operation."

The King's eyes narrowed, his mind working quickly. He was aware that the situation called for decisive action, for a response that balanced political considerations and diplomatic sensitivities in a manner more favourable to British interests.

But what he said was, "Authorize the immediate priority dispatch of a surveillance aircraft to find MacLeish," his voice was decisive, his words leaving no room for doubt. "Have military support in the form of an SAS Assault Team and anything else you think appropriate sent to Nigeria now so as to be available when Reaper asks us for it. Send young Oliver Beaumont-Blackwood if he is available. Have our people within SIS arrange this immediately. The Nigerians can put any fireworks down to Boko Haram. I will smooth out any diplomatic problems which arise."

The words were spoken with a conviction that reflected the King's deeply held belief in the importance of duty, the sanctity of loyalty, and the unbreakable bond that united the Crown with those who served it. Sir Rupert, his face reflecting his understanding of the King's position, nodded in agreement. "I will arrange that immediately sir," he assured, his voice too now filled with determination.

As Sir Rupert took his leave, the King made a secure call to Abuja, Nigeria.

120) <u>Sunday 03:18</u> A Learjet 75 Over Lagos, Nigeria

The RAF had not sent a Boeing E-7 Wedgetail, the most advanced and capable early-warning, signals interception and battlefield command centre on the planet. They had reacted to their orders with typical British understatement by sending a small, inoffensive business jet to look for Mac.

From the outside the aircraft looked like a standard civilian Learjet 75 complete with red and white livery; it even had a number on its tail which belonged to its apparent twin. A ground observer looking through a good telescope with built in night-vision, or an inept pilot passing dangerously close, would see nothing but an executive jet, a toy or a tool for a very wealthy flier.

If an aircraft had come upon the Learjet tonight, they might have noticed that the transponder was switched off. And if they had it on radar… well they wouldn't have it on radar because it was coated with a patent radar absorbing paint which gave it the reflective signature of an anorexic seagull at all civilian and military radar frequencies. And the performance specifications were not what might be expected either: The range of 2,060 nautical miles and speed of 432 knots were considerably improved. The aircraft represented a serious case of books and covers.

Within the cabin it was a little different too. A crack RAF crew of 5 SigInt (Signals Intelligence) operators, together with their kit, filled the rear compartment which would ordinarily seat eight business people in comfort. Every man and woman present had Enhanced Developed Vetting as their security rating. That is the level required to be entrusted with the control of nuclear weapons.

The pilot called back casually to the signals crew over the joint net, "ETA Lagos figures 3 ladies and gentlemen." There was no perceptible reaction, all eyes remained glued to their screens as they knew where they were. And they knew why they were there too. To pick up the incredibly weak signal from a tracker implanted beneath the skin under a captured operatives arm. Time was of the essence, and failure was not an option.

A red light began to flash on a crowded dashboard. The operator facing it spoke into her microphone, "We have a signal, sir." An older man spoke without turning from his screen, Get me a plot sergeant."

A heavily built sergeant flicked a switch and ran his fingers over a keyboard. The map on the screen in front of him had a small flashing red light now. He expanded the view and pressed a button on a piece of equipment to his left. "I have a lock and a grid reference, sir."

The officer spoke again, "Clear, recalibrate and confirm please."

A few minutes passed in silence. "Confirmed."

"Very good. Call it in."

121) <u>Sunday 03:32</u> An Airbus A220-100 Off The Nigerian Coastline

E Squadron was an elite within an elite. They were the squadron of the Special Air Service which was tasked with supporting British intelligence operatives, usually MI5 or MI6 people, when they required bodyguards locally, when they were working in unfriendly parts of the world or when they were in need of other close military support.

Despite their talent for extreme violence and destruction, it was a prerequisite of joining E Squadron that an SAS Trooper be capable of blending into the background of an apparently civilian setting. So they did have to at least look reasonably civilised.

This restriction meant that those Troopers of a distinctive appearance due to excessive height, musculature or scarring were unable to join. And their reputation may be summed up as follows: Regular SAS Troopers used to joke that E Squadron were kept in a hangar at the bottom of the parade square and thrown raw meat occasionally. The parade square, of course, was a euphemism for the regimental car park.

Mac was still a member of E Squadron, and a well-liked one, despite his semi-permanent attachment as bodyguard to Colonel Mike Reaper. And his mates were coming for him.

The Airbus A220-100 had been flying all night from Bristol Airport, UK in the confident expectation of Mac's position being discovered. Now it was approaching a spot 35 miles from the Nigerian coast.

With a cruising speed at 40,000 feet of 550 miles per hour and a range of 4,000 miles the RAF pilot, Squadron Leader Andrew Henderson, had covered the 5,000 mile trip down the West Coast of Africa in just over ten hours despite head winds and a mid-air refuelling RV off Mauritania. Now he was thinking about another refuelling rendezvous on the trip home and considering where he would have to switch his transponder back on before he did so.

Again, this aircraft was not quite what it appeared to be. On long charter to the British Ministry Of Defence, it was used to transport up to a hundred fully armed troops wherever they were required at short notice. A requirement called upon more regularly than some might be aware. It was painted in the same radar absorbent material as was the Learjet 75, so that it would not be noticed overflying most sensitive targets.

It its current configuration, the 220 had one row of seats running down each side of the fuselage as this left plenty of room for equipment and extra

men could always sit on the floor. Tonight there was no need for this as there were only nine passengers, Captain Oliver Beaumont-Blackwood and eight men, together with the usual three airmen of the dispatch crew.

There used to be a time when men of good family could buy a commission in the British Army and so there were a certain proportion of aristocratic types in the military who were neither very bright nor very tough. Those times have long since passed, and in any event, Oliver was very much one of the other kind of aristocrat. The kind that grew up in a harsh public school situated in the highlands of Scotland. A school which enforced cold showers after a bracing run in the sleet every morning. The weak pupils typically died. The ones that didn't die were used to expand and manage the British Empire.

Today their employment is more subtle; they work in merchant banks and the like. Or they join the British Army and play polo between stints pacifying the locals in various parts of the world. This type of aristo thinks selection for the SAS is like being back at school.

The troopers were all following the timeless British Army dictum; eat when you can, shower when you can, shit when you can and sleep when you can. They were asleep to a man and the fuselage reverberated to the snoring. Oliver checked his watch, just before Henderson called through the internal net, "Captain, we have an ETA of minutes three zero. Thought you might want to wake your beauties up. Over."

"Thank you Captain." Oliver shook his head at his sleeping men. Taking a breath he called out, "Come along chaps shake a leg." He knew his men joked about his "posh" background and he played it up for the humour. His men were quickly awake and alert. It came with the job description. Now they watched him carefully, expecting a final briefing.

All members of the SAS are trained in static-line parachuting such as airborne soldiers do, and many are trained in HALO parachuting, where a man jumps from about 40,000 feet, which is over normal radar, and free-falls to less than 1,000 feet, which is under normal radar, before opening their 'chute. This is fine for a covert entry into a country so long as the aircraft can get quite close to the target.

For this operation it had been decided not to risk compromising security for no advantage by overflying Nigeria and these men would jump HAHO. That is high altitude, high opening. So the men would jump at 40,000 feet, but 35 miles off the Nigerian coastline. And they would open their ram-air long-distance steerable 'chutes immediately and fly them to where they wanted to land. This might be as much as 40 miles from their jumping point so there was a great deal of flexibility in the event of unhelpful winds at altitude.

With their parachutes strapped to their backs, wearing black jump suits proof against long exposure to a temperature of -60 degrees, and with a small tank of compressed air for breathing strapped to their chests, the men were almost ready to go.

One last thing, clip their containers to their harness to fit between their legs. Military paratroopers pretty much always jump with a tubular sleeve or container of some kind on a cord. This is to carry weapons, ammunition, explosives, water and all the other kit which might obstruct the use of a parachute if strapped directly to the body. With HALO and HAHO jumpers the mounting of the container is somewhat different to static line as there is an element of free-fall involved and the luggage can get in the way of the air-flow and affect stability before the chute opens.

As one might expect, for this operation the SAS men's containers were crammed with all manner of equipment. When they jumped their containers would be clipped close to their crotch but when close to landing a clip would be released and the container allowed to hang some thirty feet blow the parachutist so that it would land first and his 'chute would have time to slow up from the accelerated rate of descent caused by the extra weight in the container.

The men checked each other's equipment.

Then the dispatchers checked it again.

122) **<u>Sunday 03:38</u> Unit 17, Apapa Industrial Estate, West Of The Lagoon, Lagos, Nigeria**

Within the warehouse Maxwell lay sleeping in the cab of his truck. In a corner, Mike had sought the embrace of sleep on a makeshift bed of blankets, his head and body both aching from recent wounds, his mind burdened with concern for his captured friend.

The silence of the night was shattered by a sudden alert from Mike's laptop, a harbinger of news. In a swift, practiced motion, he rolled to his feet, his body reacting with military precision even as his mind struggled to shake off sleep's lingering haze. He staggered at the blinding pain in his head and chest. He pressed a button and the screen flickered to life, it was a message from the Palace:

"Mac has been located. See attached.
Your request anticipated: E Sqdn Team arriving 05:30
HAHO to your landing loc.
Beacon and clearance if convenient.
Good luck,
Beefeater"

Mike's eyes scanned the links on the message, his mind desperate to see the details. Mac was at a warehouse within the Lagos Port Complex, a mere two and a half miles away. There was a hi-res photograph from the air with an arrow, the building was marked on Google maps and there was an 8-figure grid reference to put in the GPS. It was good work by someone.

"My fairy godmother has sent me a message, Maxwell," he exclaimed dryly, a note of hope in his voice.

"Oh, that is good," Maxwell replied, his puzzled smile filled with support, though the meaning of Mike's words eluded him.

"My people have found Mac and are sending soldiers to help rescue him."

Maxwell considered, "Your boss changed his mind did he?" he asked, his tone light.

"The big boss over-rode him, more like," Mike replied, a smile playing on his lips.

"Ah, the big chief has spoken," Maxwell mused, his eyes twinkling with satisfaction.

"You never spoke a truer word, Maxwell. We have to prepare a welcoming party by the beach for 05:30 this morning. And we will take the truck to bring our people back here," Mike declared, his voice filled with a newfound energy.

Maxwell patted his truck affectionately, his eyes filled with pride. "The great She-Erin (Lead Elephant) is ready for your command, Mike."

123) Sunday 03:42 Unit 23a, Badia Industrial Park, Lagos Ports Complex, Lagos, Nigeria

Saturday had been a long day: Mac had been visited every hour or so and usually knocked around a little for the amusement of the guards. He had reacted very little, acting semi-conscious. Now he sat on the steel chair, hands in front and cuffs around the pipe just as he had been left. His head was slumped forwards onto his arms and a little blood had dripped onto the concrete floor where it had run from his broken nose and split cheek.

There was a rolling metallic click as the key turned in the lock and the door opened once more. Though it remained night, the burly guard who had been wielding the rubber hose was clearly on night duty too, and bored, as he had come to pay him yet another visit. And this time brought a smaller friend with him to gloat.

“Hey, English, you sleep?” His tormentor swaggered across from the door to stand beside Mac’s chair and began to bend as if to bring their faces together.

With the speed of a mongoose on amphetamines, Mac’s hand whipped around from beside the pipe and he jammed two fingers deep into the man’s eyes. The guard rocked back clutching his face, his mouth open but remained silent as men do in such cases. The open cuffs slid down behind the pipe to the floor.

Before the guard’s companion had time to think, let alone move, Mac swung himself to his feet, turned and lashed out with a booted foot, catching the other man in the groin and causing him to double over. Taking the first man as being no danger, Mac grabbed the second man by his neck and belt and ran his head into the concrete wall, hard. He crumpled to the floor, dead, his head smashed in at the crown like an egg.

Turning to the blinded man, still staggering and clutching his eyes, Mac smiled grimly and side-kicked one leg at the knee with a certain satisfaction, breaking it and causing his tormentor to topple straight to the floor. Mac took a couple of steps as a run up and jumped. Coming down with both heels onto his chest he broke the man's ribs and ruptured his heart.

"A thought ye might like a wee scrap, no?"

He first shook blood and life back into his hands then scanned the room for cord and found nothing Taking off the men's trousers Mac tied the ends together to make an effective strap some eight feet long. He stopped and listened for a few moments, checking for signs of movement within the unit. Nothing. Opening one of the main windows he saw that there was a drop of a little over twenty feet to the ground.

Fastening one end of his make shift rope to the window mechanism with one of the men's boot laces he threw the remainder out and saw that it stopped some ten feet from the floor. Like a bed tempered ferret Mac was through the window, down the strap and dropped fairly lightly to the ground. Looking around, there was no one in sight; and still no one inside seemed to have noticed his escape. Satisfied that there would be no immediate pursuit, he set off through the night at a jog for the port exit. Fortunately, the gate guard checked people on the way in, not the way out. Strange but true.

124) <u>Sunday 04:01</u> An Airbus A220-100 Off The Nigerian Coastline

The Airbus A220-100 was now approaching a point ten minutes from its target, a cross on the map over featureless sea, 35 miles South of Lagos, Nigeria.

Flight Lieutenant Graham Bagley's eye caught the green indicator light signalling their arrival at the last way-marker before their target. As co-pilot and first officer he was responsible for admin of this kind. Of every kind, really. He turned automatically to the pilot and captain of the aircraft, Squadron Leader Andrew Henderson, "Figures ten to target sir."

Henderson did not turn, he continued to concentrate on the wall of indicators in front of him. "Very good, number one, make sure our passengers are wrapped up warmly and have them let us know when they want to lose the air."

In the rear of the aircraft, by the specially adapted exit door, the Jump Master caught Oliver's eye, "Are you ready to lose the air sir?" Sergeant Major "Punchy" Stevenson was a grizzled old Warrant Officer in the RAF Regiment and had supervised the parachute training of all the men in this SAS unit since they took their first balloon jump. His skin was like teak, dried and hardened with sun and age.

Oliver stood opposite the door and his men stood in a line running up the aisle of the aircraft. Every man was ready to go with oxygen mask fitted. One of the jump-master's crew finished checking the kit on the closest trooper and came to check Oliver. Oliver turned to Punchy, "When you are ready Sergeant Major." With that the SAS Captain fitted his mask snugly in place.

Punchy glanced at his team to confirm they had their masks on and spoke into his microphone to the co-pilot, "Depressurise now, sir."

"Confirm depressurise Jump Master?"

"Confirm depressurise, sir."

A moment or two later the air-pressure in the cabin reduced dramatically and the men swallowed repeatedly to equalise the pressure in their ears. Punchy's two-man crew now worked the fittings on the door to move it outwards and have it slide forward parallel to the fuselage on a strengthened rail out of the way of the jumpers.

The pitch of the engines dropped and, without any obvious sign, the flaps went down on the wings as the aircraft slowed to barely above a stall in the cold, thin air at 40,000 feet.

The jump crew stood out of the way, Punchy stood by the door and patted Oliver on the shoulder and he led his men out the door.

Oliver looked up and check his canopy had deployed properly, all good, no lines crossed. Then he scanned the sky and located his men, all on open 'chutes and converging on him from an extended line to one side. Exiting the aircraft at just over a second between each man they had opened their chutes about four hundred feet apart. He flew a circle and checked out the lights in the distance, Lagos for sure. Better safe than sorry so he looked down at the navigation console on his chest, and saw the arrow pointing a gnat's to the right of Lagos.

"Number off gentlemen."

"One okay."

"Two okay."

The role call completed and the unit flew towards the coast.

Technical Notes:
The higher a plane flies, the thinner the air, and the thinner the air the faster an aircraft has to fly to avoid stalling and tumbling to the ground. At 40,000 feet, an Airbus A220-100 has to maintain a speed above 190 knots, even with the nose trimmed up and full flaps down. And given the normal jump speed for paratroopers is half that, there is quite a wind whipping by as a man exits the aircraft.

This wind grips a man and appears to throw him to the rear, following the path of any turbulence generated by the body of the aircraft and hopefully below and clear of the horizontal stabilizer, the part which all civilians call the rear wing. This lasts for a few moments until air resistance slows his lateral velocity and he begins to fall straight down. It takes longer to read than to do.

Each man left the aircraft facing forwards into the -60 degree, 200 mph gale and lay into it as they were thrown, effectively, backwards; stabilising themselves and avoiding a spin by forming the classic star shape with their arms and legs. In a normal static-line jump the airborne warriors almost run down the aisle and leave as quickly as possible so they are not spread too far by the travel of the aircraft. An aircraft plodding along at perhaps 100 knots.

In this case, the aircraft was moving fast, approximately 300 feet per second, and spreading them across the sky; but on the other hand their parachutes were not the standard round airborne jobs with minimal steerage, they were ram-air models which amounted to flying wings, effectively fabric gliders. And gliders with zero radar reflection too.

125) <u>Sunday 04:41</u> Unit 17, Apapa Industrial Estate, West Of The Lagoon, Lagos, Nigeria

Mike had just got to sleep when there was a syncopated banging on the steel pedestrian door to the unit. Groggy, he lifted his head and wondered for a moment where has was. God, his head hurt. The banging continued and Maxwell was already at the door, looking to Mike for the nod to open it. Mike eased his Glock from under his makeshift pillow and nodded.

Maxwell called through the metal, "Hello, Who's there?"

A moment of silence then, "Let me in ye daft bugger."

Mike laughed and nodded to Maxwell who then slid back the heavy bolt.

Mac staggered into the dim light, his face a mess.

"Fuck's sake, Mac, you look like you lost one." Mike was on his feet and laughing with relief.

"Och, ye should've seen the ither laddie. Fetch me a dram."

Maxwell produced a bottle of rum from Mike's stash and poured a generous helping into a mug. Mac seized it and chugged it down as if it were tea.

"How bad is it?" Mike was making banter.

"Well it's not G10 rum like the QM gets me but…"

Mike laughed in relief, "No, you daft twat, how badly are you injured?"

"I'll no be up for the video dating but I'll live." Mac held out the mug for a refill. "I thought ye'd ge'en me up, so I cam hame masel'."

"I just got a report that the Raff found you an hour ago, so we have the address, and that the heavy cavalry are coming to rescue you at 05:30. Landing at the beach where we landed."

"Jumpin' in are they?" Mac seemed pretty normal. Amazingly.

"HAHO from offshore to land about 05:30 plus or minus."

"Whit are ye gonnae dae?"

"We are going to go in the truck to collect them. Bring them back here and then work out how we are going to find the Russians' new base. I think it is certain they will have moved on the assumption that you have told our side where you were held."

"Aye, like enough."

126) Sunday 05:19 A Sandy Beach Near Akinlade, 15 Miles East Of Lagos, Nigeria

Maxwell rolled the truck to a halt on a dirt road 30 yards from the beach where Mike and Mac had landed the week before. He switched off the lights and sat in companionable silence with the men for a moment as they stared out over the dark sea.

"We are a minute or two early. We'd better take a look around. Don't want any witnesses." Mike was in jeans and a T-shirt and carried a silenced MP5DS in one hand as he climbed out of the cab. Mac pulled his MP5DS from the door clip and followed Mike. Maxwell's eyes were wide at the implication of Mike's words. He looked puzzled for a moment then climbed out too.

The early morning was still very dark, as is the way so close to the equator. Daylight would come like it was switched on in a little over an hour. Nevertheless, the two men held their weapons close to their bodies to avoid a scary silhouette if anyone was around. Mac took a turn to the East for a few hundred yards and turned to come back. Mike set off to the West and saw a couple laid under a palm tree, presumably courting. "Shit."

Mike scanned the sky as best he could over the dark sea. Nothing, but then there wouldn't be until there was. He set off almost at a jog back to the truck. Maxwell and Mac came to meet him. "Maxwell, we have a young couple under a tree a few yards from the landing point. I really don't want to kill them."

Maxwell's eyes stretched.

"Any ideas to move them?"

Maxwell thought for a moment, "You are not the only people to use this coast for private business Mike. People land drugs here all the time. Offer them some money to go away and give the impression you are waiting for a drugs shipment. They will say nothing."

"Brilliant! How much should we offer them?"

"Dollars or Naira?"

"I have a wad of dollars in my wallet."

"Twenty dollars would be plenty, Mike. More than that might be thought odd."

Mike opened his wallet and counted out fifty dollars in tens and twenties. "Take that and sort them out. And get yourself a drink tonight. You saved me a nasty job."

Maxwell trotted off about his task.

Mike's headset sprang into life, "Hello Crab, this is seagull, over."

He replied, "Crab send over."

The headset spoke in the plummy voice of Captain Oliver Beaumont-Blackwood, "Locked on your beacon, Crab. Confirm clear over."

"Crab, clear over."

"Seagull, copy that. Will be with you in figures 10 to 15 over."

"Crab, copy out."

twelve minutes later a line of black shadows appeared over the sea and nine men made an almost silent landing on the beach in a fairly close grouping around Mike and Mac. Immediately they touched down every man detached his container, grabbed his 'chute and bundled it up over one arm. Within a minute all the men were gathered around Mike and Mac.

Maxwell had the truck turned around and Mac walked up to meet the soldiers on the sand. Mike scanned the assembled men; dressed identically in black, it was not obvious who was the officer and the two waited for someone to speak.

One did in a Liverpool accent, "So, Mac, we've had to come and bail your sorry arse out again, you ugly bastard."

Mac didn't miss a beat, "I'll have ta' keep ma hand on ma wallet no' you're here ye Scouse git." The men laughed at the banter that marked a strong bond.

Captain Beaumont-Blackwood spoke through a smile and extended a hand to Mike, "Beaumont-Blackwood, Captain, sir."

Mike shook his hand, "Oliver! Good to see you again. Call me Mike. We have a lift for you behind the trees but you would be as well in civvies."

Oliver nodded to the men and they carried their bundled 'chutes and kit to the truck, threw them in the back then quickly changed into various riffs around the theme of jeans, desert boots and shirts. Then they followed Mac to climb up into the open back of the truck themselves. Oliver joined Mike and Maxwell in the cab.

"Drive on Macduff." The quote was lost but the intention was obvious and the engine roared into life.

127) <u>Sunday 16:33</u> Unit 17, Apapa Industrial Estate, West Of The Lagoon, Lagos, Nigeria

Inside the bare confines of Unit 17, two trestle tables had been pushed together side-by-side to serve as the hub of operations. Oliver was seated next to Mike, eyes fixed on a laptop screen, while the rest of the men settled around the table. Mugs of hot sweet tea were handed around by Maxwell.

Mike filled the men in on the situation: "The Russians will have moved their operation immediately following Mac's escape. Unit 23a still shows life, but it's a ruse. We don't yet know where they have gone."

He continued, laying out the challenge ahead, "The Russians will be obliged to keep their operation going as it is so important to Moscow, so their new base will be defensible. They will know we are looking for them and likely to find them so they will be ready for us. There are less than a dozen of them but they are GRU."

He then turned to the plan, "The British Embassy will try to find the Russians' new base for us by tracking the movement of rice from the next shipment landed and by people traffic at the Russian Embassy. They do need fresh supplies of the Additive regularly from the embassy for sure. They might be able to move it all in one go."

With a thoughtful pause, he added, "I am going to proceed as if we will know where the Russians have moved to by the end of this week, so I have some little jobs to keep you all occupied. Then we can move forward as soon as we know both where the Russians' new location is and that they have a delivery of the Additive there. I want to catch them in the act of doctoring the cocaine if I can as it will make for better photos."

He looked around the room, his eyes meeting each man's, "This is what I want you to do...." His voice was firm, his instructions clear. The men listened intently, knowing that the success of the mission depended on each man's actions over the coming days.

128) Tuesday 11:19 Sir Henry Attwood's Office, Whitehall, London

In Whitehall Sir Henry Attwood sat back in his expensive carved swivel chair and stared blankly at the dark screen of a laptop sitting lonely on his expansive green-leather topped desk. The china cup on a side-table held rapidly cooling tea. His mind was obviously elsewhere. The speaker on his laptop clicked and spoke, "Permission to action operation Butterfly, sir?"

"Permission granted."

Henry came back to life and pressed the space bar on his laptop which brought the screen to life too. He touched a few keys and the view from a camera appeared, looking down into a quiet London street scene. He watched the video feed carefully, sipping his tepid tea.

129) Tuesday 11:31 Lower Sloane Street, London, UK

Yelena Ivanova strolled down Lower Sloane Street with the gentle roll of a fashion model. Head back, her long blond hair hung loose over a pale jacket, her long legs accentuated by tight, expensive, blue-jeans. To tone down her traffic-stopping appearance she had concealed her dazzling emerald eyes with fashionably oversized dark glasses. A passing red Ferrari stopped in the road nevertheless and the swarthy, young driver stared. She ignored him, but missed nothing and smiled inside.

She drew abreast a shop selling over-priced clothes for the anorexic and stopped to gaze in the window for a minute or two, taking in her surroundings from the reflection. Her actions habitual after all these years.

A small white van, sign-written for a plumber, pulled up on the red tow-away lines behind her and the doors opened. Two men in cheap tracksuits climbed out, they were wearing surgical masks – a not-so-common relic of the pandemic nowadays. She tensed slightly at this. Then caught her breath as the men quickly closed on her from either side.

A long killing blade appeared in Yelena's right hand, and she turned to fight like a cornered cat, but the men were too quick and far too well-trained. One caught her wrist and folded her hand in against the arm, stretching the tendons and causing the knife to drop from the opened hand. He caught it in his spare hand. The other smoothly threw a cloth bag over her head and pulled the cord tight around her neck, pressed his hand over her mouth to keep her quiet. There was a sharp prick in her arm as a needle entered. A hand protected the top of her head as she was forced into the back of the van.

Two passing women stopped, one raised her hand to her mouth in shock. But the whole event had taken seconds and the van was now some way down the street and lost amongst the traffic.

130) **Tuesday 11:31 Sir Henry Attwood's Office, Whitehall, London**

Sir Henry watched Yelena's efficient collection on his laptop and smiled like a well-bred lizard. He sipped the last of his cold tea from the antique china cup and exhaled gently with evident satisfaction. Looking around the elegant office which had somewhat confined him in recent years he spoke softly to himself, "Now we can have an honest conversation, madam."

131) **Friday 09:27 Unit 17, Apapa Industrial Estate, West Of The Lagoon, Lagos, Nigeria**

Unit 17 was quiet and had been all week. No 'phones were allowed as their use might be picked up by Nigerian or Russian intel. Oliver read a copy of The Times collected by Maxwell from an Expat bar. The men were gambling at present. Watching a competition from their beds between Scouse and a trooper of the Yorkshire persuasion to establish who could hold a position for the longest. Thighs parallel with the ground and back vertical against the wall. A test of leg strength which had just passed the 23 minute mark according to the timekeeper. Scouse grimaced and the other trooper said something in Yorkshire. Someone asked Scouse if he was, "Made up."

Mike was reading a book, "The Traveller's Guide To Lagos" Only two of the men were on duty; One was a trooper watching a laptop connected to the security cameras, which were in turn watching the perimeter of Unit 17. The other watched Mike's laptop whose screen showed a view of the walled compound to which the Russians had moved their operation.

The Russians' new home had been found by the British Embassy people on Tuesday. The invisible embassy operators, doubtless MI6, had followed shipments of rice from a Columbian freighter as they were distributed to wholesale warehouses. One delivery site had stood out because it was run by Russians and it was defensible. Drones had confirmed the intel.

The new Russian compound consisted of one residential unit and two small warehouse-type buildings with an 8 foot wall around them. It was situated in a busy residential/light-commercial area off Okorogbo Street and only a mile or so from the port as the crow flew. Yet it might as well have been fifty for the winding roads and crush of buildings between the two sites. The live feed showing their comings and goings was beamed in from a tiny drone parked inconspicuously on a nearby rooftop.

The mood of the room switched instantly as the Trooper on drone-watch called out to Oliver, "I think we have a delivery Boss."

Oliver and Mike leapt to their feet and stood behind the man, craning to see what the screen was showing. A few moments of consideration and Oliver commented, "Looks like a delivery to me. What do you think Mike?"

Mike shook his head, "We are never going to be sure but it certainly looks that way. A package coming in by car from the Russian embassy by its plates. They are not bringing a takeaway."

Oliver pulled a face, "It is such an amateur move to use an embassy car. I'm looking for a trick. But I can't see what they might be doing other than a delivery."

Mike thought aloud, "If they knew we were watching they would pause the operation. Could they know for sure? I doubt it."

Oliver considered for a moment, "If they knew we were watching there would not be a genuine delivery but why would they set up a fake delivery? Why bother?"

Mike's tone changed, "I think we have no option but to take it as real. If it is real we catch them with their hands dirty, and if it is not a delivery but something else then we will likely still get a result. And we shut them down either way. We will go in tonight."

132) <u>Friday 09:33</u> Car Park, Hotel Sota, Elblag, Northern Poland

MI6 Officer Colson opened the rear door of the Range Rover and stepped back for Pilot Officer Alexander Kuznetsov to climb in. He closed the door then opened the front passenger door and boarded the vehicle himself. Officer Drake was already behind the wheel and pulled out of the car park leaving the comforts of Hotel Sota behind.

They had only stayed one night in the very modest circumstances allowed by their expense account but the bar was good and the three men had spent a pleasant evening chatting with Alexander about his family. In Russian, of course. Alexander was obviously not trained in counter interrogation and they picked up a few tid-bits which were now forwarded to GCHQ.

Drake drove them South East out of the city of Elblag and took the E28 North East for the border with Kaliningrad Oblast. (Province) Technically Kaliningrad was a Russian semi-exclave, a diplomatically arranged Russian holding of land to give them a port on the Baltic; and surrounded by Poland on the South and Lithuania to the North and East.

As they drove through the pleasant, green but completely flat, farmland, Colson drew his Glock 19 with its lightweight polymer frame and pulled the slide back then let it go forward, chambering a round for instant action. A look of surprise crossed Alexander's face and Colson saw it in the second over-screen mirror as he returned the weapon to his shoulder holster. In explanation he said, «Ty milyy mal'chik Alexander, no my ne znayem tvoikh druzey». Roughly, "You're a lovely boy Alexander, but we don't know your friends."

Drake pulled the vehicle into a long, double-width lay-by just short of the border between Poland and Kaliningrad. A low-end, beige Mercedes 4 door saloon lay ahead, at least two people inside and the only other vehicle in sight. Drake stopped fifty yards short of it. Both the front doors on the Mercedes opened and two serious men in long, dark coats and hats stepped out. Likely FSB. One focussed his stare on the British vehicle and the other turned to a rear door and opened it from the outside. Likely a child-lock switched on. A heavy-set man of probably Indian extraction stepped out and waved.

Colson waved back and turned to Alexander, "You know the drill?" It was a statement, a reminder more than a question. Alexander nodded seriously.

Taking up station either side of Alexander, the British agents walked him half way to the Russian vehicle and stopped.

The Russians did exactly the same and came to a halt ten feet in front of the British. One Russian called out in Russian, "Pilot Officer Alexander Kuznetsov?"

Alexander replied, "Da."

Colson called out, "Faris Iqbal?"

Faris replied, "Yes."

Colson continued, addressing his opposite number, "Dovol'ny li vy prodolzheniyem obmena plennymi?"

"Are you happy to continue with the prisoner exchange?"

"Da!"

Colson nodded to Alexander and the young man began to walk forward.

Faris began to walk towards the British agents.

Without warning, the Russian agents drew their MPL pistols, the Russian ersatz copy of the Glock 17. The man on the left fired one round into the centre of Alexander's chest. The strike made him stagger backwards but his heart was destroyed by the expanding bullet and he was dead on his feet. The man on the right fired across and hit Colson in the centre of his chest. More importantly, in the centre of his ballistic plate.

Before either Russian had time to get off another round Drake had straight-drawn his Glock 19 from a quick-draw side-holster and shot both Russian agents, each in the middle of his face to avoid any body armour. They died where they stood. By the time all three corpses had hit the ground Colson had his pistol out in a slower cross-draw from a shoulder holster. "Bloody Hell that was fast Billy."

Billy Drake shrugged and smiled modestly as he put his pistol away.
Faris was less restrained, "What the fuck happened there?"

"At a guess, Faris, the Russians didn't want their man back and would rather it looked like bad faith on our part. Deniable murder anyway." Colson shook his head in mild regret, "Shame, he was a nice boy."

133) <u>Friday 23:48</u> A Truck Leaving Apapa Industrial Estate, West Of The Lagoon, Lagos, Nigeria

Maxwell dropped straight onto Mobil Road from Unit 17, all the men in the back under canvas and the two officers at his side in the cab. It was late but the traffic was still heavy with a mixture of hustlers still working and people going out for the evening.

He drove West with the eponymous Mobil Depot sprawling to his left, a mass of warehouses and oil tanks. Next, the Army barracks and they arrived at the bridge over the "canal", a fifty foot wide dry ditch full of bushes and running North to South. This bridge was the only way across the ditch locally in a motor, a tactical consideration in case of interference in their mission.

Half a mile further and a turn right onto Bale Road heading North. Their route went right and left as Maxwell found his way by memory through the maze of dead-end roads which led eventually to their destination. He pulled up opposite an electrical shop on Okunola Street, with the Russian compound just around the corner. Either side were ramshackle huts and abandoned vehicles. Junk and scrap vehicles lay everywhere. In this part of the world a great many people slept where they worked. The battered old truck was camouflaged amongst its peers in this low rent neighbourhood. Here they would wait.

Oliver called quietly through the back window of the cab to the men behind him, "Stand easy guys."

134) **Saturday 04:01 Shell Oil Storage, West Of Lagoon, Lagos, Nigeria**

The Shell Oil storage facility covers some acres of ground close to the lagoon and is surrounded by various naval facilities including the Western Naval Command Headquarters complex. Besides the ubiquitous large sheds, the facility hosts dozens of oil storage tanks standing like truncated pillars in various sizes ranging from huge to enormous. They were holding tanks for various grades of oil and the many kinds of spirit distilled from crude. All of them were highly inflammable, if not potentially explosive.

At 04:01 there was a sharp crack as a high explosive cutting charge sliced through the metal wall of a tank holding some thousands of tons of naphtha, a highly volatile distillate commonly used as paint thinners. The blast not only blew a hole in the tank wall closest to the detonation point but the shock wave, which travelled through the liquid filling the tank, split open the far side and a flood of burning naphtha surged out and across the facility, surrounding and igniting other storage tanks as it spread.

A few minutes later and acres of tanks were blazing and sending black smoke in a towering column to the sky. But more deadly was the wave of invisible, toxic chemicals in the air, the product of this uncontrolled combustion. Specialist fire crews tumbled from their bunks, put on their fire proof suits and oxygen supplies but there was little they could do; overwhelmed by the wall of flame and the tide of poison gas flooding the site and spreading across the surrounding area. They called for support from the city fire service and the police.

In less than ten minutes more fire crew and police arrived by the score but all they could do was cordon off the area and watch it burn.

135) **Saturday 04:10 Area B Police HQ, Apapa Road, Lagos, Nigeria**

Area B Police Command Headquarters is sited on Apapa Road some half a mile South of the junction with Mobil Road and nearly a mile South of the explosion at the Shell facility. Ordinarily it would be fairly quiet at four in the morning but today it was a hive of activity due to the blast at the Shell site. Sleeping officers were roused from their bunks and others called in from home as Police Commander Hadi Akume did all in his power to support the fire crews and keep the public safe from the spread of fire and noxious gases.

Then the second blast came. A sharp crack demolished a section of the police compound wall just where the landline cables entered, cutting all telephone communications with their sub stations. Taking over the radio room, Commander Akume ordered his police to fall back to their stations and assume a defensive position against what now looked like a coordinated terrorist attack.

136) <u>Saturday 04:15</u> The Nigerian TV Broadcasting centre, 1 Lateef Jakande Rd, Ikeja, Lagos, Nigeria

The Nigerian TV Broadcasting centre is at 1 Lateef Jakande Road, Ikeja, and looks like a small, modern town. Though there are a number of TV production companies in Lagos, their products are all broadcast through the state system from Lateef Jakande Road. At four in the morning on a Saturday, the station was quiet as there was no overnight broadcasting.

Even with the advent of the internet, TV remained an important way for government to speak to the people in times of emergency and so this little town had its own electricity generation plant to ensure this could be achieved in times of emergency, or just to keep going when the regular mains electrical supply failed.

On this particular morning the generator room was not in service and there was no one around. Which was fortunate because at 04:15 an explosion disabled the generating system and put it beyond easy repair.

137) <u>Saturday 04:20</u> Regional Electricity Control Centre, Ayobo Road, Lagos, Nigeria

The Power Holding Company Of Nigeria is a forward thinking, national organisation which supplies electricity to the whole of Nigeria across a Balanced Grid System running at 330,000 volts. The actual electricity is generated from hydro, oil and gas; the gas turbines, with their rapid spin-up time, being used to balance the load across the grid. Lagos itself therefore, both receives power from up country via the national grid and generates its own from oil and gas to support the grid locally.

The Regional Electricity Control Centre on Ayobo Road in Lagos keeps the local grid balanced with their gas turbine generators according to load requirements, and distributes all the incoming power to end users by stepping it down from the high-voltage transmission levels of 330,000 volts to supply homes and small businesses with power at 230 volts and 50 Herz similar to Europe and the UK.

All this has resulted in there being a forest of pylons around the Ayobo Road Control Centre, where power comes in from up country and out again onto the local supply. Three of these pylons were key to the viability of local supply and, following six sharp cracks, these particular pylons collapsed amidst showers of sparks. Small fires broke out where the cables touched anything which might burn.

Lagos went dark and all internet and mobile phone relays went dead. Communications were effectively shut down. All that could be seen was a wall of fire in the distance, taller than the skyscrapers, and a sky lit up by the flames. And, of course, now the government could not speak directly to the majority of the people.

138) <u>Saturday 04:20</u> A Quiet Street Near The Russian Compound, Badla Industrial Park, Lagos, Nigeria

As the lights went out across Lagos Mike tapped the rear of his magazine on the truck dashboard to settle the 9mm rounds to the back and reduce the chance of a stoppage. Then he put the magazine back on his MP5SD and followed Oliver out of the truck cab. Maxwell remained behind the wheel waiting for the signal.

Both of the officers walked around to the back of the truck and looked in the rear. All the men were dressed in the distinctive combat gear of the feared Nigerian Army Special Forces and their hands blacked up with camouflage cream. Under their helmets they wore black balaclavas and attached to their helmets AN/PSQ-22 night vision goggles which combined thermal imaging and light intensification to give very reasonable vision in any kind of light plus the ability to highlight warm targets.

In the isle of the truck-back a trooper was testing a quick-assembly armed drone about three feet across. It too carried a modified MP5SD, mounted below the body. Mike and Oliver stood clear as the drone launched and flew unaided to its programmed staging point on a roof by the Russian compound.

Mike waved the men out and set off along the deserted, dark street. The men followed in staggered file either side of the road but even if they were seen, no one was going to trouble a unit of the local SF as they were known to lack finesse when dealing with civilians. Behind them, Maxwell started the truck and set off back the way he had come, heading for their rendezvous.

Oliver pulled a tiny screen out of his pocket and checked the view from their recon drone which sat opposite the Russian position. It was still on station, hidden in plain sight, a scruffy item in a gutter on a corrugated iron roof. The Russian compound was dark and quiet despite the night's disturbance and the sudden power cut. Were the Ruskies asleep or were they at stand-to and waiting for them?

A left turn and they were on Okorogbo Street. All remained quiet and the Russian compound was 50 yards ahead on the right. From here, still no movement, no hot targets indicating bodies in the night.

The line of men tucked in to the right side of the road and made their way from shanty-stall to stall. All closed and shuttered at this time, such occupants as were awake hiding for their lives now there were Nigerian soldiers prowling around.

Mike turned, caught the men's attention and pointed to an alley. Oliver led his 4 men down it, the men covering alternate sides of the path with their weapons. Over the wall to their left was Russian territory.

Mac crept forward followed by the other four troopers and crossed the closed-up front gate in silence. Mike scanned all around for anything unusual, anything at all. Nothing. The team were now spread across the front and one side of the compound so as to be able to deliver effective cross-fire. But nothing so far had shown any sign of life.

Mike dropped his pack and pulled out a box similar to the one they had used in Colombia. Fired it up and looked through the block wall to check where the occupants were. "Bugger," they were crouching inside, behind their weapons and waiting for them directly behind the wall where he knelt.

Mike whispered into his throat mike, "Drone Op, on my grenade take out the two men on the North side of the compound." A thumbs up indicated he was understood and the drone operator tucked himself into a corner of the alley behind Oliver. He opened the mike and spoke to the men, "There are two more behind here", he pointed to the wall, "And two more unaccounted for."

"Ready for go." Most of the men produced little spring-folding grappling hooks with stirrups on an attached line. They readied to throw, Mike took the pin from a Russian fragmentation grenade and held it lever up. He released the arm, which flew away, the striker went down, and he counted,

"One thousand and one," Then tossed it over the wall to explode in mid air on the other side.

As one man, the team threw their hooks and climbed after them, the armed drone skimmed over the wall and two soft thuds indicated it had taken down its targets, now it was hunting for more. Two shots rang out from inside the compound and Scouse fell forwards from the top of the wall to land by a dead Russian.

Mike was over the wall in moments and saw one of the troopers checking that the Russians downed by his grenade were dead by the simple expedient of shooting them twice each in the head. Someone offered the same service to the armed drone's victims while the remainder of the men surrounded the building used as a dormitory, recognised by all from study of the recce drone's efforts earlier.

There was the detonation of a stun grenade and the men entered the building. A couple of soft thuds and it was over. Mike hurried up to find another dead Russian and Colonel Dimitri Petrenko pinned to the floor by two troopers. They looked for orders. Mike supplied them, "Plasti-cuffs and gaffer tape. Bring him with us. Good effort lads."

Mike stepped outside to see the compound held securely by the team from several fire positions. Now the action was over, a trooper was tending to Scouse. Mike walked over and saw he had been caught by one shot that went in over his left eye and out in front of his left ear. He was alive but that eye was swollen like a tennis ball and the trooper was applying a dressing to keep out the dirt and hold in the white matter which had come out of the exit wound. Scouse jerked a little.

Mike looked to find Oliver and saw him with a camera in his hand coming out of a shed. "I have lots of good pics of the additive, and the coke, plus samples."

"Very good Oli. Will you get me some head shots of the Colonel, just in case we lose him on the way home?"

Oliver nodded, sombre at Scouse being hit, "I'll do that for you right now."

Mike called for the drone operator, still outside in the alley, his charge sitting quiet in the middle of the compound, "Drone, send your bird home please."

"Wilco that boss." The drone rose into the air and took its pre-programmed route to land quietly at unit 17.

Mike saw the gaffer tape ripped painfully from across the Colonel's face to allow a good photographic head shot by Oliver before a fresh strip assured the man's silence. Into his microphone, Mike gave the order to leave, "Okay guys, out through the front gate and over the ditch."

With two men dragging their prisoner by the shoulders, two more carrying Scouse and others carrying their kit, the team jogged around the back of the compound and Eastwards through the mud, junk and bushes which marked the canal. This brought them out to a lane where Maxwell waited for them in an extension of their own industrial park, the engine already running. As the last man climbed in they set off for the few hundred yards through back lanes which would take them back to Unit 17.

139) <u>Saturday 04:33</u> Aso Rock, Presidential Villa, Abuja, Nigeria

In the heart of Nigeria's capital, Ajuba, the Presidential Palace stood as a magnificent symbol of power and authority. Inside, President James Oluwa, a seasoned general himself, was already awake and in his office trying to get ahead of the paperwork. The phone rang, always a harbinger of trouble so early.

The voice on the other end was General Adekunle, head of the army, his tone strained with tension. "Mr President, sir, Lagos is under attack. Explosions. Power cuts and chaos across the city. It must be terrorists."

"General, remain calm," President Oluwa instructed, his voice clam and measured. " I was expecting this attack from Boko Haram, in conjunction with Islamic State West Africa Province, and I have already taken steps to have their leaders arrested. Mobilize your troops to defend Ajuba. Have the police and army take up defensive positions at their bases. Alert the air force to be prepared for action. We must be ready but not hasty with our military response."

"Yes, Mr. President," General Adekunle acknowledged, a touch of relief in his voice at the steady voice and clear orders. The President put down the phone and was left with time to think in the quiet of his study.

The President picked up the phone again, summoning his top advisers. Plans were set in motion, orders given. The heavy machinery of government lurched into action, guided by the cool hand of a leader who knew the stakes.

Outside the palace, the sky was just beginning to lighten, a new day dawning. But for President Oluwa, the challenges of another day had already begun.

140) Saturday 06:03 A Sandy Beach Near Akinlade, 15 Miles South Of Lagos, Nigeria

The time was 06:03 and it would be first light at about 06:30. The beach where the SAS had landed a week earlier was quiet, the air devoid of wind, and the moon's faint glow barely pierced the darkness.

The SAS team were hidden amongst the palms, packs by their sides, weapons ready in case of emergency. A thick, black plastic body-bag held Scouse. Mike and Mac stood vigilant in civilian clothes at the head of the beach, their bags at the ready too, their senses attuned to the night. Mike's hand held a small military VHF radio, a lifeline to their offshore support.

"Hello Dolphin this is Crab, over," Mike's voice broke the silence, crisp and clear.

"Hello Crab this is Dolphin. Comms fives, do we have a clear, over?" the reply came, professional and to the point.

"Crab, Comms fives, All clear, over."

"Dolphin. With you in figures five, out."

The exchange was precise, a practiced exchange of formal words that conveyed all necessary information. Mike pocketed the radio, his gaze fixed on the dark horizon, his thoughts momentarily his own. Mac, sensing the opportunity for a brief connection, ventured, "A penny for yer thoughts?"

Mike's response was swift, his focus unbroken. "Nothing really, I'm not about to get all introspective on you buddy."

Mac retorted, "Thank fuck fae tha'." An attempt at humour that entirely failed to lighten Mike's mood. Their friendship was evident, but the death of Scouse was on everyone's mind. They just showed it in different ways.

"I can see the boat," Mike announced, his eyes picking out the faint silhouette in the distance. His words were a call to action and the men made their way down the beach, carrying their packs and their dead comrade.

Mike hoped the Captain of the submarine would not make an issue about taking Scouse home. There might be a problem if he did.

141) The Ahmed Family Home, Oxenhope, West Of Bradford, UK

In a quaint little town near Bradford, the modest but welcoming home of the Ahmeds stood third along a row of identical houses. Today it was filled with warmth and anticipation because Faris, their eldest son, was coming home after many weeks of absence. The scent of an exotic meal was in the air.

The door opened and Faris stepped in and dropped his case. His face was thin and showed the stress of his secret life, a life his family knew almost nothing about. His parents now knew that he worked for MI5 but that was all they knew and they kept even that to themselves. To their friends, Faris worked for an oil company, in a technical department on a rig in the North Sea.

"Where have you been, son?" his father asked mid hug, concern in his eyes, suspicion and fear mingling with relief. The family had feared the worst, of course.

"I'm alright, Dad," Faris replied, evading the question with practiced ease. "I'm home now, and that's all that matters."

His mother embraced him, tears in her eyes, while his younger siblings looked on, their faces a mix of joy and confusion. They sensed something different about their brother, something they couldn't quite put their finger on. It must be tough working on the oil rigs.

The evening wore on, filled with laughter and the sharing of mundane family news. Yet, the shadow of Faris's secret life lingered, unspoken but palpable. As the family retired for the night, Faris remained standing by the window, his mind on the risks he had taken, the secrets he had kept. He looked at the photographs on the wall, the faces of the people he loved. It was for them that he had chosen this path.

142) A Luxurious Dacha, Rublyovka, West Of Moscow, Russia

In the seclusion of a luxurious dacha outside Moscow, two Russian Generals had convened, their faces lined by years of service, their chests adorned with bands of medals. Both were in dress uniform, and despite being old friends, the air was charged with tension. They had arranged to meet to talk about keeping order on the streets of Moscow.

General Alexei Ivanov poured chilled vodka over ice into crystal glasses, his eyes meeting those of General Viktor Petrov. He proposed the toast to Russia in the traditional long form which the circumstances demanded. The clink of their glasses rang a not-so-subtle reminder of their allegiance.

"Have you heard about Nikolai Kuznetsov?" Ivanov asked, his voice betraying no feelings, one way or the other. Petrov nodded, his expression equally guarded. "Under suspicion, despite his loyalty. His wife gone, his son missing."

They sipped their vodka, the silence heavy with their unspoken thoughts.

"The unrest is spreading," Ivanov continued, his words measured. "From Moscow to other cities. The war in Ukraine has lit a fire amongst tinder."

"The common people are unhappy with the President," Petrov added, his voice low. "They say he is weak and unlucky. He is growing unpopular."

"Perhaps not just the common people are unhappy" " Ivanov said carefully, his eyes fixed on Petrov's, looking for his reaction. "Russia needs a strong leader… Perhaps someone stronger."

The meaning hung in the air, the implication clear yet unspoken.

The two old soldiers continued to talk, skirting around the issue, their habitual discretion avoiding anything approaching a dogmatic statement. The views they were sharing would likely be passed to other men of seniority to test the water further. Before anything of a practical nature was done.

The room was filled with the aroma of fine cigars and the soft clinking of the ice in their glasses. Outside, the snow fell silently, thickening the soft blanket of white which already covered the landscape, as if nature itself was conspiring to keep their conversation a secret.

The meeting ended with a firm handshake, their faces showing no sign of the weighty matters they had discussed. They were soldiers, patriots, men of action. And they knew that the time for action was approaching.

They parted, each returning to his own world, their thoughts on the future of their country. The dacha stood silent, witness to a conversation that never happened but which might change the course of history.

143) General Nikolai Kuznetsov's Dacha Outside Moscow, Russia

Outside, the stars shone with cold indifference, their light reflecting off the smooth, flat snow that covered the grass and trees. Already the single track of footprints was covering.

In General Nikolai Kuznetsov's luxuriously furnished drawing room, the aftermath of violence lay stark and bloody. The icy wind had pushed its way through the open garden doorway, scattering dry, blown snow across the thick, Turkish patterned carpet.

The profound stillness was punctuated by the mournful crying of Laika, the General's old Borzoi wolfhound. Her whimpers filled the room as she attended her fallen master, licking his face with an instinctual blend of affection and confusion.

General Kuznetsov lay motionless, his life extinguished by a wound to the centre of his chest. The blood had spread across the carpet, a dark stain that told a tale of betrayal and death. His eyes, once filled with intelligence and energy, now stared vacant and unseeing.

The room itself, once a place of comfort and elegance, had been transformed into a scene of grim conclusion. The furnishings, so carefully chosen and arranged by Natalia, were now witnesses to a tragedy that would send ripples through the halls of power.

In the cold silence of that room, with only the soft crying of the faithful Laika to mark the passing of time, the enormity of what had occurred settled like a heavy shadow. A chapter had closed, and the implications of that closure would be felt far and wide.

144) The Streets Of Central Moscow, Russia

Rioting had erupted in Moscow, a city now engulfed in chaos and discontent. Men and women, young and old, were united in their protest against the war in Ukraine against the President. What had begun as peaceful demonstrations had escalated into violence, a reflection of the people's deep-seated anger and frustration.

The streets were filled with the sounds of shouting, gunfire, and sirens. Young men, their faces flushed with fury, had armed themselves, challenging the black-clad riot police. The police, in turn, responded with force, their batons and shields and now guns were used to push back the surging crowds.

Buildings were ablaze, the flames leaping into the darkening sky, casting an ominous glow over the city. The acrid smell of burning mingled with the cries of the wounded and the chants of the protesters amid the now almost constant crackle of gunfire. Casualties were mounting, with both protesters and police falling victim to the violence.

Word was spreading that the unrest was not confined to Moscow. Similar scenes were being reported across Russia, a nation on the brink of something larger and more dangerous.

In the midst of the turmoil, voices could be heard, shouting slogans and demands. But above all, there was a sense of desperation, a realization that the situation was spiralling out of control.

Leaders were scrambling to respond, their words careful and measured, but the streets were beyond reason. The people were speaking, and their message was clear: Enough was enough.

As night fell, the situation showed no sign of abating. The city was a battleground, and the stakes were control of Russia. A nation watched and waited, uncertain of what the dawn would bring.

The turmoil was a stark reminder of the fragility of order and the power of collective action. It was a moment that would be etched in history, a turning point that would shape the future of a country at a crossroads. That would shape the world.

145) Freedom Park, Behind Marina Road, Lagos, Nigeria

Freedom Park in central Lagos, once a colonial prison, had transformed into a trendy gathering place for the fashionable young. Its lush greenery, water features, and fast food kiosks made it a pleasant area for an evening rendezvous. Friends and lovers mingled, creating a lively yet safe atmosphere.

At 20:00, it was early by local custom and the park was relatively quiet, providing an ideal setting for a private meeting. George had arranged to meet Phillip in a public place. A common ploy used by those of certain occupations to avoid being overheard. And it which would add to the mystique.

Phillip waited on a bench which marked the spot, concealed in shadows cast by a venerable tree. His grin was broad; he found the intelligence game both effortless and very profitable. He was well pleased with himself and with how his manipulation of his two foolish income sources was progressing. When George arrived, Phillip stood, confident and expectant.

The handshake was firm, but George's troubled expression did not escape Phillip's notice. The informant inquired about his payment, and George's reply was swift and clear.

A suppressed Glock 19 emerged from under George's coat, and a single shot was fired into Phillip's chest. The hollow point bullet did its work efficiently, tearing through Phillip's heart. He was dead before his head touched the ground.

No one in the park reacted to the sound. A single shot rarely draws attention in any event. Anyone who hears a single shot listens for the second and, in the absence of a second, discounts the first and goes about their business. George walked briskly away, his face set like marble, The stone in his stomach heavy with the weight of his actions. This was his first kill, his initiation into the darker side of intelligence work.

The park continued to host friends and lovers, oblivious to the violence that had just occurred. Life moved on, but for George, something had shifted. A rite of initiation had been performed, a line had been crossed and there was no going back.

146) The Dog & Barrel Public House, Westgate, Bradford, UK

The Dog And Barrel, scene of Mike and Mac's "arrest" some few weeks earlier was filling up. The early evening crowd was already rowdy, a mere precursor to the violent chaos that would take over when more alcohol had been consumed.

In a shadowed corner, hidden from prying eyes, a transaction was taking place. Faris Iqbal was engaged in the wholesale purchase of cocaine. The importer opposite him, a man accustomed to the shadows, eyed Faris with a mix of suspicion and hope. The potential for regular business with this new, background-checked contact was lucrative, promising him substantial profits.

Their conversation was terse, filled with the coded language of the trade. Money and sample product exchanged hands with practiced ease. Both men understood the stakes, the balance of trust and treachery that defined their interaction. It was over quickly, a brief exchange, one of many in a place of this kind.

Faris left the establishment, his face impassive, his mind already moving on to the next phase of his operation. The dealer returned to the thrum of the bar, blending into the crowd, another hard face in a room filled with secrets.

The Dog And Barrel continued its nightly performance, a place where alcohol and disorder mingled, where operators and criminals crossed paths, all under the watchful eye of a building that had seen it all before.

147) Liverpool Railway Station, London, UK

Outside Liverpool Station in the centre of London, the morning rush was in full swing. Commuters, bound by timed routine, scurried towards their destinations, a blur of briefcases and hurried conversations. Among them all, a small kiosk stood as a beacon of calm normality, offering newspapers and a few friendly words from the vendor.

Today, however, something was different. The headlines on every paper were dominated by one staggering story. Bold letters announced the capture of Colonel Dimitri Petrenko, a Russian operative caught shipping cocaine into the UK. But this was no ordinary drug trafficking case. This cocaine was laced with a deadly additive, a substance that transformed the drug's users into frenzied murderers and explained all the recent attacks upon innocents, mostly around the North of the UK.

Betty Marsden was recognised by the vendor as she paused to read the headlines and make her purchase. Her eyes widened as she took in the news, a mixture of shock and disbelief playing across her face.

Colonel Petrenko's stern image, now widely disseminated, stared back from the front pages. His capture, executed by the British Secret Service, and supported by the Nigerian Government, was a triumph celebrated across the nation. The implications were profound, reaching into the highest echelons of power and international diplomacy. Perhaps even the Prime Minister's job was safe for another week.

The vendor, accustomed to the ebb and flow of news, engaged Betty in the brief snippet of friendly conversation that people came for, "Terrible ain't it darlin'? But the Ruskies have form for poisoning people don't they?"

"Oh, its awful! But aren't they clever, our secret agents, catching the Russians like that?" Betty continued on her way, the newspaper tucked under her arm, her thoughts consumed by the revelations. The vendor returned to his duties, greeting the next customer with a practiced smile.

The gates of Liverpool Station continued to witness the unending stream of humanity, each person a part of the larger tapestry, each story interwoven with the next. But on this day, the news of Colonel Petrenko's capture shone a light into the shadows and was a reminder of the hidden world that lurked just beneath the surface.

148) Defence Science and Technology Laboratory, Porton Down, UK

Yelena Ivanova, strapped into a restraint chair, was now wearing army issue green coveralls. Somehow she still managed to look magnificent. The laboratory's work continued around her as she was left to her thoughts for a while. The young men present stole glances at her when they thought they were unobserved. Yelena's face was beautiful but blank, perhaps she was considering her options.

Ralf watched her from out of her field of view, fascinated by the tigress in his cage. He approached, "I have never seen to much kit packed into so little clothing Yelena."

"We Russians have learned to do a lot with little, Ralf." She smiled half heartedly. "Why have you brought me here? You could give me sodium pentathol anywhere and learn all that I know."

"Of course I could Yelena, but the excellent Professor Tribble likes to do our interrogations when he can. He says it keeps him in practice. But I think he has another reason myself."

Yelena smiled, fearless, and her eyes dazzled Ralf. "I suppose he never meets real women."

Ralf remained deadpan, "Oh, I think you would be surprised."

Professor Tribble returned from supervising a young lady at a work bench and picked up a loaded syringe. "Ah, Ralf, would you like me to prepare the subject for interrogation now?"

Ralf glanced at Yelena before answering, "Yes, Professor, please go ahead."

"Oh, and can I have her when we are finished? The drug dealer didn't last long at all and you know I am always short of test subjects." Professor Tribble looked at the beautiful woman restrained in front of him dispassionately, as if she were a lab rat.

Yelena's mask cracked for the first time.

149) The British Consulate, 11, Walter Carrington Crescent, Victoria Island, Lagos, Nigeria

British Diplomatic representation in Nigeria is run from Number 11, Walter Carrington Crescent, Victoria Island, Lagos. This is about 2 miles South of Freedom Park and a mile East across the water from Unit 23a.

It says "Deputy High Commission of the United Kingdom" on the wall, and it is actually a Consulate in status, but in the usual British way it is universally known as "The Embassy."

From the outside, the first floor of the building looks something like a huge desktop computer with air vents that are actually vertical slit-windows against the sun. And they make it defensible in case of public unrest. This box sits upon a larger ground floor unit which shares the same style but spreads over a greater footprint. There is a vehicle turning circle out front and a couple of pillars supporting a portico to keep up appearances.

Tucked away around the back, on the first floor, was the office of Brigadier Andrew Hartley, the Military Attaché. Andrew was an ex-Guards officer with some grasp of diplomacy beyond the use of gunboats and a notable talent for selling Britain's military wares. He was aged in his mid fifties and over 6 feet tall. Once he had been a 7 handicap polo player but age, easy living and the endless formal dinners had taken their toll; he had spread out a little.

Andrew sat back in his chair, put his hands behind his head and considered George. He smiled like a kindly uncle, which was a role he tried to play with this pleasant young man and relatively new recruit. It was not difficult, George was a nice boy and reminded him of the son he had lost in Afghanistan.

"It's the same for everyone, George." He said with an air of finality. "Just the way it is. The first time you kill a person, I don't care how tough you are, you stop and think for a while. Probably your brain cells are re-arranging themselves or something."

George shuffled in his chair. He almost said something.

Andrew continued, "Unless you were some kind of low-life, it goes against all you have been taught all your life. The standards of religion and society and everything."

George spoke softly, "It feels like murder to me."

Andrew went on firmly, "Its not murder, George. People murder out of anger or for gain. You killed an enemy of our country as much as if it had been on the battlefield. He has already sold information about what we were looking out for and led two of our men into an ambush. Who knows what trouble he would have caused if he had not been silenced."

George sighed quietly, "I feel dead inside."

Andrew was more brisk now, "Everyone feels like that for a couple of days after the first one. Then I guess your mind sorts out its position. I don't know where your career will take you, but if you have to kill again, the rest will be like switching off a light bulb. Trust me on this. Did your Glock reload properly with those hollow-points I gave you? Didn't feed a round across the breach and jam?"

150) The Clocktower, Credenhill, Hereford, UK

There is a grey clock tower near Hereford. It stands between Stirling Lines, the old SAS base, and the new site at Credenhill. It is a memorial which looks somewhere between a huge grandfather clock and a carved monolith. It does actually have an odd shaped clock at the top. Beneath it there are always wreaths of poppies, renewed as they fade, and always fresh on the 11th November. Though the names of fallen SAS soldiers are carved with pride in other places, this is the place where the men remember their lost friends.

There is a winged dagger, badge of the Regiment, half way down the pillar, and below that an inscription from the poem, "Golden journey to Samarkand," "We are the Pilgrims, master; we shall go always a little further; it may be beyond that last blue mountain barred with snow across that angry or that glimmering sea."

On occasion, old SAS men, old Pilgrims and not so old, gather there to remember times past and comrades who have failed to, "Beat the clock," as the SAS men say.

On this Autumn morning Mike and Mac had come for some quiet time.

Soldiers, by and large, don't do the showy stuff with wailing and tears, staple of TV shows; they toast their lost friends in a bar, and some drink themselves to oblivion to remember them. Today, the two men were thinking of Scouse and his funny ways. Product of an orphanage, like so many special forces soldiers, another good man gone and no one to mourn him.

"A good man, Scouse," Mike said the obligatory words staring at the lines of poetry.

"Aye, bat he widnae huv wanted tae go ony ither wye, big man. Ah knew him 8 years, an' we've bin some places, seen some hings..."

"We see things, do things other people only dream of and the price of it is that we play Russian roulette with the Devil."

"It could ha' been either one of us." Mac's fatalism was bullet-proof.

151) Security Council Chamber, United Nations Conference Building, New York City, US

The Russian Federation succeeded to the Soviet Union's seat at the United Nations, and its membership of the United Nations Security Council otherwise known as "The Big Five", in 1991 after the fall of the Soviet Union.

The big five, the nations which earned their seats on the Security Council by the possession of nuclear weapons after WWII, or in China's case by 1964, consist of the USA, France, the UK, China, and Russia.

NATO may be thought of as fostering peace by preparing for war, whereas the United Nations might be said to foster peace by preparing for peace. This being the case, there is a lot of talk and hot air at the UN General Assemblies. It can be a place for virtue signalling by the great and the good.

The decisions made by the Security Council, however, have a very different status. In contrast to decisions made by the General Assembly of the United Nations, which a country can safely ignore, as a rule, decisions made by the Security Council will be backed up by force if compliance is not forthcoming. For this reason, the Security Council's twice yearly meetings at the seat of the United Nations, a huge, be-flagged building in New York, are a serious matter. But extraordinary meetings of the Council can be called when there is a significant threat to world peace.

This extraordinary meeting had been called by the UK in furtherance of their allegations that the Russians were smuggling modified drugs into the UK with the intention of destabilizing the state. It was a very serious matter and one of intense concern to all the members because they were all potential victims of a similar plot. In support of their allegations, the British had photographs, captured papers, samples of the drugs and of course the chief officer on the ground himself, Colonel Dimitri Petrenko.

As per the Security Council's statues of operation, notarised documents detailing these proofs had been distributed to members' representatives in advance and now these representatives met in open council to debate the issue. They spoke in an order decided by chance with the nation temporarily in the chair speaking last.

By "chance" the French and Chinese had spoken carefully, the British had restated their position and the threat to governments everywhere, the US had called the Russians names not often heard in diplomatic circles and finally the Russians had their turn to defend themselves.

The Russian delegate blustered and bluffed, the British were lackeys of the US and trying to frame them, to turn world opinion against them and benefit from the resulting loss of gas sales. The US delegate looked uncomfortable for a moment. His country had benefitted greatly from the Russians inability to export gas since the US had blown up the undersea pipeline running from Russia to Germany off the Swedish coast. Everyone knew this and no one said anything but the Russians.

The French were impassive, as were the Chinese. The latter were selling huge amounts of military hardware to the Russians at vastly inflated prices being almost the only state who could stand the objections of the US. Nevertheless, the Russians knew that everyone else knew they we caught with their hands in the till and no amount of denial would change that. The Russian delegate ended with a final call for justice against the US oppressor and sat down.

An aide whispered in the ear of the British delegate, “Sir, I think they will have to stop their operation against us.” The delegate nodded without looking around.

An aide touched the shoulder of the Russian delegate and whispered, “They will not vote for further sanctions as punishment but we must end the operation.”

152) The King’s Private Office, Buckingham Palace, London, UK

The King sat in his private office at Buckingham Palace and reviewed edits to a speech he was giving to a reforestation charity. As was his habit, he glanced at the gilded clock on the mantle. It read precisely 13:59; he expected a call shortly.

Right on schedule, the apparently vintage telephone on his desk rang. Recognizing the name on a screen beside the phone, he smiled as he answered, "Hello, James. Its good to hear from you, old friend. How the devil are you?"

A familiar voice responded in the same public-school English, "Charles, you old rapscallion. I'm well. And the family?"

The two old friends exchanged warm pleasantries until the President of Nigeria broached his reason for calling. "I wanted to thank you for resolving that little problem with the Russians last week. Your people made a bit of a mess, but you did me a great favour. I've been able to crack down on the Boko Haram terrorists, and their associates, without so much as a peep from the clergy."

The King smiled. "Think nothing of it, James. What are friends for? I'm just pleased we could provide some discreet assistance."

"It will not be forgotten," replied the President. "Give my regards to Camilla. Hopefully we can catch up at the Commonwealth meeting this spring."

"I look forward to it. Keep well, my friend." The King set down the receiver gently. Crisis averted, for now. There was always another fire to put out.

153) The Traveller's Rest Public House, Anderston, Glasgow, Scotland, UK

Auntie Moira's pub had an old fashioned "snug", a room set apart from the main bar where patrons looking for a quieter time could sit with their friends or their drinks. It was not a large room, there was just space for half a dozen small tables on moulded cast iron legs and a bar the size of a broad man's shoulders in one wall. There was an open fire on another wall and in it there burnt a belly of coals topped with a thick log from who-knew where in this city? In front of the fire, on a thick old rug, lay Snuffles, now a rather portly Pit Bull, snored gently in his security.

Mac sat at one of the two occupied tables with two old men playing dominoes. He sipped a pint of Guinness and glanced around the room, then at the dog, "They'll be daein' up this auld place sometime soon, aye?"

Without looking up one of the old men replied, "No' in ma lifetime, ah think."

154) The King's Private Office, Buckingham Palace, London, UK

A tall and unusually handsome footman, arrayed in the livery of Buckingham palace, opened the door to the King's office and bowed Mike inside. "Did he smile at me?" Mike thought as he went in.

The King stood behind his desk and extended a hand in greeting. "Good to see you again Colonel."

"Thank you, Your Majesty. I hope you are well."

"I am very well, thank you. Relax and sit down Colonel." The King indicated a chair which Mike pulled into position. "I wanted to see you as soon as convenient following your return to thank you for sorting out a tricky little problem for us."

"It was nothing, sir," Mike stepped down from "Your Majesty" to "sir" as is correct form after the first salutation. Oliver had taught a him great deal about how to behave in royal company.

The King continued, "You have graduated from being useful as an extra pair of eyes within SIS to being our agent of change in a matter of great importance to the nation, Colonel. May I call you Mike, I understand everyone else does?"

"Of course, Sir."

"In future I shall arrange for you to be given more jobs of a sensitive or trying nature if you are happy with that arrangement Mike?"

"Very much so, sir."

"And I would like to give you a little something to show my appreciation of your efforts."

"That's not necessary, sir," Mike appeared slightly uncomfortable, mumbled and indicated as much with his hands.

"No, I want you to have this, Mike. It is a sort of master key to my estates and may be of some help in getting things done when you are struggling for co operation with the sort of jobs-worths we all come across now and again."

The King produced a small embossed card, something like an ID card, with Mike's headshot and name on it. But the words were less usual, "Please give the bearer whatever access, assistance or support he may require without question. He has my full confidence." It was signed, "Charles R" and accompanied by both the Royal Cypher and badge of the Palace Security Group.

XXXXXXXXXXXXXXXXXX

If you enjoyed Kill Or Capture please give it a 5 star review on Amazon and you will help us get it in front of more people.

To access the higher quality maps and photos relating to this story, plus other Goodies, go to our website http://robertdalcross.com

Best wishes from Robert and all the team at Military Press

Cap badge of The Palace Security Group

XXXXXXXXXXXXXXXXXXXXXXX

The next book in this series is:

Enemy Action

An SAS / MI6 Mission

"Once is happenstance. Twice is coincidence. Three times is enemy action"

— Ian Fleming, Creator of James Bond and ex-British Intelligence Operator

- **A nuclear inferno engulfs Missouri.**
- **Thousands are incinerated in a New York airport holocaust.**
- **The Hoover Dam becomes a shattered tomb destroying Arizona and Nevada.**

The US is on fire.

The media blames China. The hawks circle, screaming for war.

Riots consume cities.

The President calls DEFCON 2.

Nuclear missiles lock on. The major powers' naval fleets face off. The brink approaches.

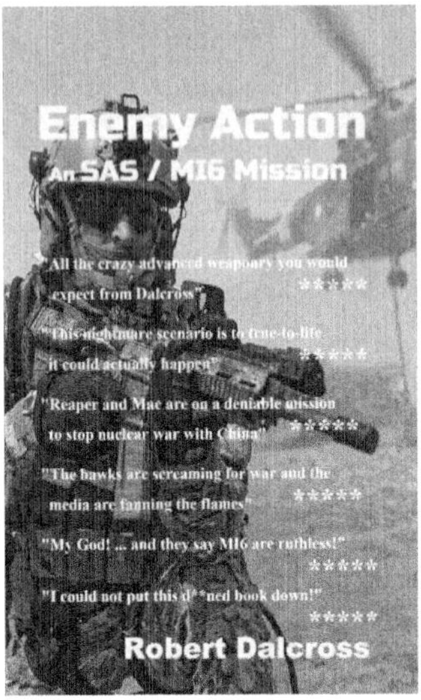

Then London burns. A dirty bomb. Tens of thousands with radiation poisoning

Enter Mike Reaper, MI6 Operator, and Don Mac, his fearsome Glaswegian SAS bodyguard.

Their mission: Stop the countdown.

Who profits from Armageddon?

- **A rogue state?**
- **A power-hungry general?**
- **The war machine?**
- **Or a master manipulator pulling the deadliest of strings?**

Reaper and Mac must outrace time, outsmart enemies, and outlive betrayal.

The CIA is in bed with Chinese terrorists.

Russia's hungry eyes scan the map for a land-grab.

Gaza's bombers dance to a billionaire's tune.

In a world teetering on the edge of oblivion, they are the last line of defense.

Just them and their MP5SDs

To storm an enemy stronghold and save the world.

And a SEAL wet-work team has been sent to kill them…

Enemy Action is a white-knuckle ride into a future of terror. Packed with heart-stopping action, mind-bending twists, and moral dilemmas, this is a techno-thriller that will leave you breathless. For fans of Robert Ludlum, Tom Clancy, Lee Child, LT Ryan, Dan Brown and James Herbert, this is your next obsession.

This book has 3 maps and is about 5 times as long as Extraction Under Fire.

Read Enemy Action now!

Available from Amazon

XXXXXXXXXXXXXXXXXXXX

Printed in Great Britain
by Amazon

49454228R00136